THE MERRY
WIDOW

Meagan McKinney

THE MERRY WIDOW

WHEELER
PUBLISHING, INC.
ROCKLAND, MA

★ AN AMERICAN COMPANY ★

Published in Large Print by arrangement with Kensington Publishing
Corp. in the United States and Canada.

Wheeler Large Print Book Series.

Set in 16 pt Plantin.

Library of Congress Cataloging-in-Publication Data

McKinney, Megan
    The merry widow / Megan McKinney.
       p. (large print) cm.(Wheeler large print book series)
    ISBN 1-56895-863-3 (hardcover)
    1. Explorers—Fiction. 2. New York (N.Y.)—Fiction. 3. Large type books.
I. Title. II. Series

[PS3563.C38168M47   2000]
813′.54—dc21   00-028327
                                                                        CIP

To Tommy Roberson
and Clare Elizabeth Leigh Glenn
(and me, Johnnie, Mary, Jay,
Logan and Kate)
—FRIENDS FOREVER—

AUTHOR'S NOTE

Small license has been taken by the author concerning the exact time of actual events set herein. The wherabouts of the lost Franklin party were more east and north of Herschel Island and York Factory. For nonfictional reference, the author recommends *Frozen in Time* by Owen Beattie and John Geiger.

*Drying a widow's tears
is one of the most dangerous occupations
known to man.*

—Dorothy Dix

PART ONE

TOO COLD TO SLEEP ALONE

CHAPTER ONE

Herschel Island, Beaufort Sea, Canada
Just Before Midnight
February 13, 1857

"Noel Magnus—has—failed," the man whispered in paranoid starts and stops. He looked behind him as if expecting Satan himself to be smiling at his back. All around, his cronies huddled at the plankboard table in the only saloon north of the sixtieth parallel, their rough, ice-deformed hands clenching tankards of home brew.

They didn't nod or disagree. They seemed frozen by the words. The unspeakable words.

"He is not a man who fails," another one whispered. He placed his dark head in his hands and looked wildly about the tiny hovel that posed as the Ice Maiden Saloon. "He swore to Lady Franklin that he would find her husband. He's been North for three years doing just that. And then there is the reward...oh, the sweet mountain of gold; oh, the soft fragrance of Paradise. Don't say now 'tis all lost..."

"This fierce place has not yet conquered Magnus." A young man with cropped pale-gold hair hunkered defiantly down inside his caribou parka. Gone unnoticed was the wind that blew against the log walls in a pounding baritone. Ominous layers of ice banked the two squares of glass which served as windows in summertime, but even that didn't seem to daunt the young man; nor the insidious icicles that formed like stalactites from the windowsills to the wooden floorboards despite the fact that the outside shutters had been closed weeks ago to shield the barroom's mad inhabitants from the never-ending night.

"The rumors from Fort Garry of his death will be proved false. Magnus will be here, and soon. Our ice maiden will force him to return—for would not our great friend Magnus rather die a slow brutal death than never lay eyes upon such beauty again?" A last man, Alexander McIntyre, his face old and weathered, peered across the cabin to the dim figure of a woman.

She was a white woman and the only other inhabitant of the saloon, but she made no effort to listen to the conversation. Instead, she leaned against the makeshift plank counter that served as the bar and stared morosely at the frost that grew like mold along the chinks in the log wall.

The ice maiden's clothing was like that of a native. A fringed *amautik* covered her from neck to ankle, and she wore the garment as if it were the only kind she'd ever known. Thick duffle leggings and *mukluks* of polar bear fur completed her attire, along with the ancient flintlock pistol she kept ready in her crude leather belt.

An Englishman untutored in the ways of the

4

North might have been shocked at the woman's appearance, but after the initial disconcert wore off, a certain kind of charm, no doubt, would overtake him. Certainly the bleached moose-hide *amautik* complemented the woman's fair coloring, for the garment was the exact color of her blond hair. The huge wolverine-lined hood at her back held a particular kind of fascination also—her present audience included. The hood artlessly displayed her unbound gold curls; it also signaled she was not married. The *amautik* was a garment designed for females to carry their babies in the enormous hood, but this woman's hood held no sleeping babe, and sometimes the younger men who frequented the place liked to imagine that there was a rather forlorn look that crossed her face whenever she glanced behind her.

In any other society, at the age of twenty-seven, unmarried and childless, Rachel Ophelia Howland would have been considered an old maid. But in the godforsaken North, there wasn't a man for two thousand square miles who wouldn't gnaw off his own leg for a chance to give Miss Rachel a baby.

"Rachel appears especially fine tonight." William Mark, the young man with the pale curls, gave her a gloomy stare.

"Look. She's even washed her hair. Can you believe that? Why, the last time I saw hot water was June." Inigo Weekes, his Spanish blood showing in the dark flash of his eyes, grimly took a swig of his tankard. "Bet she wouldn't wash her hair for none of us." He wiped his mouth with his sleeve. "Oh, please God, say Magnus isn't dead. If he is, not only will Lady Franklin be bitterly disappointed and withhold the reward, but we'll have no choice but to continue this fool's expedition for her husband until we're all dead and froze, too. Worse than that, if Magnus never shows his face here again, Miss Rachel will be treating us like the nastiest wolf-bitch that ever crossed the muskeg."

Rachel Howland took out her father's old flintlock pistol from her belt. Discreetly, as if it were second nature, she slammed the butt of the gun into a large chink between the logs. From outside the cabin, a strange grunt followed, then an odd chuffing noise. When she removed the gun from the opening, the leathery black nose that had almost plied itself between the logs was gone; in its place was an enormous white bear paw with claws the size of sharks' teeth.

"Take that, you rotten cur!" she cried, dueling with the paw that searched blindly for a target. She batted at the paw until it finally pulled back. The polar bear was ripe for round two when she pounded a green glass whiskey bottle into the chink and ended the fray. All that was left was the sound of bear teeth on glass, a strange kind of music that was quickly eclipsed by the scream of the wind.

Rachel paused. Her dark blue eyes turned to the four men huddled around the table in her saloon. She cocked an eyebrow as if to say,

"What are you looking at?" Chastised, the men tore their gazes away.

"He's already four weeks late in picking us up to return to ship. Maybe we need to accept that...something has happened." Grimly Weekes emptied his tankard.

Luke Smith, the fourth man in the group, nodded. "Do you recall what happened the last time he was here? For as many years as the man has been in the Arctic, Magnus has made his journey to the Ice Maiden Saloon. But that last time—last year after her pa died, remember?—Miss Rachel was feeling so low. Magnus seemed to finally break a little; he wanted to cheer her so badly. He even talked about maybe marrying her and taking her from this wretched place. I've never seen the man so tore up. No, he'd be back here if he could. If he could, he'd be back, I know it."

"Would he?" asked William Mark, a cynical gleam in his eye. "And do you recall how she's been ever since that last visit? She's been really put out. *Really* put out. I wager Magnus might not be showing his hide because he left her behind last year, marriage promises and all, and he knows what kind of temper Rachel has."

"She gets a might testy," Alexander McIntyre agreed, "but all the gel wants is to go back to civilization, to marry, to have children. She wants what every female I've ever known wants—and it's all been denied her because her father was a whaler, and then he had to go and buy this saloon, and now he's gone and died on her here on Herschel."

7

"You think Edmund Hoar might have finally struck old Magnus down?"

The dark question seemed to sober them all into silence.

Inigo Weekes looked around the table at each man before he spoke again. "Hoar's been wanting Magnus dead for years. They're mortal enemies. Hoar has sworn to find Franklin before Magnus."

"The land may have conquered Magnus; too, his old foe Edmund Hoar might have taken him down at last..." McIntyre took another glance at Rachel. "But I fear more a woman. A woman can fell a man like no other." He met the other men's gazes. "Magnus will be here. 'Tis all I know. If he's got a beating heart and didn't fall through the ice at Wager Bay as rumor has foretold, then he'll be here. He's driven to it. Trust me."

Inigo frowned. "I agree Magnus isn't the kind to go and fall in the ice. He's too experienced for that, but Edmund Hoar might have set a trap for Magnus. Maybe the rumors are true. Maybe Magnus is gone—" Weekes's words were cut off by the chiming of the clock bell. After twelve rings, the room fell dead silent.

Each man in their turn took a glance at Rachel. The reverberation of the last chime was so strong and vital, it seemed to rise over the wind and echo through the small log room until it turned deafening. Rachel held her breath. Her gaze fixed on the battened door and she stared at it, as if to look away would turn her into a pillar of salt.

"See the will at work in her...if she were a witch she would conjure him to appear at this very moment..." William Mark whispered darkly.

Inigo took another deep dram. He looked away from the door as if it disturbed him.

"Her father was cruel to bring her up here, and even more cruel to up and die and leave her vulnerable to the likes of Magnus." McIntyre gazed down at his drink. The sight of Rachel's face taut with hope rocked him to his core. "Someone else needs to melt the ice maiden. Someone other than Magnus. Magnus likes the North far too much for any true flesh-and-blood female. Rachel deserves better."

"Any one of us'd take her home, but she wants him and only him," Luke Smith grumbled.

"I want no man!" a female voice cried out to him.

All four men turned to stare at Rachel.

Inigo cringed and whispered to the group, "Great. Now she be listening to us, the she-wolf of the tundra..."

She was a sight. Her face was snow white beneath a mass of golden hair, the only color on her at all was the lightning blue of her eyes, which flickered beneath the lamp only to become blurred in a pool of unshed tears.

"Maybe Magnus's ship became fast in the ice near Bathurst—"

"Maybe his dogs didn't hold out from the trip overland—"

9

"We're lost, too, Miss Rachel. He was supposed to fetch us back to the ship when the ice melted this spring. He told us we could keep the Franklin reward if we found—"

Alexander McIntyre raised his hand and silenced the lot of them. He stood and looked at Rachel. "You can sell this place to Edmund Hoar. You know his Company of the North owns everything on Herschel. Sell the Ice Maiden to him—"

"I despise Edmund Hoar," Rachel declared. "He's a greedy, dark-souled pig of a man. I'll never give him what my father wrought with his blood, sweat, and tears." The planes of her face hardened.

"Go south, Rachel. You needn't stay up here. Any young man'd have you—" William Mark interjected.

She sniffed back impending tears. "I don't know anyone in the South. All I had was Father. Now I have nothing but the Ice Maiden."

"Sell this place and go find your way. You'll die up here, Rachel. Oh, you might still breathe and walk and talk, but, inside, you'll be froze just like the landscape." Alexander stared after her. His heart was breaking for her.

She turned away. Alexander heard another sniff, then another.

The bear chose that moment to push the green glass bottle from the chink in the logs. The bottle hit the floor with a loud, nerve-peeling crash. Rachel wiped her hidden tears, reached for another half-empty whiskey bottle, and tried to seal the crack in the daub with it, but this time she seemed unable to do it.

The other men stood to assist her. It was then, at the height of the drama, that the batten door to the saloon flew open.

Snow and ice swept in with all the violence of a warmonger. A large figure of a man entered with the fury. He shoved his bulk against the door and shut out the storm. When all was silent, he leaned back against the battens and slowly allowed his exhausted form to slide to the floor.

It was Noel Magnus.

Most wouldn't recognize him. His face was all but hidden in a wolverine hood. Like the Esquimaux, he wore a plate of ivory over his eyes, with two small slits cut into it to allow him to see even in a whiteout. His dark beard was covered with thick icicles, especially around the mouth where his moist breath froze at the point of exhale.

He drew off the ivory plate. His eyes were dark and wild as if they'd seen too much death, too much hardship. Outside his dogs began to bark and squeal. They smelled the polar bear. A dog would be missing in the morning; such was the hard luck of the North. No second chances.

Magnus's gaze found the woman across the room. He stared at her—stared hard—then his eyes closed in exhaustion. He leaned his head back against the door.

Rachel said nothing. She peered at the great hulk of ice, caribou fur, and man lying prostrate in the threshold of the door. Slowly, on silent polar bear *mukluks,* she tread over to the form.

She looked down at him.

Alexander McIntyre stood motionless with the other men, watching her.

An aching tenderness haunted Rachel's expression as she took in Magnus's face. His eyes were still shut as if he were too exhausted to reopen them, but even slumped over in a heap, his face covered with hair and ice, he was indeed a handsome man. His brow was fine, his nose large but supreme. And then there were his eyes. Lined by laughter and long, harsh winters squinting from snow blindness, even unopened as they were, they were the kind of eyes that seemed to long for a feminine hand to caress their corners, the kind that beckoned a soft pliable mouth to kiss away the harshness of them.

Rachel uncorked the whiskey bottle. With a pale hand, she touched his cheek.

The eyes opened. Dark eyes, the color of exquisitely aged sherry, stared up at her. Despite the strength in Magnus's expression, his eyes pleaded for mercy. Compassion. Forgiveness.

"I missed you. It's been a year," she whispered to him, her words all womanly softness.

The eyes pleaded even further.

She straightened. She was beautiful in her fury. She poured the half bottle of whiskey over his head, all the softness seeping from her expression until she looked as cold as her nickname.

"You dare to come back here, you breach-of-promise bastard?" she cried, tears welling again in her beautiful blue eyes.

"Rachel, you've got to understand—I didn't exactly promise. And I couldn't take you with me. Even now, the ship is locked in the ice off Victoria Land and, nigh, seven weeks ago I had to bargain for another team of dogs—" Magnus growled through the rain of whiskey.

"You promised me a wedding." She pressed her lips closed as if choking back a sob.

"One of us'd be happy to marry you, gel. You know we would be," Alexander chimed in wickedly, though all prudence told him to stay out of it.

"I did the best I could, Rachel." Magnus squeezed the whiskey out of his eyes—his red, wind-burned eyes. "You've got to believe me. I couldn't take you with me."

"No. I won't believe you. I won't." Choking back a sob, she pulled open the batten door. The wind nearly knocked her off her feet but that didn't deter her. Not even bothering with the hood, she slipped past Magnus and the batten door, and ran outside into the white, blowing oblivion.

Rachel slammed the door shut to her cabin and quickly lit the lantern. Next she fumbled to light the stove. It would take at least a half an hour to warm the tiny room, so she didn't remove her *amautik*. Toasting her hands over the flame, she watched helplessly as tear after

13

tear fell and sizzled on the scorched iron top of the potbelly.

Noel Magnus was never going to truly love her. If he truly loved her, he'd have married her after that last visit, and he would have taken her away from the life on Herschel Island.

But he was never going to do that. Because he didn't have to do it.

And she couldn't make him.

The hard-bitten realist in her told herself to accept this fact and get on with her life, but even now it seemed impossible. The hurt—the want—still balled in her chest like a lump of ice on the Beaufort Sea.

She touched her cheeks. In the frozen cabin, her tears had become nothing more than rivulets of ice on her skin. It was a fitting end for a snow queen who should prefer cold and alone. But Rachel Howland didn't.

Dismally she sank down onto a rickety wooden chair. She melted the ice on her cheeks with her palms. Her eyes clouded with despair.

Perhaps it was just that since her father died she'd been focused on all the wrong things. Certainly, Herschel Island was hell on earth eight months of the year, but there was a five-or-six-week period around July when the place was quite habitable, a time when Arctic wildflowers graced the raw tundra and musk ox rummaged the hills. Her father always used to take her exploring during these weeks. They'd walk the muskeg and pick up pretty stones along the coast, and sometimes find a horn needle or a bone carved in the shape of a man, the residue of the ancient peoples who used to live there. In the Arctic, she'd seen the sight of two hundred thousand caribou crossing the Porcupine River; she'd watched the heart-melting play of two polar bear cubs. There were not a whole lot of white women who could say that. None of them in the fancy ladies' magazines ever got to see such sights, she'd wager.

A small frown creased her forehead. She gazed over to the table where her only edition of *Godey's Lady's Book* lay. Unable to stop herself, she picked up the issue and tortured herself anew.

The color plates spoke volumes. There were pages and pages of fashionable ladies to study. In their lace caps and horsehair crinolines, they perched on tuffets and chatted amiably, always in a surrounding that was both luxurious and pretty. Her favorite was of a lady in a rose taffeta gown studiously painting the portrait of a young girl. Behind the woman stood a passel of her female admirers, all equally fitted out, and behind the entire tableau were magnificent white satin draperies looped up like the train of a wedding gown.

Depressed, she crushed the magazine to her chest and swatted away fresh tears. There was a whole life out there she could only imagine. When she'd been a child, she remembered her mother in a gown such as those in the magazine. She lived with her mother in

Philadelphia in a house that possessed such amenities as red wool carpet and mahogany furniture. But at the age of ten, she watched her mother die of yellow fever. There was no one else for her except her father, who roamed the cold seas in search of whalebone, the integral structure of the picture she had just admired.

Her sole issue of *Godey's* was from 1849. One of the seamen who visited the saloon had brought it to her when it was only a year out of date. She cherished it like a Bible. She knew every piece of furniture upon which the ladies perched, she knew every hemline of their gowns, every swag, jabot, and ruching of the drapery that graced its pages. Even the occasional potted oleander didn't miss her hungry eye. It was a world she knew in the dark reaches of her memory. It was filled with grace and comfort, and the tender hand of a mother who loved her little girl.

But now it only existed in fantasy, printed on the static pages of worn paper. Even so, she'd had it in her head for so long, it seemed real. Somewhere, there was a parlor with bridal satin drapery and a lady painting the portrait of a little girl. There had to be.

The door to her cabin banged open. She reached for her pistol and half expected to see the bear at the threshold. Once, she'd seen a polar bear knock a door down with one swipe of his broad ivory-furred paw.

But it was not the bear come to call. It was Magnus.

"Get out." She raised the pistol and took aim with one eye closed.

He ignored her. With an arrogant cock of his head, he shut the door, barred it, then began to unlace his parka. "Are you going to shoot me?" he asked gruffly, not pausing. "Well, shoot me then. Put me out of the bloody misery I've endured just to get the hell here."

"You dog, you don't know misery until you've been seduced and abandoned like I've been." Her lower lip quivered, betraying her. "That last time, you promised—"

"That last time I was here you were sobbing over your father's death. You were afraid, you were cold and lonely. You begged for comfort. You know what I told you. I told you the truth." His deep voice crackled with ire.

She lashed at the tears that now fell freely down her warm cheeks, but her anger deflated into dejection. "You loved the North, that's what you told me," she whispered, almost to herself.

"That's not all I told you," he answered, throwing his parka on the table. Without invitation, he bent to her and gripped the pistol barrel with both hands. He pressed the muzzle to his heart, then looked at her. "It took me two and a half months to get here. Ten weeks of hunger and cold and darkness, and unrelenting thoughts of you. So, shoot me then, Rachel, for if you send me away like this, I won't be able to endure the cold and the hunger and the darkness to get home."

A sob caught in her throat. Her gaze locked

with his. She couldn't shoot him. Not when she loved him. And had secretly for all the years he had frequented the Ice Maiden.

Reluctantly she lowered the pistol.

"Good girl," he whispered. He lifted her chin and gazed down at her face. "Now give me the kind of welcome I've dreamed of these past ten weeks." He lowered his head. Lips brushed hers in a ghost of a kiss. She briefly felt the cold wetness of his beard where the ice had melted, but then he pulled back as if he feared displeasing her.

As if he could. As if he ever could when she loved him so.

"Is that ship of yours what you call home?" she asked sullenly. "Is that where you would go if I turned you away from this settlement? Back to the *Reliance* locked fast in the ice? Oh, why do you do it? Why would you love this place so when you could have a real life and a real house in New York?" She lifted her hand and touched her cheek, the expression in her eyes distant. "Why would anyone give up the gentleness of a warm wind on his face for the violence of that?" Her eyes turned to the door that moaned beneath the onslaught of wind.

His hand, rough and callused, replaced hers. He caressed her cheek, her temple, letting one large finger sensuously outline her lips. "If I were not here in this place, I would not have found you, my beautiful, sweet Rachel. So you mustn't blame me for loving this land."

"But you've found me now. We don't have to be here any longer."

Magnus's sherry-colored eyes darkened. "I have to find Franklin. I can't leave. I'm so close."

She tore away from his hand. "Franklin, Franklin. He's been missing for ten years. You've been North half as long, and now they're starting to send search parties for you." She reached under his discarded parka and drew a crumbling yellow newspaper from the table. It and her *Godey's* were her only artifacts of real life.

She tossed the newspaper to him. "Here, you can see for yourself the turmoil you're causing. And it's already over a year old."

He stared down at the headline of *The New York Morning Globe* dated January 25, 1856. It read: **Publisher Noel Magnus Pronounced Lost in the Frozen Wastelands of the North. Lady Franklin Weeps. Reminded of the Final Voyage of Franklin's H.M.S. Erebus.**

Slowly, he placed the paper back onto the table. His face was wiped clean of expression, but she could see the irritation in his eyes.

"See? Even your benevolent Lady Franklin believes you dead." She studied his expression. The shock and surprise she'd expected never came. He didn't seem to mind being thought dead at all. "Don't you care that people are worried about you?"

"My demise might be making the papers, but it's of no account. There certainly is no one down there worrying about me." He laughed. If there was bitterness in his voice, he hid it

19

well. He then stared at her; his words were gentle. "You think you know cold, Rachel, living up here as you do, but far colder than this place is a home where no one mourns your passing."

She frowned and locked gazes with him. "Surely there is someone there to miss you. Lady Franklin weeps—"

"Because she fears there's now one less man looking for her husband." He grinned.

"But surely someone in New York is worried. You must have family, Magnus—"

He ran his rough hand down her cheek. "My mother ran away when I was three. My father educated me to all her woes soon enough. He gave me nothing but directions and the whip if I didn't do it well enough, and he doled it out because he said he wanted a son who would be tough enough to take over his role and run what he thought was a glorious empire." He paused. His face hardened. "So here I am, sweet Rachel. Tough enough to run an empire now that its creator is no more, tough enough to weather the worst frigid wind, tough enough to know this place is the place I want to be because you and my men are the only ones who would mourn me should something happen." He smiled. His teeth were white and even—another thing she loved about him. "You would mourn me, Rachel, would you not?"

She fought the urge to slap him. He knew the answer all too well, and it was cruel of him to mock her with it.

Turning matter-of-fact, he said, "Of course,

I do own the *Morning Globe,* and I confess, they're probably fretting about who will inherit."

"You own this newspaper?" She went to the table to look at it. It seemed much like other newspapers that found their way to Herschel. The fact that it was well over a year old was of no consideration; it was as timely a newspaper as they could lay hands upon. "I thought I knew you well, Magnus. Every year when you arrived here, Father always greeted you with a smile. He liked you; you know that. But I see now we didn't know much about your other life." She grew pensive and stared at the paper. "If you own a newspaper, Magnus, does that mean that you're a rich man?"

The question was ridiculous. Whether he was rich or not meant nothing to her. The only thing that did was that he would marry her and take her with him when he was ready to go. She loved him. That last time they were together, he'd promised her the moon and the stars, and she'd believed him. But all he really needed to produce was a wedding.

"Would it melt this cold heart sooner if I told you I was rich?" His fingers played with the front lacings of her *amautik.*

She looked down and realized she was suffocating in the dense fur. The stove was suddenly working much too efficiently. She whispered, pulling away, "Last year, when I told you I had given you my heart, I never asked to see your bank notes, did I?"

"I've never taken advantage of you. You told

me you wanted marriage and I held myself back because of that. It doesn't become you, Rachel, to be pious."

"Still, I won't be a whore. Not even *your* whore." The tears fell again. "I just want you to marry me. It's only right that I reserve myself until I have such respectability. I don't beg for your promises. No, you give them too easily. But now you have to make good on them. It's what Father would have wanted. You know that. He didn't raise me to—to—" With trembling hands she set his own aside from the rawhide lacings of her *amautik*.

"I'll marry you when I can leave this place. I promised you then, and I promise you now. I will do it."

"Marry me now and take me with you to the *Reliance*. I've been on a ship before, Magnus, you know it."

"The life is difficult out there, Rachel. You're no longer a child ready to take a ship-board adventure. You'd have to go with me as a wife, and with that would come all the cares of perhaps finding a babe inside you. No, I think it would be better that we start our marriage in civilization."

"And will you be saying this ten years from now? Twenty? Is that the excuse you'll be telling your bastard sons and daughters?" She couldn't stop the bitterness from edging into her voice. "I hope you really do become lost and end up like Franklin. It's the end you deserve."

"Don't be harsh. I can't bear you harsh, Rachel, when I know how soft you can be."

She met his gaze. His eyes were impossibly warm and expressive. They seemed to see right into the secret corners of the soul she'd always thought she had so well hidden. That was the power he had over her. "I want to be soft for you, Magnus. You know I love you. I'd give you everything I have to give just for a tiny band of gold." She began to shiver though she was not cold. On the contrary she was beginning to perspire. "Oh, but I can't stand the thought of New York just waiting for you and you not wanting to return. Your house, the one on the Hudson Bay—no, the Hudson River, you said—why, if you're a rich man, there must be five or six rooms to that house, all empty with no one to live there. Just an empty house with no one to appreciate the gentle breezes." She laid her head in her hands. "The profanity of it."

He stroked her long, blond hair. "It anguishes you, doesn't it, my house standing vacant while you dream of a better place?" His words grew more pensive, more tender. "Five or six rooms would seem a mansion to one who's lived most of her life in one room, wouldn't it?" He raised his hand and let his knuckles graze her temple.

It was then she noticed his hands were cut and frozen and bleeding, a byproduct of his long journey. She took them in her own and led him to the stove. "Come warm yourself, Magnus, and I'll get Father's salve." Gently, she inspected each wound, as if by memorizing them she would memorize him.

"I don't need Howland's ointment. My hands only want this as their balm." He slid his palm up one side of the *amautik*. She didn't move. She didn't breathe.

"No," she whispered, but did not remove his hand.

"Do you remember what I told you last time?" he whispered into her hair.

"No, I won't believe your empty promises again. I'm not weak. I won't fall prey to this. Not without marriage."

"I'll marry you, sweet Rachel, I promise. One day you will be my wife."

"Not one day. Now," she almost whimpered as his mouth nibbled on her tender earlobe.

"I've got to find Franklin."

It was like ice water being thrown on her again and again. She pulled away and drew her arms over her chest. "Why must you continue this search? All you're bound to find is a bunch of bones. What worth are they to Lady Franklin now? They won't keep her warm at night."

"She's not just searching for her husband's remains," he grunted while he stooped to unlace his sealskin boots. "There's a secret to my journey here, and if I tell you, you're to tell no one." He straightened and began on her front lacings. He seemed to barely notice her reticence. "Lady Franklin's not so in love with Sir John as she might appear in the press. It seems her husband left her side with the family fortune in tow. He called it his good luck charm, a precious opal the size of a walnut. It was a strange black stone he obtained when he was governor of Van Diemen's Land. The gem is very valuable, my love. But of more value, if I find it, is the story that goes with it."

"What is the story?" she gasped, hardly able to believe he was already done with her laces.

"The gem is associated with disaster," he answered, pulling her *amautik* down around her shoulders. "They call it The Black Heart. There's rumor that Franklin took the stone from the native who showed it to him, and now they say it's cursed. To the pure of heart, it will bring great fortune, but to the black heart, it will bring only sadness and death." The corner of his mouth lifted in a smile. "Think of it, my beautiful girl. A gem as big as your fist. I've always thought when I returned to the city I would give the piece to a museum. The opal will be my finest treasure within it. And just think of what my paper could do if I find the stone in the midst of all the Franklin carnage. Lady Franklin is convinced The Black Heart did in her husband. She believes he discovered the northwest passage just as he swore he would, but it was the misfortune of the opal that took his life, not this land."

"It's too fantastic. Don't waste your time any longer on this, Magnus. Think of your empty house on the river...that beautiful empty house where the wind is soft against your face..."

"I never think of that house, Rachel. Up here,

I can only think of you and the stone, that stone as dark as all night, with a flashfire in the center like lightning."

Rachel looked up at him sharply. "What did the stone look like?" she asked, frowning.

Magnus kissed her. The beard was dry now and she trembled wondering how that beard would feel brushing against her most holy places. "What did it look like, Magnus?" she repeated, her mind groggy from his kiss.

"It was described to me as almost midnight blue with an iridescent fire exploding in the center. I picture it like the explosion inside me that has been forced to wait for you, Rachel." He bent his head and tongued the fine hairs on her nape.

She shivered. Deliberately, she grabbed him by the beard and forced his head up. He was twice her weight and more than a foot taller, but she saw the female bears protect their dens in winter; she knew how to handle a bear like Magnus. "Tell me true. If you found this stone, what would you do with it? Would you first return to New York?"

"If I find the stone this spring, I'll—"

"No, no. If you discovered this stone this very night, what would you do first? Would you return to New York and your house full of six empty rooms?"

He smiled down at her and stroked her hair. He had a master's touch with a woman. To her eternal damnation, she always found herself succumbing to his particular kind of caress.

"You sound as if you know where this stone is. Did old Howland in his meanderings on this island find the Franklin party where seven ships of men have already failed?"

"If I found The Black Heart for you, would you take me from here right away? Tell me true, Magnus," she whispered breathlessly. "Would you marry me and take me to New York right now?"

His expression turned bemused. "Eventually we'd do that, but if the stone were here right now, I'd still have to return to the *Reliance*. My men are counting on me. I can't leave them there to sail the ship home alone."

"And after that, you'd return for me?"

He raised one eyebrow. In the yellow light of the whale oil lantern, his dark-brown hair had a decidedly red cast to it. "After that, I'd have to take the ship to New York for supplies. I'm running low, you understand. It's been three years since we last saw that port."

"And after that?"

"After that, winter would be upon us again. I wouldn't be able to get here to Herschel except by sledge. I'd have to make you wait until spring when the *Reliance* could sail."

"That would be a year and a half from now. I wouldn't even see you next winter." She pulled away from him, a saturnine expression darkening her face.

"Rachel, are you toying with me? Do you have this stone? If you do, you must hand it over."

She stared at him. "Hand it over? Why, if I had the thing and gave it to you, I'd never see you again. Never again, though you've made me lover's promises and tried all sorts of seductions."

"You want to go to those places. You know deep down inside, you want to. So why don't we go there tonight?"

She crushed her balled fists against his chest. "I want them, yes. You know that only too well, you wretched man. But I'll have them with all the benefits of marriage. Marriage, do you understand me? It's how I was brought up and it's how I'll be until I go to my grave, no matter how lonely and torturous my existence."

"Give me the stone—or what you think to be the stone. Let me see it this instant."

"I don't have it," she burst out, all the while staring at him, taking in his handsome face, his broad, hard, yet impossibly warm chest encased in a thick coat of gray duffle cloth. "I don't have your damn stone, but I think I know where it is. You come back for me this spring with the *Reliance* and I'll show you it."

"Don't be a child. I can't come back here this spring just to chase your wild dreams. Franklin was never this far west. He would have found the northwest passage if he were ever here on Herschel."

"I am a child, so you have to please me. You'll come for me *this* spring."

"I will not. I've got to get supplies. I'll not risk my men just to try to get here because you have a silly woman's notion."

She stared at him. A doomed yet triumphant smile crossed her mouth. "You're never going to leave the North, are you, Magnus? There will always be a reason to stay here. You'll find your wretched opal and the story won't be lurid enough for your reader's tastes so you'll remain here until another expedition disappears under even more tragic circumstances." She looked toward the newspaper tossed haphazardly onto his parka. "You might even be that very next expedition. And why not? The civilized world already thinks you dead. Just by staying up here, Magnus, you gain more readers and more money. Just by staying here and lying to me."

"I'm not lying to you. I will marry you, Rachel. I *want* to marry you. You're the most extraordinary woman I've ever known."

"Am I beautiful to you?" She cocked her eyebrow and almost smirked.

"Oh, God, yes. You're beautiful."

"How you turn my head, Magnus. You, a man who hasn't seen a woman in nigh six months." She looked forlornly toward her issue of *Godey's,* then released a bitter laugh. "No doubt I, with my cracked lips and sooty face, would put all of those dazzling ladies to shame."

He stared at her, a tenderness in his eyes. "But you do put them to shame. Every one of them."

"So you've seen women like them before? Beautiful, poised women who rustle of silk and smell of French perfume? And forever you would

29

give up the likes of them for the likes of me?" Tears welled in her eyes again. "Me, who reeks of woodsmoke and moosehide?" She pushed him away. "I think you're presenting me with another lie, Magnus. Have you no conscience?"

" 'Tis no lie. You're perfect, Rachel. You're lovely. I dream of you every night. I think of only you."

She brushed away a flood of cold, silent tears. "Me? Prettier than those women in their beautiful parlors? Me? With my wind-burned hands and my chapped, bleeding lips and my despicably weak virtue you chip away at each year? I think not."

"Your virtue is intact. But if you surrender it this night, I tell you, I will cherish and keep it safe within me. And one day, when I'm your husband, none of this will matter."

"Liar," she whispered softly, her heart fracturing beneath his gentle caress.

"Enough of this talk. Let's go to the bed. I fear we will communicate better there." Gruffly he took her hand.

She pulled away. "No, give your lust to one of the native women in the settlement. They'll lay by your side without complaint and hand you all that you deserve and desire."

"I only want you, Rachel."

"Then marry me," she said coldly.

He stared down at her. "Remember what I told you last time? I'll be with you and only you. And you will be with me and only me. We will marry in time."

"Oh, why must you torture me like this?

Wasn't I good to you? Haven't I proved it year after year by shunning all others and holding out for only you?" She wept as he sat on the edge of her small bed and pulled her onto his lap. He ran his strong, tough fingers through the silken strands of her hair. It was a soothing touch, but she took no solace in it.

"You were meant for me, Rachel, as I was meant for you. Fate will find me right in the end," he said, his disturbing sherry-colored eyes locking with hers.

She moaned. She leaned ever so gently against him, and his lips took hers in a deep kiss. His tongue filled her mouth, but she didn't fight. For what was the point when the war was near lost.

"Is this why you love the North, Magnus? Is this why?" she whispered darkly.

"I love all the violent beauty here. I love the wind and snow. The here and the now. But mostly I love the thought of being with you on these exquisite nights. I dream of lying next to you when it's too cold to sleep alone."

"Bastard," she wept as he pushed her down against the mattress and kissed her between her breasts. "I hope one day you freeze your member off. It's what you deserve for masterminding my downfall."

He tongued the sensitive hollow in her throat. His laughter tensed his entire body. "I've bad news for you, ice maiden. At last count, I hadn't lost a digit." He raised his hands and wiggled his toes. "All twenty-one of them are still in good order."

31

"I'll hate you forever, Magnus, if you force this. I'll take my hate to the grave. I swear I will," she whispered until his dark head covered hers and the words melted into silence.

But soon the fire inside her rekindled. With a harsh moan, she shoved him away and rose from the bed.

"Get out," she said, not looking at him. Not daring.

"But it's so cold, and you're so warm. Don't make me sleep in the saloon. Show me this little mercy."

"Get out." She brushed her welling tears with the back of her hand. "I'll have a wedding first, or I'll give you nothing."

"But yours is the only true bed for miles. If you won't join me in it, will you lend it to me, just for a few sweet hours?" He looked at her with pleading eyes. "I've come so far."

She tossed him a dubious glance. "Fine. Take your few hours in a real bed. But I won't be here. I won't have those scurrilous dogs back at the saloon wagging their tongues over something that isn't true. When you awake, I'll take my turn. Until then, I'll be in the Ice Maiden." She grabbed her *amautik*, slipped it over her head, and slammed the door behind her.

Rachel returned from the saloon and looked at the man in her bed. Magnus lay in exhausted sleep, his feet dangling out of the polar bear coverlet, his arm flung across the mattress where she should have been.

But she held her ground. Still, a frown marred her satisfied expression. It boggled her mind why life had to be so difficult. She loved this man. She needed to be with him, but there was no way to do it unless he took her with him, and there was no place for a woman by his side.

Depressed, she walked over to the crude table where the *Godey's* still lay. She thought again of her mother and how she had once dressed as the ladies dressed on the cover. Sarah Howland had had a wide-skirted gown with black braid along the cuffs and bodice; even now Rachel could recall her mother's dress with all the detail that she could her mother's dear face. Noel had said women still wore silk gowns back in New York. Rachel looked at the magazine cover and couldn't stomp back the jealousy whenever she thought of Magnus, her beloved, sitting in a New York parlor surrounded by such belles as those in the *Godey's*.

If he took her back to the real world, she wondered if her crudeness and lack of social manners would embarrass him. Maybe that was why the marriage wasn't forthcoming.

Suddenly, she became so distraught over the idea, she found she couldn't even look at the bed with him on it any longer.

He was never going to marry her or take her back home. She was stuck on Herschel forever.

But there was always...

She tiptoed to a makeshift shelf and opened a large walrus ivory box. Dumping the contents into her hand, she then held up a rock the size of a small potato. It was black with hints of blue—almost the color of the winter sky—and shifting through its center like the most magical display of northern lights was an aura of fire and color that took her breath away.

The Black Heart. It had to be the same notorious stone Magnus was obsessed with finding. He was looking far and wide for his treasure, and it was right here all along. She believed her father had found it long ago. He'd once told her the strange black rock was amongst the ruins of a campfire and tied to a small fragment of a letter written in English. Her father hadn't known what to make of it, but she now knew it had to have been Franklin who left it. The letter said to leave the stone where it lay, but her father hadn't paid any mind to the warning.

And thank God he hadn't. If Magnus didn't want her heart, she knew at least he wanted the opal. The Black Heart.

He stirred in the bed. Grumbling, he cursed, "Where the hell are you, Rachel?"

Hastily, she dropped the opal into the ivory box and crept to the edge of the bed.

"I'm here, my love," she whispered to him.

"Have you set out to kill me? I'll freeze to death without you next to me to warm me. I don't cherish the thought of making you a widow."

"To make me a widow, you have to make me a wife first."

He grabbed her by the waist with one meaty arm and drew her to him beneath the polar bear rug. "Details, details."

He kissed her, but she rolled on her side and grew pensive.

"Are you thinking of New York again?" he growled.

His gruff question irritated her. "If you must know, I am. I'm thinking of the life we could live there. I could take care of you and your six rooms. We could fill them with children. We could be happy."

"I'm happy now. Very happy," he whispered, all the while stroking her hair.

"There must be someone who mourns you in New York, Magnus. There must be someone you want to see again."

"There's no one. So, shall I send you there to mourn me? You could pose as my widow. It would make great drama for the papers." He laughed.

"Be serious." She jabbed him.

"Oh, I am serious," he chuckled. "I'd half do it too, if just for a joke, except that if I were to send you to New York I'd miss you too much next winter when I arrive back here. So I can't even consider the notion."

"Next winter! It's an entire year from now." Her soul felt the weight of her depression. "I shall decline your next visit just on principle."

"As you declined this one?" he asked, his tongue running down her spine.

She pulled away.

He quieted. "Do you think I don't care for you, Rachel? For you're gravely mistaken."

"You can leave me for a year; it says a lot. I couldn't do it. Not how I feel."

"I confess, it will be harder to leave this time than it was even the last."

"Then don't do it."

His silence gave her the answer she expected.

"I might not be here when you return, Magnus."

"Where would you go, love? You're as alone as I am." He kissed her shoulder.

She opened her mouth to retort, but there was nothing she could say. He spoke the truth. She had no one to go to, and nowhere to go.

Then suddenly a strange idea came to her.

The absurdity of it. The very idea. Her going all the way to New York to live in those six empty rooms posing as this man's...as his...Oh, it was too funny. Too ridiculous.

She turned and stared at him.

Of course, to all civilization, he was conveniently dead.

His probing gaze locked with hers. "You've got mischief in your eyes, Rachel," he murmured. "You're not to leave me. Ever. You understand?"

She playfully tweaked his nose. It was cold, as hers was.

"You look positively gleeful. What's going through your mind?" He scowled. Bearded and dark-eyed as he was, his scowl was fabulous.

She laughed. The very idea in her mind

was a wild fantasy. To go and live in his empty house in New York posing as his widow. Things like that were not done in this world.

But she couldn't shake the picture of it. Her, in a wide-skirted black dress, waiting for company in his splendid house next to that river in New York. And there was no way she could really get in trouble, either, because he was probably never going to go home to it anyway. New York was nothing more to him than a harbor in which to obtain supplies for his next expedition. And on the slim chance he should return to his home, she'd already be there, waiting to greet him with all his promises of marriage dangling about her neck like his esteemed opal.

But, of course, there was also the possibility that he could discover her ploy and be murderously enraged.

She shrugged off the trepidation. There were risks, of course, but she had age and pride motivating her. She was twenty-seven years old, no longer in the market, and the love of her life was probably never going to marry her. There were times, too, when she wondered if Magnus was avoiding his promises because one of those beautiful belles like the ones in *Godey's* was still a memory in the back of his mind. It was not hard for her to imagine that when he got tired of Rachel Howland and the North, he was going to find himself trotting right back to New York to court one of its beauties.

She studied him. The words whirled in her

mind and clawed at her heart. *Marry me, Magnus. Marry me and make me your wife. I'll go with you anywhere on this godforsaken land. Give me hardship and all that goes with this life, but let me stand by your side and spare me from this death of loneliness.*

"Rachel, it bothers me when you look at me so. It makes me think of the time I found a starved grizzly watching me from atop an esker."

"I'll give you one last chance, Magnus. One last chance to ever see me again. Take me with you when you leave tomorrow. Take me with you and I'll be yours forever. Leave me behind, and God save you."

"I'll marry you one day, Rachel. I promise."

Marry me now, my beloved Noel. Take me with you, I beg of you. Don't make me do this. Don't make me even think it.

He kissed her. His mouth bade hers open; quickly the kiss turned deep and hot.

He rolled on top of her.

She stared up at him, all the while her insides howled and begged for his love.

But love couldn't be asked for or demanded or even earned. It had to be given. And freely.

So, outside, the ice maiden remained silent.

PART TWO

THE MERRY WIDOW

CHAPTER TWO

Herschel Island
July, 1857

"**Y**a can'a be leavin' us, gel. What'll we do wit'out ya?" Ian Shanks said at the mooring of the *Sea Unicorn*. Hat in hand, he squinted in the bright July sun.

"The saloon is yours, Ian. I give it to you. I won't be back," Rachel told him, a thick lump in her throat.

"But all your fat'er's work, you'll be givin' it to me free and clear? What would he be sayin' in that grave o'er yon?" Ian nodded to the rise of hills past the ship's mooring. There, in the barren distance, lay a dozen graves, some native, some white, all containing victims of smallpox.

"I've got to reach for something better, Ian." Rachel frowned and clutched the small carpetbag which held all her worldly possessions. She nodded to the distant graves. "I think he would understand. I really do."

"Do what ya have to, gel." Tears welled in the older man's eyes. "But if'n you e'er come back here, the saloon is your'n. I'll dub it the Ice Maiden until then."

Rachel hugged him, tears springing to her own eyes. Ian Shanks had been with her father as long as Rachel had been on Herschel Island.

Ian, the trustworthy old salt that he was, had hauled kegs of whiskey, intervened in a hundred bloodthirsty brawls, and still found time to scrimshaw fairy tales on whalebone for the bored little girl playing with her cloth dolls behind the illicit bar her father managed. She would miss Ian. He was probably her only real friend and mentor left in the world.

Certainly he'd been more faithful than Noel Magnus. The man had handed her so many unkept promises, she was out of faith. When he'd left her, he'd said he wouldn't make port again at Herschel without bringing her a ring. This last time, Rachel knew not to believe him. It was now his turn to be disappointed. When he arrived—if he arrived— she would be long gone. And his empty words and excuse why he came back without an engagement ring would fall to the cold deaf ears of the tundra, and not her own.

"Forgive me," she whispered, staring at him.

He stood, meeting her gaze with a sad, fatalistic expression. "Come next July, gel, I want to know how ya are. If I don' get a letter and hear from ya, ya know I'll come fetch ya."

She nodded, unable to acknowledge the tears streaming down her cheeks. With a nod, she said, " 'Tis more than Magnus has cared for me. I certainly haven't heard from him these past months, now have I?" She choked down the rest of her tears. Quickly, she picked up her skirt and embarked upon the gangplank of the clipper, *Sea Unicorn.*

"God's speed, Rachel. And God bless you!" Ian cried out.

Rachel said no more. Her tears streamed down upon her cheeks until they froze in the sub-zero breeze of the midnight sun.

Herschel Island
August, 1857

"Whoa, Magnus. You look as if you could swim to the dock. Be patient, man. You've been gone five months from this place. Surely you can spare another fifteen minutes?" Captain Luke Jacob laughed and slapped Noel on the back.

Beyond the schooner, *Lady Rupert*, lay the bald hills of Herschel. Already, though it was not yet fall, the land was aflame in red, yellow, and orange. Even the lichen that covered the rocks along the coast had turned into the autumn colors of chartreuse and prune. A thick ominous layer of ice had built up along the shadowed crevices along the island's perimeter, foreshadowing the weather to come.

"Let me see the ring again, will you, old boy?" Captain Jacob asked him as the ship entered the tiny bay. Around them, men climbed and clung to the rigging, taming the ship's sails.

Magnus gave the captain a sideways suspicious look. "In all the years up here that I've known you, Luke, I never figured you to be susceptible to sentiment."

"It's not often up here that a man gets to make an honest proposal of marriage—with that ring, you don't look to be after a native marriage." He glanced over Magnus's broad shoulder as if to see the treasure.

Magnus reached into his shirt pocket and pulled out a thin gold ring set with three tiny marcasites. "I'll be buying her a real fancy ring once we return to civilization, but this was all I could get from the trading post at Wager Bay. They told me they took it off the corpse of a preacher's wife. The preacher died next to her. The Cree took it and sold it for whiskey."

"I wouldn't go bragging on that story, Magnus. Women don't like such things. They don't think it romantic."

Noel lifted his dark brows. "As if you would know, you old bachelor. But I suppose you're right. I'll just tell her I bought it."

"Good thinking, man."

"Can't we hurry this ship to the mooring?" Magnus asked impatiently.

Jacob snorted. "What? And crash into the ice with the only load of flour, sugar, and liquor these people will see until next July? I'd rather burn down my own house than damage the fair *Lady Rupert.*"

Noel leaned on the ship's rail and stared into the settlement. The saloon was easy to pick out. It was by far the smallest wood building and yet the busiest. Men walked in and out of the doorway, all eyes on the schooner making its way through the middle of the bay.

He frowned. "I would have hoped she'd meet me on the dock, but I don't see her."

There were a few women in the crowd, but all were native, their little babies strapped securely inside the hood of mother's summer *amautik*.

"You'd think she'd have the courtesy of meeting the ship, since her future husband is here on it with a ring in hand," Noel muttered.

Jacob shook his head. "I've got to see to the mooring, but don't fret, Magnus. She's probably been too busy serving up the happy bastards in the saloon. Now that a new supply of whiskey's arrived, they're sure to feel obligated to drink up the old as quickly as possible."

Magnus laughed. "Yes, I suppose you're right."

"Of course I am," Captain Jacob said confidently as he took the wheel.

"What the hell do you mean she's not here?" Noel growled, slamming his fist down on the bar.

Ian Shanks trembled like a newborn calf. "She's left, Magnus. Gave me the saloon an' took off."

"To where?" he demanded.

Behind him, the inhabitants of the island, native and white, stood in deathly silence, as if they were watching Thor cast down his thunderbolts from the highest hill on Herschel.

"She went sout'. Caugh' a ride on the *Sea*

Unicorn when she docked here in July. I don'a know where she was headed to."

"Seal shit!" Magnus roared, grabbing Shanks by the lapels of his jacket. "You know where she went on the *Sea Unicorn,* and you'd better damn well tell me or I'll be roasting your bones by evening."

The blood left Shanks's face. "She mentioned goin' to one of the states. I don'a remember which one."

"You'd best spit it out or I'll reach in there and grab the news for myself."

"I really don'a remember."

Magnus took his large hand and pressed open Ian's jaw.

In terror, Shanks pulled away and cowered by the wall. "The gel said somet'ing about going to a house. Some kind a house she heard about in New York."

Dumbfounded, Magnus stared at the old man while everyone around him, including Captain Jacob, held their breath.

"She said she was going to live in a house in New York? My New York?" Noel repeated.

Ian's eyes nearly popped out of his head. "The gel said not'in' 'bout you bein' t'ere, t'at's for sure."

Noel lowered himself into one of the few rickety wooden chairs. Pain and a distant sense of anger crossed his harsh features. "Can you believe that woman? I tell her about my house in New York, and the next thing I know she's foolish enough to think she can just go live there in my absence."

46

Jacob placed a hand on Magnus's shoulder. "You know as well as I, the people do that up here all the time. If a cabin is empty, it's the unspoken law any man may live there who needs shelter. I suppose it's all that she knows, Magnus."

Magnus put his head in his hands. "Do you realize what this means? Even if my suspicions prove correct, and she's where I think she is, I have no way to get to her. Your ship can't get out of the ice before freeze-up. You always winter here at Herschel."

"You could dogsled to Fort Nelson. But not for another month or so, until the ground is covered in snow," Ian piped in.

"But I'll still be months behind her. Months." Suddenly furious, Magnus fished out the ring from his shirt pocket. Betrayal ran deep within the gleam of his eyes. "And I was going to give her this. The lying, thieving baggage! I should make her choke on it now."

"She just got tired of waitin'," Ian whispered as if trying to remedy the situation.

"Tired of waiting! The little fool," Magnus's eyes flashed. "How the hell is she going to get along in New York? She knows nothing about the world out there. Nothing." In a sudden fit of panic, he stood and barked, "Shanks, get over to the company house and hand over all the supplies you can spare. And get me some dogs. Some good ones." He looked down at the cheaply made ring; nonetheless, an immensely rare item way up North. "I'll pay with this ring. I don't need it now. Serves the

47

bitch right for abandoning me and trying to steal my own home."

"Magnus, haven't you heard a word that's been said. You can't get out of here until freeze-up. And even then, it would be a crazy thing to be trying for Fort Nelson in October. You'll hit the worst of winter way before you get down there."

Magnus looked at the captain, despair creeping into his voice. "But how is she going to manage alone? That big city—she has no protection, no guidance. Something terrible may happen to her there. I may never find her. I may never see her again." He dropped his head into his hands once more.

The room fell silent.

"We'll make sure you get out of here first chance, Magnus," Jacobs said solemnly. "First chance," he whispered to the bowed head.

Ian and the rest of the saloon patrons nodded. But still no one said a word. No one dared.

CHAPTER THREE

South Street Seaport
New York City
December 15, 1857

Rachel's new life had finally arrived. All her hopes, dreams, and visions of a perfect future were no longer intangible vignettes within her imagination but now the terrifying palpable vision of a busy New York dock.

She had wanted to be back in civilization, dreamt and schemed to return. Her father had taught her to be independent, taught her that she was no man's puppet to be toyed with and forgotten. Her escape was partly due to her father's wish for his daughter's self-worth, partly due to the longing for her mother's world, the world she'd yet to forget.

For years she'd cherished the stark memories of her childhood: of the room she shared with her mother in the luxurious Philadelphia townhouse where her mother worked as a cook; of white laundry snapping beneath a warm June breeze; of pink blooming dogwood and dresses the same delicate hue; and finally of death, of yellow fever and bedside promises and the voyage to join a father she'd never even met.

At the age of ten, Rachel's world had

imploded into little more than snow and ice and the all-consuming cost of a shot of whiskey. Now she was free of it. All she wanted was the warm sun on her face, and perhaps a new dress, and, lastly, a place to live where she could find peace. A place that didn't depend on fighting off frostbite and polar bears, and, worse, the constant advances of drunkards twice her size.

But now the civilization she had longed for spread out below her in an incomprehensible rush, and she had to admit the chaos frightened her. For several long moments she even had a twinge of regret that she had left the harsh but predictable frozen tundra.

Trembling at the rail of the *Sea Unicorn* she forced herself to look over the new land. Spread out as far as the eye could see were the upright rectangles of tenements, their brownstone facades black with the soot from hundreds of thousands of coal grates. Gray, tattered laundry crisscrossed the space between buildings; pigeons or their refuse clung to window ledges. The entire tableau was dank, unsanitary, and depressing. The beautiful ladies from *Godey's* were nowhere in view.

But more disconcerting than the scenery was the population. Below, the docks teemed with hundreds of rough-hewn stevedores and slick-suited brokers. Everyone seemed busy and way too important to be bothered with a shivering girl in a worn-out fur *amautik* who didn't even possess a crinoline to wear beneath her thin skirt.

But Rachel Howland was a fighter. If the unforgiving North had taught her anything, it was how to survive. And so far, so good.

Bracing herself, she squared her shoulders, clutched the worn leather handle to her threadbare carpetbag—the entire stash of money she'd accumulated at the Ice Maiden was inside it—then she walked down the ship's ramp. The air smelled of salt and rotting cod. A breeze kicked up and sprayed her with city dust. All around, men stared at her, their curiosity a threat that gleamed through their harsh, grimy faces.

"Where you from, woman?" one man asked, walking toward her, his smile showing a mouth full of gum and empty spaces.

She backed away, but another man quit his task of weighing fish and came from behind her. He touched the large hood of her *amautik*. "You sure are a strange-looking gel. What kind of fur is this?"

"Ringed-seal," she stammered, shrinking from his touch.

"Never heard of it." He stepped closer.

She turned and walked away, hoping her stride proved she was no stranger in town, and that she knew exactly where she was going. The men didn't follow, but their stares stayed with her until she turned from the docks and took her first walk down a New York street.

Her senses filled to overflowing; everything by its newness was magnified: the slap of wagon wheels through a puddle, the scent of bread from a bakery, the rainbow colors of ribbon at the milliner. She walked for blocks, unable to form a plan of action when the shop windows lured her like a prostitute to gin. If she dreamed of a fantasy land, she now could see the land existed behind the polished windows of the endless New York shops. Bolts of French silk in Persian blue, canary green, and sunflower orange beckoned her into one shop. Silver-backed hairbrushes and jasmine perfume lured her into another. One shopkeeper was even able to turn winter into spring as she passed by a florist and inhaled the fragrance of a hundred jonquils crammed into buckets.

"So sorry. Excuse me," she blathered to the pedestrians who crushed her rudely and mindlessly. The people out on the streets were almost all men, dressed in dark wool capes and black hats, and looking very important and rushed. The few women about were escorted by men, and they gave her insulting looks, as if she were offal beneath their fine leather boots.

She leaned against a toy store window and surveyed the street. From the wrought-iron sign affixed to the gas lamp she was on Broadway, whatever street that was. Another woman gave her a killing stare, then clutched her companion's arm as if for dear life and stepped around her. Rachel found she couldn't blame people for giving her strange looks. She must look odd in the sea of dark woolens, as odd as one of those *Godey's* butterflies alighting on the top of an igloo.

Two children suddenly caught her eye. They were a boy and girl, raggedly dressed in patched dingy osnaburg. Rachel surmised that neither one of them was older than eight and that there was blond hair beneath all the soot. They appeared from the corner and seemed very interested in Rachel until she realized it was the toys that had caught their attention.

Rachel moved from the window front and allowed them a better view. The little girl's blue eyes widened at the gold carousel that danced with pretty horses. The boy seemed determined to keep his sights on the wooden train with a fancy set of polychrome lithograph papers glued to its sides.

"Perhaps if you're good, your father will bring you a trinket from inside this very shop," Rachel announced to the boy.

He looked at her, his eyes a vivid azure in a face dark with grime. "Me father? Ain't got me one of those."

Rachel nodded in understanding. "I don't have a father anymore, either. But take heart. The people who care for you might buy you a trinket for Christmas."

It was the little girl's turn to stare. "Would you buy us something?"

The boy, clearly a born salesman, chipped in, "You're such a pretty lady. We'd be mighty grateful to you."

Rachel laughed. The children smiled and crowded closer.

"I wish I could buy you something, but all

I have in the world is inside this very bag." She lifted the threadbare bag to show them. "I'm afraid I barely have coin for lodging until I reach my house."

The girl nodded, resigned.

The boy only stared. At Rachel, then her bag.

Before she knew it, he bumped her and took off running. The girl followed, terror and exhilaration on her face. In shock, Rachel looked down and realized they'd taken her carpetbag.

"Hey!" she cried out to them angrily. Pulling up her skirt, she dashed after them. They might have gotten away. They certainly knew the shadowed, twisting alleys off Broadway better than Rachel, but Rachel was an agile runner, her legs honed by long walks on snow and spongy muskeg. Besides, she was furious, and all the fear and energy of being cooped up on a ship for six months exploded like a Roman candle.

"You hooligan! You wretched little child! Wait until I take you back to your elders and let them teach you a lesson!" she cried out when she had the boy by the collar.

Rachel snatched back her bag. In terror, the little girl crumpled next to him, her face a fragile mask of fear.

"They can hang me for stealin', but I won't go quietly!" he shouted.

"They'll have to hang me, too, then, Tommy. I won't let you go without me," the little girl mewed.

Rachel gasped. "Hang you? Your elders

might dole out a whipping, but no one's going to hang you."

"The police'll see me hang. And be happy to see it, too, I figure," the boy spat.

All Rachel could do was shake her head. The entire situation confused her. A thieving child made no sense. All the native children she'd ever known were cherished to a fault. Not one of them would have to steal when everything their parents had was given to them freely. "I won't take you to the police. Just show me where your people live. They'll give you a fitting punishment for stealing, I've no doubt."

"Me people?" the boy said, looking as dumbfounded as Rachel felt.

"The people who care for you. I know you haven't a father, but where's your mother?"

"Gone," answered the boy matter-of-factly.

"You have no family?" she asked.

"Me sister." He nodded to the little girl who clung to him.

Rachel stared. "But who is it who cares for you? Who took you in when you lost your mother? Someone has taken you in, I know it. Someone is always there to take in a child. There must have been somebody who took you in. Who are they?"

"Why must someone take me in?" The boy's face wore genuine curiosity.

"Why?" Rachel felt as if he'd slapped her. The boy's total ignorance of compassion was obvious, but she couldn't understand it. In the North, there was no such thing as an orphaned child. The natives gladly adopted any child who needed it and treated them as gifts from their god, as they treated their own children. It didn't seem possible in this land of gold carousels and bakeries and unimaginable riches that two children could go without even the barest necessities.

"Tell me true now, I must know who cares for you."

"No one cares for us. No one." The boy answered with such cold hardness in his voice, Rachel felt as if he'd fisted her in the heart.

"I don't understand. I can't believe it. This makes no sense. Tell me true now, I know someone must care for you," she whispered, sympathetic tears thick in her throat.

"I care for him," the little girl said, her voice barely audible in her fear.

Rachel studied the two of them for a long moment. The last thing she needed on this journey was two little children clinging to her skirts. She was unsure of her abilities to take care of herself, let alone others. But there was no way she could turn her back on these two strays. She wouldn't have done it up North, and she wouldn't do it now.

She straightened and clutched her bag tightly. "Show me where you live. I want to understand how you can get along in this land with no one to look after you."

"Why should we?" the boy snapped.

Her mouth twisted in a dark smile. She liked his defiance. It was probably the one thing that allowed him to survive, and she knew very well how that felt. "Show me where you live, hooligan, or I'll take you to the police and let you show them!"

The little girl cowered. The boy's face grew rock hard. "I'll be showin' you then." He tugged on the girl. Together the two wandered down the alley with Rachel bringing up the rear.

Three blocks later, they turned into another alley that had yet to be cobblestoned. The dank frozen mud was rutted a foot deep with wheel tracks. At the end there was a set of ramshackle stairs that led to the back of an old brick building. The boy nodded to the stairs. Rachel began to mount them.

"Where are you going?" he demanded.

Rachel stopped and looked up at the unpainted door at the top of the stairs. "I want to see where you two live. And who you live with," she said.

"We don't live up there." He tugged on her skirt and pointed to the stairs again. "We live here."

Rachel dismounted the steps. She thought there must be some kind of basement door underneath the steps, but to her dismay there was nothing underneath the rickety staircase but a tightly rolled-up blanket that was wedged beneath the first step so that no one might see it to steal it.

"You live here?" she asked, disbelieving.

"Now will you please let us go? And don't be goin' to the police?" the little girl begged.

Rachel looked at the little girl shivering before her in cold and fear. The last thing wicked Rachel Howland needed was two more weights around her neck, but she couldn't walk away now. Not when home was a threadbare blanket wedged beneath the step. "How old are you?" she asked gently.

"Seven, I think," the girl answered.

"And you?" she asked the boy.

"At least eight," he answered smartly.

"And your names?" Rachel demanded even though her heart was twisting.

"Me name's Tommy. And this is Clare." The boy stepped in front of his sister as if to protect her.

"Are you hungry?"

Tommy looked confused, as if he weren't used to conversations going this way. "Maybe," he said with caution.

"Let's go eat." Rachel surveyed the alley. There was nothing there for two children, just mud and the leavings of the chamber pot. It was a wonder the children had survived at all.

Rachel walked out of the alley. The two children stood frozen behind her.

"Come along now. Won't a hot meal make you feel better?" she said to them in the same kind voice she'd used to coax a white fox from its den.

"But we stole your bag," Clare answered.

"I know that very well," Rachel said.

"And we'll be stealin' it again if we can get our hands on it," Tommy announced, using a strange mixture of polite warning and brutal honesty.

"I understand," she answered resignedly.

The two children watched her, unsure.

"Then you still want us to come with you?" Tommy asked, his voice hopeful and yet beaten from a life of constant disappointment and despair.

"Yes. You must come with me." She looked out to the bustling street that was called Broadway, amazed that all the people she saw had no time or tenderness for two orphaned children.

"Come along. We'll have a good meal, then I'll tell you about the house we're going to live in." She held out her hand. In her heart, she wanted to smile kindly, warmly, but instinct told her not to. Overt kindness would have to come later. Right now both children would suspect it, and the last thing Rachel wanted to do was chase the children back into the dark alleys where she could never find them again.

"You have a—a—house?" Tommy stammered.

Rachel nodded. "Yes. I don't know if it's big enough for the three of us, but I can make room. I know how to do that. I'm from a very special place and I can make room for anyone. I'll tell you about it at supper."

Warily the children followed her. Rachel kept one eye on them, and the other on the city around her that had hundreds and thousands of people, but not one who was willing to take in two starving children. She didn't want to hate her new land, but she couldn't stop herself worrying. If there was no compassion for two small children in this city of plenty, then

59

perhaps hell was preferable. Up North, what little one had, one shared. It was the law of the land and everyone knew it. So how could all these people have missed such a basic human principle? What kind of life would she have here if they were so cold-hearted? What kind of wretched ungodly place was this pinnacle of civilization called New York?

CHAPTER FOUR

Noel cursed her very name. His oaths echoed across every mile of ice and snow in his way. Even the dogs that fanned out on their lines in front of his sledge seemed to yelp at his despair.

Fort Nelson was a thousand miles to the east and bitter, unforgiving winter prevailed. At the rate he was going, if he didn't get caught in a sub-Arctic chill of fifty below, he would arrive at Fort Nelson in a month's time. Then, if he was lucky and the weather didn't turn too ferocious, he could take the dogs through Rupertsland until he reached Quebec and transportation to New York.

But he was months behind her. Months. Months. Months...

He released a growl; the dogs went faster, veterans of their master's moods.

Ahead, two ridges of rock had inverted on

the horizon, a typical phenomenon when the air was saturated with suspended ice crystals. Jaded to the hallucination, he closed his eyes, numbed to the pain of needlelike cold hitting the parts exposed on his face. He thought only of her.

There was no peace for him. He knew he was making a hellish journey at the worst time of the year, only to be stuck in Quebec until the thaw. He was also well aware that he might get to New York and never find her. There was no guarantee she made it. She might have fallen ill on the journey. A young sailor in any one of the ports where the ship stopped might have coaxed her into running away with him.

Then there was also the possibility that she might have met with foul play. Rachel Howland might have arrived safely at the port of New York, only to be taken by thieves and murderers. Even now she could be cold and hungry in Five Points, selling herself for a half-loaf of stale bread.

His misery was like a fire inside him, forcing him onward when no mortal man should be able to make it. But *he* would make it. He had to. For Rachel. If he ever doubted his abilities to feel for a woman, he could no longer do it where she was concerned. The very thought of her destitute on the streets of Manhattan made him want to break the neck of every thug in New York. So he had to go onward. He had to find her; save her. No matter the hardships on him now, she was in

61

more peril. She couldn't make it without him. She couldn't make it.

"Another confiture?" Rachel asked Tommy as the three of them nestled cozily in the leather seat of the train. Rubbing their full tummies, both children declined an offering from the violet-papered box of sweets. Satisfied, Rachel tucked the box into her carpetbag, keeping it ready should one of them want more.

Outside the window, the countryside was iced in white frosting, presenting a passing tableau of picturesque villages and farms that seemed right out of a Currier lithograph. Every now and then the porter would walk down the aisle and place some more coal in the potbelly stove at the back of the car. Rachel had never traveled in such modern luxury, and it was so reasonably priced, unlike travel in the North. Even with paying the fares for the two children, she still had enough coin left to keep them in bread until she could get some kind of work.

Now, if only the house would be there for them. It was a gamble. For all Rachel knew, the house could have burned to the ground. Or worse, it could be occupied by someone Noel neglected to mention. Then they would all three be back out on the streets. But if that was the case, Rachel had to harden herself to accepting her lot. She'd been a wicked adventuress to come so far on a gamble. If it didn't pay off, she would just have to find work and a place to stay until she could get enough money to return to Herschel and the saloon. She'd die a frozen old maid up there after her disappointment, but at least she wouldn't be alone. There was no doubt Tommy and Clare would go with her.

The three of them were fast becoming trustworthy companions. Rachel found it wasn't hard to win the affections of the two street urchins. All one had to do was feed them often and promise them when their eyes grew heavy at night that they would stay warm and protected by her side. They were a ragtag threesome and Rachel wished desperately that she had something other to wear than her worn seal-skin *amautik* and a patched skirt for her introduction as Magnus's widow. But the money she thought would go to a new dress had been spent at an inn for baths so she could scrub the lice from the two children. Clare hadn't been hard to bathe. The little girl had mentioned a mother who once cared for her and saw to her needs before the girl had been left out on the street. But Tommy was a different story. He'd yelled and fought during the whole process, so much so that the innkeeper had had to come and help her. When the helacious bath was over, Rachel was certain he was a spawn of the streets, and no blood relation to Clare. He obviously had no memory of either parent to civilize him.

Poor and worn, the children were now nonetheless clean, fed, and well rested. Another couple of bonbons in her own belly, and Rachel realized she just might forget about her desire for a new dress.

"Rachel?" Clare's blue eyes peeked from beneath the thick railway blanket.

"Yes?" Rachel answered, a smile gracing her lips. She was still amazed that under all the grime, Clare possessed an angel's head of long blond hair, and along with it, a sweet personality. Rachel was already quite attached to the little girl.

"When we get to the house, if someone is living there, do you think that maybe me and Tommy and you could ask for work there? That way, we could stay near the house. You know maybe they've a stable or something that we could sleep in when it rains."

Rachel touched a wisp of gold hair at Clare's brow. "I plan on us doing better than that."

Clare looked worried, as if she couldn't quite bring herself to believe in dreams. "I don't want to go back to the orphanage. I don't want to ever go back."

Rachel looked at her, confused, but finally Tommy explained.

"We both sprang from St. Vincent's. It was an orphanage, but no orphan could live there by choice," he offered bitterly. " 'Twas hell on earth, there. We won't ever go back alive," he vowed.

Rachel patted his hand. It was all the physical contact he'd allow her. "You won't go back to that place, then. Never fear."

"But if the plan doesn't work to get the

house," Clare broke in, "then we could still maybe stay near the house and—"

"—And circle it every day like a bunch of vultures just waiting to get at the carrion?" Rachel laughed. "No. If the house is occupied, then we'll have to go somewhere else. But I'll figure it out. We'll find another place to stay, and somewhere to work. And then, we'll go back to where I came from. It's not so bad there. The winter lasts a long, long time, but then all at once it's summer and the lichen turns emerald green, and we can go hunting for white swan feathers that cover the muskeg."

"That's a fairyland you're talkin' of, isn't it?" Tommy cut in, the usual suspicion blanketing his face. The boy just couldn't seem to settle down and accept that someone was finally taking care of the two of them. He continually looked for the flaw in the plan or in Rachel, and seemed disconcerted that he hadn't found one yet.

Rachel hadn't even known he was listening to their conversation. He, too, had curled up beneath the train blanket. The children napped like trail-worn ponies.

"No, it's not a make-believe place. It's very real. Not always a kind land, mind you—the weather is ferocious. But her people—" Her voice caught in her throat. "Her people are good. Of that you can be sure. You'll never go wanting as long as another has something to share."

"Then why don't we go there now? I've a bad

feeling about this house. 'Tis too good to be true. No one has houses they don't live in." Tommy scowled and stared out the window. The train was slowing down. Rachel's heart skipped a beat. From the window, she watched the sign at the train station pass. N-O-R-T-H-W-Y-C-K. She spelled it out.

The train lurched and hissed to a stop. The porter brought the steps from the rear of the car. All the passengers began to shuffle around, collecting their belongings.

Numb to it all, Rachel did nothing. She didn't move to collect her carpetbag, nor to help with the blankets covering the children. She only stared at the Gothic-lettered sign heralding the small Hudson River town as if memorizing it. The moment of reckoning was upon her. There was nothing now to do but collect her things and go forward with her plan—as insane as it suddenly seemed now.

"Have you some more luggage, miss?" she heard the porter ask her.

Focusing on his thin, lined face, she could only shake her head. "This is all." She could barely whisper. A quick, engulfing terror seized her. She'd come so far to see this wonderful house of Magnus's, but it didn't seem likely that it was sitting empty just waiting for the plucking. There were going to be problems with the scheme, she knew it instinctively. There was so much she didn't know about Magnus and his house and New York. It was only logical that she come across obstacles, especially when the going had been so smooth so far.

"Is this the house?" Clare asked once they descended the train to the wooden platform. Staring at the train station, she seemed dwarfed by the heavy ogee arches adorning the one-room station building.

"No, I don't think it's the house," Rachel answered, her despairing gaze fixed on the line of wagons and coaches waiting to pick up passengers.

"What house are you looking fer?" A man in a grimy oil coat stopped grappling with a trunk and paused to wipe his forehead.

"We're looking for a house in Northwyck." Overwhelmed, Rachel looked around her at the wagon traffic and the dozens of passengers loading onto the train. Northwyck wasn't a house, it was a town. They might never find Noel's house in the many buildings surrounding the town square and beyond.

"I know ever'one hereabouts. What's the name?" he asked.

"Noel Magnus." She held her breath.

The man nodded. "Then you'd be wanting to go to Northwyck House." He eyed them. "What are you here for? Have you got a hope for work?"

"Someday...perhaps," she said in an unsure voice. "Right now we just want to go to the house. We've heard so much about it, you see."

"I suppose the place must seem like a dream to the likes of you," he said with unmasked pity, his gaze traveling over their worn clothes and tired faces. "If I was going out and not coming in, I'd give you a ride there in my wagon." He pointed to the road out of town. "But the road there is just under a mile in that direction. You cannot miss it. 'Tis at the iron gates."

"Thank you," she said, taking Clare's hand in her own. With Tommy at the lead, they stepped from the platform and wandered down the ice-rutted dirt road in the direction he pointed.

"This must be a wonderful house," Clare exclaimed as they passed by trim little cottages adorned with wooden scrollwork and a thick layer of snow and icicles. "The man even knew of our house, didn't he, Rachel?"

"Don't run too far, Tommy," Rachel called after the boy as he impatiently scouted ahead. Returning her attention to Clare, she answered distractedly, "I do hope it's wonderful. Oh, I do hope so."

They came to a bend in the road about a mile from the center of town. Oak trees glistening with ice obscured their view, but then all at once, they found themselves in front of a short iron fence surrounding a four-gabled cottage. Lead windows with tall Gothic arches graced the tiny structure, along with deep shadow-filled eaves that made the structure appear to be nestling down in the snow.

Rachel stopped in her tracks and stared at the house. Breathless, she took in every detail. Northwyck was far more glorious than she'd imagined. In fact, it was a castle. The building had to possess at least six rooms, and there were two chimneys, more than enough fireplaces to keep out the cold for a woman and two children.

"Are we to live there?" Tommy whispered in front of the little iron gate, his defiance for once humbled.

"I hope so. I hope so," Rachel murmured, and strode through the gate to the door.

Afraid and yet wanting, she took a moment before she knocked on the arched batten door. Waiting with her heart in her throat, she gave a silent prayer of thanks with every second that ticked by and no one answered the door. Maybe the house was empty indeed.

"Perhaps I should knock again," she announced with far more confidence than she felt.

Again she knocked, this time louder.

But there was no answer.

Pounding until her dry skin cracked and bled on her knuckles, there was still no answer. Tommy and Clare stared at her, silently asking, what next?

"If the master of this house has not returned in years and they think him dead, of course there is no answer here. I say we enter and see for ourselves what Noel Magnus has left behind."

The two children nodded.

With a trembling hand, Rachel twisted the doorknob. For one second, she worried the house would be locked and they would not find entry, but the door opened on well-oiled hinges, welcoming them into a room that was warm with the scent of freshly baked bread.

"Curse it!" Tommy scowled as he ran to the

hearth where a coal fire still glowed red. "There's someone here before us. We'll never wrestle the place from them now."

Tears of disappointment welled in Rachel's eyes as she scanned the beautiful interior. A ruby velvet settee was placed near the fire with a silver Argand lamp for added light. On the seat, a pretty piece of Berlin work was being worked in a palette of lavender wool and the unfinished piece sat discarded on the seat of the settee as if put aside for just a moment. Several prints of French roses graced the walls framed in gold leaf and on the floor was a plush floral carpet that luxuriously covered the room from one wall to the others. In truth, it was the most delightful room Rachel had ever seen, and by the look of awe and disappointment on the children's faces, it was their assessment, too.

A clock on the mantel chimed. A small door over the clock face opened and a miniature monk swung out and tripped a small bell that tolled four times. Fascinated, Clare and Tommy inched forward, watching the small figure disappear behind church doors at the top of the clock. Rachel desperately wanted to stay and watch the monk ring in five o'clock also, then six o'clock, and more again until the rest of her life was chimed away, but it was getting late and they would have to figure out what they were to do now that they'd lost the house.

That was when they heard the door open and a pleasant voice humming.

Rachel spun around. The children backed into her skirts.

"Good Lord!" cried the plump older woman. Shocked, she snatched back the shawl covering her head and let her fine heavy cloak fall to the floor unnoticed.

"Who are you? What are you doing here?" she asked, alarm in her voice but no real fear.

"I—I'm so sorry," Rachel stammered. "There's been a terrible mistake. We didn't mean to come in here, only—only—" She couldn't finish.

"Only what, my dear?" the woman prompted. She absentmindedly patted the snow out of her gray curls while her eyes studied the two children.

"Only..." Rachel had to catch her breath. Her heart pounded so fiercely she wondered if she would pass out. "Only we thought the house was empty."

"Empty? Why on earth would you think that?"

"Because Noel Magnus told me it was," Rachel answered, defeated.

"Noel Magnus? Noel Magnus? How do you know of him, child?" the woman demanded, her eyes wide.

"I know of him from up North. That's where I'm from, you see."

"That certainly explains your choice of fashions," the old woman commented, a twinkle in her eyes as she scanned Rachel's ringed-seal coat.

"But it's clear you got here first," Rachel conceded. "And that is the law of the land, and I will abide by it."

"What made you come here?" the older woman asked, clearly wanting answers. "Have you seen Mr. Magnus lately? Could we dare hope that he's still alive?"

Rachel found she could say nothing. There was no purpose in telling all and sundry that Noel was still alive, because she had no reason to believe he would ever return to New York. His soul was as bound up with the ice as his black heart was.

"What brought you here, child?" the woman prompted, sensing Rachel's conflict.

"Noel told me about the house. I thought I could come live here since he was no longer in need of it."

"By what right? Did he bequeath it to you on his deathbed?"

Now was the time for the big lie, but it didn't seem so bad any longer to explain her trumped-up right to the house now that the house was taken and the stakes had erased themselves. She would get nothing out of her story except the right to make a hasty departure, so she blurted it out.

"I'm Noel Magnus's wife. I just thought since he wouldn't be needing this fine house any longer that we might come to live here. You see, he never mentioned that he left it to you."

The woman gasped. She stared at Rachel, then returned her gaze to Tommy and Clare.

"Could it be true?" the woman mumbled to

herself. She walked up to Tommy and placed her hands on his face. "Is this Magnus's son? Yes, yes, I see the likeness now."

Tommy's gaze shifted to Rachel. He said nothing underneath the old woman's perusal, but Rachel could see his astonishment and uncertainty.

"I—I—" Rachel couldn't get the words out, and what words they were, she didn't even know. There'd been no plan to pawn Tommy and Clare off as Noel's children and she was as shocked as they were to see the woman surmise.

"Nathan! Nathan!" the woman suddenly burst out. She trammeled to the front door and called outside. "Nathan, come quick! Leave the packages, tie up the wagon! You won't believe what's happened!"

"Good God, Betsy! You nigh gave me a heart attack! I'm right here at the door!" A man of at least seventy appeared at the door. He stared at Rachel and the children.

"Nathan, this is Noel's widow. And his son and daughter, too! I can't believe it! I simply can't believe it!"

Nathan didn't bother to unwrap the shawl around his head. He walked right up to Rachel, pulled off his steam-covered spectacles and studied Rachel with his own twinkling blue eyes. He touched the odd fur on her hood and said, "I guess you are from way up there, aren't you, miss?"

"*Mrs.*, Nathan, *Mrs.*!" Betsy interjected.

Rachel didn't know what to say. The whole situation was more than she'd counted on, and it was growing larger and more complicated by the second. Suddenly, she wanted very much to be on the next train out of Northwyck.

"Noel never mentioned what good friends he had here," she offered, unsure what the next move should be.

"Why," exclaimed Betsy, "we've both known Noel since he was born. We loved him like a son." The woman turned inexplicably sad. "I don't suppose it's a wonder he doesn't talk about Northwyck much. Not all his memories were good ones. But his father is dead now, and, unfortunately, Noel along with him." Betsy seemed to blink tears from her eyes as she gazed down upon Clare and Tommy. "But now maybe Northwyck has a fresh chance to raise a new generation." She turned to Rachel. "We'll do all we can for you, love. I promise we'll do that."

Holding her breath, Rachel took her opportunity. "Well, I do have one problem right now. With the house being lived in by you, I was wondering if you could find us a place to stay for the night. I only have a few coins left after our train trip. I can't afford a very nice inn, but if you know of a room that I and the children could stay in while I look for work—"

"Work?" Nathan interrupted. His face drained of blood and he was forced to lower himself to the settee, shawl, cloak, and all.

"What are you speaking of, child? You can't be looking for work like a common scullery." Betsy looked as if she were about to wag her finger.

"But I've got to find something! We're running out of coin and we've no place to live!" Perhaps it was weariness and disappointment, but Rachel couldn't hide the panic in her voice.

"My God, you don't have to worry about those things. Not ever." Betsy frowned. "I don't know what that cad put you through living in the savages of the North, but here you'll not want for a thing."

"But I've got to get work," Rachel implored her. "Me and the children can't live here with you. You got the house first, and it's only fair you get to keep it."

"Why are you so taken with this house, love?" Betsy finally inquired.

"It's just that I only knew to come here because Noel often spoke about it."

A wave of pity and tenderness seemed to engulf the older woman. "If Noel spoke of a house, he spoke of Northwyck, not this cottage, my dear."

"This house isn't Northwyck?" A newfound hope came to Rachel. Maybe there was still a chance for a life here.

"Good Lord, no. This is the groundskeeper's house. You didn't go far enough down the road."

"Well, we'll go right away," Rachel said excitedly. "And we'll be happy with it if we can live there even if it isn't as wonderful as this house. I promise you. Isn't that right, children?"

Nathan stood. He looked bewilderedly toward Betsy.

"We'd best take the girl and the children to Northwyck, Nathan. We'd best show them their new home." Betsy nodded and picked up her cloak, which had been forgotten on the floor.

They all followed Betsy out of the cottage and down the road another hundred yards. All at once Betsy stopped. She took Rachel's cold hand. "Look through the lane to your left, love. I think my cottage can't quite compare to your new home."

Rachel turned. Towering over the birches and oaks loomed a spired slate roof the height and breadth of a mountain. She took a step forward and peered through the trees. On the facade of the sprawling building, she counted six stories, forty windows, and eight men shoveling the snow and ice on the walkways that led from the carriage yard.

She looked at Betsy, not quite able to comprehend the reason for the woman showing her the enormous building. When Betsy answered her unspoken questions, Rachel felt the blood drain to her cold feet.

"That, my dear, is your new home. *That* is Northwyck."

CHAPTER FIVE

"**B**ut you must stay! What better place have you to go? You can't go back to that godforsaken land and properly raise the children. What about school? The children have got to get an education." Betsy patted Rachel's hand and studied the younger woman as if she was worried about her sanity.

Certainly that was prudent given how Rachel felt at the moment. She was either living a dream and soon to awake, or she was immersed in a nightmare the likes of which even Dickens couldn't have fashioned.

"No, really. You don't understand. We cannot live here. We didn't think the house would be so—so—" Rachel swallowed another wave of terror. Never in her wildest imaginings did she think she'd find herself in the middle of this situation. To her, Noel had always seemed rich, with his interminable expeditions and empty, forgotten house, but she realized now she never knew what truly rich was. If the parlor she sat in now was any indication of Noel Magnus's wealth, then she had been a fool to think she could come to New York and live in quiet solitude in a purloined cottage by the road. Her arrival, nay, her very existence as Mrs. Noel Magnus, was now going to be trumpeted across the countryside. She could see the headlines to *The New York Morning Globe* right now: *Wife of long-lost publisher found!* It would take a year, maybe two, for Magnus to see that headline where he was, but surely he would see it, and then he would come back to New York and have her head put on a platter.

She gazed around the parlor that Betsy and Nathan had brought her to when she nearly fainted on the roadside. The windows, fourteen feet high, were swathed in bronze and pine-green velvet plush. A burgundy-and-green-figured carpet lay in broad strips completely covering the parlor floor just as she remembered the parlor done in Philadelphia as a child. But even the memory of that luxurious townhouse was nothing compared to the enormous room she sat in now. This room had a black walnut parlor suite of twenty-five pieces. It had paintings by Jean Louis David and an antique gold frieze of trefoils and quatrefoils encircling the room. And there was not a chance that she, Rachel Ophelia Howland, was going to commit the kind of fraud that claimed her to be rightful occupant of a castle.

"Let's have some tea and see if that won't clear our heads," Betsy offered when a maid in a black dress and white apron entered holding an enormous silver tea tray. The young woman placed the tray on the table in front of Betsy, then she stole a glance at Rachel who was still in her seal *amautik*. Rachel had no doubt she was going to trot right back to the kitchens and get the whole household to listen to her description of the new lady of the house.

"Thank you very much, Annie," Betsy said to the maid. They seemed to exchange meaningful glances. Annie nodded her capped head toward the tea tray, then she silently shut the huge mahogany parlor doors behind her.

Rachel began to shiver, though the room was anything but cold with its four coal fireplaces. Trembling, she pleaded, "But even if, as his widow, I've the right to live in this magnificent house, I can't manage it. I haven't the strength to keep a house of this size clean. It would take me half the year to do it. I thought perhaps there was a cottage to look after. But this..." Rachel's words trailed off into despair. In front of her, Tommy and Clare had refused to sit down or even to touch anything. They kept their eyes trained on her as if any second she was going to yell, RUN!, and they would be on the ready.

"Child! You don't have to handle the house. That's why you have me and Nathan. He's the groundskeeper and I'm the housekeeper. We know how to manage it all, and we *will* manage it all should you wish to continue our employment."

"I would never fire anyone! Never!" Panic engulfed her. Calming herself again, Rachel said, "No, you don't understand, I can't stay here. I can't. It's too much. I can't."

Betsy handed her a steaming cup of tea in a paper-thin French porcelain cup. "It's not just about you, love." Her bright blue eyes turned to the children. "You've got to think about them, you know. They can't live as

79

you've lived, like heathens. They've a right to an education and to the things their father's legacy can provide for them. What right have you to interfere with that?"

Rachel opened her mouth, but there were no words to help her. She couldn't very well snatch the children away after letting everyone think they were Magnus's. The law would come after them if she tried to keep them from their "inheritance." To further her troubles, the law was surely going to be hard on her if she blurted out the truth now and told everyone she and the children weren't connected to Magnus. She would have dragged Tommy and Clare into her schemes. Instead of the two children sleeping beneath a cold and damp staircase, they'd be in the workhouse alongside her until they dropped from hunger and despair.

There seemed no solution to this nightmare. No way out of the maze. She was a hapless fly in a web of her own making.

"I can't stay here," she whispered in a small, defeated voice.

"Drink your tea, love. You're distraught. I suppose it is quite a shock, after where you've been, to arrive here and see how changed your life is destined to become, but it won't be for the worse, I promise you. I was Noel's nanny when he was first born, the dear one, and I'll see that his wife and children find a good life here, even if he could not." Betsy patted her hand again. Meaningfully, she said, "Now drink your tea. That's a good girl."

Rachel sipped the heavily sweetened tea. She

swore it was laced with brandy, or something else even stronger, but she found no reason to complain. Certainly she was distraught. Maybe with a little spirits in her, she could find the courage she needed to confess her crime and take the punishment she deserved.

"Now, do you mind if the nurse takes the children to their rooms? If it be true, I think they're hungry. I'd like to see them fed and tucked beneath the quilts before they fall asleep on their feet." Betsy stared at her, silently waiting for her approval.

Shutting her heavy eyes for a second, Rachel gathered herself, then turned to Tommy and Clare. "Nothing can be done about the situation tonight, so I think Betsy is right. Let's get you some food and a good night's sleep before we settle this tomorrow. Is that all right with you two?"

Clare said nothing. She just stared at Tommy with her wide blue eyes as she was wont to do when they lived by their wits back on the streets.

"Me and Clare think that maybe we should all stick together," Tommy said in his tough little voice. He frowned and looked at Rachel.

"Tommy, love"—Rachel took his hand— "I know this place is frightening us all out of our wits, and truly—truly—" Her voice broke a little. "Truly I am sorry for this awful fright. But I will make it better, and you can help me if you're rested and fed. So do as Betsy says. I trust her." Rachel stared into his eyes. "I do trust her," she whispered.

Tommy nodded.

Betsy pulled a heavy red silk tasseled rope. The maid Annie appeared again and spirited the children away to the unknown reaches of the mansion Northwyck.

Rachel downed her tea. Already her eyelids were so heavy she could hardly prop them up.

"Now, you, my dear, are next. Let me take you to your suite while you can still walk there by your own means." Betsy took her hand. Rachel followed like another child.

Her suite of rooms was unimaginable. Festoons of thick blue satin draped the full tester bed. A matching parlor suite of rococo laminated rosewood furniture fitted out the receiving room; the dressing room was four times larger than the saloon on Herschel Island; it had hand-painted wallpaper with scenes of old Paris. Rachel could hardly believe her eyes.

"I've ordered a bath for you. Mazie will lay out your bedclothes. Let me just take this, will you?" Betsy reached for the carpetbag still in Rachel's grip.

"No, please. Let me keep it," she told the older woman.

Betsy laughed. "I guess it's like an old friend now. All right. Keep it with you. I'll ring for Mazie."

Within minutes, a sentinel of maids brought hot water for the bath. Rachel had never been scrubbed so clean. Her hair was washed and she was wrapped in a thick Turkish robe and placed near the fire. Nodding off, she was finally persuaded by Betsy to surrender to the bed. She climbed into the towering, intimidating bed, the carpetbag safe beside her.

Betsy lowered the gas sconces and departed the room. Rachel swore her last words were, "Thank God we have some of you back, dear Noel."

Dazed, exhausted, and most likely even drugged, Rachel raised herself to a seated position and tried to rub the sleep from her eyes. She was as bone-tired as she had ever been, but now that she was alone, she had to think. Searching through her grimy carpetbag, she extracted the stone. The fiery black opal. The Black Heart.

The weight of it felt good in her palm. She'd worked hard at the saloon to ensure she didn't have to sell it on her long voyage to New York, and she knew she would work hard in the future to keep it. If it was to bring her bad luck, she couldn't see it as having happened yet. Especially every time she looked around the bedchamber that was fit for a modern-day Marie Antoinette.

But no matter what the omen, she knew she wouldn't relinquish the stone. She had to keep it in case Magnus ever came looking for her. It was her small revenge for his rejection. He would find all he wanted when he finally came to her side.

But he didn't know it yet. And maybe he would never know it. She had to face the very real possibility that he might never return to

New York again; that he would die a happy man in his beloved North.

Her hand tried to crush the wretched stone. The thought of her never seeing Noel, never hearing his deep voice, never kissing his hard lips, brought pain to her very soul, but there had been no other way to get him than to leave him. If she'd waited for him at the Ice Maiden she would have waited until they either brought her his dead body stiff from the cold, or until they came with the message that Noel had decided to return to his spurned New York after all and failed to take her with him.

She was destined to lose him up North. But here, she had a chance. By running from him, he just might decide to chase her. And when he caught her—if he didn't kill her first, he might realize he loved her.

And if she never saw him again...

If not, she had Northwyck. It was no small succor.

Holding her breath, she gazed at the dim cavern of a room. Never in her life had she believed such a room existed, with gold-cherubed cornices over satin drapery the perfect color for her, the pale-blue shade of ice.

But here the room was, along with forty others just as splendid. And she was in it, cuddled beneath the eiderdown quilt, her heart wanting to stay, her mind telling her it was madness. No one could take such wealth with a lie and not get caught, and the penalties would be equal to the wealth stolen.

"Off with her head," she whispered out loud, her words not comforting her, but not frightening her, either. It was the stone that gave her courage. She didn't want it or the dark palace that was Northwyck. All she wanted was love from the worthy man of her choosing, from her beloved Noel Magnus.

But if he didn't want her, then she would take his leavings. And take the punishment for the three of them should they get caught.

She fell back against the silk pillows, declaring herself insane. Maybe the stone was cursed. Maybe that was why she had acted upon this ludicrous scheme. If the time came, she would have to pay for her crime, probably with her mind, body, and soul. But at least her jailers wouldn't get her heart. Alas, it was no more. It had been given to Noel Magnus, and by all evidence, it had been tossed aside like that ill-fated opal her father had found on the tundra.

The Black Heart.

The black heart indeed.

CHAPTER SIX

Northwyck House
Hudson River
August, 1858

"Tommy! Clare! Come back! We have to ready ourselves for our company! We're finally to meet Mrs. Steadman! *Please* don't dally!"

Rachel swept back a hank of hair. The children were far down the hill almost to the river. Clare had already started toward her; Tommy was running to catch up, a toy sailboat in his hands as tall as he was. The miniature clipper ship's sails puffed out in the wind, giving the appearance of a kite ready to launch the boy into flight.

"Are you going to actually wear the pink dress, Rachel?" Clare asked, out of breath and plunking down in the grass beside her.

Rachel gave a derisive glance down at the elaborate silk widow's weeds she'd been wearing for almost six months. "I am. Today, I am officially out of full mourning and into half mourning. No more black for me. Just purple. The pink dress you mention, Clare, is actually an approved shade of lavender."

Clare nodded her blond head. The girl looked charming in a dress made of layers of powder-blue muslin, the waist tied with a wine-colored satin ribbon as wide as Rachel's hand. Her hair was pinned, and cascaded in artful ringlets down her back. Even the way she had fallen into the grass was mannered and poised. Clare was becoming a young lady underneath all of Northwyck's tutelage, but what surprised Rachel was all the refinement the child naturally had inside her. With some trust, along with many a good meal, Clare had blossomed. It was as if the child had always been to the manor born. Rachel almost wondered if it was possible that this girl from the streets had some kind of aristocratic blood in her after all.

But such was not the case with Tommy. He was still as scrappy as ever. He took elocution lessons now, and he didn't burst out with any more "ain't's" and "me's," but his tutor had a handful with him. Often Rachel would find the twenty-year-old man striding down the hallway, Tommy's ear in his grasp as he tried once again to retrieve the restless boy for his studies. Even now, Tommy didn't fool anyone. He wore the finest black linen for his sacque and trousers, but his cambric shirttail hung out and the large black satin buttons were fastened off kilter. He was a mess.

"We can't be late!" Clare scolded him.

Tommy panted to catch his breath. "I'm not late. Not late at all...at least not very late."

Rachel clasped his hand. A strange joy built inside her, and as much as she wanted to scold, she couldn't. Life had started to become quite fine for them. Everything seemed to be falling into place. At least for the children. They were looking quite plump and content; very different from the wide-eyed waifs that had attempted to steal her purse but mere months before. And for that small triumph, the struggle was worth it.

"Come along," Rachel said sternly as Betsy had taught her to do whenever she had wanted to laugh and encourage the boy. "You, Tommy, are going to need the most work of all to get ready. Mrs. Steadman isn't to be disappointed. We haven't been allowed a visitor in the entire time we've been here because of our mourning. We can't chase our first caller away, now, can we?"

Within minutes, she deposited the children in the nursery, then she went to her dressing room, where Mazie, her personal maid, was ready with a hairbrush.

"Oh, finally!" Betsy said, standing in the doorway with her dress freshly pressed in the laundry. "I was beginning to worry. We can't keep Mrs. Steadman waiting. If we lose her patronage, we lose everyone's."

Rachel stared at her from the mirror. "I know I sound terribly foolish, but tell me again why she is so integral to my success here at Northwyck?"

"My dear child, she will gain you entry not only to society here along the Hudson River, but in Manhattan as well. And if you add Newport to the mix, well, you might as well give up if she shuns you, because no one will accept you. There will be no invitations, no calls, no reason at all to get the carriage and go for a drive."

"It's so complicated here," Rachel said wistfully. "I wanted friends, but I had no idea this was how they were acquired here in New York."

Betsy sighed and gave her a wry smile. "I know things must seem very strange here compared to the life you've known. But you must understand, Rachel love, you're not just anyone. You're Mrs. Noel Magnus. There's no escaping the social obligations that go along with being the wealthy widow of a newspaper heir."

Rachel swallowed her rising guilt. "I guess I understand, but I really feel that I've enough friends as it is. Everyone here at Northwyck has been so kind. I certainly count you and Mr. Willem as my friends."

"And so we are, love, but you can't count on me and Nathan to introduce you to society. That's Mrs. Steadman's job."

"But what if I have no need to be introduced to society."

"But you must. How are you planning to find another husband if you don't?"

Rachel jerked her head around so quickly, Mazie took half her hair with the brush. "Husband? I don't want a husband," she protested, panic in her voice.

Betsy laughed softly. "I understand you were devoted to Magnus. I see the love for him in your face every time you speak of him. And of course you don't have to remarry.

But a woman must have her options. With Mrs. Steadman your ally, you cannot lose."

"But what if I don't make a good impression upon her? What if I can't live up to it all?" Rachel mused, stepping into her lavender tea gown with Mazie's assistance.

"She'll adore you. As we all do. You won't make a mistake, I know it."

It was Rachel's turn to smile wryly. "Me? Commit a faux pas?"

"All right. I'll admit the first six months haven't gone as smoothly as one would like. But the cultural differences between where you've lived and here were bound to take some time to overcome. You just never knew that a lady doesn't explain how much whiskey goes into a shot and the necessary amount of beer to chase it. But don't think the knowledge went unused. Why, the stableboys have taken your direction to heart. Nathan finds them drunk every evening by seven o'clock."

"I just wanted to be helpful," Rachel answered, chastised.

"And you were, dear child. But now it's time to embrace a whole new existence. To do honor to Magnus, I know you will succeed."

Rachel stared at herself in the mirror. Her hair was neatly combed back and pinned, and the coil of blond tresses was tucked into a black crocheted snood. Her tea gown was of tissue-weight dead-colored lavender silk, with five tiers of it flowing across her horsehair crinoline to the floor. In any other color she would have loved the dress. But the *Godey's* butterflies still hadn't fluttered into her life, dazzling her with their beautiful colorful gowns. Certainly it was a just punishment that all of Rachel's gowns be the same depressing shade of death and shadow that the last one was.

"I guess I'm ready to go to the parlor." Rachel met Betsy's gaze.

"You look lovely, my dear. It's not the most cheerful shade of purple, but at least your gown's no longer black. I know Mrs. Steadman will approve."

Rachel tipped the side of her mouth into a dark smile. "Pray your education works."

The grand Mrs. Steadman arrived in full fanfare of a coach and eight gray Thoroughbreds and her own liveried coachmen adorned in Steadman blue. Rachel watched her arrival from the parlor window, then she rushed to the far corner where Betsy had told her to wait until her guest was announced.

"Your guests are here to extend their condolences on your departed husband."

"Thank you very much. Please show them in," Rachel said to Betsy, all the while thinking how silly all the formality was. She'd just been chatting with Betsy before the coach arrived.

Mrs. Steadman was the tallest woman Rachel had ever seen. She herself was only a hair over five feet tall, but she had towered over the Herschel natives and, save Noel and few other white men, most she was able to look in the eye. But not Gloria Steadman. The woman was a foot taller than herself, with a lustrous chignon of fox-white hair she held with tortoise pins. Her gown of royal-blue cashmere with black velvet trim only accentuated her intimidating bosom and no amount of Brussels lace in her chemisette could mitigate it.

The gentleman with her, however, was not dwarfed by Mrs. Steadman's commanding size. He stood an inch or two taller, but with his slim build, he appeared taller than he actually was. The expression on his face, far from being welcoming, was dark and intense. The silver in his black locks indicated he was near fifty years of age; the fine worsted jacket and foulard silk tie dotted with green gave evidence that he was no pauper.

"Mrs. Steadman. You were so kind to think of me." Rachel extended her hand and glanced at Betsy, who had yet to excuse herself. The twinkle in the housekeeper's eye conveyed her approval.

"How tiny you are! How frail! The way they spoke of you, I expected a looming creature with club in hand ready to kill its dinner."

Rachel's mouth dropped open, and she couldn't quite seem to gather her composure enough to close it.

"Mrs. Magnus, let me introduce to you Mr. Edmund Hoar. He is your neighbor, and he was most anxious to give you his condolences on Magnus's death. He owns The Company of the North, and knew Magnus ever so well." Mrs. Steadman turned to the gentleman at hand. "Edmund, let me introduce to you Mrs. Noel Magnus."

Rachel could hardly believe her ears and eyes. The Company of the North was as familiar to her as the devil was to Faust. She knew every detail of Edmund Hoar's notoriety, but she had never met the man. He never came to his kingdom, despite the fact that every casket of whiskey, every bag of dry goods, had had to be purchased from The Company of the North. Edmund Hoar was the ultimate authority for a company that thought nothing of extortion and outright robbery of the individuals who relied on the company for the very basics of life. And he was Magnus's mortal enemy. It stunned her that he could show up at Northwyck and give condolences to Magnus's widow.

Repulsed, but knowing she couldn't show it, she put out her hand, palm-down, as Betsy had instructed whenever a gentleman should call.

Hoar took her hand and placed a dry kiss upon its back. "I'm ever so delighted to meet you, Mrs. Magnus." He gave her a small, secretive smile. "In all the years I knew him, Noel never mentioned taking on a wife."

Mrs. Steadman brushed him aside. "Heavens! The man was busy, Edmund, you cad! He was battling the elements and, clearly, even death itself, to find Franklin. A man can die no greater death than that of a hero's." The matron looked fondly to Rachel. "You must ignore Edmund, my dear. He was also Noel's most notorious competitor."

"I see," Rachel commented, hiding the fact that she knew far more than both of them.

"I vowed to find Franklin first." Edmund raised one dark eyebrow. "I plan on sponsoring another expedition this spring now that Magnus is gone. Winning's still in my blood."

"Tea will be served shortly," Betsy announced, her eyes meaningfully turning toward the settee.

"Won't you please sit down?" Rachel said. Despite her shock at meeting Hoar, she was still able to stick to the social script Betsy had rehearsed with her.

"I will." Mrs. Steadman lowered herself, keeping watch on her crinoline so that it didn't get crushed in the back.

Okay. Now the compliment, Rachel said to herself. "What a marvelous breast you have, Mrs. Steadman." Before the words were even out, Rachel's hand flew to her mouth. "I mean—mean *brooch*. It's a bird, isn't it?" she sputtered, blood rushing to her face, her gaze darting to her guests.

"The common house wren done in yellow sapphires. The piece encompasses both my love of jewels and nature, birds in particular." The woman seemed unperturbed by the error. She smiled and watched Rachel take a seat. "Now, you must tell me how you've managed during your mourning. Have you found everything at Northwyck to your satisfaction?"

"Oh, yes. Everyone's been so kind. I don't know how we would have acclimated to all the changes if everyone in the household hadn't been so patient. I do hope you'll extend us the same generosity, Mrs. Steadman. I'm certain we'll need it."

"And how are the children? May we see them?" Mrs. Steadman continued in the drama.

"Of course." Rachel turned to Betsy. "Mrs. Willem, would you bring in the children?"

Betsy curtsied. Within two minutes, the children were presented in their best muslin and linen. Tommy's hair was macassared and Clare's face scrubbed pink. They looked like two little angels—another lie, another nail in the coffin of the deceit.

"What darlings!" Mrs. Steadman cooed. "And what an ordeal they must have had to go through in order to get here. Why, come here, you dear children! I want to make sure you're all right!"

Tommy and Clare edged toward the woman. Tommy had the old look of suspicion on his face; Clare had one of adoration, as if she was already planning a brilliant matronhood like Gloria Steadman's.

"So, what exactly did old Magnus die of?" Edmund Hoar whispered while Mrs. Steadman entertained the children.

Shocked, Rachel glanced at him. The expression on his face was one of intense interest in her answer and naked ridicule; it was clear he didn't believe her fraud for one minute.

"I—I confess I'm as much in the dark about his disappearance and death as everyone else in New York is," she said, her heart pounding in her chest. She'd never counted on Magnus having a foe to challenge her, but she supposed it only served her right.

"His death was reported only in *The New York Morning Globe*," Hoar commented. "Since Magnus himself owns the paper, I think I have to doubt the veracity of anything printed about Magnus within its pages."

"What are you saying, Mr. Hoar?" Rachel asked, her voice barely above a whisper.

"I'm saying—" He closed the distance between them and whispered in her ear, "Magnus left behind a very beautiful widow whom I'm afraid might be vulnerable to certain gentlemen if she isn't watched closely."

She stared into his pale-jade eyes, unable to hide the trepidation in her own. "Here at Northwyck I know no vulnerability, sir."

The shadow of a smile graced his eyes. "You must pardon me if I take it upon myself to oversee your protection also. Noel Magnus was like a brother of the Arctic to me. Granted, we despised each other, but he knew I wanted Franklin as much as he did, and we both accepted a grudging respect for each other."

"How many times were you up in the Arctic, Mr. Hoar? Herschel Island did much business with your company. I never recall seeing you."

"If I'd known such beauty waited for me on Herschel I would have found a way up there, but, as it is, I financed the expeditions. It's up to other men to endure frostbite, not me."

From that moment on, Rachel knew she could never like the man. It was bad enough that his company sucked the lifeblood out of every northern trading post, but he lacked the bravery of daring his own adventures, and instead hired whoever was in need of the silver.

"If one thing can be said of Noel Magnus, it was that he was a great explorer. We wouldn't have the maps we have today without his prudent ability to live among the natives, and, therefore, endure the harsh climate."

"How prudent a man was he? He perhaps lost his life in search of The Black Heart—an opal the color of midnight with one brilliant star at its center. Was it worth a life just to recover one little rock?" Hoar smiled with teeth too small for his face. "But then, I understand you know the stone well, Mrs. Magnus. It's been rumored that you used just such a jewel to identify yourself as Magnus's wife."

"I know The Black Heart," she answered, wondering what he would make of her necklace should he ever see it. Betsy had insisted the precious stone be mounted so that she might be able to wear her husband's legacy. Rachel had found no way to protest.

"They say it is cursed," Hoar taunted.

"It is cursed," Rachel answered truthfully. The stone had certainly brought her father no happiness, and now that she had it, what did she really have other than a black heart to match it?

"I'd take a chance on it anyway," he told her, his gaze penetrating. "Anything that Franklin valued, I must value, too."

97

"I almost think it was that Magnus valued it," she challenged.

He laughed. "We had our testy moments. I do admit I didn't like the editorials he wrote about our slaughter of the blue whales in the Beaufort Sea. Imploring women to wear steel corsets instead of whalebone was an outright declaration of war, as far as I was concerned."

She recalled the long talks with Magnus about The Company of the North decimating the blue whales. Even now, here at Northwyck, when she'd had the choice of the best attire, she'd requested steel corsets. The visions of the massive corpses that would wash ashore in the springtime melt was alone enough to make her decide on steel. Blue whales were God's largest creatures on earth. It seemed wrong to eradicate them for fashion, even as much as she had yearned for fashion, and now finally had attained it.

"Ah, at last, our tea!" Mrs. Steadman exclaimed, bringing Rachel out of her thoughts. "The children will stay, won't they, my dear? I want to tell them about the wonderful ball I have planned to bring their mother out of mourning."

"A ball?" Rachel repeated, forgetting that she must be the one to pour out.

"Yes, yes. I've even got a promise from Mrs. Astor that she will attend. This will get you accepted right away, and you'll be able to put your dreadful tragedy behind you."

Betsy nudged her before she took her leave. Rachel shook her herself and immediately took up a cup and saucer. "Lemon?" she asked, hardly hearing herself, her thoughts were whirring so loudly. She had never imagined herself at a ball, let alone one in her honor. Fear and joy almost strangled her.

"I hadn't heard of the event," Hoar mentioned, casually watching Betsy exit.

Mrs. Steadman glanced at him. "Oh, don't be a scoundrel, Edmund. Of course you'll be invited. You're the most eligible bachelor in Manhattan now that Magnus is gone." It was the matron's turn to realize her faux pas. "Oh, please accept my apologies, my dear girl, I didn't mean to imply your marriage is unrecognized. Certainly not."

"Please don't worry another moment. I thought nothing of it," Rachel answered, handing out the cups.

"Certainly no one would think her marriage unrecognized. I'm sure Mrs. Magnus has the marriage certificate to prove herself." Hoar stared at her from beneath lowered eyelids.

Rachel dropped the cup. It went tumbling to the rug. Tea splattered across her skirt. "How clumsy of me," she murmured. "Let me clean myself up. I'll ring for Mrs. Willem to get another cup."

"We're in no hurry, dear. Please don't strain yourself," Mrs. Steadman said as she stole a tea cake and passed it to Clare.

Rachel excused herself again. She exited the room, but before she could reach the staircase, she found a hand on her arm, stopping her.

"Really, if I had such an idea he had you stashed up there on Herschel, I would have thrown away all hopes of The Black Heart and stolen you instead."

Rachel gave Hoar an unwavering stare. "You don't mean to imply you would stoop to stealing, Mr. Hoar."

"To get what I want, I would do anything. Anything," he emphasized.

An unfamiliar tingle of fear coursed down her spine. Rachel had encountered lusty men before, even threatening men. But Hoar was different. He was a man with power. On Herschel Island she had the power. She owned the Ice Maiden, and, therefore, all the whiskey. She had yet to meet a man who would threaten the closest supply of liquor within one thousand miles.

But Hoar didn't want whiskey. Worse, he seemed to be questioning her very right to be at Northwyck—and his suspicions might prove correct if she weren't careful around him.

He gave her another one of his smiles, the disingenuous kind fashioned with his mouthful of creepy doll teeth.

The tingle crept down her back again.

"I do want us to be friends, Rachel." He gazed at her. "I may call you Rachel, mightn't I?"

"What is it truly that you want, Mr. Hoar?" she asked in low tones. "You couldn't possibly be jealous of a man who's long found his Maker—"

"Magnus dead?" He laughed. "As I said in the parlor, *The New York Morning Globe* reports such news, but it has the foul odor of a lie. My agent who works the MacKenzie territory wrote to me that he had a cup with Magnus just last spring, well after the reports of his death hit the front page. So, lovely Rachel, I'm afraid that I question not only Magnus's death but also his marriage." He pulled her toward him until her chest crushed against his. "How is it you two were able to tie the knot when there hasn't been a preacher on Herschel in all the time I've supplied the post there?"

"Perhaps one slipped by your keen interest—an interest, I might add, that was never keen enough for you to ever set foot on Herschel." She shoved away from him.

He nodded. "Is this how our relationship is going to be? Full of contention? Fine. I'll take the fighting as long as I get the surrender." Pointing a finger at her, he said, "Just remember, I could take all this away in a flash if you're ever found out."

Her hands began to tremble. "What do you want from me? Is it the famed opal you want? Is that the price of this blackmail?"

"The opal, I desire. Who wouldn't want it? But it's still just a cold, lifeless rock. Maybe what is more desirable now is to own the flesh that gave Magnus pleasure. To find my own pleasure within it." His finger rested on her collarbone. He drew down the lavender silk taffeta of her gown until he met with the rolled top edge of her corset.

"I am not an 'it,' Mr. Hoar. I'm Rachel

Ophelia Howland, and not an object to be owned and used and discarded." The ice in her tone would have warned many a man away, but Hoar seemed to like it. His eyes gleamed with excitement.

"I'll see you at the Steadman ball, Rachel Ophelia Howland. And I take note that you still call yourself that and not Rachel Ophelia Howland *Magnus.*" He bowed his dismissal to her.

A maidservant entered the hall and curtsied to both of them. Rachel walked up the stairs as quickly as her dignity and her skirts would permit her. She didn't dare look back at Hoar for fear she would run.

Noel Magnus wasn't dead and Edmund Hoar knew it. The very earth and the weather were not so kind to him as to rid him of his mortal enemy. No, Noel Magnus was very much alive. He felt it in his bones, and in his heart where the hatred lived on.

Edmund sat in a leather chair by the library fire, Gloria Steadman's hand-scribed invitation to the ball held in honor of Rachel cradled in his palm.

He wanted Rachel Ophelia Howland, wanted her with a tightness in his loins he hadn't felt since his first time with the bar wench in back of the stables. Looking at Rachel in the short time he'd been at tea with her, he suddenly found he was a young man again, with all the vigor and yearnings of a virgin.

But it wasn't just her beauty that consumed him, or her defiance, or her intelligence. It was all of that and more. She encompassed everything to him. And mostly, she'd been Magnus's, and just for that alone, if she'd been ugly as a ragpicker, warts on her nose and all, he'd still want to possess her because she'd once been coveted by Magnus. And Magnus wasn't going to win. Edmund was.

Edmund crumpled the thick card in his hand and tossed it into the coal grate, watching the flames turn angry scarlet. He didn't need it. The date was burned into his mind. One week from the day and he would be at Rachel's side, guiding her in a waltz, planning for the moment when they could be alone and he could unhook her satin gown and ease himself within her fully.

She was going to fight him, but he didn't care. She was just a woman. A commodity. There was no one to fight for her honor, nothing but her wealth to see to her safety. And he didn't plan on hurting her. He planned on owning her. He would no more mar her face with a bruise than dash the famed opal on the rocky cliffs of the Hudson River. He took care of his possessions.

In silence he glanced around the cavernous room of his library, surveying the most valued treasures of his collection. There was the Rubens monumental painting of Mary Magdalene that took up the entire west wall, enclosed in a bell jar was the wax casting of Napoleon's death mask, and, at last, his greatest find of all, the Franklin Expedition diaries found strewn about the Arctic, hundreds of miles apart. The tragedy was that Franklin lived too long. Long enough to write about his interminable slope to the grave, but not careful enough with his accounts to leave a telltale map of his final resting place. It was the mystery of the century, and he was in a race to find Franklin and he would do it before Magnus, counting on the fact that the bastard was still living and breathing up North.

He looked across from him at the empty velvet seat near the fire. Rachel would look lovely perched there, drying her hair by the flames, her silk robe parted obediently while her owner assessed his treasure. She had to have been valued by Magnus or he never would have revealed the opal to her, let alone put her in possession of it. When Magnus found the piece he'd been so tight-lipped about it, even his spies among The Company of the North agents hadn't heard about the find.

But now here she was, opal in hand. A wondrous beauty who claimed spousal rights to Noel Magnus. Edmund could ruin her in minutes. Theirs had been a native marriage at best. But it was to his advantage to keep her respectable. She was that much more of a treasure that way. Besides, he didn't want to shame her in public. Let her shame come in the bedroom, where only he benefited. That way he would have his wildest pleasures fulfilled, and find ultimate retribution for

Magnus's cheating him. *The New York Morning Globe* had been his birthright. Charles Hoar had founded the lucrative newspaper and it was only Magnus's father's double dealing that had brought them to the point of bankruptcy. Afterward, the impoverished son had had to go it in the world alone. The only way to make up the family fortunes after they'd been lost was to start The Company of the North. But then, to have Noel Magnus, heir to the newspaper that had been rightfully Edmund's, write inflammatory editorials about Edmund's company was beyond the pale.

But he would get even now. To marry beautiful Rachel would entitle him to the newspaper once again. He would have the triple thrill of acing Magnus out of his own newspaper, his own home, and, mostly, his own wife.

Edmund could taste the revenge like the sweet cream of a woman. Dragging Rachel to the marriage bed would be the ultimate achievement. He could even see himself falling in love with her, with her defiant eyes and thick tangle of blond curls. And he would make sure nothing went wrong; that every incident was worked to his advantage.

He would have his enemy's wife, mind, body, heart, and soul.

And if Magnus were truly not dead? If he should show up to claim her?

Well, if Edmund couldn't have her, he would see her dead first.

CHAPTER SEVEN

R achel was ready for the Steadman ball. Never in her life had she been so terrified. Despite her better judgment, she downed the last of the sherry Mrs. Willem had sent up to calm her nerves. The last thing she wanted to do was appear at the ball with a snoot full, but the very idea of meeting so many strangers, especially with her head crammed with instructions, lessons on etiquette, and the numbers of steps in a waltz, Rachel truly wondered if she would endure the entire event without fleeing like Cinderella at the stroke of midnight.

"Oh, you do look lovely," Mrs. Willem said in a reverent whisper.

Rachel turned and gave her a timid smile. "I feel lovely, but I fear it's more the dress than me." She patted the voluminous skirt. Her ballgown was made of puce satin edged in matching *tulle-ruche* trim. A chemisette of Maltese lace covered the hefty expanse of skin exposed by the low-cut gown. Wrapping it all was an enormous shawl of garnet-red velvet edged with ermine. Rachel couldn't have dreamed of such clothing on Herschel, and now she was actually wearing it.

"The last item left." Mrs. Willem handed Rachel a large black leather case.

Opening it, Rachel took out The Black Heart. Now set on a gold chain, the opal was the perfect ornament to nestle in the shadow of her cleavage beneath the mesh of Maltese lace.

"You're perfect," Betsy exclaimed.

Rachel clasped the older woman's hands. "I must thank you for all you've done for the children and me. We couldn't have been so happy these six months if you hadn't been patient with us, and so very kind. How would I hold my head up to these people if you hadn't taught me and smoothed out my rough manners?"

"Your manners weren't so terribly rough, my child; they were just unformed from living in that wild place," Betsy soothed.

"When I first came here to New York I have to admit I thought the people cold and cruel. I couldn't understand their disregard for others. But now I see I was wrong to judge so quickly. You have changed my mind."

"I did it for Magnus as much as for you, my dear." Betsy stared at her with her warm blue eyes. "You know he was as much a son to me as he was to his mama. But she only had him three years. I, at least, was fortunate to have had him much longer."

"Did she die in another childbirth?" Rachel asked, hugging the ermine-trimmed shawl to her as if she were suddenly chilled.

Betsy shook her head. Her old-fashioned cap of figured lace comically bobbed. "No, no. It would have been a blessing for all concerned if she had. No, dear, the woman ran off. Magnus's father was a cruel man and the young woman could take no more suffering.

I wouldn't have blamed her a whit for what she did except she left her three-year-old son here to endure her husband's wrath. Noel would have been much different if not for the wretchedness of his father."

"Is that why he left here, never wanting to return?" Rachel asked quietly. So many things made sense suddenly.

"Most certainly. I couldn't blame the man. What did he have here?"

"He had a fine home to raise a family. All he had to do was marry and settle down," she said, wondering if she was giving away too much.

"Oh, but he couldn't see life as that simple and good. He was afraid, I think, that maybe the bad seed of his father was in him. He vowed never to have children." Betsy frowned as if she were deeply saddened, but then all at once she brightened. "So you can understand how thrilled we were to have you here, and the children. It was as if all our dreams had come true. Magnus in his way returned to Northwyck. And you've all made it such a happy place now. I love hearing the children running and laughing about in the corridors. Every house needs that, no matter how big or how small."

"It does," Rachel answered, her own heart twisting. For a long, silent moment she wondered what her and Magnus's child would have looked like. Would she have had blond curls like her mother? Or would he have had a dark scowl like his father? Without knowing it, she released a sigh.

"But tonight isn't the night to dwell on the tragedies, love. Tonight you're out of mourning for good, and it's your duty to go to Mrs. Steadman's and be the belle of the ball. You never know. Tonight could be the night you meet your next husband."

Rachel felt her heart stop. She'd never even thought about another husband. It wasn't conceivable to her to find a new love when the man she wanted was still very much alive.

And how would she explain that when she was walking around play-acting as his widow?

She closed her eyes a moment to gather herself. The web of lies seemed to choke her.

"There you go, my dear. No time for thinking about the past. The carriage awaits." Betsy held the door for her.

Numb inside, Rachel thanked her and walked down Northwyck's magnificent Gothic tracery staircase to the butler who held open the enormous front door. She was helped inside the carriage, and when her ermine-trimmed shawl was snug around her shoulders, the carriage took off for the Steadman household.

"They say she was some kind of heathen creature who just showed up at the doorstep asking about Northwyck."

"I heard she even had shoes made out of white bearskin. Have you ever heard of *white* bearskin? I think they made that up."

"The tale I heard tell was that theirs was a

native marriage. The children are quite old, aren't they? Almost too old for Magnus to have properly married her and conceived them."

The titters behind the rainbow of glittering fans was almost more than Rachel could bear. She knew she was being gossiped about and derided, but there seemed no other remedy than to hold her head up high and ignore their rudeness.

It was probably only natural that they be curious about her. She was the widow of a very wealthy and notorious man, and she had come from so far away they couldn't even picture the land. But very few of the guests actually spoke to her, and she found it depressing. If not for Mrs. Steadman's graciousness, she would have spent her first ball hiding behind a marble pillar so that no one could see her embarrassment.

"You look lovely, Mrs. Magnus. Enjoying the ball?"

Rachel looked up from her seat, startled by the familiar voice. Towering over her was Edmund Hoar. He looked dashing in a white silk vest and black swallowtail coat, but she could barely hide the fact that she wanted to recoil from him. Her memory of their conversation in the hall at Northwyck was still vivid in her mind.

"Edmund, you had better get your name on her dance card before it's all full up," Mrs. Steadman interjected from a thick circle of her admirers.

Hoar's black eyebrow lifted. "I plan to do just that."

His attention once more riveted to Rachel, he said to her, "Before I squeeze into your line-up, allow me to introduce to you a dear friend. Mrs. Noel Magnus, I'd like you to meet Miss Judith Amberly."

A woman, blonde and slender, stepped forward and nodded. Rachel felt as if she should stand or something. Instead, she held out her hand in greeting, and the woman looked at her extended hand as if it were a dead mullet.

"Miss Amberly has much in common with you, Mrs. Magnus," Edmund commented.

"And how is that, Mr. Hoar?" she asked, still trying to be pleasant even though her hand had to be lowered to her lap.

"Well, you are the widow of Noel Magnus, and Miss Amberly was his fiancée. How ironic, don't you think? His last visit here he had promised to wed her upon returning to New York. You see the lovely ring she has? He gave it to her." Hoar smiled with those tiny teeth. "How old did you say your eldest child was, Mrs. Magnus?"

If a poison could have seeped into her blood and killed what was left of her insides, Hoar's words did just that.

Numb, she looked down at the beautiful diamond glittering on the young woman's left hand. Judith Amberly was younger than herself. The woman would have no trouble picking up her disappointments and triumphing in the end. But Magnus had given Judith Amberly an engagement ring. He'd given this thin, hard-eyed blonde a diamond ring while he'd given Rachel only a bagful of lies. On his few trips to New York he'd been courting a fiancée while Rachel had been waiting for him, as she had waited for years.

"I'm pleased to make your acquaintance, Miss Amberly," Rachel choked out, the pain inside her too deep for tears.

"Likewise, I'm sure," the woman answered, a pinched expression on her face.

Hoar seemed to enjoy the encounter as if he were a cat lapping up the last of the entrails of a mouse.

Rachel looked away. It couldn't be easy to be Miss Judith Amberly. To wait all these years for a man who was never coming was a kind of agony she knew well. But then, to have the world think you were going to marry, only to find out your fiancé already had a wife and two children, indeed, Rachel had yet to suffer that pain.

Nonetheless, she knew she was never going to like Judith Amberly. Never. Certainly Rachel looked like the winner of the contest, but if the truth ever be told, she was the one betrayed, not Judith. Noel could still arrive and marry Judith. Rachel didn't have the luxury of wearing Noel's promise on her hand. She'd been denied that as surely as she'd been denied most everything Noel had promised her.

"I see this next waltz is not spoken for.

112

Would you care to dance, Mrs. Magnus?" Edmund bowed, his eyes glittering with evil amusement.

Rachel had no choice but to allow him to take her hand and lead her onto the dance floor. It was that or chat with Miss Amberly, and have her soul die just a little bit more.

Her every movement wooden and cold, she went around the dance floor with Hoar, but she spent all her time looking at the other waltzers rather than at her handsome partner.

The Steadmans had spared no expense in creating the marble ballroom. Creamy white stone relieved only by gold pilasters and gold mirrors was the precise foil in which to showcase the beautiful gowns of its attendees. The *Godey's* butterflies did exist, Rachel realized, when she had first been escorted to the ballroom and stood in the doorway. She'd been utterly dazzled by the ladies' gowns, which seemed to float by their crinolines. The colors were beyond the rainbow in vivid colors of fuchsia, emerald, and peacock-blue satin. Rachel felt almost dowdy in her subtle puce satin until she looked up and met Edmund Hoar's hungry gaze as he led her around the ballroom.

Suddenly, she felt she wasn't dowdy enough.

"So you never answered my question. Are you having a good time, Mrs. Magnus?" he said in her ear through the din of music and the crush of dancers.

"Yes. Mrs. Steadman was quite gracious to invite me."

"Invite you?" He laughed. "You, my lovely Rachel, are the guest of honor, or didn't you know that? Why else would Gloria Steadman ensure that you were seated to her right on the dais with Mrs. Astor?"

"I never thought about it. I just assumed she was being kind in seeing to my comfort. She knows I know no one," Rachel answered.

"Society matrons such as she don't extend their kindnesses to just anyone. Mrs. Steadman has taken you under wing because she likes you. There are others here who've spent years currying her favor and have never had the reception from her that you've had at tea."

Rachel was aghast. "But I don't need special attention. I never asked for it."

"You may not have asked for it, but you have it now. Don't be surprised if it has made you some enemies."

"Would that include you, sir?" She knew the question was inflammatory, but she couldn't help herself. Bluntness was in her nature. Life had been too harsh up North to hide oneself from the truth.

He grinned. "No, indeed. It wouldn't do to make enemies of the woman I intend to make my wife."

"You don't even know me, Mr. Hoar," she answered, ice in her words.

"I know enough," he said as his gaze lowered to a place beneath her chin. "The Black Heart does you justice, fair Rachel. You took my breath away when I saw what you wore around your neck. Where did you find it?

According to my diaries, Franklin must have had the stone at his last resting place."

"My father found the opal," she answered cryptically. "If he found Franklin's remains with it, he took the secret to his grave."

"You know more," he stated, his gaze holding hers.

"Perhaps," was all she offered.

"I think you don't want to betray your husband. Am I not correct?" He held her more closely, more brutally. "But yet, according to you and the rest of New York, Magnus is dead. So why not tell where your father found the opal, if not for Magnus's sake?"

She refused to comment.

"Lying, fraudulent little whore," he spat under his breath. "But I'll get the information out of you before Magnus. I promise I will."

"That could be a very long time, if Magnus is dead, as everyone thinks he is," she countered.

He smiled, his grip loosening. "I'm not fooled by you, love. In fact, I look forward to you telling me the whereabouts of Franklin." His eyes lowered to the opal. "And I look forward to the time when I can hold that infamous stone in my hand and caress its cold beauty."

"At what time would that be appropriate, sir?" she derided.

He locked gazes with her. "When I finally have you; when I can make you wear nothing but it."

Her breath caught in her throat. She wanted

to retort, but there was no denial strong enough with which to backhand the man. Without another word between them, the waltz ended and he led her back to her seat on the dais.

"I've got Fredrick Wing lined up next, so don't take all of her time, Edmund," Mrs. Steadman admonished.

"I wouldn't think of it," Hoar replied, leaning down and kissing Rachel's hand.

It took all her courage not to snatch her hand away, especially when she felt his tongue wiggle hotly upon it.

"Until later," he said.

Rachel refused to answer. But the worry built up inside until she wondered if coming to Northwyck was going to be more dangerous than running the Ice Maiden up on Herschel.

"I think he's quite taken with you," Mrs. Astor said to her when Hoar had gone.

"He doesn't know me," Rachel answered like a mantra.

"Let me give you some advice, my dear child. His family is of Knickerbocker stock just as mine is. You could do worse..." The famed young matron lifted her fan so as to cover her mouth. "Especially considering the vulgarity of your background."

Without a clue as to what a Knickerbocker was, Rachel still knew she'd just been mortally insulted by the woman. From that instant onward, she decided she was never going to like Mrs. William B. Astor, Jr., no matter what Gloria Steadman and the rest of the world thought of the woman.

"If Mr. Edmund Hoar and you are related, please forgive any imagined insult. Believe me, I wish no further hardship." With that, Rachel accepted the next name on her card and left to walk back onto the dance floor, leaving behind Mrs. Astor, whose face had hardened with anger.

"Magnus's widow is certainly an independent thinker," she commented to Mrs. Steadman.

"You and I will always differ there, Caroline. I admire a woman with backbone." Gloria smiled and opened her fan. "In all the years we've been friends, you've certainly tolerated mine."

"You deserve to be respected. Your family's impeccable and you've triumphed as a hostess," the famous society matron commented.

"Ridiculous. I've never done half the things Rachel Magnus has had to do just to survive. I bow to her greater accomplishments." Mrs. Steadman's expression turned devious. "If you won't accept her, I'll bring up the family history of the name Backhouse—revealing the *true* reason why you insist on being called Mrs. William *B.* Astor, Jr."

Mrs. Astor looked ill. "All right. I'll accept the girl. But I insist there be no more scandal. If we work hard enough, we can make people forget where she met her first husband and," the woman moaned, "that she worked as a barkeeper for a living."

"That's all I ask." Mrs. Steadman nodded to Rachel as she passed on the dance floor with her latest escort.

"But no more scandal. No more. If I'm to give my social approval of the girl, you must promise me she will live a scrupulous existence."

"No more scandal," Mrs. Steadman promised.

When the French clock in the Steadman hall chimed exactly ten o'clock, Mrs. Steadman stood. All the ballgoers silenced as she raised her goblet in the air and began her speech.

"Fair ladies and gentlemen, I welcome you to my home," she began, "I have given this event in order for you to become well acquainted with our new neighbor. Allow me to introduce the lovely Mrs. Noel Magnus to our abode." Mrs. Steadman took Rachel's hand and pulled her up from her seat on the dais.

Nervously, Rachel stood by the woman's side, her gaze traveling across the two hundred guests. She had no idea they would treat her so well, and her heart was filled with relief at their acceptance, and terror at the lie she had promoted to this point.

"If you would all raise your glasses to toast Mrs. Magnus, I will be the first to drink to her happiness in her new home." Mrs. Steadman put the goblet to her lips.

A long silence ensued while the rest of the guests took sips from their goblets.

All the while Rachel was sure they could hear the fierce drumming of her heart. She was mortified to be the center of attention, and it was even worse that the attention was manufactured out of a fraud. If she could have melted into the dais to form an inconspicuous puddle at Mrs. Astor's feet, she would have.

But suddenly all eyes were turned away from her toward the ballroom doors. A man's loud voice and scuffling noises could be heard in the grand marble-and-gilt hallway beyond.

"—and take that for your trouble!" the voice boomed. A split second later, one of the footmen who had obviously been trying to contain the man from entering the ballroom was unceremoniously hurled through the door.

Rachel froze. It couldn't be, her mind kept telling her, but her soul knew who was at the door. The deep voice, the gruffness, the strength. She would know it anywhere.

A chorus of gasps rippled through the crowd. In the doorway appeared a tall man. His caribou parka was black with grime and his features all but obscured with an unruly mass of black hair and beard. With a crazed look in his sherry-colored eyes he scanned the room until he fixed on the dais. On Rachel.

"Good God! Is it you, Noel? Are you not dead after all?" Mrs. Steadman cried out.

He pushed his way through the crowd. The ballgoers parted in terror as if there was a monster in their midst. His gaze never wavered from Rachel.

"You!" he cursed.

Rachel said nothing. Her voice was gripped with a fear she had never known before. She could feel every drop of blood in her body waterfall to her toes.

"I've come for you, *Wife,*" he spat.

She wanted to say something; to flee; to protect herself. But nothing moved. No limb cooperated. All she could do was stare back.

His wild gaze moved downward to her neck.

She thought his mind was on strangling her, but then she realized he had glimpsed the opal.

Recognition, then another bout of poker-hot anger, flashed over his face. He reached for it, to yank it from her neck; perhaps to choke her with it if he could.

Then she finally found the escape she desperately sought. The air she could not quite suck into her lungs got the better of her. Between the terror and a too-tight corset, she sank into blessed unconsciousness, falling into a dead faint at the feet of a horrified Mrs. Astor.

PART THREE

TAKE NO PRISONERS

CHAPTER EIGHT

He would kill her. When the physician finally told him she was ready to receive visitors, he would go to her bedside and personally wrap his hands around her neck.

Noel ran his hand through the freshly cropped mass of black hair. In the time it took for Rachel's limp body to be carried to the Northwyck carriage and driven home, the town's physician had been summoned to check on her. He was with her still, though Magnus had had time to bathe and have his old valet trim off the wild mane of hair. All that was left for him to do until the physician told him he might see her was to pace and think.

The Black Heart. The baggage had had the stone all along. She might have had it for years while he battled hurricane-force wind and temperatures cold enough to fracture bare skin. She must have laughed at him when he dragged in his near-dead body and talked incessantly about his search for Franklin and the fabled stone. And all the while she had it in her possession, thinking it a trifle when compared to marriage and a home.

A trifle. He snorted. The most famous find of the century and she didn't bother to mention it. Instead, all she harped on was marriage. Marriage. Confounded marriage. She was mad. She had to be. Rachel Howland didn't know the value of anything.

But, of course, to all bystanders, he was the one who appeared crazed. He'd come after her like a lovesick suitor. The great explorer Noel Magnus had arrived back at Northwyck in a froth; he'd pushed himself so hard to arrive quickly, he hadn't bathed or changed clothes in the entire journey. No one had ever seen him so feral. But when he'd heard from Betsy that Rachel had arrived at Northwyck in one piece and was so well cared for that she was even then at a ball given to her by Gloria Steadman, Noel had only felt sweet unspeakable relief. She wasn't dead. She wasn't stranded in some godforsaken port forced into prostitution just to keep bread in her belly. She was alive and he'd found her. Well, almost found her.

Instead, she was off at a ball given in her honor as the suddenly very available widow of—of himself.

That was when the rage came to him. The burning need to feel her soft throat between his hands. The ignitable need for revenge.

And he was still put off from getting it. The damned woman had had the cowardice to faint on him, and he was left to the tiny hours of morning to pace in his library like an expectant father.

A knock came at the door.

He yanked it open.

"She's coherent, but the physician said she's had quite a shock. Tread gently when you go to her," Betsy told him.

His fists curled into cannonballs, but he moderated his voice. "Let me see her."

Betsy led him up the stairs, lighting the way with a gold candelabra. The physician met him in the upper hall, a vial in his hand.

"She's in a fragile state. I tried to give her cocaine but she wouldn't take any. Perhaps with your pleading, she might relent. It would be good for her." The tidy little man gave Noel the vial and left with Betsy for the front door.

Alone, Noel took a moment at the door before opening it. Revenge was foremost on his mind. He wanted retribution for all the deceit, all the lies, all the anguish. He would get it, too. His expression turned cold. She had wanted him as a husband, and she had wanted this unholy ground for a home. Maybe he should just let her have it. Let her see the hell of a society wife; let her endure the torture his own mother had lived through and finally escaped.

It would be almost fitting to let her get her dream. He smirked. Yes, after the nightmare she'd put him through, let her get her dream.

When Rachel saw the looming figure at the doorway to her bedroom, she wanted to slip under the covers and hide herself. She wanted to pretend that if she didn't see him, he might not actually be there. He might go away. He might not kill her as she so very much deserved.

"I'm sorry," she burst out, tears stinging her eyes. "I didn't mean to be so deceitful. When

I arrived here, I thought the Willems' cottage was yours and when they thought I was your wife, they were so kind. So very kind..." Her voice trailed off into nostalgia, but then she shook herself and continued. "I wanted very much to keep that kindness—and—and it was hard to tell them about my lie, especially after they showed me your real home and— and how much they wanted me here." She swallowed the knot of hysteria rising in her throat. There was no point in it; no point in crying. She didn't deserve mercy. She deserved everything he gave her.

"You had the opal all along, didn't you? All those years I spent looking for it, it was tucked away in the Ice Maiden, wasn't it?" His voice was low and harsh. Like a growl.

She kicked at the covers in frustration. "I longed to present it to you. My father found it the summer before he died. But where would it have gotten me if I had handed it over to you? I would be up there still, dying inside, and you would be here with your fine set of friends, making great ceremony in giving it to a museum."

He walked to the bed and snatched her jaw up in his rough hand.

She locked stares with him. She'd forgotten how big he was, how muscled and strong. Even in the dim gaslight of her bedroom, she still felt the same attraction for him. He leaned down and she noted that he was clean shaven. She'd never seen his true face, but far from being disappointed at what he hid beneath the rough hair, she was that much more drawn to him. He possessed a face more handsome and hard than she could have imagined. Even now she wanted to reach out her hand and touch it. He had Gabriel's face with the devil's dark hair and eyes.

"I spent years in the cold and the dark looking for that stone. Years. Do you know what that's like, Rachel?" His hand became a vise on her chin.

She shoved him away. "Yes," she hissed, though her cheeks were wet with despair, not anger. "I know all too well what it's like to wait years for something—something you're not bound to have." She reached out to her night table. The opal was there where she had left it.

"Take it then. It's yours," she spat. "It's more than enough payment for the use of your home these few months. Just provide me passage back to Herschel and I'll be gone at first light."

He sat on the edge of the bed, his eyes glittering with anger.

She kicked at him, but in a flash he took her hands and pressed them back on the pillows, pinning her down. She felt naked beneath him. The sheer batiste nightgown didn't offer much coverage when stretched taut across her breasts.

"You dare to think the damage you've caused can be erased with even that costly rock?" He shook the bed as if to wake her. "It's not one-tenth payment for the fraud you've made of my life."

"Tell them I'm a criminal. What do I care? I shall never see them again." She heaved against him to make him let her go, but he didn't budge.

"No. To let you run back to Herschel now would be too good for you."

"Then you want me in prison." The words came out in a fearful little whisper even though she still fought him.

"Prison is where you belong," he said frigidly, her struggles not fazing him.

She looked away. The shadows filling the corners of her bedroom offered little comfort. "I can't deny you that," she conceded, a tear slipping down her nose before the fight in her began anew.

"But if I send you to prison, I can't watch your torture. I can't see your loneliness. I can't revel in your despair." He almost snarled. "No. What I'm going to do is give you this wonderful life you've stolen for yourself. Let you live out the next months as my wife. Let me see if you can take it."

Her eyes turned to him. "What are you thinking?"

He laughed without mirth ever touching his eyes. "What I'm thinking is that you should go on playing my wife. That way I'm saved from looking like the fool, and you will get every punishment you deserve."

"What kind of punishment is this? I've made friends here at Northwyck. I've every comfort here, and every indulgence. Why would I suffer should it continue?"

"Because you haven't yet had a husband to please, have you?" he said ominously.

Again she locked stares with him. Her breath came quick and hard from struggling. "What—what do you mean?"

"You were the one who announced this marriage. So, let you experience the pain of it—beginning with the marriage bed." He freed his hand by clasping both of hers in one. Then he flung back the bedclothes and studied her, his gaze caressing her body, which was revealed in intimate detail beneath the sheer cotton.

"But you can't. You know I won't do it," she gasped. "We're not married—"

"Says who?" he retorted, the corner of his mouth lifting in a diabolical smile.

"I say it," she protested.

"That's not what you told everyone else in this town." He placed his hand on her thigh and slid the gown up until it caught in the intimate triangle between her legs.

"I've given you your opal. I'll leave here to never return. You can tell them the shock of seeing you alive killed me." She pushed away his hand.

He ignored her. Slowly he ran his knuckles across her breast, teasing her nipple beneath the paper-thin batiste.

"No," she gasped, struggling to release her hands from the manacle of his hold.

"As my wife, you have no right to say no. Not ever," he whispered against her hair, his tongue licking the soft place behind her ear.

"No legal right, but a moral one," she spat. Finally, in desperation, she turned to him. He bent to kiss her and she bit him on the lower lip.

"Damn you," he cursed, releasing her hands as if throwing her away.

"You deserved it," she said, burrowing back into the pillows for protection.

"I should have remembered how confounded difficult you can be," he mumbled as if his lip was sore.

"I've offered my peace to you. I can't—nay, I won't—give you any more than that," she told him, crossing her arms across her chest.

He studied her with a dark, baleful stare. "You make me into the laughingstock of all New York, and yet you find limits to your reparations. Good God, you are a brazen wench. I can't believe I ever thought you were worth the trip back here."

"Why did you come back?" she finally asked, needing to know. "Was it that you finally tired of the North as I predicted? Did you want more refined company? Named Miss Judith Amberly?" A ball of tears weighted her chest, but she vowed not to give him the satisfaction of seeing her cry. The war had been lost. There was no point in giving the victor any more satisfaction.

He stiffened. "Where did you see her?"

She wondered what his question meant; if he wanted all the details of his fiancée like a long-lost lover would. But she only offered, "I met her tonight at the ball."

He ran an exasperated hand through his newly shorn locks. The firelight from the dying coal hearth lit the hard planes of his cheek. Truly, he was the most handsome man Rachel had ever seen. The picture of him arm-in-arm with Judith Amberly was more than she could bear.

"Why didn't you tell me about her, Magnus?" The words lay between them like a stone fortress.

His ire returned. "Why didn't I tell you about her? You sit here in my own bedroom pretending to be my wife and you ask me about my transgressions? Ridiculous."

She studied him. Was there any guilt flashing in his eyes? Did his voice weaken when he spoke? She couldn't tell. She only heard anger.

A knock came at the door. Noel rose and pulled it open. "What is it?" he growled.

Betsy stood there. "Sir, the doctor said she needs her rest. I know it's been a while since you were reunited, but I must remind you, she's had quite a shock. She must take what the doctor prescribed."

He glanced back at Rachel, an expression on his face that said, "I'll deal with you later." Gruffly he walked past Betsy and disappeared into the velvet blackness of the hallway.

"I'm so sorry. I didn't mean to keep you apart." Betsy came into the room, her cap crooked from so much bustling about.

"It's all right," Rachel answered darkly, her gaze still on the doorway as if any moment she might find him returning to her.

"Will you take some of this?" The house-keeper lifted the blue glass vial the doctor had handed out.

"No, I really don't want anything." Nothing would make her sleep that night anyway. She had plans to make, such as how she was going to get back to Herschel, and how she was going to get through the rest of her life without Noel.

She rolled onto her side and stared into the fractured red glow of the dying coals.

Betsy came alongside her and stroked her hair. " 'Twas quite a shock seeing him again, wasn't it? I swear, even I could not believe it when he strode into the hall earlier this evening looking like some wild creature." She released a small laugh. "I didn't recognize him at first. I'd never seen him so hairy and unkempt. I thought we were being robbed, truly I did."

"Oh, Betsy," Rachel moaned. In all her heartache, she'd never thought how to tell the kind woman that she and the children must now leave Northwyck because they were a fraud.

"Don't speak, love. You've truly had a terrible shock. But everything's going to be all right now. Noel is back. *He's back,*" Betsy emphasized as if it were a miracle. "And you shall regain your intimacy with your husband tomorrow when your state is not so fragile."

"I fear Noel is not happy with me right now—" Rachel began, but Betsy interrupted her.

"He's had a lot to manage, love. His trip here

was harsh, I understand. He's certainly slimmer than I remember him. But you should have seen his face when I told him you were here and were safe. The relief on his face was unbearable." Betsy sighed with satisfaction. "And he himself carried you up here when you were unwell. According to the coachman, he wouldn't let anyone help him with you at Mrs. Steadman's. He only ordered the physician to meet him here and he tended to you himself."

Rachel found that almost hard to believe. But, of course, he wouldn't want her to die on him. Not when he could revive her to torture. "That's a wonderful story, but I fear—"

The other woman was incorrigible. "I've never seen him in such a state. When we told him you weren't here but at Mrs. Steadman's he wouldn't wait for you to return. He wouldn't even bathe and have some food, all he wanted was to see you."

I'll bet, Rachel thought bitterly. "Mrs. Willem—"

"He brought that package for you. See it yonder?" Betsy nodded to a large fur-wrapped bundle on the chest of drawers. "While the doctor was tending to you, he couldn't be persuaded to leave until you started to revive. Only then he would go to his room to bathe and have some supper. But he came right back with this bundle, and when I asked him if I should unwrap whatever was inside it, he told me it was a surprise for you. That he'd brought it all the way from Herschel for you."

Rachel stared at the large bundle. Half of

her wanted to dash to the thing and rip it open; the other more prudent half didn't want to know what was inside it at all for fear it held more retaliation.

"I'll leave you now, love. You get some rest. You've a grand day tomorrow. You'll need it. Why, poor Noel has been so distraught over you, he hasn't had a moment to see the children yet." Betsy frowned. "Why, Rachel, dear, you look so pale, won't you take some of the doctor's tonic?"

"No, no—" Rachel gasped, her mind recoiling in horror. She hadn't even thought about how Tommy and Clare would react tomorrow. Of course, they'd be kicked out with her, but Noel probably knew nothing about them yet. They would be another ferocious lie to deal with in the morning.

"Sleep well, dear Rachel. Think good thoughts of tomorrow," Betsy said lightly before passing from her room.

Alone, Rachel had no other option but to pray for death to take her while she slept. That was the only escape possible. Otherwise, in the morning, she was going to have the unpleasant task of introducing to Magnus his previously unknown son and daughter.

CHAPTER NINE

"Good morning, Mrs. Magnus," the maid said as Rachel timidly entered the breakfast room the next morning.

"How well you look, Mrs. Magnus," Mr. Forest the butler announced while he poured her coffee.

"Doesn't she though?" Betsy agreed as she gathered up the help and shooed them back into the pantry.

Alone, Rachel looked at the beast sitting opposite her at the large gleaming expanse of mahogany. His urbane handsomeness still shocked her.

He looked nothing like he had on Herschel. Gone was his pointed obsession to find Franklin, and in its stead was a focus on her, on anger and revenge. Gone, too, was the bear and the wild hair. His shorn black hair now matched the color of his trousers; the austerity of his white shirt was relieved only by a fir-green silk necktie that had to have been barrel-knotted by a master valet. She had the strange notion that it was probably impolite of him to come to the breakfast table without his jacket, but it was no surprise that he was unconcerned about offending her. By his baleful stare, he looked ripe for throttling her if only she would be so considerate as to move to his end of the glossy mahogany breakfast table.

"Please don't let me keep you waiting," she said, facetiously glancing at his nearly empty plate of eggs and bacon.

He said nothing, but picked up his coffee cup and drained it.

Rachel ignored her own lavish breakfast. She would never be able to touch a bite of it. Reaching for the coffee, she realized her hand trembled so much she wasn't going to be able to drink it.

"I came to give you this, nothing more." She rolled The Black Heart toward him. The opal gleamed like the depths of hell against the nunnery white of the tablecloth.

Clearing her throat, she said, "If that settles the accounts, then I only ask that in return you give me enough coin for the journey back to Herschel. I haven't any of my own left. It took all I had to get here."

"You've helped yourself to my name, my home, my fortune," he bit out, his eyes glittering. "You mean to tell me there's more you need?"

Anger built inside her. She had done it all only because she had loved him, and while he had promised her everything, he'd given her nothing.

"No. I don't need anything more," she answered quietly. Looking down at her lavender linen dress, she said, "I'll send you the funds for these clothes when I have them, unless, of course, you're so spiteful you'd have me leave this house bare naked?"

By the taut expression on his face, she was sure he was pondering the idea.

Unable to take any more, she spun on her heels and headed for the door.

"You haven't been dismissed."

Her hand stopped cold on the doorknob. She turned to him and stared.

"What's more to be said? I've given you all the payment I have in this world." Sick and wounded inside, she said, "If that's not enough, then the only thing left for you is to call the jail and have me hauled away. But then do it, and be done with it. I find I'm as anxious to be gone from this place as you are to see me gone."

"But I don't want you gone. Do you see my point?" A wicked little smile graced his lips. "You want your punishment for your bad behavior meted out and over with. 'Be done with it.' Those were your very own words."

"Well, why don't you do it then?" she asked, barely leashed fury in her words.

"Because I'm just not that kind, Rachel. I'm not that merciful. My vengeance won't be had with the quick slam of the jail's iron door or by casting you from Northwyck into the cold cruel world without even the clothes on your back. No. I've got worse things for you. Much worse."

"And what would that be? You'll need persistence to overreach those cruelties," she shot back.

"Ah, but I've got that." Maddeningly, he lifted his napkin and wiped it across his hard, handsome lips. He placed it at his plate's side with all the care of a disciple leaving the last supper.

"Then what is your plan?" Her patience seeping away, she fought hard to hide the hysteria in her voice.

He grinned. The white of his teeth matched the white of his shirt. His smile was dazzling and utterly devoid of mirth.

She had no choice but to think him exquisitely evil at that moment.

"If I throw you in jail for fraud, I look duped. I will not have that. If I cast you to the four winds and have the devil take you, then I don't get a seat with which to view your oncoming wretchedness." He paused. His gaze locked with hers. "So you will be my wife. You will play-act and perform your duties for all and sundry to witness. You will do it or die trying."

Her head seemed ready to explode with all the confusion inside her. "But if you recall, that's what I've wanted all along. How can you make that into punishment when I've fought this hard to try to have it?"

He refused to meet her eye. "Because it will be play-acting. It won't be real. You'll not be my wife, but you will learn what that vicious role would have been like—like my own mother learned it. And if your penance is thorough, my better side may just rear up and show you mercy. When you beg to be free of your bondage, and you've earned it, I'll see to it you're taken back to Herschel."

"You're going to be that purposefully cruel? Just to make a point?" She shook from suppressed rage.

His voice grew low and harsh. "I'm going to give you a dose of the truth. The truth about marriage, the truth about Northwyck, the truth about me."

She stared into his eyes. The tenderness she had found there in Herschel seemed gone, replaced with the frigidness of a dark Arctic winter. It took her several deep breaths in order for her to calm down enough to say, "It won't work. Even if I am cast into the role of playing your wife, there are other complications you haven't considered."

"You mean there's more to this deceit? I find that hard to believe, *Mrs. Magnus.*" His words oozed sarcasm.

"Well, actually, I thought to tell you last night, but—"

"So sorry to interrupt!" Betsy popped her head through the wainscoted breakfast-room door. Her face beamed with delight. "I wouldn't be so bold, but I've two anxious little visitors here."

Rachel opened her mouth to protest, to wave Betsy back, but it was too late.

"What are you talking about, woman?" Magnus boomed.

Rachel interjected with, "She's a bit premature but—"

"But what?" he bellowed, throwing his napkin onto the table and standing.

"I don't think it's the right time, Betsy,"

Rachel begged, hoping against hope the woman got the message.

The kind housekeeper didn't know what was going on. Bemused, she said, "But they've yet to see him, Rachel. And here, the poor darlings thought he was dead all this time. It's quite a surprise to wake up and suddenly find he's returned, don't you agree?"

"I agree, and certainly all logic would tell you that, Betsy, but, really, now is not the time," Rachel pleaded.

"Time for what?" Magnus turned to the housekeeper. He gave Betsy one of his penetrating stares. "Who wants to see me?"

"Tommy and Clare, of course. They haven't seen you since forever. They thought you were dead," Betsy offered.

"Tommy and Clare," Magnus repeated, looking to Rachel for help in understanding.

"Now is not the right time, Betsy," Rachel mewled.

"But when's the right time to see your father when you've long thought he was dead? I can't be so unfeeling as to tell the children their father would rather not see them now."

"Children?" Noel choked out. "Father?" If looks could slay, he would have cut her dead with one rapier glance.

"Yes." It was all Rachel could utter. She looked at him, almost daring him to strike her. Seconds passed.

He shut his eyes as if doing so would offer escape.

"Betsy," Rachel began, "would you please take the children to the parlor?"

"I'll surely do it, but"—the housekeeper turned to Noel—"but when shall I tell them they'll be seeing their father, sir?"

Noel looked as if he was going to explode. "I'll see them shortly. I just need another moment with *my wife*." His words were a threat and a curse all in one.

Betsy closed the door.

Rachel gathered her courage. Alone with him once again, she said, "I tried to tell you—"

"What the hell is this? You and I have no children. No children," he ranted through gnashed teeth.

"I found them in the streets of New York, starving. I couldn't leave them behind—not in that unfeeling place. So I brought them here to share the wealth. It was only logical to tell everyone they were yours. And now, if you don't allow us to leave right away, this farce will only grow larger."

"You think you've won, don't you? You think you thought of everything—of every protection—by dragging two street urchins here with you. But it won't work. I'll match you eye for eye, tooth for tooth. We'll see who can hold out the longest before begging for mercy."

"But, Noel!" She grabbed his arm. "You can't use Tommy and Clare in this war between us. You can't hurt them. They're not to dispose of so easily, as I might be. They're just children. Tommy's no more than eight."

He shook off her touch as if it burned him. "Watch me."

In despair, she ran after him as he stormed into the parlor. "Please," she begged.

Tommy and Clare looked ready to run for their lives. Like the old days, Clare ran to Tommy, and Tommy's face took on the toughness she'd seen that first day in New York.

"Me and me sister ain't done nothing to hurt you, and we'll be leavin' now if you let us!" Tommy cried out, six months of diction lessons melted away by sheer terror.

Magnus stopped.

Rachel couldn't erase the picture of his tall form towering over the two children who cowered against the very civilized damask-covered settee. The contrast was sickening.

"Please, Magnus," she said softly to his unyielding back. "I'm the one who's hurt you. I'm the one who should pay. Not them. They had your luxuries, but only for a little while. And it was only their right as children to have such things, so can't you forgive them? Can't you turn your anger to me instead?"

"It's never been in my nature to have children wanting," he said tightly, still not looking at her. "These two shall not pay for your sins."

Clare and Tommy slumped down on the settee. Relief graced their expressions like an angel had just passed over.

"But you, you're not above my wrath," he said, turning on Rachel. "And you'll pay twice. Once for them and once for this outrageous lie." He took an ominous step toward her.

"I'll pay, then," she whispered, holding her ground.

"She won't!" Tommy cried out.

Before Rachel could see what was happening, Tommy hurled his small body toward Magnus with all the force of a train. And Clare, her face pale and her blue eyes wide with fright, ran behind him, ready to fight also.

"What the hell are you doing?" Magnus said, holding Tommy up by his jacket collar.

Clare butted him, and he grabbed her as well.

"We won't have you beatin' her. We won't have you breaking her pretty face, because we'll be breakin' yours first!" Tommy swung at him. He spun around like the ribbon from a maypole.

"What kind of vermin have you picked up here, Rachel?" Magnus asked, his voice as calm as death while Tommy swung at him.

"Run, Rachel! Run!" Clare cried out, her long blond curls falling from their pins until she, too, looked like a wild animal out for blood.

"No, no, release them, Magnus." Rachel then implored the children. "He won't strike me. You mustn't think he will," she said, pulling Clare down from Magnus's large fist.

Tommy fell to the floor in an undignified heap. Panting, both children stared at her as if they needed to be sure what she said was true.

"He won't hit me. I promise you," she reassured.

Tommy growled at Magnus, "If you touch her, I'll be settlin' with you. I'll be settlin' wit' you good."

Magnus ran his hand through his hair. His expression was tight and unreadable.

Rachel noticed she'd seen that gesture, that expression, more than once since he'd arrived back at Northwyck. All the frozen tundra and hungry ice bears in the world hadn't brought Noel Magnus to the breaking point. But maybe she had.

"These creatures were passed off as my children?" he demanded.

"They haven't been in a brawl of recent. That is, until just now," Rachel answered apologetically. "Usually they're quite good and spend their time upstairs in the schoolroom with the tutor. Mrs. Willem's been giving them lessons, too. Really, they've been much polished since they arrived."

"Call Betsy and have her take them back upstairs to their tutor." He dismissed them with a nod to his head.

"We won't go without Rachel. We won't go anywhere without her," Tommy said.

"That's right," Clare added.

Rachel went to the two frightened children and kneeled in front of them. Patting their hands, she said, "I got us into this mess, and it's up to me to get us out of it. But I promise you, you needn't worry about me. I can take care of myself."

"Then let's go, Rachel. Let's get out of here and be gone," Clare begged, her eyes still haunted by old fears, and then, when she glanced over at the towering angry master of the house, by new fears.

"I would like to go, but—" Rachel looked over her shoulder at Magnus. "But I'm afraid he's not ready for us to leave just yet. And we owe him time in order for him to get out of the bind we've put him in, making up him having a wife and children. You understand?"

"We don't want to see your face broken, Rachel," Tommy said, his voice cracking.

"No, love," she soothed, her own voice filling with tears. "I don't know all that you've seen and experienced, but as I've told you since we first met, you have to start new here. This is a different world than the one you and Clare came from. It's better here. Much better. Men don't do such things to women here at Northwyck, I promise you that. I promise you."

She turned to Magnus to see if he would back her up.

He was staring at the two children, a gleam of pity in his eyes.

"Rachel's face is beautiful, and I'd have her stay that way. I'd never lay a hand on any woman in any account. I never will," he said sternly to Tommy, adding under his breath for Rachel, "no matter how provoked."

"There? You see?" She hugged both children. "I know it's frightening what I've gotten you into. But now you must promise me that you'll trust me. No matter what happens, you must trust that I'll see you taken care of.

I told you I would and I mean to keep that promise."

"But what if you can't, Rachel?" Clare choked out.

"Then others will do the task for me," she said gravely. "Betsy won't see you two cast to the streets. I know it." She turned to look at Noel. "And there may be others who will step in and do what's right." She stared at Tommy and Clare. "But you both must trust. It's the only way you can heal, and believe. You must trust. I've told you that all along. Trust is what's most important. So promise me," she insisted. "Promise me."

Clare flung herself into Rachel's arms. Rachel hugged her tight. Tommy as usual held back, but the tightness left his face; the toughness left his eyes.

She wiped a tear that had slipped down her cheek. Straightening, she said, "Now if it's all right with Magnus, I want you to run upstairs for your lessons. Mr. Harkness will be waiting for you to begin your geography about now."

Tommy and Clare paused. They stared at Magnus, waiting.

"Go," was all Magnus said before he ran his hand through his cropped mane of thick, dark hair.

When they were alone, Rachel took the initiative. Haltingly, she said, "I meant to tell you about them, but there were already so many complications that I wasn't sure how—"

"Don't." He held up his hand. He refused to even look at her.

"I don't care what happens to me, but I can't let them pay for it. Take it all out on me, but I won't let them suffer. They're just children."

"I see that."

She grew silent. Staring at him from across the room, she finally said, "I really need you to help me find a place for them somewhere. I know they can't stay here, but I would do anything to see them happy and well cared for. I'd pay any price, endure any punishment."

Looking around the room, she dug for the correct words to convince him. "If you'd only see what wretched, emaciated things they were when I found them. They've had nothing but horror and want in their lives. They've had so little happiness, I can't stand by and watch what little they've had slip away now." She paused. Her voice trembled. "I would have you break my face rather than see them back on the streets again. That's how much I want them happy." She tried to laugh, but it was a miserable failure. "What need have I for a pretty face anyway? On Herschel it was only a liability in any case."

"You know I would never lay a hand on you," he said darkly. "Besides, whether you know it or not, there are worse things than for a man to destroy a woman's beauty. Worse still is for him to destroy her spirit. Much worse still." His thoughts seemed a thousand miles away.

"I would have you destroy either before hurting them. No price is too high. No price."

He finally looked at her. He seemed to

want to reach out and touch her cheek. His hand lifted, but then it fell again to his side. "Leave me."

Torn, she shook her head. "But how do I arrange for the children if I leave now?"

"No. Go up to your room. I don't want to see you."

She released a shaky breath. His hatred burned and scarred more deeply than a lash. His prophesy was already coming true. She would pay for her indiscretions. He had taken her heart, so how did it matter that he might bruise her body or trample her soul. She'd already paid for her mistakes, because her first one had been to fall in love with him.

"Very well," she whispered. "I'll play your nasty game if that will make things better. But when it's over and you've won, when you've had your fill of revenge, you must make arrangements to send Clare and Tommy to the best boarding school in New York. When I return to Herschel I want to know that something good came out of this. Something good..." She was unable to go on.

"I'll see them taken care of." He didn't look at her. In a monotone, he said, "Now be gone from me."

She fled the room in tears.

CHAPTER TEN

Rachel swung open the leaded casement windows to listen to the crickets. Night gathered in deep shadows in the valley. From the window seat, she could see far into Northwyck's fields, which lay shrouded in an early-evening mist that billowed up from the Hudson River.

The nightscape fit her mood. She laid her tear-stained cheek against the cool glass and let her gaze drift to the horizon. Daydreaming, she pictured herself disappearing into the fog, the nightmare over.

Instead, she was a prisoner of her own making. And she had no one to blame but herself. She had brought herself here. She had schemed and performed. Now all that was left for her was the luxury of her jail and the wrath of her jailer.

Wearily she shut her eyes. Love had been snatched from her father by the strange plague of yellow fever which had mysteriously arrived one summer in Philadelphia. By the time Rachel had been put on the ship that sailed for Herschel in the fall, the plague had subsided as quickly as it had begun, sweeping away its numerous victims as with the ebb of the tide. Perhaps that was how love was meant to be. Instead of sustaining the soul, perhaps it ate away at it, leaving a weakened spirit, a ready victim for whatever tragedy waited around the corner.

But if that were true, she had only felt invigorated by her feelings for Magnus. Whenever he arrived at Herschel, she had felt more alive than she had ever felt. Every breath was deeper, every view of the ice and snow around her more white and heavenly than the day before.

Every touch was hotter and more wanted.

Her red eyes opened.

She wanted to scream in denial that it wasn't so, but it had been so. She had left Magnus, left Herschel, because it had been getting too hard to say no. Her downfall was destined to be Magnus, and now, instead of raising a bastard child beneath the counter of the Ice Maiden, she was here at Northwyck sporting two children of the street as the master's own, and play-acting as his widow in order that she might carry off her fraud and live in peace.

But there would be no peace for the wicked. Nor, it would seem, for the ones who dared to love.

She turned away from the lavender twilight fields to assess her prison. The bedchamber door wasn't locked. It wasn't even closed. The gaslight from the hallway flickered into her room. In theory, she could depart at any time. But there was no point in lingering upon the thought. A lock made no difference when will and circumstance made far stronger bondage. There was no easy way to extract herself from the situation. To leave would be to abandon Tommy and Clare, and she would never do that. To take the children with her would mean that Magnus could track her that much easier. If he wasn't satisfied with her penance, he could find them and make their lives hell for many years to come.

So she would have no choice but to stay and take her punishment, and let her heart be trampled once more. Destiny fulfilled.

Her depressed gaze lit upon the bundle of fur that had been left the night before. Her curiosity piqued. Rising from the window seat, she went over to it and took the large package in hand.

Caribou and wolverine covered it layer upon layer. There were more than ten pieces of fur to be peeled from the precious center and whatever lay inside it. She unwrapped another fur, then another, but a shadow in the doorway made her pause.

Magnus stood there. He wore the same clothes he wore at breakfast, only now a dark silk vest blacked out the brilliant white of his shirt. There was a weariness around his eyes she never remembered on Herschel. All the harsh winter crossings, all the nights of bad whiskey and days of blizzards in a sub-zero chill hadn't left their mark in his eyes. Magnus's eyes always glowed a warm sherry brown, but not now. Now they seemed permanently cast in the shade of his anger and disapproval.

"You left this here." She held out the bundle to him.

"I brought it from up North." He nodded gravely. "For you."

"I ran from there. What could you have brought me that I could possibly want?"

"Open it."

She unwrapped the last two furs and almost missed it. Nestled within the last wolverine pelt lay a glistening shard of ice.

He walked to her and picked it up. "This is all that's left of the huge block I placed on the sledge. This tiny sliver—and it's melting still. In another few minutes it'll all be gone."

"Why?" she gasped softly.

"Why?" he repeated, watching it form a small puddle in his hand. He lifted it to her mouth and slipped the fragment of ice between her lips by the force of his palm. "Because it could have been good, Rachel, our life up there. It could have been as sweet as the water you swallow now."

The sliver melted in her mouth. The last of the pure Arctic water disappeared.

He turned angry. "But that life can no more exist in this place than a block of ice in June."

"I could be happy with you anywhere, Magnus. Anywhere. I told you that," she pleaded.

"No," he answered darkly. "You brought me back to this vile house, this place I wanted to be gone from." He pushed her away as if he could not bear to look at her. "You've awakened the beast I wanted dead and buried forever."

She watched him leave. He didn't look

back. The pelts lay in a sodden pile on the floor, mocking both of them with their emptiness. The ice was no more.

"Why does Magnus hate this house so?" Rachel asked Betsy when the woman had come to oversee the chambermaid turn down the bed.

Dismissing the maid after her duties were completed, Betsy twisted the key on the gas sconce. All the lights were out except for a lone candle on the nightstand.

"You've a long day tomorrow, love. Magnus is setting out for the city. He wants you to go with him," the woman said.

"I know, I know," Rachel said, climbing into her bed. "But I don't understand that either. He no more wants me tagging along with him to the city than he wants me to be his—" She shut her mouth. She'd almost said "wife." Betsy still didn't know her trickery and she wasn't up to telling her yet. Not when the housekeeper was their only real friend. It was going to kill Rachel to have to one day tell her the truth, and perhaps suffer the loss of the woman's kind regard.

"It's only right a wife accompany her husband when he's about to go under the knife."

"What?" Rachel gasped, convinced she'd heard incorrectly.

Betsy frowned. "He's going into the city to have surgery on some old wounds. They were aggravated by this last journey, I presume."

"But what kind of wounds?"

"The kind more injurious to the heart than

153

to the body, I'm afraid. The master was only a child, no more than Tommy's age, you see, and his father in a fit of anger threw a whiskey bottle at him. The piece broke and some of the shards stayed in his back and neck. He now wants them out, and he's found the doctor to do it."

Rachel hugged the pillow to her and shivered in her thin nightrail. She never remembered seeing any wounds on Magnus, but in truth, she had never seen the man fully naked, nor had he seen her. He could have had all kinds of marks on his body that she would know nothing about.

"So that's the terrible secret of Northwyck. His father's cruelty." She said the words to no one.

Betsy pulled the counterpane over her. "There was little good in the man. After his wife ran off he accused Magnus of being a bastard even though the child was the double of his father. Magnus paid the price for everything. I never blamed him for wanting to leave. I'd just always held out the hope that things would change." She smiled softly. "And now they have changed."

"I want them to change, too, Betsy," Rachel said as the woman departed. "But I don't know how to make things better."

"You've already brought him back from the dead, and now home. You will have to be patient, dear Rachel, if you want more than that." The woman laughed. "Now, get your sleep. It's going to be a long ride to New York."

Rachel blew out the candle and snuggled down into the sheets. She wanted to sleep, to find the respite in sweet oblivion, but her mind was racing. It never occurred to her that Magnus had his own tale of tragedy. He always seemed larger than life, bigger and stronger than anyone around him. It was foreign to think of him as a small boy Tommy's age, vulnerable to his father's rage.

She recalled all his visits on Herschel. No one ever brawled at the Ice Maiden when Magnus was there. He wouldn't stand for it. But now, thinking back, she couldn't recall him ever putting a fist to another man. He maintained order around him without violence, but with commanding words of iron and a will to match. The promise of retaliation was just as feared as the retaliation itself, so no one dared ever to defy him.

Until she did.

In the dark, her gaze found the door outlined in yellow light. When she had first arrived at Northwyck, Betsy had seemed to know which bedchamber should be Rachel's from the first night. Only now did Rachel understand that her bedroom suite was for the lady of the house, and had been built adjoining the master's. It was Magnus's door that glowed in outline in the dark of her room. The light in his room was still burning.

She rose from the bed. Why she was drawn to his door, she didn't know, but once there, she was surprised to find it unlatched and open just a fragment. Enough for her to push

155

it a quarter inch more and find a view of the bedroom beyond.

He was there. She was surprised he didn't brood in his library or the hundred other rooms of the mansion. Instead, he lay in the middle of his bed, dressed only in a pair of dark trousers, his naked upper half propped up on down pillows. A cut-glass beaker of whiskey sat ignored by the bedside. From his brooding stare into the fire, he looked a thousand miles away. Perhaps back in the cruel Arctic where he had found his peace.

He slid off the bed and grabbed the beaker. Determined that it should cure his melancholy, he filled it higher with whiskey from the decanter on top of the marble fireplace mantel.

It was then she saw the scars. Ugly white ridges that scattered across his back like the trail of a shooting star. Several of the thick scars were red and irritated; she figured these were the ones giving him trouble. Any old wound would be irritated with the unforgiving cold of the Arctic. She'd seen fifteen-hundred-pound bears die from a paltry wound that froze and thawed in the climate, ultimately festering and taking the animal to its grave. Now pity rose inside her at the thought of his being struck by his own father. The big towering Noel Magnus was like those magnificent bears, still walking wounded by the cruelties of the past.

As if by some instinct borne out of the northern wilderness, his head turned toward the door where Rachel stood in the shadows. The door was open only a sliver, but he walked to it, determined to see if he was being watched.

She backed away. Her room flooded with light. She covered her hurting eyes with the back of one hand.

"Were you spying on me?" he asked, his form filling the doorway.

"I didn't know that was your room," she blurted out.

"Liar. You're here as my wife. Of course your bedroom would be next to mine."

He studied her. She stood shivering with her back against the silk curtains of her bedstead, helpless to stop the roving of his gaze.

In the thin nightdress, nearly all the details of her figure were revealed; the narrow curve of her waist, the generous spheres of her breasts, the dusky silhouette of her nipples taut in the cold night air.

He seemed torn by her fragility. As if it aroused and disturbed him at the same time. "You were watching me," he confirmed in a low tone.

"No. I only wanted to know what was beyond the door," she said, though her teeth chattered.

"Did you see me take my clothes off? Did the sight of my back make you recoil? Or do you want to see more of this man, this man who plays your husband?" His hands went to the hook at the front of his dark trousers. He unlatched it.

"No! I didn't spy on you. Please, I won't do it again," she promised.

He reached out and grabbed a handful of cotton nightgown and drew her toward him. "You and your propriety, your maidenly sensibilities. How ridiculous I've been to respect you when all you were doing was scheming to rob me."

"No!" she vowed, her head tilted back so she could look at him. "I had no idea you had so much. I would never rob you—or anyone. I only wanted to use what you so cavalierly discarded. I only wanted your remains..."

He snorted. "Then who are you to spurn my offers—even of sex? You who have nothing. And no one." He looked down at her. His other hand ran alongside her face as if he relished the feel of her. "You should have thanked me for the flattery of my offer, then opened your legs." He paused and the anger lashed out. "You are no one, Rachel. You run a saloon at the end of the earth. Who do you think you are to want from me?"

She turned her head away in anger. The sight of him was suddenly more than she could bear. "I—I may be nobody," she said, her voice begrudging and tight with unleashed fury, "and I may have nothing. And I *have* wronged you. That I will concede. But I won't let you take what I will not give. I will not."

"If we were married, you would give every time. It would be my right to have you."

"You would have rights under the law, perhaps. But I wouldn't recognize them. You would have what I give and you would earn my generosity, or you would have nothing."

"What makes you think you can defy me? I could break you with one hand."

"You will not become your father, Magnus. I know it."

"You know nothing. You are nothing. You have no one."

The tears she thought were dammed suddenly overflowed. They streamed down her cheeks; her shoulders slumped. "The Noel Magnus I knew those nights at the Ice Maiden would not have said that," she whispered. Starting again, she said, "I can't deny what you say is true, but I've the strength my mother gave me and the convictions of my father, and that is why I won't perish at your hand."

He pulled the wad of thin batiste nightrail until she pressed against his bare chest. "Don't you see? The man you knew is not capable of kindness in this madhouse."

She stared up at him, holding his gaze. "This is just a house, Noel. In the hallways where you see your father inflicting his tyranny, I see Tommy laughing and chasing after Clare." She reached up and touched the hard plane of his cheek. She swore it relaxed for one split second. "It's just a house, Magnus. The memories can change. They can grow sweet if you only let them."

"They are not my children. You are not my wife," he said.

"We could be. We could be," she whispered until his mouth captured hers in a deep kiss. His free hand cupped her bottom so that she was thrown into him, helpless to resist. His thick, hot tongue invaded her mouth, filling her again and again in counterfeit penetration.

Her legs grew weak; a moan emanated from her throat. She wanted to pull back, but he offered a tantalizing glimpse of love, of security and bliss the likes of which she could only imagine. And she wanted those things. Wanted them with every fiber of her soul.

Because she was nobody. She had no one. Nothing.

"Please, Magnus, don't," she whispered, breaking free of his kiss.

He didn't answer. His arms fell to his sides. The bunched-up nightrail slowly unwrinkled and covered her to her toes once again.

"You want to be my wife," he droned, the anger in his voice still seeping out the edges. "Tomorrow you will get your chance."

"Magnus, I'll show you what a fine companion a wife could be," she promised.

He laughed, but there was no joy in it. "Is that so?" He finished with, "And I, Rachel, will show you what a villain a husband can be."

The message just came from his stableman. They were going to Manhattan in the morning. Noel and Rachel. Together.

Edmund ordered his carriage without delay. He'd planned a night of reading, but he would go instead to New York and be there before they ever arrived. He knew the hotel Magnus frequented. The man's mistress had had

160

apartments there for years. He would be at the Fifth Avenue Hotel and he would greet them with all the warmth of an old friend.

And if Magnus took his eyes off his wife for a minute, he would lose her to Edmund, or find he was the grieving widower.

CHAPTER ELEVEN

The Fifth Avenue Hotel was a far cry from the rat-frequented dockside inn where Rachel had spent her first night upon arriving in New York City. Tommy and Clare's alley home was but blocks away. Rachel knew the children must have passed the conspicuous white marble building before, but never could the two urchins have dreamt they'd reside in a mansion more glorious than its velvet interior.

She and Magnus shared a suite of rooms on the ground floor overlooking the bustling avenue. The view was astonishing. A stream of coaches, omnibuses and wagons clogged the street. At five o'clock in the evening, the congestion was even worse. Several drivers lost their temper altogether and shouted obscenities which Rachel would have heard had not the drapery been so thick and the windows so well constructed.

"I suppose with the traffic, I should be

grateful the surgeon will be late," Noel said, grumbling over a large goblet of whiskey.

Rachel let the drapery fall back over the window. "You'll have more time to dull the pain, certainly." She gave his glass of whiskey a dubious look. "I should think if this doctor is so renowned, he will know how to manage the operation."

"The man is a surgeon; therefore, a butcher." Twisting his lips in resignation, he lifted the goblet.

She'd never gone under the knife but had seen the gruesome results of some of the sailors who had; she couldn't quite argue with him.

Nonetheless, hoping to cheer him, she said, "At least you're not having to go to a filthy hospital. This is a splendid place to recuperate. The surgeon will be here soon. You'll heal and then the wounds won't bother you on your next trek north."

"Ah, yes. My next expedition." He smirked. "I first went up there to find Franklin. I now plan on going so that I may return you."

She stared at him, feeling like a strayed piece of baggage. He was certainly a bear and had been ever since they left Northwyck. Indeed, his back might be hurting him, but she secretly thought he was just using that as an excuse. What he really wanted was to torment her, and he was doing a brilliant job.

A knock at the door announced the surgeon. Behind him came three valets who the hotel had sent to assist. They carried a long table and sheets. The surgeon's young assistant produced a black leather bag of instruments.

Without much introduction, the surgeon went to work. Noel lay on the table, his bare back exposed to the bright evening light from the window, a thin sheet all that covered his lower half.

In less than an hour, the efficient surgeon had Noel bandaged and sitting up. Noel had endured the pain with only a deep grunt or two announcing his agony, but now his strength seemed gone. He weaved when he got to his legs. The sheet dropped and Rachel sharply looked away. The maleness nestled between his muscular thighs had been more than she'd bargained for.

Wrapping the sheet around his hips, the valets placed him stomach-down on his bed in the bedchamber. The laudanum and whiskey were finally winning against his iron constitution. He seemed to fall right asleep.

"Thank you, Doctor," Rachel said to the surgeon as he placed his bloody utensils back into the same leather case they were brought in.

"Let him sleep as much as he can. The less he moves, the more quickly he will heal. If he gets to be too much of a handful, send a message to my office and I'll chloroform him." The doctor tipped his hat.

Rachel walked to the door to see him out.

"I'll be back in two days to check on him. Until then, do not let him move." The surgeon nodded. He left with his assistant and the army of valets.

The blessed quiet was not marred, not even by a small groan from Noel. Going to his bedchamber, she stood in the doorway and watched him. His breathing was so quiet she would have wondered if the good doctor hadn't killed him except that she could see his chest still moved up and down.

Going to the bedstead, she knelt by his side and touched a lock of his dark, cropped hair. His face was relaxed in slumber, he looked boyish and handsome, far removed from the grizzled iceman she knew on Herschel.

"My Noel," she whispered, more for herself than for him. The sound of his name on her lips was soothing to her. It meant something to her heart, if only she could have reclaimed it.

Blood was already seeping through the snow white of the bandages. The surgeon had been quick, but he had had to probe, and Rachel couldn't imagine the agony of enduring that.

"My love," she finished, touching his strong lips.

"May I bring in some supper, Mrs. Magnus?"

Rachel looked to the bedchamber door. Mazie stood there, the usual anxious-to-please expression on her face.

"No, thank you. After all that, I don't think I could touch a bite," Rachel answered in low tones so as not to disturb Magnus.

"Mrs. Willem will have my hide if I tell her you didn't eat while in New York." Mazie's Irish eyes pleaded.

"You win. Send in a tray if just so that I may

assure Mrs. Willem that you did your best, as you always do, Mazie." Rachel gave her a tired smile.

Mazie brought in a silver tray prepared by the hotel. Porcelain-covered dishes sat in the midst of a teapot and cups.

"Shall I pour you some tea, madam?" Mazie asked. "I find it always lifts me up a bit."

Noel took that moment to groan.

Rachel shook her head and led the maid to the suite door. "That'll be all for the night. Thank you so much for your care. You're always so kind."

Even after more than six months of employment, Mazie still looked surprised by her apparent good fortune. "Madam, you're a pleasure to work for. A true pleasure. After my last mistress, I cannot thank you enough for all your patience and consideration."

"Your last employer was a tyrant, was she?" Rachel wanted to make light of it.

"She went after me with the back of a hairbrush day and night. I never knew a woman could be so black-hearted. But it was running to Northwyck that saved me. Mrs. Willem, saint that she is, took pity on me and my situation, and let me come to work at the house shortly before you arrived."

"I see. You were a lady's maid before. So that's why you're so proficient at your work. I always wondered that you were at Northwyck our first night even though no lady lived in the house." Rachel smiled. "I suppose you worked for a lady nearby?"

"No, madam. I worked right here in New York City, I did. But—" Mazie suddenly turned tight-lipped. Nervous, she said, "Well, if that's all, Mrs. Magnus, I do believe I'll be going now. I don't want to be keeping you from the master."

Rachel let her out, suddenly succumbing to the stress. Without another word, she watched the maid depart and locked the suite door behind her.

Mazie knew something she wasn't telling. Rachel wanted to know what it was, but she knew instinctively she wouldn't get it from the maid by probing. Mazie was the kind to reveal all, but only in tangent conversations one must piece together to find the truth. It would take some time, but Rachel knew eventually she'd discover who the former employer was. She already knew she wouldn't like it.

Sighing, she looked at the tray, then turned away. Food wasn't what she needed. Even tea seemed like too much to bother with.

Her gaze rested on Magnus, on his long, lean legs and the tight curve of his buttocks beneath the white sheet.

She went to him. He was still passed out, but she noticed the muscles in his wide shoulders seemed to quiver as if he were cold and shivering.

Taking the satin quilt from the daybed, she placed it over his shoulders, but even its light weight seemed to cause him agony. He moaned until she drew it off his back.

His shivering continued. She felt as if they

were back at the Ice Maiden, and she was once more in her room, bargaining for her body warmth.

Slowly, she unhooked her dress and let it fall to the carpet. Her corset was next, then her slippers, then her petticoats. Finally, in just her chemise, she crawled beneath the quilt and curled up against him as close as she could get without hurting his back.

He sighed and turned to her as if by instinct.

She lay next to him, thinking of all the nights they'd shared just so, each aching with an unnamed need that had yet to be satisfied.

"What you need, Noel Magnus, is a woman who loves you." She touched his hard, handsome face. "If only you would open your eyes and see..." she whispered before heartache took her words away.

Rachel wished she had dreamt. She wanted to escape to glittering palaces along deep rivers, to cities with roads paved with their wealth, to lands that stretched green and warm to the horizon. But she got none of that. She awoke from a dreamless sleep only to stare at the heavy, closed-draped window that led out to Fifth Avenue.

It had to be morning. She felt she'd slept for days. But there was no telling the hour by the room. The gaslights still burned. The aubergine velvet draperies effectively blocked out any daylight that might have crept in.

She took a deep breath. Every muscle was

relaxed and she was wrapped in delicious warmth. She didn't know if her limbs had the strength to move. In the night, Noel's arm had flung across her chest. Now it captured her within a cocoon of heat and security.

Turning her head, her gaze sought him out, to gauge how he had fared during the night. He was staring at her, his shadowed eyes piercing, yet heavy-lidded with drugs.

"Are we North, Rachel? Is that why you lay next to me?" he whispered, his voice rough.

She tried to pull away, but his hand clamped down on her arm.

"Are you thinking to run from me? But it's so cold. What man could keep you as warm as I might?" Beads of perspiration coated his brow.

She bit her lower lip in apprehension. He was burning with fever. But even brought down with that, he was more than twice her size, with the strength of an ox.

"Sleep, Magnus. You need sleep," she soothed.

"Then stay next to me. Don't leave," he demanded.

"I won't. I won't," she placated, feeling him press her against him.

Without another word, he closed his eyelids once more and fell back into a morpheus sleep.

Trapped, she had no other choice but to close her eyes as well, and for a few hours more, relish the liberties a wife takes for granted.

"She has not gone out, sir. Of that I am certain." The hotel's valet stood in Edmund Hoar's own suite at the Fifth Avenue Hotel. His hand was not extended for a bribe, but Edmund thought it might as well be. The man looked as eager and greedy as an insurance salesman.

"Very well. I want to know the minute she leaves the suite. The very minute."

"It may be several days. Mr. Noel Magnus is down with fever. The talk is that Mrs. Magnus is quite the devoted nurse."

"I'll be here waiting until she leaves the suite. I want to know the minute she makes a public appearance. Am I clear? I want no mistakes," he growled before handing the man several silver dollars.

"Yes, sir. You're exquisitely clear," the valet chimed before he bowed deeply and departed.

CHAPTER TWELVE

"It feels good to feel the sun again." Rachel laughed. "I never thought I'd say that down here."

Mazie walked by her side down Fifth Avenue.

"You've been cooped up in the hotel for five days straight. I should think it would do the soul good for you to feel the sunshine."

"I'm just relieved Magnus is doing better," she said softly.

Mazie almost snorted. "If sitting up in a chair and shouting out orders like the worst sort of tyrant is getting better, then he's most certainly in the prime of his health."

Rachel tried to hide a smile. Magnus was a handful. The valets despised him, the chambermaids ran in terror. But the beast was far better than the feverish, delusional man she'd cared for the past few days. Even the doctor was at a loss as to how to contain him. But five days of fever wasn't bad for his kind of surgery, according to the physician, and though paler and weaker, Magnus was finally cool to the touch, with an abominable disposition to go along.

"At least he's healing. The doctor says we might go home in less than a week if things progress as they should," she commented.

"Aye, that may turn out. But don't be surprised if the master likes his new temper. It happened to Miss Harris. Some say she went down with a fever and it changed her completely. She was an angel, but from that moment on, she was a devil."

"Is that her name? Miss Harris? The woman you used to work for?" Rachel knew Mazie would reveal more without a show of curiosity, but she couldn't help it. For five long days she'd had virtually no one to talk to. Now she wanted conversation with someone who wasn't raving in a delirium.

A range of emotions crossed Mazie's face. All the way from affection to despair. "Oh, madam, please don't let on I told you anything about her. I'll be fired if you do. Truly, I will be."

"Fired? How could that be?" Rachel said as they passed the cowcatcher at Twenty-third Street.

"Just—oh, please let's not talk about my past, madam. I beg of you. Will you show me that much mercy? For I will be fired if you don't. I will be." Mazie pleaded. But the fearful look in her eye didn't diminish no matter how much Rachel reassured her.

"We'll not speak of it again, I assure you, Mazie," she finally said, nodding to the hotel brougham which had escorted them on their walk.

"Oh, thank you, madam. Thank you." Mazie looked torn. "You have no idea how much I value your employment. You've been a kind and considerate mistress. I only want to please you. Not displease you."

Rachel allowed herself to be helped into the carriage by the driver. "As I said, we'll not speak of it again."

But the whole way home, Rachel's curiosity burned with all the heat of Magnus's fever. Miss Harris. Mazie's former employer. She desperately wanted to know what the controversy was about. Something told her the complications were difficult and that was why Mazie wanted to keep her in the dark. But she also knew it was imperative she know all the conflicts around her. That way, she had a much better chance of self-protection.

And something told her she was going to need it.

"Do you, perchance, know a Miss Harris? Is she a neighbor?" she asked Magnus just as soon as they sat down to dine in the suite.

He stared at her across the fine mahogany table. "How the hell do you know that name? I never told you it."

By his very reaction, she knew she'd touched a nerve. Her curiosity and her dread doubled.

"I've just heard talk about her. I was curious if she lived near Northwyck, that's all." She looked down at her filet. It was done to perfection with a demi-glace. She couldn't eat a bite.

"Your curiosity does not serve you well," he sniped, refusing to look at her. "Since you insist on playing the part of my wife, I'll tell you now that poking around will only get you what you deserve."

She shoved away from the table. The man was impossible. She couldn't even eat a meal with him. Angrily, she walked to the windows. Fifth Avenue glistened with a sentinel of vibrant gaslights. Dozens of coaches went by, their lamps lit and weaving from side to side as the vehicles negotiated the rough pavingstones of the street. Even in the rain it was a sight to see so much activity, so many people involved in the pursuit of living. It was different from the lone tundra, where one counted days by dropping stones into a bucket, where one treated a visitor as if he was as exotic and precious as royalty.

"Damn it," he cursed behind her. She heard the screech of his chair and the whine of the table's casters as he pushed it away from him.

"Shall I ring to have the table taken away?" she asked, still not looking at him.

"Yes," he hissed.

She went to the wall and pulled a lever which was attached to a bell at the concierge's desk. Knowing the call was from Noel Magnus's suite, the concierge would have the table and its uneaten contents hauled away in seconds.

When the attendants left, Rachel still found herself fascinated by the view of the avenue. Magnus prowled behind her, pacing and rummaging through bookshelves, discarding every diversion like a bear searching for honey.

"The doctor says we might return tomorrow if he deems it acceptable," she broached. "I would very much like to see Tommy and Clare—make sure they're not getting into a scrape or anything."

"They're dirty little orphans from the street, and yet you treat them as if they were your own children," he sneered.

She wasn't willing to spar with him. Not tonight when she wanted to know who Miss Harris was and why the name had made him agitated. "All my life I felt cheated. My mother died of yellow fever when I was eight. I had to leave the fine house where she was working and join my father on his wretched whaling vessel. I'll never forget the *Shona*. Her cargo stank of whale's blood and vomit. Even though he was her captain, my father's cabin was so small, I had to sleep on the floor. Until the *Shona* sank in the harbor one winter, I didn't see a real bed until I was twenty." She released a dark smile. "And then, there was the pleasure of the Ice Maiden, and all the charms of running a saloon."

She finally turned to face him.

His gaze held hers.

She laughed bitterly. "Yes, for pretty much as far back as I can remember, I've felt sorry for myself, Noel. Sorry for my lot in life. So sorry that I came up with this insane plan to take over your 'cottage'—and what a fine prank you played on me there, I must tell you—and then I get to New York, this big, terrible, wonderful city. And I find two children living in the mud beneath a staircase." She held open her hands as if in surrender. "Don't you see? I was a wretch to have ever felt sorry for myself. My mother and father loved me. They saw to my care until their dying days. I had it so much better than Tommy and Clare. They humbled me, Noel. I need to care for them, because they in turn need me so much. Do you see?"

"No, I do not see," he said, his jaw tight and clenched. "But you've done so many foolish things, I must count these ragamuffins in with the rest of your deeds."

"If you don't like the children, Noel, we can leave at any time. I'll work for our passage back to Herschel if I must. You can count on it." She lifted her head in defiance.

"But then you would have deprived me of my just retribution, and I won't have that. No, indeed," he snarled. "Not when you owe me so much you can never repair the damage wrought to my name and reputation."

"Name and reputation don't matter as much as food. Have you lived beneath a stair, Noel? Have you run begging dirty and cold through the filthy mud of this city? No, you have not. So, take your retribution of me, but leave out Tommy and Clare. What little faith and innocence they have left is mine only because I earned their trust. I'll now go to my grave to care for them."

"They don't deserve it," he mumbled.

"You're an awful, man, Noel. The devil take you then, if you can hurt a child."

He was silent for a long moment. Then he said simply, "I would have yearned for a life beneath a staircase, for the filth and the mud, if only I'd known of it."

Astounded, she watched him walk to the bedroom, his movements stiff and sore.

Realization hit her like a locomotive. Here she was casting him as the villain to little children, when he'd fed and clothed those very same children he disparaged, when himself had been so wounded by his father, even decades later he was having to undergo surgery to heal it.

Suddenly, she was struck by how little she knew of him. He was the bigger-than-life explorer, Noel Magnus, the man whose name was bandied about saloons in revered whispers. He was big and strong, his body was warm beneath the caribou skins of her bed, but the heart of him, the little boy who'd been cast aside by his own father with a broken bottle, that man she knew very little about. He was a stranger.

"Noel, I'm sorry," she said, going to him, her chest aching with some unnamed emotion.

"Sorry about what?" he snapped, his gaze raking her. "Sorry about all your mischief? Sorry about those two street wretches? You ought to be." He left her and went to his bed-chamber.

She didn't want to follow, but something compelled her.

Watching him ease himself onto the edge of the bed, she briskly went to the nightstand and retrieved bandages and ointment.

"Come. The doctor said it's important to keep changing your dressings. You'll feel better if we don't wait until the morning."

"Go on then, and be done with it."

She knelt next to him. Slowly, she unwrapped the length of soiled linen that bound his torso. If she hurt him, he hid his pain with a series of steely glances and a clenched jaw.

His back was riddled with barely closed slashes. The lips of the wounds were swollen, but pink flesh, not the feared black, greeted her when she cleaned them.

"Finish it and leave me be," he lashed out when she tried to wipe the largest of his wounds.

"Yes," she soothed, her throat choked with emotion. She dressed his back once more, wrapping a new linen bandage around his hard torso.

"Now get out," he said when she had finished.

"Yes," she whispered, placing the soiled bandages in a chamberpot and shutting the door to the nightstand. Quietly, she strode to the door to leave him to his thoughts, but his words stopped her.

"It could have been good, Rachel. It could have been."

She faced him. Even from across the spacious chamber, she could see the bitterness etched upon his face. His lost faith and innocence, the wounded boy inside him, pierced her soul.

"It can still be good. All is not lost," she answered softly. For a long moment she was silent, then she offered, "The only thing I knew about you, Magnus, was that you were the big famous explorer. You would arrive at the Ice Maiden like a great winter storm, and everyone braced for your arrival." She met his gaze and held it. "Now I find you're mortal, so mortal that I seem to have discovered you're almost like myself. I must say, Magnus, it heartens me."

"It does not hearten me," he answered, ice in his tone.

She laughed gently. "I can see that."

"You mock me?" He stood; his hands balled into fists.

He was certainly strong enough to kill her with one blow, but she wasn't frightened. She was beginning to know him by now. "No, I'm not mocking you. I'm welcoming you, Noel. Welcoming you to earth where the rest of us live and muddle through, just like you'll learn to do if you try." She walked to him. Without invitation, she wrapped her arms gingerly around his waist and hugged him.

It was the most natural thing for his arms to go around her, for his hand to stroke down her hair. As he held her, she closed her eyes and for a moment she was back on Herschel, believing in his promise to make her his wife.

She recalled that night in the Arctic when his words meant everything to her. He'd asked her to undress and lie naked with him in her bed but she'd refused, too afraid. But to appease him, she'd peeled off her furs until she had on only her linen shift, then she'd slipped beneath the covers and allowed his body to lay against her own, his maleness hard velvet against her bare thigh.

They'd gone too far then. She should have never allowed more, but he was devilish in his knowledge of the female anatomy. Sliding his fingers between her thighs, he'd found that precise sensitive place and began stroking, his fingers soft and rhythmical, soothing in their gentleness.

But soon she found he quickened. Yet, instead of pushing him away, chastising him for taking liberties, she ached for more, and then more, and then much more...

Her eyes flew open. The picture of her collapsing against him, her thighs wet with perspiration, her pleasure coming in sweet slow waves was more than she could bear. She'd acted like a fool. Not only had she allowed his torture of her, she now spent nearly every night before bedtime replaying the scene in her mind until she thought she might go mad from it.

His exquisite torture.

He tilted up her head. His movements were stiff and he was obviously still in pain, but he kissed her then, in the dark, his chest warm and rippling with muscle beneath the bandages.

"No, Magnus," she whispered, pulling away.

He refused to let her go. Weakened by pain, he was still a force to be reckoned with. His arms were like a steel cage and no amount of struggling would release her without a key.

Like lightning, she recalled the rest of the night she'd spent with him, how she had denied him his pleasure even though she had received hers. She told him it would come with the promise fulfilled. He'd told her she was selfish, but he'd given her the promise, nonetheless.

"I'll keep you to your word," she vowed now,

even as his fingers worked open the buttons down the front of her dress.

"I can break you." In the shadowed light, a smile tugged on the side of his mouth. "Enough nights together, and you'll be begging me to not keep my promise to you."

"There won't be any nights together," she panted, watching his hand as it ruthlessly parted her dress.

"Rachel, you forget everyone thinks you're my wife." He continued the dark smile. "Remind me when we return to Northwyck to have my things moved to your suite. I think I sleep too far from my wife's room, and I like to have a woman next to me, keeping me warm at night."

He caressed the plump top of her breast that couldn't be tamed by her corset. Staring down at her, admiration in his eyes for the tight black satin that held her chest in a cage of erotic iron, he said, "I like this corset. It's perfect for you. You must keep this one as a reminder of your wicked widowhood. And wear it when I ask," he said, his mouth moving down on hers, giving her a full deep kiss before his lips lowered to her breast where his hand had been stroking her.

Her heart hammered in her chest, her mouth grew dry. "You cannot have it all, Magnus, without your promise to marry me."

"I can have it all when you beg me to break my promise," he said, his fingers playing with the pretty lilac ribbons that adorned the top edge of the black satin corset. Without warning, he roughly pulled her dress down to her hips, running his hands along her cinched waist as if he could span it. He brushed his lips along her shoulders, letting his tongue play with the delicate structure of her collarbone.

"I won't let you break it. I'll lay with you tonight, but it'll be just like on Herschel. Nothing for you. Nothing," she moaned when his hand tugged at the laces of her corset. She wanted to fight him, but the memory of pleasure was as close as the sudden dampness between her thighs. The corset loosened and his mouth hotly covered her nipple.

Sanity bade her break away. She moved across the room, as far from him as she could get. "I'll keep to my word, Noel. I swear I will."

His answer was diabolical. He stared at her with those dark eyes and said, "Then I'll take the wager. Let's see how many nights it takes before there's something for me, shall we, Wife?"

A loud knock at the door woke her. Magnus was already sitting up and cursing.

"What do you want?" he barked, his hand holding Rachel down in the bed, though she wanted to bolt for her clothes.

"There is an urgent message for you, sir. I thought it unwise to keep it until the morning," came the voice of the hotel manager.

Magnus stood. He didn't even bother to cover his loins as he snatched open the bedchamber door, took the written message and slammed the door in the man's face.

"Is everything all right? Is it from Northwyck? Is there something wrong with Tommy and Clare?" Rachel clasped and unclasped her hands.

He strode over to the gas sconce. Opening the note, he gave it a cursory read. Then, in exasperation, he crumpled it and tossed it on the top of his bureau.

"Everything's all right at Northwyck?" she asked.

"Everything's all right at Northwyck," he repeated.

She released a sigh. It was then she noticed him beneath the dim, flickering light of the sconce, the bandages and his long, tapering thighs a perfect frame for his obvious desire.

"Have you given up yet, Wife?" he asked, raising one infuriating eyebrow at her.

She glanced away, then turned and faced the wall, her answer clear.

But he had his own ideas. He slipped beneath the fine Egyptian sheets, sliding more and more onto her side of the mattress until she thought she might have to fall to the floor to avoid him.

But just as she was considering doing such, he threw his arm over her and held her against him in a rock-hard embrace. Finally, he scooted just two more inches toward her and pressed himself against the pliable flesh of her bottom, and held her tightly against him, daring her not to feel him.

She did.

Frozen, she forced her mind not to wander

from anything but the most mundane, lest temptation weaken her.

But her gaze wasn't so easily tamed. In the dark, she made out the form of her black satin corset and laces dropped upon the light background of carpet. The pale lilac ribbon edging the top glowed in the lamplight coming in from a crack in the drapery.

The sight of the corset tortured her. Thoughts of release flooded her mind. The heavy hand that rested against the curve of her waist promised caresses the likes of which she had never known.

But there was no succumbing. She knew she had to be strong or lose all. So she shut her eyes tight and thought of home; ice and snow, bleeding chapped hands and raw blubber.

Through it all, the hand on her hip, the hardness against her bottom, remained.

It took her a very long time to go back to sleep.

CHAPTER THIRTEEN

Rachel walked by the crumpled piece of paper a hundred times. Whatever was written on it was none of her business. Certainly it hadn't concerned Noel, for he had tossed it off as quickly as he had read it.

But she wanted to know what it said. By the

very fact that he had refused to tell her, she was left burning. Noel finished breakfast in the parlor. She had excused herself to look for the rest of her hairpins still strewn within the sheets. This was her only chance to see what the note had said, perhaps to discover one more hidden facet of the man she desperately loved.

She uncrumpled the small sheet; every noise convinced her Noel was going to pounce on her any second. The handwriting was in pale-gray ink on cream paper.

Darling—
  I must see you! The very thought of you dead left me distraught. Now I ache to find you once again in your rightful place as my lord and master.
  I'll wait all night with brandy and a bath.
                    Your beloved Charmian

Rachel crumpled the paper in her hand. Stunned, she could hardly breathe. It had been bad enough finding out about his fiancée Miss Amberly, but this woman Charmian was more. Much more. Noel clearly had a relationship with the woman. Charmian was his mistress. She was his Arctic equivalent of a native wife. Charmian had been performing the role Noel had tried to cast Rachel in, and so far, unsuccessfully.

"I see I needn't explain to you who Miss Harris is," Noel said, acid in his words as he stood in the doorway staring at her.

184

In her shock she hadn't heard him rise from the breakfast table. Nor had she heard him walk to the bedchamber.

She handed him the balled-up piece of paper.

In a low tone, she said, "Forgive me. I see it was none of my business." She meant to walk past him, but a touch to her cheek made her stop.

"If I'd wanted you to see the note I would have shown it to you. I didn't want to explain Charmian Harris. But now I suppose I must do so—"

"No," she interrupted harshly. "I don't require an explanation. I've no right to it. I'm not your true wife. I'm not even your lover. If you have a mistress, then it's your business and her business. Not mine." She gathered her emotions. He went to touch her cheek again and she drew away as if he burned her.

"I didn't go to see her last night, did I?" he offered.

"I don't want to hear about her. Truly," she said, still cringing. "I see now that last night was a mistake. I've made so many mistakes." Her eyes stung with unshed despair. "I want to help you return to Northwyck, but then I must leave. No matter how much you may demand me to stay, I see now that I must leave."

He grew angry. "Rachel, I will not have you dictate to me. Charmian Harris was my mistress, but I haven't seen her since—"

"Since when? Since five years ago when you visited New York? Those same five years ago when you were visiting me and my father on Herschel, promising me love and devotion? Then trotting back here for supplies only so you could mount..."

Knowing she was going over the line, she tiredly went to a rosewood chair and sat down. "This life you lead here, full of mistresses and wealth and excess—" She placed her head in her hands. "I don't want it. In fact, I don't remember ever wanting it." *Because all I ever wanted was you,* she thought blackly.

"Rachel, she was my mistress for ten years. I knew Charmian long before I knew you," he said coldly, without contrition.

She gave a cynical little snort. "I suppose then she should be jealous of me. You asked me to be your mistress while you were still maintaining her. And now you refused her offer last night to stay with me." Her gaze turned to the bed. That delicious place where she had found security and at least the imaginings of love. "But you must send a note to her right away, Magnus. Tell her you'll come to her right away." She rose from the chair. "Because certainly I never will."

"You've come here wanting to be my wife," he snarled. "Well, have a taste of what being my wife is going to entail, Rachel. A man of my station takes on a mistress. Judith would have accepted this."

"She would have been a fool then," Rachel murmured.

He looked at her. "You don't understand the ways of society."

"My father was at sea most of the year, and yet he stayed devoted to my mother until the day she died. Don't tell me I know nothing of society, because I know how love should be." Her eyes flashed.

"Your father was a seaman, your mother a cook. Bourgeois morality plays no part here. None whatsoever. And you in your innocence don't see that," he scoffed.

She stared at him, unblinking. "I know how love should be," she repeated.

"And now you have a taste of how love is." The hardness left his expression for a moment. "You don't belong here; I could see that up on Herschel. You should have heeded my caution, Rachel. You should have stayed away from those things of which you know nothing. You should have protected your silly notions of love and stayed away."

She wanted to lash out at him, to pummel some feeling into him and rid him of his cold attitude, but before she could utter a word, a knock came to the door of the suite. They both stood there, frozen, as the door opened and a man walked into the parlor.

"I pray I've not come at a difficult time," Edmund Hoar said as his gaze found them in the doorway to the bedroom. "I saw your valet, Magnus, and he told me you were finishing breakfast. I just wanted to see how you were doing after your operation." His pale-jade eyes fixed on Rachel. "Good morning, Mrs. Magnus. I do hope I haven't intruded."

Rachel said nothing.

Noel, however, looked as if he might crush the man's face with his fist. "Get out," he said to Hoar with no thought to manners.

"I take it your animosity results from your wounds and not my company." Hoar perched himself on the edge of a desk. He looked dashing in black trousers and a bottle-green coat, and by his affectations, he knew it. "I've got to confess, I've come to inquire about The Black Heart. I'm burning with the desire to know why you have not announced its whereabouts to the newspapers, Magnus. Was that not the infamous stone I saw around your wife's neck at the ball?"

"I will not provide you with information. Now, get out," Magnus growled.

Hoar's gaze turned once more to her. "My dear woman, do you not know what a terrible stone you have? And do you not heed its curse?"

"I fear no curse," she answered, not caring anyhow. Her life was beyond the point of doom.

"But this one is so very wicked. The stone came from India. The raj put a curse on it when his favorite consort ran off with a servant. It's said that whoever owns the opal is destined to kill that which he most loves. Do you believe in such things, Mrs. Magnus? Because Lady Franklin did not. She gave Franklin the opal as a way to break the curse, and now

188

she is spending the rest of her fortune to find her beloved in the hope that her actions did not ultimately cause his death."

Helplessly, Rachel thought of her father. He'd given her the opal with the thought that one day it would bring some money. But now, with Edmund's ramblings, she wondered if he had been the owner of the stone at the time of his death, or if she had been. Certainly she'd loved no one as much as her father, and after he'd died, there was only Magnus to love.

She would not see a curse cut him down, too.

"It's useless to warn me off, Mr. Hoar. I no longer have the stone. It's now fully Magnus's to do with what he wishes."

Edmund gave a dramatic intake of breath. "Is that wise, Magnus, now that you've finally been reunited with your lovely bride?"

Rachel almost wanted to laugh had it not been so painful. Her life was in no danger. Noel was not prone to giving her an outpouring of love. At best, he viewed her with occasional affection. At worst, she was just an unattainable object of lust which he would not quit until he conquered.

"Mr. Hoar, may I remind you that I've told you to leave this suite." Noel stepped toward him. Edmund slid down from the table and ventured toward the door.

"I'll pay whatever price is asked, Magnus. You know that," Edmund said.

"The Black Heart is going to the museum. I announced that when I was setting out on my first expedition, and I intend to keep my promise. Now, good day, Hoar." Magnus shut the door behind him.

Rachel began to laugh with all the furor of a madwoman. When she was done, she went to the suite door and said, "I'll see that the carriage is ready for our journey."

"First you will explain what is so amusing." He placed his hand on the door, blocking her exit.

She turned despair-filled eyes toward him. "I was just thinking that it was most fortunate I gave you the opal."

"Why so?" he demanded.

"Because I love too many, Noel. Don't you see?" She tilted her mouth in a sad smile. "Many lives would be endangered if the curse was real and I owned The Black Heart. But you! Why, you're the perfect match. No curse could touch you." The tone of her voice deadened. "Because you love no one."

"Then perhaps it's destiny that I find Franklin's opal," he answered sarcastically. "I'm making the world safe again."

She looked at him. As if directed by a will outside her own, she lifted her hand and placed it on his beard-roughened cheek, caressing it with all the tenderness of the night before.

I would take the risk of all the curses if only you would love me.

She wanted to cry out the words but reason choked her. The curse wasn't real. Franklin had surely perished, not from a cursed opal but from bad judgment in the world's worst climate.

And Magnus wouldn't imperil her with his love because he didn't love her. And probably never would.

CHAPTER FOURTEEN

"Mrs. Magnus, how have you been holding up? You're the talk of the town with all you've had to endure these past weeks."

Rachel looked up from the hotel desk. Edmund Hoar was at her elbow, the same ever-helpful grin on his face she'd seen earlier.

"Mr. Hoar," Rachel said, succinctly turning back toward the concierge.

"Is he well enough to travel? How pleased you must be at the thought of returning home." Hoar took his hand and placed it at the small of her back like a husband would do. Then he whispered for her ears only, "Meet me in the oriel of the hotel ballroom. I've some information for you. Information concerning Magnus."

In a harsh whisper, she said, "Mr. Hoar, why would you believe I would meet you any-where—"

He cut her off. "Magnus is in trouble. Dreadful trouble. I fear for his life."

"In trouble? In trouble with who?" she demanded, her voice still locked in a hush.

"Charmian Harris is a spiteful woman. She conceded to being his mistress, but for him to not see her has made her livid. She told me herself she wishes him dead and she has the venom to carry out her threats."

Rachel remembered how cowed Mazie was when she first went to work for her. Beatings with the back of a hairbrush was energy well spent on a lazy servant. But that kind of person would go to the ends of the earth to punish a man who had rejected her.

"Meet me in the oriel," he repeated. "You can then warn him about Charmian and what she's about to do."

Torn, she watched Hoar walk away, a confident lilt in his stride as he nodded farewell.

Twenty minutes later, Rachel found herself opening the door to the unused hotel ballroom. The cavernous room was dark; the draperies were pulled shut, but daylight streamed through the part in the fabric. She could see the oriel at the east corner behind a ghostly sentinel of sheet-clad chairs.

"Brilliant girl. You've come." Edmund stepped in front of the blue velvet curtains that enclosed the oriel.

She said nothing and went no closer.

"You want to protect him, don't you? You love him." Edmund looked at her. She swore she could see his jaw muscle tighten in anger.

"I only know secondhand of Miss Harris's temper, but I know he refused to see her last night. From what I understand, any imagined transgression is cause for a backlash." She waited for the information she'd come for, a sixth sense telling her to go no nearer to Hoar.

"Charmian Harris is known for her tantrums. The servants despise her." Edmund laughed. "You stand there, Rachel, your eyes as fearful as a child's, and yet you came here. For him." The last words were like an oath.

"Magnus is a powerful man. He can protect himself. But I know nothing of a woman's fury. I feel it my duty to make sure he was warned." Her words were all Hoar needed to know: nothing more, nothing less.

"Charmian is a witch with her servants, a trollop in bed, and most importantly, an impotent little fool. No match for Magnus."

"Then why did you lead me to believe otherwise?" The question was as impotent as Charmian's anger. The only answer was that she'd been lured there and she shouldn't have come. She'd opened herself up for trouble now.

"Come sit in the oriel with me, Rachel."

Rachel took a step backward. She was about to flee to the closed door, but he was more swift. He took both her hands and pulled her against her will in the direction he wanted.

"Come, sit with me, my love." He dragged her toward the black yaw of the interior of the oriel. She struggled and struck at him, but to no avail. Her thin leather slippers slid along the waxed parquet, assisting him.

"You didn't tell him you were meeting me, did you?" He chuckled. "Good girl. Otherwise he'd be here in your stead, making me eat his fist." He slammed her against the wall and ran his hand down the side of her corset. "And I'd rather be feasting on something else."

"Please," she panted as he slid his hand from her mouth to her cheek. "I don't have the opal for you, if that's what you want. Magnus told you the truth. He possesses it now. I can do nothing for you."

"But which treasure does he value most? You or The Black Heart?" His breath was hot against her ear, reeking of tobacco. He clamped down on her jaw and tried to kiss her. She violently turned away.

"I found out from the help that you shared the same bed last night. He declined Charmian's offer for you. *You.* So, tell me. Tell me which he prefers."

"Why do you hate him so? He's your rival, I know, but there have been times when you've won the rivalry, Mr. Hoar. You owned all The Company of the North. The company tried to thwart Noel constantly. Sometimes you won, Mr. Hoar. Can't that be enough?"

He shook her so hard she wondered if she would ever see straight again. "He will not have the opal and you, do you understand me? So which does he prefer?"

"He prefers the opal! The opal, I tell you!" she cried out, her voice thick with humiliation.

He let her go. She slumped against the ornate gilded plasterwork.

"You wretched little girl," he whispered, panting. "You've fallen in love with him, haven't you? And the sentiment isn't returned as passionately, I wager?"

She refused to answer him.

He laughed. "He doesn't deserve you, Rachel." Slowly he brought his body against hers, pinning her to the wall. "But what joy you would give me to leave him. He'd appreciate you then."

Struggling to make him let her go, she finally quieted and said, "If I leave him, it will not be for the likes of you. I'd take a toothless peg-legged seaman before I'd choose you."

The slap came hard across her face. She moaned, but her defiant gaze never left him.

His hand stroked her cheek as if in apology. "It's no secret I find you desirable, Rachel. Perhaps we could have an arrangement—"

"You only find me desirable because you believed Magnus desired me. Well, I tell you now, he desires The Black Heart more. Now that he possesses it, I plan on returning to Herschel Island as soon as I manage to find the funds necessary to take me and the children back there." She finally managed to push him off her.

He stood back and studied her. "I don't know if I can believe it," he insisted.

"It's true. As you suspected, our marriage is a sham. He has only dallied with me. Now there's no reason for me to remain in New York."

Under his breath she swore she heard him say, "If this is true, you may well have saved your life, beautiful girl."

Frigidly, she said, "If I may go, I'd take kindly to never seeing you again, Mr. Hoar. For if I do, you may just be praying that Charmian Harris take her fury out on you instead."

He laughed. The little teeth seemed to glow in the dark. "You say it's my covetous nature that makes me want you, but I see now that's not all it is. You tempt me every time with the pleasure of breaking you."

"I won't be around for you to try." She turned and walked across the ballroom.

"How do you plan on securing the funds to leave for Herschel? I take it Magnus controls the purse strings?" He followed her.

"I'll find a way," she answered, not looking back.

"You want to leave soon, don't you? He's broken your heart, hasn't he? And now you long to escape so that you needn't be tormented by his lack of love any longer. Am I not right?"

She ignored him.

"You could be on the next ship leaving New York Harbor. I could give you the money to leave. Did you hear me?"

Her hand paused on the rococo door handle. "Do you want the money to leave now?"

Without looking at him, she answered, "It would be suicide to be obligated to you."

"No obligation. You do me a favor, I do you one. Then we wipe the slate clean."

"What do you want?"

"The opal."

"I could never get that for you."

"You could try."

"But—" She closed her mouth. It was sheer stupidity to explain to Hoar that she had given Magnus the opal and would not ask for it back. Hoar would never relent then. "Fine. I will try," she lied to him.

He stroked her arm. "In the meantime I expect you to reconsider our liaison. Perhaps we might both get our revenge on Magnus that way."

She pulled her arm away. Without a retort, she opened the ballroom door and left him.

"You seem unusually quiet. What's brewing in that head of yours?" Magnus stared at her from across the compartment. The train rolled at a steady twenty miles per hour. They would be back at Northwyck by the end of the day.

"I'm just anxious to return to Tommy and Clare. I miss them." Rachel studied him. He sat stiffly on the tufted leather seat, not daring to relax. More than once she'd watched him let down his guard and suffer the pain of his wounds crushing against the luxuriously upholstered seat back.

"I sent word of our arrival. With any luck, the two snipes should be there to meet you."

The ghost of a smile touched her lips. "It's a good thing you can afford this private compartment, Mr. Magnus, so that all and sundry can't hear your conversations. Those two 'snipes,' as you call them, are believed to be the fruit of your loins."

"Ha!" He gave her a dark glance. "My children will be twice as smart and twice as handsome than those street wretches."

"Tommy and Clare are both brilliant, and as beautiful as any child you might bring into this world, Noel. And don't forget, your children will look half like their mother. Judith Amberly, with her all-too-slender form, should produce several nice stick insects for you."

"Easy there," he growled, a strange emotion twinkling in his eyes. "You sound jealous, my love."

She turned her head to look out the window. There was no refuting what he'd said. She'd given everything in order to win his love. With Edmund Hoar's pointed questions in the hotel ballroom, she realized it was not possible. Noel Magnus was never going to love her. He loved his precious opal more than her. The realization cut her to the quick.

"What is it about your cheek, Rachel? It's red. You look as if you've been struck, yet I vow I haven't laid a hand on you." His gaze locked with hers.

She put a hand to the cheek Hoar had slapped. It was still tender. She was almost tempted to tell him his enemy had done it, but then thought better of it. There was no use. All the revelation would secure her would be Noel's further testimony of her worthlessness.

"You haven't struck me. I'll agree to that should anyone ask," she said lightly.

The honesty in his words pierced her. "But I would never strike you. A man striking a woman is something I cannot abide. I watched my father do it enough. Now I think I might kill the man who raised his hand to a woman."

She wondered how he would meet Edmund if Noel had seen the way he'd treated her.

"But I must know. How is it that your cheek is red? Did you fall? Bump into something? I'll see to it the hotel is notified if their rooms are a hazard," he told her.

An uncomfortable moment of silence passed. "It was my own fault. Please don't notify the hotel." She pleaded with him with her eyes.

He looked away. "You should be more careful, then. Take care of yourself. If you were more wise to the ways of the world, you would know a woman's face is her fortune."

But more so her mind and her heart, she wanted to cry out.

Instead, she turned her attention back to the windowscape.

She had to return to Herschel. Not even her obligations to maintain appearances until he could extract them from this fraud of a marriage was enough to make her stay.

Tomorrow, she, Tommy, and Clare would be back on the train, this time heading back to New York City. It was leave him, or betray him with Edmund Hoar's obsessive plotting, and she would never do that. Not even to rid herself of the despised opal. The Black Heart that was so much more worthy in Noel's eyes than her loving one.

They had reached the mountains near Northwyck and the train rocked as it swerved around a curve. The entire car shuddered. Noel slammed back into his seat. Pain cracked across his expression. He cursed.

She watched him, aching to ease his torment, aching to love him. But he sent her one of his dismissive glances and she knew the futility of it.

She would not betray him; so she would leave him.

CHAPTER FIFTEEN

Rachel grabbed a kashmir shawl to chase away the chill. The soft lightweight warmth around her shoulders was something she had begun to take for granted. But no more.

She pulled out her old carpetbag. The seal fur *amautik* was still inside, along with her polar bear *mukluks*. The smell of bear grease and sweat sent her back on her heels. It didn't seem possible that only six months ago she didn't have violet water to bathe herself with, and silk gowns to announce her with their rustle.

"Child, what are you doing? Heavens! Did Mazie forget to dispose of the chamberpot in this room?" Betsy entered her bedroom carrying a pot of chocolate on a tray. She placed the silver tray on the nightstand and started poking around the cabinets.

"It's not the chamberpot, Betsy," Rachel confessed. "It's my old clothes. I've gotten them out."

"I wonder if it's finally time to cease the nostalgia and burn them, don't you?"

"I—I can't burn them." Rachel bit her lower lip. It was time to confess her crimes to her only true friend. Only then could she get the help she needed to leave.

She began. "I have terrible news, Betsy. I pray you won't hate me when I've finished, but until then, may I ask you to sit down?"

Betsy lowered herself to a chair, her aged blue eyes wide with trepidation. "I fear I'm not going to like this, am I?"

"I'm sorry. I can't make the truth pretty. I've been trying too hard to gild all these lies. Now I just have to be out with it."

"Out with what, my dear?"

Rachel stared at the woman. There were so many things she would miss about Betsy: her kindly features, her pretty lace morning caps, her slavish attention to everyone's comfort. But mostly she would miss her female friendship. Not since her mother had died had Rachel known the dear companionship of another woman until she'd arrived at Northwyck.

"I—I've been lying to you. To everyone. I'm not Magnus's widow. He has not married me—it was only my desire to have him as my husband that drove me to come to this place and live here. And commit this terrible fraud." A tear escaped her eye but she brushed it back, unwilling to let emotion mitigate her crimes. "I did it out of despair, for I never thought Noel would come back here. He'd been declared dead and seemed happy to stay that way, but I was a fool. Naturally, with a fiancée and mistress here, he would have returned eventually. I see now he had no desire to marry me, because he'd planned his wedding long ago with Miss Amberly."

Betsy stared at her for a long moment. Rachel didn't know what to expect; anger, betrayal, ridicule. She did not expect the woman to rise from her seat and wrap her arms around her.

"You poor child, abandoned in that wretched frozen wasteland, pining for Magnus's love when he'll be happy to leave you starving for it. I don't know how you've survived."

Rachel felt as if she'd imbibed too much even though she hadn't touched a drop all night. "Mrs. Willem, perhaps you haven't understood me. I—"

"Save your explaining. I think I suspected as much. Certainly when Magnus arrived and he didn't even remember his own children. No, I couldn't quite reconcile that, but now it makes sense."

Her soul weighted down with sorrow, Rachel said, "I'm sorry I tricked you. It wasn't for wealth or greed or anything of the sort. I thought to live in his cottage with the hope that one day he might look for me there. I had no idea Northwyck was a mansion. No idea I'd find such kindness here from you and Mr. Willem, and Mazie, and everyone."

"There, there, my dear. I'm sure it does your heart good to confess. And this certainly clears up a mystery or two—such as the children?"

Rachel shook her head. "Tommy and Clare tried to rob me in the city the day I arrived. They were sleeping beneath a stair in an alley. I couldn't just turn away. I thought I'd be fending for myself in a small cottage, and I figured I could fend for them, too. I never meant for this to get so out of hand."

Betsy laughed. "Heavens! What a story for you and Magnus to tell the grandchildren about!"

"I'm so glad you're not angry. I think it would have killed me to lose your friendship. Your kindness has meant so much these past few months, and it means double now that you know you were kind to a charlatan."

"You're no charlatan. You did what you had to to survive. And Noel's hardheartedness drove you to it."

Rachel hugged her. "It's no excuse. I was wrong, but I'm ever so grateful not to have to leave on bad terms. I'd like to write you, if I may, once I return to Herschel."

"Herschel? What are you talking about? You can't leave." Betsy's dismay was genuine.

"Magnus wants me to continue the charade until he can find a graceful exit for it, but

I find I can't continue here. He—" Her voice cracked. "He doesn't have any regard for me, and I see now he never will. Knowing this, I find staying here more than I can bear."

"Then don't stay here, love. Go to Paris for a while. Newport. The city. We've seven houses. Don't go back to that unholy island in the ice."

Rachel wiped the tears that were flowing freely now. "I can't continue to live on his goodwill. He has none for me. No, I must return home. My father left me a saloon. I wager it will still be standing when I return."

"A saloon." Betsy visibly shuddered. "You can't do it. I won't let you."

"I have less right to be here than you or Mazie. I'm not even a servant here. Not even a guest. I've got to return to the place I belong, and the only place for me is the Ice Maiden Saloon." Rachel took both the woman's hands in her own. "After this wretched confession I have only one last thing to ask you, and I pray that you take mercy upon me."

"What is it, child? What do you need?"

Rachel groped for the words. "I came here with nothing. The last of my father's coins brought me and the children to your doorstep. The opal that I said Magnus gave me was in truth one my father found. It belonged to me, but now I've handed it over to Magnus for restitution. I have nothing now. Nothing. He forbids me even to take the clothes on my back if I should flee and not live out this charade until he plots the appropriate finale.

So I must have funds. The children and I can wear rags, but we'll have to eat on our journey, and have money to get us there."

"I can give you the money, Rachel. But you must let me speak with Noel before I do it."

"If you let him know I want to leave, he'll hold me prisoner here and see me die before he'll let me interfere any more in his life." Rachel's breathing locked up. Panic engulfed her.

Betsy studied her, compassion glowing in her faded periwinkle eyes. "I know he's difficult. I know he rants and glowers and sinks into melancholy just being here in this place that holds so many bad memories. But I know him better than anyone on this earth, love. He's more my own son than he could ever be my master. You must trust me with this. I have to talk to him. I'll try to keep your secret, but you must give me this chance. And if I see fit, after I've spoken to him, I'll send you and the children back to Herschel first class."

"And if you do not see fit?" Rachel asked, her voice small and worried.

"Then I will do as he asks." Betsy squeezed her hands. "Because I know him so well. And his reasons for my compliance will be good ones."

"I can't stay here, Betsy. Please believe me, I cannot stay here." She trembled from the emotion wracking her. "I know about his mistress, I know about his fiancée. He could never love me. Never. I see that now and I cannot bear to even think of him, let alone see him..." Her words dwindled to nothingness. The same nothingness inside her.

"Give me some time to speak with him. Then the trip shall be yours."

"I'll repay you," Rachel blurted out, grasping at straws. "Please know that as soon as possible I'll send you the funds. The Ice Maiden doesn't do too badly as long as the summer ship arrives from The Company of the North."

Betsy released a sharp laugh. "Perfect. You can repay me as long as Edmund Hoar sends his ship in to rob you. The irony of it all."

Defeated, Rachel slumped to a chair.

Betsy patted her cheek. "Take heart, child. You haven't lost all your friends. I'll be your friend whether Noel wants you to stay or allows you to go."

"But don't you see, he'll never allow it. He enjoys torturing me." She hung her head in her hands.

"We'll see about that. We'll see," Betsy said enigmatically before she departed.

"May I see you?" Mrs. Willem knocked softly on the half-opened door to Noel's study.

"What is it?" Noel answered, sitting in a leather barrel chair, his hand cradling a glass of whiskey.

"It's about your wife, sir. I must speak with you." Betsy closed the heavy double doors.

He pulled another barrel chair in front of the fire. Taking the seat with all the comfort of an old friend, Betsy looked at him and said, "She wants to leave."

He snorted and took another swallow of whiskey. "What has she told you then?"

"Everything." She frowned. Lines of concern carved into her face. "She wants to borrow the money from me so that she and the children can return to Herschel Island."

"I won't permit it." He stared grimly into the fire.

"Do you love her?" Betsy leaned over and tenderly stroked his brow. "I've no right to ask, I know. I'm nothing more than a servant here. Just Northwyck's housekeeper. But we've always been more to each other than servant and master. I had no children of my own; I was the mother when *your* mother left you. You've given me and Nathan our cottage. You've been as kind and devoted as any son. I certainly could love you no more than my own."

He stared at her. "Where's this leading to, Betsy? Somehow I don't think I'm going to like it."

"She loves you, Noel. Pure and simple. If you do not love her in return, in the name of humanity, you've got to let her leave this place. It's not good for the soul to do to her what you're doing. But—" She paused and studied him. "But I saw that man who arrived here from the Arctic to find her. I saw the fear on his face when he thought she wasn't here, I saw the pain and torment he'd put his body through so that he could get here quickly and ease the torment in his mind."

She gave him a soft, beautiful smile. "I know that man loves me, though he has never told me. So I wonder if I should give Rachel the money—or if I should give that man more time to say what I think is in his heart."

"She tricked me. She came here enacting a fraud," he bit out.

"I know. She told me all that."

"Then she must do as I tell her. She's beholden to me."

Betsy laughed. "Yes, she told me all that, too. But that's not what I'm asking, Noel. I'm not asking what's owed and who deserves restitution. I'm asking if you need more time. Because if things are never to change between you and Rachel, then let her be on her way."

He glanced away, anger in his eyes.

Betsy looked at him, weighing and gauging all the nuances she knew so well. "Love is difficult for you, Noel. A man can't master a soufflé when all he's known his whole life is starvation. No one knows that better than I do. I was the one you came to when as a toddler you cried for your mama. I was also the one who first cleaned the glass from your back when he threw the bottle at you. I blame myself for the incident even now. You didn't want him to send you to school. You didn't want any more loneliness and privation than you had at Northwyck; and mostly you didn't want to leave me. So that's what you told the old man. You didn't want to leave me, the worthless, faceless housekeeper, and in his rage over that, he threw that bottle at you, the scars you bear even

208

now." A sadness engulfed her. Slowly she rose from the chair and crossed to the door.

She gave him one last study. "I don't blame you for being afraid, love. I just need to know if you need more time. A yes or no will do, and I shall act accordingly."

He didn't want to answer. Refusing to look at her, he gripped his head as if his father's own rage was bottled up inside him.

Then, all at once, he hissed, "Yes," and it was over. And Betsy knew what she needed to do.

"But did she say anything? Did she need to speak with me?" Rachel's questions seemed absurd in the context of her being the mistress of the house and Betsy being the housekeeper, but when Mazie arrived to dress her for dinner, Rachel was crawling the walls with anxiety.

"No, Mrs. Magnus. Betsy simply told me it was time to help you get ready for dinner. Just like any other evening." Mazie stared at her mistress as if she wondered about Rachel's sanity.

"I couldn't eat now. I can't go downstairs. Please give my excuses." Rachel paced the room, ignoring Mazie who obediently curtsied and left through the servants' door.

She would go mad if Betsy didn't give her an answer about the money tonight. There was no way to face Noel at dinner when any moment she might be surprised by Betsy's betrayal. Rachel wouldn't begrudge her for it;

the woman was devoted to Noel, but she swore the housekeeper had understood her pain. She had faith the woman would do everything within her power to free her from the hell she'd gotten herself into.

Resigning herself to a night of worry, she nestled into the window seat.

Her nerves crashed at the violence of the door flinging open.

"I understand you're not feeling well?" Noel walked into the room and went to the mahogany wardrobe carved with intricate Gothic tracery. He opened it with a lurch.

"I—I'm not up to dinner after the long train ride," she stammered, unsure of him and his mood.

"Don't be ridiculous. You've got to eat." He glanced at her, barely leashed fury in his dark eyes. "Look at you. You're wasting away. Soon there'll be nothing to you." He returned his attention to the contents of the wardrobe. "Every garment's black in here."

Mentally cringing, she said, "The gowns are for a widow."

"Tomorrow send for the dressmaker." He looked at her. "Tell him I want you in dresses the same delicate color as those damned magazines you used to fawn over in Herschel."

She rose from the window seat, her guard up. "I don't plan on staying long enough to wear any more of your dresses."

He met her gaze. "How do you figure?"

She took a deep breath and gathered her courage. "The opal alone has more than made up for any embarrassment and cost to you. Edmund Hoar certainly seemed to think so when he asked if he could get me to take it from you. He has quite a lust for the piece, I understand." Her voice turned husky. "Almost as much as yours."

His eyes turned stormy. His tone proved he was at the razor's edge of self-control. "When did you see him to discuss the matter? Certainly it was not in my presence."

"He made the offer in New York. At the hotel."

He was silent for an interminable moment. "What other offers did he make to you?"

She glanced away, not expecting him to be so blunt. The blush rose up on her cheeks even as she fought it.

Noel stared at her, enraged and yet, for some reason, manacled. "I understand he was a visitor to the house while I was away. Was he a...frequent visitor?"

Quietly holding her own emotions in check, she said, "Does it matter? After all, I'm not your wife."

His rage snapped. He went to her, grabbed her in his arms and forced her to look at him. "Everyone thinks you're my wife. Everyone blessed this unholy union but myself because it was thrust upon me—"

"But no more. No more! I'm leaving, I tell you! You clean up the damage and accept my apologies, and take that as the end of it." She shot him a defiant look. "The charade is over, Magnus. It's over."

"It's—not—over," he gnashed out. He raked her with his gaze, then pushed her back to the window seat. Striding to the wardrobe, he ran his hands through the dresses until one suited his purpose. He yanked it out and went to her.

"Put this on. Be ready for dinner in ten minutes, or so help me, I'll dress you myself." He looked down at the gown in her hands, a black watered silk with an ink-colored net fichu over the bosom. Reaching out, he ripped the fichu from the dress and balled it in his hands. "There. That's better. It's the way you should be dressing for your husband. Now put it on and don't keep me waiting."

Aghast, she looked at the ruined gown. The neckline was tattered and so bare as to be nearly obscene. "I can't wear this. I can't," she repeated, almost begging.

"You've got"—he took a gold watch from his pocket—"a little more than eight minutes." With that, he stormed out. She heard every furious step as he descended the stairs.

"Miss?" Mazie asked softly, appearing like an angel from the servants' door.

Like a ragdoll, Rachel stood and allowed the maid to hook her into the black dress.

CHAPTER SIXTEEN

Rachel walked into the private dining room thankful for the soft candlelight that might mask her shame.

Looking up from the table, Noel assessed her brutally. His eyes followed her as she crossed the room and stood at her place at the table.

A footman helped her with her chair, then he removed the hot silver cover from her soup.

"Leave us," Noel said curtly.

The footman bowed and exited through the jib door.

She stared at the fine watercress soup as if it were the meanest gruel.

"Eat," he ordered.

Her gaze locked with his.

"Why are you doing this?" she asked, not touching her spoon.

"What? Asking that my wife wear something other than the chaste widow's weeds of a fraud offends you, my dear?" He enunciated every word as if they gave him pleasure.

"No decent woman dresses like this." She looked down and felt the blood rise to her face. The dusky aureoles of her nipples were almost exposed at the edge of her neckline. Her breasts were generous to begin with, but corseted and barely covered by a tight, low neckline made them appear twice as big. Mortified, she covered her nudity with a splayed hand. But he would have none of it.

"Put down your hand," he told her.

"Why not just demand that I come to the table naked?" she gasped, pulling at the frayed edge of the bodice to no avail.

"My wife will do as I say. That's the lesson here, Rachel. You long to be my wife, then you long to be property, and as my property I may dress you as I please, treat you as I please, take of you as I please." A muscle bunched in his jaw as he gazed down at her chest. "If I had the notion to pin you to this table, throw your skirt over your head and force myself inside you, as your husband I'd have the right. And no one, not you, not even the law, could prevent me from having my way."

He seemed to grow melancholy and pensive. Staring deep into her eyes, he said, "I wanted something better for you, Rachel. I didn't want you to live like my mother did. My thoughts were always how to keep you, not run you off. I didn't want to return here. You were keeping me away from this hell, and now look what you've done. You've managed to land both of us in the middle of it."

"There are other kinds of marriages, Noel. Other kinds of life. You're not destined to duplicate your father's existence though you live in this house and walk in his footsteps."

"I have him in me." He glanced away.

"How do you know that?" she offered, forgetting her dishabille for the moment.

He looked at her, his hungry gaze raking

across her bosom. "Because now that I'm a man I can understand the desire to possess a woman. My father was obsessed with my mother, and when she ran away from him he labeled me as her bastard. He wanted nothing to do with me, and do you know why? Because he figured if my own mother wouldn't stay by my side, then I must be flawed to the extreme. He blamed her leaving on me, not him. And thus I was cursed."

"No woman in her right mind would leave her child, Noel. If she left, she was probably being driven mad by abuse. Her thinking was damaged. I'm sure she regretted it later."

"We'll never know. The fine woman who was my mother died in a crib in New Orleans, a half-empty bottle of gin still clutched in her hand."

"I'm sorry," she whispered, lowering her gaze.

His own settled on her hand, which was still splayed out over her breasts. "Remove your hand, Rachel. Don't make me ask you again. You should be grateful for my patience. My father would have ripped the dress away by now."

She stared at him, devastated. Slowly, she countered, "I cannot get used to baring myself. I tell you I can't display myself like this. Please let me go get a shawl and I'll be happy to lower my hand."

He shook his head. "You only accentuate that which you're trying to hide." He gave her a piercing stare. "So, put down your hand or I'll put it down for you."

With her nerves peeled raw, she forced her hand to her lap. "If this humiliation brings us even in the game, then so be it."

"This isn't a game. This is a lesson. A lesson in being my wife."

"And what would be the lesson if I were your mistress as you've wished all along?"

"There would be no lesson needed. You would already appreciate my lust for all the wonderful things it buys you, not to mention your own greedy pleasure."

"Lessons, games, pleasure, and purchases. You've mentioned everything but love. Where is love?"

"Love isn't necessary."

"To you, but not to me." She stood. Without another word, she walked to the door to leave him.

"Where do you think you're going?" he asked, suddenly at her side.

"You don't need me, Noel. You've got Judith and Miss Harris. You say I forced you here, that I'm keeping you here to clean up the damage I've wrought? Well, no more, I tell you. The children and I plan on leaving on the train at the first light of day. You may tell anyone you like that I left to take care of my sick parent and won't be back for some time. Then close up Northwyck and return to your wretchedly cold North. This episode will then be behind both of us."

"How do you plan on financing this escape?" he asked, his voice soft and diabolical.

"I've a loan set up already."

"I think not. You'd better check with your source."

She swallowed the lump of dread in her throat. "I don't think I'll be denied unfairly."

"No. You won't." He put his hand to her still-tender cheek. "I still want to know how you did this to yourself. I don't like my property marred."

She turned away.

His hand lowered to her collarbone. He traced the delicate structure until his fingers slid to the plump flesh just below it. "The only thing missing is this." He produced the opal. Soon The Black Heart was nestled between her breasts, the stone warming against the fire of her skin.

"Are you giving it back to me?" she asked.

"What? So that you can pawn the thing for three ship fares to a frozen hell? Not likely."

"Then you keep it, and its curse." She went to remove it.

He stopped her. "It's not cursed. For every fatality to its owners, there have also come riches. Louis XVI bought it from a thief who claimed to have stolen the stone from the eye of an Indian idol. The thief became rich."

"And Louis XVI lost his head to the guillotine." She placed her hand at her throat.

"Lady Franklin gave it to her husband as a protective talisman. She thought by giving him the stone, the curse would fall upon her as his beloved, thus ensuring his safety in the harsh environment up North."

"Bad insurance, I think. Now she is the one grieving."

"The stone is not cursed, Rachel. Some say it is, because it was used on a religious symbol that had been profaned." His eyes warmed. "But gracing it as you do, you don't profane it, you exult it."

"My father gave me the stone and he died. The one I loved most on this earth. I think the curse must be very much alive and well inside its fiery center." She looked down at it; she wanted to break the chain and throw it across the room, and watch it shatter on the hearth.

His thumb brushed across the edge of her neckline where the dusky half-crescent of nipple almost peeked above the torn black silk. She tried to push his hand away, but he was adamant. "I'll take the curse. All of it, if only you will wear the thing for me and me alone."

She pressed back against the wall. "If I must, I'll wear it tonight, but come morning I'll be gone."

"Not yet." He bent down to her.

She knew the maneuver well. He would touch his lips to her gently at first, testing, wondering. Then, at the first enthralling sign she wanted his kiss, he would unleash his passion, press against her and begin the seduction until she forced a halt.

She'd resisted until now, because always there was the prudent voice inside her mimicking her father's admonitions. *He must marry you, gel. You're too good to be any man's puppet. You want the man and the strings that he holds. If he marries you, then you'll have both, and I can die a happy man knowing you're well cared for by a husband, good and proper.*

But her father's advice worked on hope. Now that she had none, she didn't know what was left for her to cling to.

"You're as cold as you were up at the Ice Maiden, aren't you?" he said, nuzzling the white flesh of her neck.

"You know the price of having me, Noel, and you've spurned the offer. It certainly won't come free now," she answered with more than a little petulance to her voice.

His mouth touched the top of her breast. She knew the heat of his kiss there well. Her weakness. She always had stopped him from going too far, but with each passing day, her curiosity, her urges, grew stronger. Each time he touched her, they went farther. She found it more and more difficult to gather her senses and stop him.

"Let me retire, Noel," she said to him, her voice trained with no feeling.

He smiled against the generous swell of bosom over her bodice. "You come to dinner in this whore's dress and you think I'll dismiss you before I'm satisfied?"

"Are you to rape me? Perhaps the law would not hold you accountable, but your conscience would."

He kissed her mouth, deeply penetrating her with his hard, masterful tongue. Massaging her nipple through the fabric of her gown, he pulled back and said, "I made you wear this dress because I like seeing you the harlot. I like

219

picturing you with your blond hair knotted from lovemaking, your lips swollen from my kiss, your legs parted in greed. Why can't you be that girl for one night, Rachel? One night and I'll give you passage home or a house, or anything you choose."

"You never mention love, Noel. Never," she said, her breath coming quick beneath his touch.

"Do you need love to feel this way? Tell me true?" His hand bunched the fabric of her full silk skirt. He snaked his way through her petticoats and the open slit between her pantalettes. Finding the jewel he'd calculatedly sought out, his fingers stroked it, slowly at first, then faster and faster.

"Damn you!" she cried, clamping her legs together and pushing him away.

"How does it make you feel, Rachel?" he whispered to her harshly as he captured her arms and pressed her back against him. "Does it make you feel good? Desirable? Beautiful?...Loved?"

Tears streamed down her face. It did make her feel all of those things and that was why she couldn't tolerate it. The lies were too wonderful.

"I hate you, Noel. I loved you once, but now I hate you." She broke from his grasp. Yanking the door open, she gave him a vicious look, then, crossing her arms over her chest, she ran to her room.

"Hush, love. It'll be all right. I know he can be a beast, but you can tame him. In fact, I think only you can," Betsy soothed as she stroked Rachel's hair.

The woman had quietly entered the bedroom only to find Rachel flung across the bed, weeping into a balled-up pillow.

"No, I can't do it. And more importantly, I won't do it." Rachel hiccuped. "Thank God I'll be gone from this place tomorrow." She grabbed the woman's hand and pressed it to her lips. "Thank you so much for helping me with the money. I don't know what I would do now if I didn't have you to count on."

Slowly Betsy removed her hand and placed it again on the halo of blond hair tumbling down Rachel's back.

"Love," the housekeeper began hesitantly. "I can't promise to help you by tomorrow. I've got to have more time."

Rachel ceased her weeping and looked up. "I don't understand. I need to leave here." She showed her the opal at her neck. "I gave him my father's jewel. I'm sure it's worth a small fortune. I don't owe him anything, and I'll pay you back. I promise I will."

"I believe you. Truly I do. But I can't give you the money this soon. That's all there is to it." Betsy's face was lined with sorrow.

Sitting up, she stared at the housekeeper, her eyes wild and flooded with tears. "But if

I wait, it'll be too late." She couldn't get her mind from Noel. He knew too much about seduction, too much about a woman's body, and too much about her needs and vulnerabilities. He would get her in bed and then she would reach the point of no return. She would never leave him. And he would have won.

"Give it more time, Rachel. Just a bit more time."

Panicked, she shook her head. "I can't. I can't." She stared into Betsy's kind eyes. "If you won't give me the funds, I'll have to get them from Edmund."

"Has he offered? How like him," the woman answered, disdain in her voice. "The villain."

"Noel is the villain. Noel." Rachel sat up. "I don't want to betray him, Betsy, but I'll have no other choice."

"I was afraid you'd be like this." Furtively, the housekeeper pulled a thin stack of old letters from her apron pocket. The yellowed missives were tied with a frayed piece of yarn, as if they held no importance. "I'll leave you with these in order that you might reconsider your need to leave. I also must ask you not to go to Edmund for help. Noel doesn't need any more enemies; he's got enough in Edmund."

Rachel took the letters, her forehead creased in a frown. "What are these letters? And why does Edmund Hoar hate Noel so? A professional rivalry is one thing, but they go too far in it."

Betsy stood and just nodded her head. "I

think if you read these tonight, so much will be explained. Then maybe we can purchase you some patience." The housekeeper left by the servants' door.

Rachel looked down at the letters in her hand, unwilling to believe they would change anything. Untying the dirty, frayed string, she scattered them across the bed's counterpane. They were all in the same handwriting, all postmarked NEW YORK, all addressed to Mr. Charles Michael Magnus.

She pulled out one and began to read:

Christmas, 1830

Mr. Magnus,
 I should very much like to come home from school. It's been a year since you sent me here and I feel much yearning to see home. Besides it being the Christian holiday, it is also my birthday. I would very much like to see Northwyck again. Please, sir, if I might impose upon your good graces, might I take the train for a visit? I won't stay but a day. I would very much like to come home. Please.

Your son,
Noel

Rachel felt a knot in her chest. She looked again at the postmark and the date on the letter. Noel couldn't have been much older than Tommy when he wrote it.

Grabbing another, she read:

June 21, 1832

Mr. Magnus,
Today is the first day of summer. I
would be most grateful to see Northwyck
in bloom. It's been so long since I've been
home I find I can hardly recall what the
place looks like. If I may make my case,
sir, I would very much like to come home
to congratulate you in person for buying
The New York Morning Globe from old
man Hoar. The headmaster told me about
it. He told me you bankrupted Hoar. If I
could come home just for that reason, I
would not stay long. I would not be a
bother. Though I have not heard from you
these years, I still very much long to come
home to see the familiar faces. Please, sir.

Your son,
Noel

Unwanted tears stung her eyes. She grabbed
another letter, then another. She read the
phrases in each one of them.

Please, sir, I would like to come home.
Mr. Magnus, if I might ask your favor to
come home. It's another Christmas and I
would very much like to spend it at home.

She couldn't read them any longer for the
holes they drilled into her emotions. Magnus's
father had abused and neglected the boy,
then he'd sent him away. Taking the newspaper

from Edmund's father explained the source of the hostilities between Edmund and Noel, but none of the letters explained how a man could treat his only child with such coldness.

She flung the yellowing letters to the carpet. Now there was no use in going to Edmund. She couldn't get money from him when she'd read these letters. She couldn't betray Noel like that, no matter how cruelly he treated her. His anathema for Northwyck made sense. For years he'd begged to come home, and was left ignored and wanting. When his father died and he could return to Northwyck, the place had only reminded him of his father, and all the heartache that came with it.

Rachel released a deep sigh. Across the room, through the double doors that led to Noel's bedchamber, she could hear him barking orders to his valet to leave him in peace.

He went in want of that from everyone. Especially her. But no one loved the man like she did. Not Charmian Harris or Judith Amberly. Her love for him was all encompassing. It was a curse upon herself, and surely the road to ruin, but it was there inside her, unable to be denied. And she couldn't betray her only love with his enemy.

"May I come in, madam?" Mazie asked from the servants' door.

Rachel nodded.

"Mrs. Willem sent this up. She said you were to drink it all. It will help you sleep. You've a long day tomorrow with the dressmaker."

225

"I won't be—" Rachel stopped herself. She was going to say she wouldn't be needing a dressmaker, but now she didn't know. Without Betsy's help, and refusing Edmund Hoar's, she wasn't going anywhere soon. Looking down at the black watered silk gown ruined by Noel's very hands, she knew she couldn't wear it again. And the rest of her gowns were a comedy, black and lavender for a widowed wife who was neither.

"Thank you, Mazie," she offered, allowing the maid to ready her for bed.

When the brew had been drunk and Mazie had left her to her dreams, Rachel cut off the gas lamp and lay beneath her comforter. Her mind was wide awake despite the warm milk. Her body ached where she had fought to stay erect all day on a weaving train and her arm muscles were sore from pushing Magnus away, but the darkness of her room wasn't soothing. In front of her were two thin rectangles of light, the outline of the double doors going to Noel's room. He was up. She could hear the studs from his shirtfront being dropped into a porcelain dish, one by one.

She stared at the doors, wondering what he was thinking and doing. Her imagination pictured him taking off his shirt, shrugging out of it gingerly so as not to unduly irritate his back.

He would then kick off his shoes.

One, two, she heard the muffled thuds as the pair hit the carpet.

Next would be his trousers. He would have

to slouch a bit to get a view of the trouser buttons. Then he would pull the buttons one by one out of their holes and yank down the waist, nonplussed by his own nudity in the warm summer night.

His steps were sure and distinct as he moved around the room. She waited for the gaslights to be keyed down; and they were. Finally she held her breath as she anticipated the distinct noise of him easing into bed, the mahogany of the full tester bed groaning beneath his solid weight.

But the sounds didn't come. There was nothing but silence that met her beyond the double doors. Silence and loud wretched thought.

Footsteps crossed his bedroom and came closer and closer still to the double doors. He reached them. Her heart skipped a beat as she saw the door's outline break as he paused on the other side.

If any noise could be louder than a man's hand on a doorknob, Rachel had yet to hear it. In the dim light of her bedroom, she couldn't see it turn, but she imagined it turning. It would be only seconds before she would see his nude form fill the rectangle of pure light as he stood watching her in the open door.

Her heart pounding, she rose to a sitting position. Facing the closed double doors, she waited for him to enter.

Inside, she endured a sudden fierce surrender. She realized she wouldn't fight him. It was pointless. Not because he was stronger or that he'd seen to it she couldn't flee, but rather because she wanted him. The only difference between his entering her bedroom with her arms opened wide or closed in rejection had only to do with a vow of love and a small gold band. As little as those things seemed, in her world they loomed large, now they seemed too large for her to aspire to any longer.

A bittersweet tear trailed down her cheek. She wouldn't turn him away, because he'd won. She wanted him near her, holding her, rendering her a woman. She loved him, and tonight she was suddenly too weak to hide it any longer.

The doorknob released with a well-oiled rotation. She waited, but nothing happened. The door didn't open. If anything, she didn't think he even had a hand on the knob any longer. Rather, he was just standing there on the other side, the breaks in the thin rectangles of light giving him away.

Then he walked away, the muffled thud of his fading footsteps on the ornate wool carpet leaving her inconsolate.

"I hate you, Noel," she whispered to the cold outline of the doors. "I hate you," she repeated as she curled up into a ball and slid her hand between her thighs as if it would ease the loneliness.

CHAPTER SEVENTEEN

"**M**adame would like this? *Ici?* Or this, *ici?*" The dressmaker, Auguste Valin, was already setting out the silks in her dressing room before Rachel was finished with her morning coffee. Mazie had said the man came all the way from the city. Since there was no night train, Rachel surmised he had come with them yesterday on the same train and had stayed overnight at Northwyck. Magnus, with his usual gall and foresight, had taken care of everything.

"I think Madame would look best in the pink net and powder blue. *Non?* And this would look so lovely against your pretty skin and pale curls." The tiny immaculately turned-out man swept before her a most lustrous rose-colored satin.

"She'll also need several darker gowns. To match this," Noel interjected from the doorway, tossing Auguste something.

The dressmaker caught the object and looked down at the magnificent black opal in his hands. His eyes gleamed with admiration. "Of course. I have a deep-blue-and-mauve changeable taffeta, monsieur. It is the latest fabric to come out of France. How do you like it?" He held the opal up to the iridescent silk.

"Excellent. But I want others. A whole wardrobe full." Magnus gave her a nod good morning, then he sat in a large chair, giving himself prime audience to the transaction.

All Rachel could do was endure. And it was two hours of it while Auguste measured her, laced her, draped her, experimenting with every color of the palette in silks and cotton voile. Magnus offered an opinion on each detail—whether the color suited her, whether the proposed neckline flattered her, or cheapened her.

Rachel was undone by his nerve, but through the whole embarrassing ordeal she rationalized that the man was entitled to an opinion because he was the one paying for the costly gowns. And he would probably do well to wear half of them himself, for she was determined not to be around that long.

The only diversion to the grueling task of satisfying Noel Magnus was when Clare ventured into the dressing room, transfixed by the oceans of fabric. She giggled to find Rachel nearly swimming among them, overwhelmed by the choices and the little Frenchman who buzzed around her like a fly.

"The little girl has good taste. *A bon goût.*" Auguste nodded pleasantly as Clare stroked a length of currant-colored silk brocade.

"No doubt she learned it from her mother," Magnus interjected sarcastically from his chair.

Clare spun around, her eyes wide. She clearly hadn't known Magnus was in the room. Even adorned in her charming dress of patterned blue organdy, the little girl wore the street waif look again, wild and ready to flee. She was still terrified of the master of the house.

Rachel went to her and coaxed her into resuming the appreciation of the fine fabrics. As the child nervously touched a bolt of blond *peau-de-soie*, Rachel darted a glance at Magnus, daring him to frighten the girl away with another acerbic comment.

"You must be a proud man, monsieur, to have such a beautiful wife and daughter," Auguste enthused. He sighed with pleasure. "In truth, I've never seen two such as them. Look at them. They are like two golden-haired angels fallen from the ceiling of the Sistine Chapel."

Clare stood a little closer to Rachel, not out of narcissism, but out of anxiety. She didn't quite know what Auguste was talking about, but she knew the attention was on them.

To ease her fear, Rachel hugged her, then beamed a smile. It pleased her to no end that Clare could be mistaken for her daughter, for she loved the little girl like a mother would.

"Yes...fallen angels..." Magnus murmured from the chair.

Rachel locked gazes with him, her instincts poised to defend herself.

But none were needed. Magnus simply stared at her and Clare, his eyes filled with a strange emotion.

"Monsieur, shall I make your daughter a dress, *oui?*" Auguste asked Magnus.

He turned to the couturier, a wry smile twisting his lips. "I have the most outrageously expensive dressmaker this side of the Atlantic, and he desires to make a dress for a six-year-old child?" He laughed.

Rachel felt Clare tremble next to her.

"By all means, Auguste. Make Clare some dresses, too. Why shouldn't the two look as much like mother and daughter as they can?" Magnus leaned toward Clare. "Pick out whatever you like, child. I can't promise the gown will flatter you"—he slid a look to Rachel—"because as your mother proves, one such as you will only flatter the gown."

Dumbfounded, Clare went with Mazie to examine the fabric and be measured. Auguste began making some sketches. Magnus rose to leave.

"If I may—?" Rachel said when she followed him out into the passageway.

"Yes?" He paused to look at her.

She raked back a stray lock of blond hair that had escaped its pins during the fitting. "I just wanted to say thank you. Clare is still quite terrified of you. I feared the worst, and then you surprised me—both of us—with your kindness."

"For all the child's wretchedness, she'll fool the world into believing she's a princess in Auguste's creations. So, why not? Let the farce continue, for I find it's beginning to amuse me." He smirked.

"I cannot pay you for her gowns." She stared at him. "But I will try when I return to the Ice Maiden."

He laughed. "Her gowns are but a trifle compared to what yours will cost."

She chewed on her lower lip. "I haven't the heart to ever ask her to give them up."

His eyes narrowed. "As you one day will give yours up?"

"It would be unwise to dress for a ball on Herschel. I fear I would only court ravishment and frostbite."

He locked gazes with her. "If you must pay for her gowns, then do it now, not when you return to that infernal saloon."

"How can I do that? You know I've no money—"

"I'll take payment in the form of a horse-back ride with me. This afternoon at four."

Her eyes widened. The unruly hank of hair fell across her face once more. "That's little enough to repay you for Clare's beautiful gowns, but I fear I can't join you. There are no horses to ride aboard a sailing vessel, nor in the tundra. I don't know how to ride."

He tucked the stray curl into a tortoise-shell pin, letting his hand rest longer on her cheek than she thought necessary. "You need to know how to ride a horse eventually. Be at the stables at four. I'll teach you."

He stood back and studied her. The warmth that had been in his eyes when he'd looked at her and Clare returned.

"Again, you astound me with your generosity." She stared at him as if seeing a ghost.

He only laughed. Then departed.

"Over there is the meadow I told you about. Ha!" Magnus chuckled. "And it's still there. The fairy ring." He halted the steel-gray Thoroughbred named Mars and pointed in the distance.

Rachel stopped her mare with a slight tension on the reins. She felt as if she'd spent years riding, and not just an hour. Her mount, a black, spirited mare named Plutonia, intimidated her at first, but the animal was finely trained and sensitive to her every direction. Rachel soon learned to relax and enjoy the view.

"Why, you're right. It is a ring." She edged Plutonia further into the hillside meadow. The ground was covered with wild violets, and in the midst of them was a large white ring twenty feet in diameter made of mushrooms.

"It's there every summer." Noel released a half-smile. "In these hills they say Rip Van Winkle went to sleep inside the fairy ring, and that's the true reason he awoke years later."

"I think I can almost believe it. I've never seen such a strange sight." She nudged her mare gingerly in and out of the ring.

"You? A woman who's lived most of her life beneath the aurora borealis, running a saloon at the end of the earth? You've seen everything. You're the one, Rachel, who should be jaded to strange sights." He watched her as if her innocence surprised him.

"We've no fairy rings up there. Not a one," she affirmed, still analyzing the strange circle from atop her mare. "The only mystical place we have on Herschel is the old *esquimaux* graveyard. And that place only gets stories told about it because invariably someone gets drunk, trips on an ice heave and finds himself face-to-face with the dearly departed who got shoved to the surface with the thaw." She laughed, then shuddered.

"I've one other place to show you. Are you up to it?" he asked, his mirth suddenly leaving.

"I'm fine. Your horse is treating me well, so much so that I might find myself enjoying a daily ride about Northwyck."

"Good. Then come." He turned his mount and strode across the meadow.

They came upon a path deep in the primeval woods. It widened and narrowed, and she finally realized it was an old road, now unused and overgrown.

"So, what is this mysterious place? Is it full of trolls and hobgoblins?" she mused, half to herself.

"No. Only ghosts," he said, halting Mars in a clearing.

The sun broke through the trees, shimmering down on the glade with pink-gold beams. Plutonia edged forward, bringing Rachel through a stone arch covered in ivy. She looked above her at the cloud-streaked evening sky. All around were the crumbling vine-covered walls of a stone church.

"This was built by my ancestors. It dates back

one hundred and fifty years," Noel said behind her.

She looked up at stone quatrefoils thick with moss, at the jewellike shards of colored glass still winking in the light. Now that she knew what the structure was, she could even find the building's exterior flying buttresses amongst the fallen trees.

"Your family must have been quite rich to have built such a church just for their own use." She looked at him. He stared at her from the entrance.

"The name Magnus originated from the conquering Romans. My ancestors ruled England, and then when they themselves had become English, they decided upon a new territory. America."

She gave him a soft smile. "And now you find America isn't enough. You have to rule all the Arctic as well."

"I guess I can't deny who I am." His expression turned hard.

Her gaze drifted to a damp stone corner where a bench was built into the stone. May apple carpeted the floor like lily pads on a pond. Clover bloomed from the cracks in the stone, covering one wall with a delicate shade of lavender.

Noel dismounted and tied Mars to a fallen beam. He helped Rachel down, her long black riding skirt nearly tripping her as she tried to walk.

"So, how was this beautiful place destroyed?" she asked.

"A fire. Set by my father."

She looked at him; he captured her gaze. "I'm sorry," she whispered.

"My parents were married over there." He nodded to the front of the church. "That was the source of his rage. After my mother left, he wanted no monument to their union."

Walking to a vine-covered mound, she realized the white stone peeking out from it was a carved marble lamb laying atop a large bowl.

"That's the font where I was baptized. Another reminder of his poor judgment and betrayal."

Her gloved hands pulled away the vines. Lovingly she stroked the forgotten lamb and looked up at the cathedral of sky streaked gold and purple with the setting sun. "Instead of destroying this place, he only managed to make it more beautiful." A wry smile graced her lips. "If I were to marry, I would do it here, beneath God and his heaven. The ruins only serve to show how weak mortal man is."

He stared at her, the emotion in his eyes strong but unreadable. "And yet by returning here, you would prove how strong the spirit."

She nodded. "Exactly."

His hand reached out. He outlined the curve of her lips with his thumb. "I fear sometimes I'm not that strong."

His touch burned her. She turned her head; his thumb moved to her cheek, then lower to her throat where her pulse beat in a sensitive hollow.

"You're far stronger than I, Noel. Herschel broke me," she confessed, her words slow and difficult.

"And now that you've fled Herschel, have you mended?" He took her chin and forced her to look at him.

"Not mended," she whispered, staring at him. "Just learning to do without."

He studied her. The sunlight narrowed to one golden beam, falling upon the lichen-covered bench. He clasped her hand and placed her there, as if he were a painter searching for the perfect setting for his subject.

"What is it about this place that haunts me so? Is it the forgotten graveyard of my ancestors, or the beauty of what was and is no more?" His voice was like warm acid.

"It's neither," she answered. "Rather, it's the pain of what could have been. Your children and your children's children could have been baptized at that same font in this same church, but your father tried to destroy it." She eyed him. "And you let him."

"I was not even four years old when he torched this place," he defended.

"I'm not talking about when he burned the church. I'm talking about now. Why mourn the loss of it when you don't ever plan on needing it? You need a family church to marry when you marry for love. But you'll marry Judith Amberly in a cathedral in New York, and you'll be the toast of the town even as you stop to spend an evening with Miss Harris." Bitterness welled up inside her, and she was helpless to stop it.

Slowly she said, "Forget about this place. Don't think of it again." She looked away. "And don't torture yourself by coming back here."

A depression, black and bottomless, fell over her. The ruins of the church was a metaphor for her own existence. Even if she returned to Herschel, Magnus would come to her again. The great Miss Judith Amberly or Charmian Harris couldn't hold him here for long. He would head up North on another expedition for Franklin, and he would show up at the Ice Maiden, and remind her of what she could not have. He would visit her just as he visited the ruins of the church, and mourn all he could have changed if only he'd had the will to change it.

"I think we need to leave. It's getting late. I promised the children I'd read them another chapter of Swift." She stood.

"What is love, Rachel? Does it wound or does it soothe?"

She looked at him. His gaze pierced her. "I loved my father with all the joy in my being. When he died he took part of my soul with him. So I suppose it's both; it's delight and anguish all in one. But it's worse to not have it. It's a desert then, and you die of want."

Without looking at him, she walked toward Plutonia unmindful of the vines and fallen beams in the way. Suddenly, her hair was yanked. With a cry of pain and surprise, she turned and found Noel rushing toward her.

"Your hair is caught in the thorns. Wait," he commanded. Removing her beaver hat, he unpinned the chignon that twisted her hair to her nape, then broke the thorn branch and slowly disentangled it from her hair.

"Thank you," she said, taking the long plait of hair from him.

He towered over her, a great muscular specimen of a man, but his hands had been as gentle as a parent's when he'd removed the thorn branch from her hair.

"Thank you," she repeated in a hushed voice, waiting for him to quit staring and to assist with their mounts.

He didn't move.

Quietly, the words spilled out of him as if they were a catharsis. "You think I duped you by my engagement to Judith and by keeping Charmian, but you're wrong, Rachel. There was never a moment that passed that I did not think of you, or picture you, or want you."

His confession struck at her soul. She couldn't think or even breathe. All she could do was stare at him with her emotions running across her face. And wait for him to continue.

"You don't belong in this place, Rachel," he told her, his voice harsh with conviction. "And I have too many responsibilities to leave it behind. So I did the best that could be done. I appeased my father with my engagement to Judith so that I could produce an 'acceptable' heir, and I kept my mistress happy so that I would have somewhere to go to ease my desires for a woman. But there was never anywhere to go to ease my desire for you."

She froze the oncoming tears, not wanting to grant him any further satisfaction. "Then you never needed all that. The answer to your problem was simple: marry me, bring me here." She released a lilting, bitter laugh. "Why didn't we think of that, I wonder?"

"I hate seeing you in this place." His eyes flashed violence. "You don't belong here. You're pure and untainted. You're not a whore opening your legs for another diamond bauble, nor are you a minor heiress plotting with your mama to deepen the family coffers. You are, in truth, simple and good, and I wish you to be gone from here—if it's not too late—before Northwyck taints you, too."

"Why force me from your side? It makes no sense," she choked out, her tears fire and ice as they tipped over her eyes.

The muscle in his jaw bunched. "You capture me, Rachel, whether you know it or not. I would have walked to the ends of the earth for one of your smiles, and I would have gladly died in an attempt to get there. I would have always seen to your protection at the risk of my own. I would have done anything for you..." His words trailed into misery. "...but foul you with this place and this life."

"This place and the life you live here can change. With love, it can change. Look at Tommy and Clare," she begged,

He grabbed her by the arms and pulled her to him. His mouth close to hers, he demanded, "What is love? What is it? How do you expect a pauper to understand a feast?"

"Love is this," she wept softly before pressing her lips against his. "And this," she whispered, caressing his nape, the other hand stroking his hard cheek.

The crook of his arm pinned her to him. He found her mouth and refused to let her go. He kissed her deeper and deeper until she moaned with the pleasure of being filled with his hot tongue.

"Lay with me here, Rachel. In this holy place. Let's resurrect it, if just once." He stared at her, the expression in his eyes hard and forlorn.

Above her, the moon had risen in a dusky blue sky. She waited too long to make her choice. His head lowered and she watched as he opened her riding jacket and nipped at her batiste-covered breasts with his teeth.

As if outside herself, she marveled at the raven blackness of his hair, and how pale her fingers looked running through it. His own hand reached up and clasped hers, his large one encasing her petite one. Their hands seemed made to fit together. She wondered blindly if their bodies would fit as well.

The horses stamped their feet and shuffled in the oncoming darkness, but she hardly heard them as he lowered her to the carpet of May apple. Her skirt billowed around her as if enticing him to make a bed of it.

"Cleanse this place," he whispered as his hands mastered the pearl buttons of her corset cover. He unhooked the front of her pink satin corset and her breasts spilled free, alabaster in the moonlight.

His strong hands filled themselves with her. She threw her head back, unable to stop him, tortured now by the idea of desertion.

His mouth worked on her nipple until it was hard beneath his tongue, then he moved to the other, ignoring her gasps and wildly thrumming heart that lay just beneath his palm. When she couldn't stand the exquisiteness of his tongue any longer, he pulled off her skirt and petticoats and lay her back on them, his hands worshiping her like a pagan his god.

"Noel." She said his name in acceptance, her body and soul needing and fearing and taking when she should have fled.

He yanked off his boots, his shirt and trousers, finally kneeling above her nude. Her heart beat faster at the fearful sight of his primed manhood. A twinge shot through her because of the imagined pain to come, but he slid his hand between her thighs and she found herself ready for him, wanting him.

He kissed her mouth and lay atop her, his thighs coming between her own.

"Rachel, my beloved Rachel," he whispered against her, his mouth greedy at her nipples, his hands pinning her beneath him. "Cleanse me," he told her as he kissed her mouth one last time and thrust deep inside her.

Her moan was muffled by his kiss, his tongue filling her above as his manhood filled her below. He moved against her, slow and calculated, until she realized it wasn't pain she was feeling but something more, something delicious and wicked and greedy.

"I'm dreaming. Surely I must be dreaming," he murmured as he swept back the hair from her face and increased his rhythm, pounding her wet thighs with his hips.

"But it must be true," she told him, making him gasp as her hands swept across his back and the tender wounds still healing there.

His gaze never left her, never wavered as his movements became slower, his thrusts harder.

Two more sent her tumbling blind into pleasure. Her legs gripped him, embraced him, until he thrust himself deep into her and he convulsed with his own tortured oblivion.

CHAPTER EIGHTEEN

Rachel fell asleep lying in Noel's arms. He'd made love to her twice more in the moonlight beneath the crumbling ruins of the church. Finally they succumbed to exhaustion and satiation while all around them the crickets sang, and the lightning bugs lit the forest with a surreal glow.

When she awoke, the moon was high in the black velvet sky. She was warm from Noel's embrace, but he had sat up, startled.

"What is it?" she whispered, clinging to him for warmth, and something more.

"There's a lantern. See it?" He pointed to

the north. A faint glow emanated from the distance, probably from the valley. "They're out looking for us, no doubt. Come. It's time we left this place."

He helped her to her feet. Solemnly he handed her her corset and chemise.

Shivering, she hooked herself, again embarrassed by her nudity. She wondered if there ever came a time between a man and a woman when shame played no part.

"Here, pin your hair. I've found your hat." Already dressed himself, he handed her the beaver headpiece.

"Will you be able to find our way back to Northwyck?" she asked as he helped her mount Plutonia.

"If I found my way to the Ice Maiden every spring, I think I can find my mansion from the bridle path." He swung up onto his Thoroughbred and reached for her reins.

"I can manage her," she told him. "I did so all afternoon."

He grunted. "You did very well, but I'm not risking her shying from a raccoon. If she gallops off in the middle of the night, I'll have a hell of a time finding you."

She said nothing. His lack of faith in her riding abilities didn't offend her. If anything, she felt gratitude that he worried about her safety. The idea of it gave her a strange, secure feeling she'd never experienced before.

They rode the fields in silence. The lights of Northwyck winked at them through the trees. Before she was ready to face it, they were delivering the horses to the stable and walking to the mansion.

"I was sure the hobgoblins got you! Are you all right?" Betsy exclaimed as she and Nathan ran out of the house.

"We got waylaid, but we're fine. One of the horses went lame." Noel gestured for them to go inside. "Get Rachel some tea, and order up a bath. I'm sure she's chilled."

Rachel followed the housekeeper into the foyer, her eyes on Noel. In truth, she was cold and tired, but she didn't want to go to her room and be separated from him, not even for the luxury of a bath. There was too much to discuss. Her very world had fractured. She needed to know too many things to just take her bath and go to bed.

"If I may, I would like to go with you—" she began, but he interrupted her.

"No, you may not. You're nearly blue. Go with Betsy and take care of it."

As if a bucket of snow had just been dumped on her head, she stared at him, unwilling to comprehend his sudden coldness.

"Did you hear me? I said, go with Betsy."

"But I'd like to stay with—"

He interrupted her again. "You're my wife. Do as I say." A muscle hardened in his jaw. He gave her a brief glance, then he looked away, as if he was doing something he didn't enjoy.

Wounded, she stared at him until Betsy took her by the arm and helped her upstairs.

"My heavens, child, look at the twigs in your hair. What a terrible ordeal the night has been," Betsy cooed as she coaxed her away from Noel.

But Rachel never took her eyes off him until they were upstairs and he was out of sight.

It was dawn before Rachel found sleep again. She tossed and turned in her bed; she walked the carpets; and she stared at the light that came from under the door of Noel's room.

She hadn't expected his coldness. In her girlish hope, she'd prayed that by giving herself to him, he might cherish her further. It even seemed so when he took Plutonia's reins to see to her safety. Somehow, she'd expected to return to Northwyck and dream in his bed that night. By his side.

But he hadn't the need to see her, to hold her, to feel her warmth as he drifted off to sleep. He'd put out to stud and his desires were fulfilled. In his heart he showed he had only lust for her, and now that his curiosity and his loins were satisfied, there was no more need to see her. Until the next time he burned for her.

She rolled to her side and fought off the tears. Her soul shrouded in depression, she found sanctuary in cold, lonely slumber, and dreamed of fallen knights, their armor pitted and rusted, their mounts pierced with the jousts of their opponents.

CHAPTER NINETEEN

"**M**r. Edmund Hoar, sir," Betsy announced quietly. "He says he's come this morning to inquire about your health. He'd heard you and Mrs. Magnus went missing last night."

Noel's eyes narrowed to slits. He rose from his library chair and stood by the coal fire. "Show him in."

Edmund entered the room, a pleased expression on his face, the old animosity in his eyes.

"Are you here to congratulate me that I didn't get thrown and break my neck?" Noel baited, not offering him a seat.

"If you had, then the paper would be mine, wouldn't it? I'd buy it from your widow as I was planning to do before your inconvenient arrival."

"Foiled again." Noel smirked.

"Now that I've reacquired the family wealth, I plan on taking the newspaper from you someday." Edmund stood by the library desk, not willing to go closer. "You see, I'm a patient man. But if you'd like to forgo all the nonsense, I'd be willing to give you a check today."

"If I sold the *Morning Globe* to you, New York journalism would sound its death knell. Spare yourself, Hoar. Get the idea out of your head. Not now, not ever will I sell you back the paper. I've got people who work well for me. You would turn it into a sweatshop again."

"Then how about you sell me that wife of yours?" Hoar opened a purse and let several gold coins scatter across the polished mahogany desktop. "Tell her I think this should be more than she asked for."

"What the hell are you talking about?" Noel's voice was a low, vicious growl.

"Why, she came to me at the hotel and wanted to make a loan." Hoar placed his palm against his front in mock horror. "You mean she didn't tell you? How embarrassing."

"She would not accept funds from you," Noel clipped.

"Oh, but she wanted them. To flee back home, if I am correct. The price was a little more than she wanted to pay, but it certainly seems she's not happy here with her long-lost husband back home. All that domestic peace just isn't enough for the girl, I suppose. She longs for the rambunctious brawl of the saloons."

Noel slammed him against the desk, Hoar's throat in the manacle of his hand. "What do you mean by coming here? My wife will not be taking your money. Not ever," he promised.

Hoar could barely choke out the words. "I think you must ask her that question."

"I've no need." Noel shoved him, then removed his hand.

Hoar slumped against the desk.

"You'd better watch yourself, Edmund. I do not plan on bestowing either my newspaper or my wife upon you."

"I only want the newspaper. Your wife I've already had."

Stunned, Noel stared at him.

Edmund straightened his neckcloth, hatred burning in his eyes. "Who do you think eased her loneliness these months you were gone? It wasn't old Nathan."

"I don't believe you." Noel laughed darkly. "I think you must be bent on suicide to come here and say such things."

"Well, then, ask her. Ask her if she wanted to borrow money from me. Ask her if she's met with me alone." An unpleasant smile tugged at his lips. "Go ahead. Send for her."

Noel shook his head. "It makes no difference. I don't believe you. I never will believe you."

"Could you really stay married to a woman who's betrayed you, Magnus? Do you love her that much?" Edmund stared at Noel as if he were desperate to read every nuance, every emotion that crossed his face.

"If what you say were true, she would have fallen in my eyes, yes. But she would have had reason to fall. I would listen to her. I would forgive her." Noel stared back at him.

"She means that much to you?" Frustration and rage passed briefly over Edmund's features. He masked it quickly with obsequiousness. "But of course she does. She's your wife. You married her. You came from the Arctic to be by her side."

"Get out and do not ever return here, or I'll run you through. I've tolerated your presence because you were an impotent fool, Hoar. You thought to take me down in the Arctic and here I've succeeded where you've only failed: I brought back Franklin's opal." Magnus paused to add emphasis to each word. "But now that you're bound for a duel, I'll warn you only this once: come anywhere near me and mine, and I'll kill you."

Betsy stood at the door, her face lined with concern. Magnus's loud voice had obviously summoned her. "May I help you, sir?" she inquired, staring back and forth between both men.

"Yes," Noel hissed. "Show this idiot out. And take heed that he is not welcome here again."

"Very good, sir," Betsy said with obvious relish.

"No need to kick me out. I can leave of my own volition." Hoar nodded to Noel. "But take heed the curse of the opal, Magnus. Take heed," he repeated ominously.

Betsy returned from seeing Edmund out. She poked her lace-capped head through the door and said, "He's well and gone, sir. And may I say you handled the situation admirably. I thought we'd be needing the sculleries here to scrub blood from the carpets."

"He's up to something. I've a bad feeling about it." Noel stared into the fire. "Get me my wife, will you, Betsy?"

Betsy stared at his handsome profile as he forlornly studied the flames of the fire. "Certainly, sir. Right away."

"You needed to see me?" Rachel asked, frost in her voice as she took a seat in the library where Noel waited for her. She'd spent the morning in her room, despondent. But upon Betsy's urgent and inexplicable summons, Rachel found her anger.

"Yes." Noel turned from the fire. He glanced at the housekeeper. "Leave us, Betsy."

Mrs. Willem closed the double mahogany doors soundlessly.

"Edmund Hoar was here. He said you've been meeting with him alone." Noel's expression brooked no prevaricating.

"He's always trying to speak to me," she admitted. "Sometimes I think he follows me in order to get me alone."

He digested the bit of information, then asked, "Have you ever asked him for money?"

She froze, suddenly realizing where the questioning was going. Cautiously, she said, "I never requested money from him."

"Did he offer you money? Did he tempt you with funds so that he could get his hands on The Black Heart? That's all he wants, you know."

Taking a deep breath, she didn't answer at first.

Against her better judgment, she let her thoughts drift back to the sweet honesty of the night before; of the simplicity of lying in his embrace, gazing at the stars, lulled by the music of the crickets. For one aching moment, she had utterly believed he could love her as she loved him, but now, it seemed, the moment had passed in the blink of an eye. Noel had thrust her back into the role of calculating her worth against that of a cold, hard stone. And again she was coming up short.

"I didn't take his money," she said finally.

"But he offered, didn't he? And you tried to bargain for Betsy's coins, didn't you?"

Wounded, she refused to comment.

He laughed bitterly. "Who am I to trust while you scheme with the help and my enemies?"

She looked away. "After last night and all that I've done to win you, I would think you'd see I'm worthy of your trust."

"But I, above all, know what you're capable of doing to get what you want," he grumbled.

"Then see me off. Give me the means to leave and I'll scheme no further." She held her breath, waiting for the inevitable reply.

"Don't be absurd. After last night, I've more reason than ever to see you stay here."

"But without love and trust I won't stay here," she answered evenly. "And even you can't make me."

"Like hell I can't."

"If I were your wife you could force me to stay, but I am not your wife. You've no legal documents to show your authority over me. I'm a free woman to do as I choose."

His gaze pinned her where she sat. "Then I dare you. Leave me." His mouth twisted in

253

a nasty smile. "But more than that, I dare you to leave all the luxury in which you've lived these months and return to the raw hell of Herschel."

"I've assessed all that you are, Noel." She returned his stare. "I've seen this great mansion, I've read your fine newspaper, I've lived in your towering shadow. But for all of that, there must be more in your character or, indeed, you're impoverished. There must be love, respect, and trust, the unbreakable bonds that secure a marriage. If you're not capable of such things, I understand. But I won't stay around for your luxuries, for they're paltry compared to that which begets true happiness."

"It's ridiculous for you to speak of leaving. You've no way to do it." His temper flared. "I won't let you continue with this empty threat."

"It's no empty threat," she whispered as she turned to leave.

"It is. I say it is. And you're never to even think you've the means or the desire to leave me!" He rose from his chair to add further intimidation to his temper.

She looked back at him, pain freezing her expression.

"I said you can't leave," he commanded, his eyes a frightful black from his anger.

She turned and walked out the door.

Behind her, she heard his decanter of fine whiskey shatter against the far wall.

CHAPTER TWENTY

"**W**ake up, darlings. Wake up. We've places to go. Get dressed." Rachel stood in the nursery, a chamberstick in hand as she softly roused Tommy and Clare.

"But where are we going?" Clare asked, rubbing her eyes.

"If Rachel says we must go, we go," Tommy answered, awake at once, his instincts overriding his young body's requirement for sleep.

"We don't want trouble here, do we?" Rachel released a soft smile. "So, let's be off before the dawn light breaks."

She pulled the little girl from her warm nest beneath the satin comforter. Kneeling, she helped Clare with her dress. It was too heavy a wool garment for the summer, but Rachel knew they'd need warm clothing at sea. She didn't plan on staying in New York long.

In minutes, Tommy was dressed warmly also, and each child carried extra clothing tied up in one of Rachel's fine kashmir shawls.

"Not a word now," Rachel whispered as she opened the door and crept into the hallway.

She led the children down the servants' stairs, very far from Magnus's room, and very far from her own room, which held the tear-blotted note explaining how she would send him money for the clothes they took.

"We'll go out the kitchen door. Then we'll

walk to town and be on the first train to our new home." She took Clare's cold little hand and pressed it. "I told you two I wouldn't leave without you. And I've kept the promise now. Do you know why?"

Clare shook her sleepy head.

"Because I love you," Rachel answered with the words she told both children often.

"I love you, too, Rachel," Clare said as if the phrase came naturally to her.

"I love you, Rachel," Tommy whispered, too low for Rachel to hear.

But she heard it anyway. And smiled.

"Get my horse," Noel barked to Nathan as the old groundskeeper stood in the doorway to the master's bedroom. The whole household was in a dither with the news that the lady of the house was missing. Betsy flitted about the room, wringing her hands like a nervous midwife.

"The stationmaster said they left on the morning train. There won't be another until four," Nathan offered, his leathery face alive with a concerned hazel gaze.

"The carriage will take too long. I'll ride alone to Martindale Depot. It's another line altogether. The train there will get me into the city on their heels." Noel pulled on a pair of black leather riding boots.

Nathan disappeared to give orders to the stable.

Betsy helped with his jacket. "I know you'll

find them." She frowned, almost talking to herself. "If only she'd come to me. Oh, if anything happens to those three..."

"I'll find them." Noel strode to the door.

"And we can't let her think she can leave ever again," Betsy exclaimed, tears in her eyes.

Noel paused at the door. Without a word, he left, hell bent for Martindale Depot.

Rachel clung to Tommy and Clare's hands. She shivered with fear, but she didn't let it show on her face. So far they'd been able to procure their transportation to New York City by bartering one fine paisley shawl for three fourth-class rail tickets. Now, stepping onto the train platform of New York, she saw the city was again a foreign place. Gone was the fine lodging at the Fifth Avenue Hotel, gone was the waiting carriage and ensuing army of servants and trunks. Now it was just her, two children, three bundles, and a hefty carpetbag packed to bursting with the clothing that would provide for their journey.

"We have to find Broadway again. We'll have the best luck there with the tailors, I imagine," she said lightly.

"It's over that way," Tommy instructed, suddenly on familiar ground again as he and Clare ran ahead.

"Why, thank you, sir. This should be a fine journey after all," she exclaimed, taking Clare's hand in her own again and following her trustworthy guide.

The hour was late. The sun had already sunk behind the five-story brick buildings that lined Broadway. But like a beacon in the night, two gas lanterns burned within a window on the other side of the street. A sign painted on the glass said JONATHAN STOUD— MANTUA MAKER.

"Our salvation." Rachel clutched the carpetbag.

"Shall Clare and I find a place to sleep tonight?" Tommy asked, a few steps behind her.

Rachel smiled at his refined accent. The boy sounded tutored and wealthy. All the education at Northwyck would do him no good with the brutes in the alleyways of the city.

"No bed of mud for us. We're going to have coin. Enough for our entire passage. I have something very special. Very special indeed. I'm sure it will bring us a fine bit of gold." She nodded for the children to come with her. Rachel entered the shop and opened the carpetbag for the corset maker to peek inside.

From far away, a clock tolled midnight. Broadway was abandoned except for a black carriage rushing to the wharves. It hurriedly clambered south toward South Street. All at once, a man shouted from within the black-lacquered interior. The driver pulled on the reins. The carriage wheels stopped rolling so suddenly they made a sound like steel rubbed across a grindstone.

The man leapt forth from the carriage. He ran along Broadway to the place where he had first cried out to stop.

There, at a mantua maker's window, as if fortune drew him to it, the man pressed his face against the glass and took in the vision of what he'd seen from the carriage.

It was there, modestly posed at the front of the shop, cinched to a linen-covered mannequin. With pale-lilac ribbons adorning the top edge, he found the rare black satin corset he knew so well.

Jonathan Stoud had never been woken in the middle of the night. Tailors were used to such inconvenience. Upon a death, no matter what the hour, a tailor would be summoned to start producing the appropriate black clothing for the widow and her children. Even when the bereaved were left penniless and adrift, custom mandated a new black wardrobe sometimes at the cost of scraping together the last of their savings in order to show respect for the dearly departed.

But a mantua maker was a completely different bird. There was never any urgent need for a corset. The fittings had to be exact. Hours were invested in stitching the boning in long, sensual rows, and in procuring the flexible whalebone that offered the most comfort. So to be awakened in the middle of the night by a madman banging at the front door to his shop was a noteworthy event that even brought the neighbors to the windows.

"Can I help you, sir?" Mr. Stoud asked as he unlocked the door and allowed the man to enter.

The man stared at him with the most astonishing eyes Stoud had ever seen. They were dark and brooked no disobedience. All in all he was a terrifying figure, tall, muscular, wearing the expensive clothes of a wealthy man used to getting his way. "I've come about the corset. That one," the man said, pointing to the black one he'd just placed on the mannequin before retiring to his back rooms for the night.

"That one?" Stoud nervously studied the creation. When the girl arrived with it, he'd been astonished by its work. It was surely the finest corset he'd ever seen. He surmised it had to be from one of the Parisian mantua makers who sewed for the likes of Mrs. Astor herself. It was strange the girl wanted to sell such a personal garment, but he surmised she was probably the abandoned mistress of a money baron and, sadly, had found herself in the family condition.

He knew from the start he couldn't resell the thing; it was custom-fitted to its owner, and over the top of his customers' price range, but he'd bought it anyway because he thought it might impress his clients. Embarrassed now at the notion, he hadn't planned on telling them he didn't make it.

"What do you want to know about it, sir?

260

I confess I didn't make it," he added hastily, seeing his wife enter the shop sleepily tying her wool dressing gown.

"Where did you get it?" the terrifying man demanded.

"Where? Why, a young woman brought it into the shop just as I was about to close for the night. She wanted to sell it and I found I could not help but admire the work. Do you know about the young lady, sir?" Stoud asked, wanting actually to ask, *Does your wife know about the young lady, sir?*

"I must find her. Did she tell you where she was off to?" A muscle tightened in the man's jaw.

Stoud didn't dare refuse him. "She said she was going to South Street to find passage in the morning away from the city. The children looked so tired I told her about a small inn near the wharf. A clean, respectable place for the children. She was most grateful. I paid her, and they departed on foot." Stoud wondered if he was hurting the girl by giving this man the information. He fervently hoped not, but he found no way out.

"Thank you. Now take the corset down. I want it," the man snapped.

"I paid a dear price for it, sir. I hope you understand I'll need my money back," Stoud offered as his wife nervously unhooked the corset from the linen-covered mannequin.

"This should cover it. It's more than I paid for the thing new." The man placed a paper note down on the work table. He grabbed the corset from Stoud's wife's hands and disappeared in his coach. The carriage took off for the inn, fading into the mist that had settled upon the city.

"Papa, who was that man?" his wife asked, adjusting the night cap upon her gray head.

"I don't know. Someone important, no doubt." Stoud looked down at the paper note the man had left, convinced he had been taken. But then he snatched the money up and looked at it carefully in the light of the chamberstick still burning in his hand.

Involuntarily, he gasped, "Mother! We're rich!"

CHAPTER TWENTY-ONE

It was a long walk to the Dovecote Inn from Stoud's shop. Rachel was tired, but the children dragged behind her like war-weary soldiers on the march.

"Not too many blocks now, and then we'll have a nice warm stew and a clean bed," she encouraged. "But if you would like to rest a bit, we can do it. I know it's been a terribly long day."

"We can keep up," Tommy said dutifully. "Besides, this is the old neighborhood. If we stop, you can be sure we'll be robbed."

"By the likes of you, eh? Well, that's bad business." Rachel commented with a small smile.

"We have to cross the street!" Clare cried out, suddenly revived from her marching stupor.

"What is it?" Rachel asked as Tommy took Clare's hand and they hustled across the cobblestones.

"It's the orphanage," Tommy whispered to Rachel when Clare walked ahead. "She doesn't like it. She won't even walk by it."

Rachel looked across the street at the nondescript building. She remembered Clare mentioning it earlier, but the horror in the child's voice didn't seem to fit with the brownstone in front of them. It was four stories high, built probably thirty years earlier, but now the building stood abandoned, boards nailed to each window, the sign that said VINCENT ORPHANAGE hanging derelict from one chain. A sloppy hand-painted sign said FOR SALE across the boards covering the front door.

"Was it a terrible past at that place?" Rachel asked Tommy, her voice hushed so that Clare wouldn't hear.

"We ran from there. The man that owned it beat us all the time. We were starving and worked eighteen hours a day in his workhouse going blind with needle and thread to make sheets." Tommy's face was pale, his mouth a thin grim line. "So one day I said to Clare that living on the streets would be an improvement. We would starve but we wouldn't be hit across the face and bleeding if our basket wasn't full of hemmed sheets. So we left." He nodded to the ghostly building. "I heard tell the man took all the money donated for our keep and he fled. After that, the orphanage shut down and the children scattered for the street. Now it's for sale."

Rachel wanted to weep at his story. She took another look back at the forlorn building, wishing she could picture it clean and maintained, with scrubbed-faced happy children on the steps, well-cared for and hopeful.

"Let's get that warm stew, shall we?" she said to Tommy, her hand sweeping across his cheek.

Clare looked back at them, her gaze trailing to the orphanage standing ominous beneath the flickering gaslight.

"It's just a building, love," Rachel said to her. "It can't hurt you anymore. The evil within it is gone." She took the little girl's hand and picked up the pace of their gait. With sorrow, she thought if Magnus had been there, she could have used the same words to him. Northwyck was just a house. The evil was gone and goodness could have returned.

If only he'd allowed it.

"I want her summoned this instant," Noel said to the sleepy innkeeper of the Dovecote Inn.

The man flipped the tassel of his nightcap away from his face. As if to flaunt him, the tassel kept slipping back into his eyes. "They were bone-tired when they arrived, sir. I don't know if I can rouse them."

"Leave the children in their beds. But I want her down here immediately." Noel slipped several gleaming gold coins onto the bar. "Will this motivate you?"

The innkeeper's eyes suddenly popped wide awake. He looked at Magnus, then nodded. In his faded nightdress, he walked up the stairs to the back of the bar and left Magnus alone.

"Miss? Miss?" the innkeeper whispered after giving the door a light knock.

"Yes? What is it?" Rachel answered the door in only her chemise and a shawl. Her hair wasn't even plaited. She'd been too tired. Behind her, in the tiny garret room, the children lay in her bed, sprawled in deep sleep.

"There's a gentleman to see you, miss. He wants you downstairs right now."

Rachel leaned back against the doorjamb. Her insides warred. Noel somehow had found them, but he didn't possess the force to keep her. Her will was the exact match of his.

She looked behind her at the small deeply breathing forms beneath the threadbare blanket. "I'll follow you."

"Thank you, miss. I was afraid to lie to him, and you didn't tell me you'd be having visitors." The innkeeper smiled wearily.

Rachel decided he was a nice man. She was sorry he'd been placed between herself and Magnus. From his expression he looked more frightened than put-upon; she guessed Noel had placed the fear of God into him with one of his ferocious glances.

Clutching the ends of the shawl to her, she followed the man down the stairs and into the bar empty of patrons.

As she expected, Magnus sat at a far table, his stare filled with rage.

"Would you like me to stay here in the bar, ma'am?" the innkeeper offered, giving Magnus a nervous study.

"Oh, please return to your bed. I'm so sorry about interrupting your sleep," she said. Smiling, she nodded toward Noel. "Believe it or not, the gentleman and myself are very well acquainted. I can manage him alone. Please don't bother yourself any longer. I'll be fine."

The innkeeper grinned with relief. He took one last anxious glance at Magnus, then trotted out the door.

Tiredly, she made her way toward Magnus. She was in no mood to parry with him. The day had been exhausting and they still had to secure passage on a ship tomorrow.

"Magnus," she acknowledged, sitting across from him at the trestle.

He looked at her, his gaze not missing her small shoulders encased in the fine kashmir, nor the tangle of blond hair that fell down her back.

"If you've come to bully us into returning, I fear you've come all this way in vain—"

He interrupted her. "I've come to make you a deal. To make you rich."

She nearly fell off the worn oak bench. In her mind she was prepared for his wrath, his

manipulations, his demands. But she
certainly not prepared to find him manag
his temper.

"I don't believe it. You've come all th
way to apologize? Have you actually changed
Noel?" she exclaimed.

"I want to start the game over—"

"It was no game," she said gravely.

He nodded. "I see that now. But you foisted
too much upon me by going to Northwyck on
your own. Still, Betsy has grown fond of you
and the children. I see good reason to try to
make a deal with you to return."

"Have you grown fond, too?" Her voice
was plaintive and unhopeful.

"I don't envision us living the happy life you
imagine at Northwyck. You know that."

She said nothing.

"Still," he continued, "I would like to try
again. I will make you this offer: Come back
and live with me as my wife at Northwyck for
one month. At midnight of the thirtieth day,
if I cannot manage married life with you,
then I will release you. I will send you anywhere
you want, with a fine dowry to go with you.
I will in effect make you a rich woman just for
trying another thirty days."

She listened to the offer carefully. Finally
she said, "And if you find you cannot live
without me?"

He locked stares with her. "Then I will beg
your hand in marriage, and if you choose to
accept me, we will unite in a quiet ceremony
at the ruins of my family church."

art seemed to stop in her chest. He
giving them another chance. She des-
wanted to take it even though she
sure the fortitude of her soul could
are another failure.

Of course, you need time to think about
." His lips thinned into a hard line. "I'll be
happy to give you time, but I ask that while
you ponder your decision, you allow me to place
you and the children in more pleasant accom-
modations."

"I only ask that you keep your word. I've only
ever asked that." She stared at him.

The lines dropped from his face. In spite of
his anger, he appeared as relieved as he had
the night he'd found her at the Steadman
ball. "Then let's return to a finer hotel where
we can negotiate the terms in the morning."

"I don't need your money, Noel. I never
wanted it."

He laughed. "Such different words than
those from Judith Amberly's lawyers."

"What are you talking about?" she asked
ingenuously.

"I'm talking about the million dollars I had
to pay Miss Amberly to settle the Breach of
Promise suit her parents filed. That's what I'm
talking about."

"A million dollars? That can't be!" The
blood drained from her cheeks.

"It cost that to the penny, but I expect
Judith will be much more cordial the next
time I see her, now that she's five times the

heiress she once was and that much more eligible."

"I've never heard of such a thing. The money even made her happy?"

"Quite happy. I expect to make you even happier, for the price to settle with you I vow will be substantially more."

She shook her head in disbelief. "I never wanted money. You know that. This was never about money. It was about—about—" Her voice faltered. "It was about love."

"Yes," he said quietly, his eyes filled with an unnamed yearning. "And I suppose it's just for that reason that if I let you go, I will make you much wealthier indeed." He stood. "Now get the children. They can sleep all of tomorrow in your suite at the hotel. I'll take care of the innkeeper and wait down here with the carriage."

She rose and clutched the shawl to her chest. "I didn't bring the clothes to stay in New York. I only brought with us the bare essentials. I fear we may embarrass you."

The corner of his mouth tugged with a smile. He reached out and caressed her cheek where lines were still imprinted on it from the bedsheet. "I'll get whatever's been completed at Valin's to be sent to the hotel in the morning. But know this: even in rags you're beautiful, Rachel. So very beautiful." He stared at her for a long moment.

She left for the staircase at the back of the bar in order to rouse the children. In minutes, she had two sleepy urchins tucked into the velvet banquette of the carriage. They took off in the night after Noel had made the innkeeper of the Dovecote Inn a very happy man.

But before they reached their destination, Rachel noticed they passed again the abandoned building that had been the orphanage to Tommy and Clare. As if by instinct, she cried out for the carriage to stop. She stood and lowered the multipaned window into the carriage-door frame, then spent several moments studying the building.

"What's this all about?" Noel asked.

She chewed on her lip, deep in thought. "Noel, living as your wife in these next thirty days, I should think I should have some kind of allowance to spend, is that correct?"

"Whatever you think you need. But what does that have to do with that derelict building?"

She smiled. "I'd like to spend my allowance on renting it. The children and I could clean it and see that it's a better place for unwanted children."

"I see now it was an orphanage. Did they come from there, perhaps?" He gestured to Tommy and Clare, huddled like pink-cheeked cherubs beneath the beaver throw.

"They ran away from it. Clare won't even walk on the same side of the street as the building. I'd like to make it better. I think it would heal the children, too, to see it returned as an orphanage again, but this time, a kind and moral one."

"I suppose this is my next expensive entanglement." He leaned back on the banquette and knocked on the board to get the driver started again.

"I can do much just with my allowance," she said. "Really, I don't expect you to get involved at all."

"We'll have to buy the building, hire a staff, clean the place up. It's going to cost a fortune."

She slumped. "I suppose you're right. It's over my head. But when I heard how abusive the place was, and how mismanaged—so much so that the children were just left to scatter on the street—I wanted to do something about it. New York shouldn't have unwanted children fending for themselves on the streets. They care for the orphans in the North where the life is harsh, why do they throw away their young here, where life is so bountiful?"

"Because some do everything they can to push life away." He didn't look at her. Upon these words, they both remained within their own thoughts until they arrived at the hotel.

CHAPTER TWENTY-TWO

Noel sat up in the parlor of the suite hours after Rachel and the children had retired to their rooms. He slowly drank a whiskey and stared at the black satin corset.

It was nothing but a piece of froth in his large hands. Again and again his fingers were drawn to the tiny lilac bows on the top edge. The ribbons were much like her, pale, soft, curvaceous, but the steel inside the black satin casing was like her, too. Nothing would break her. Not even him.

His thumb dragged along the tight ridges of steel and satin. As if on a whim, he reached inside his waistcoat pocket, retrieved The Black Heart, and threw the dark opal onto the black corset.

He had every intention of donating the piece to the museum, but somehow, he always hesitated. He was growing too fond of seeing it at Rachel's neck. He would never forget how she looked at the Steadman ball with the stone tormenting him from the shadow of her cleavage.

She had been a vision after those months of frozen hell to get to her. Now that his anger was subsiding, being replaced by an all-too-real fear he might truly lose her, he could almost view the whole scenario with humor. How delicious she had looked, clad in her modest puce gown. She was groomed and well-kempt, far from the image he had in his mind of her dirty and wandering the streets of the city trying to find another bit of coin for some bread.

She'd made him into a fool.

And now he could admit, she was his match entirely.

If only his past wouldn't rear up and ruin

the tentative truce. It was going to be difficult for him. His view of life, of Northwyck, of true happiness, would all have to be reformed. He was not a creature of change and she could not change him. *He* had to do it.

But suddenly he wanted it very much to work. Even when he'd helped her tuck Clare and Tommy into their beds, he'd found himself wondering what it would be like to be their father, to accept them as his own, to cherish them and nurture them so that they could achieve great things.

The feelings were alien to him. As foreign as the jungle to the *esquimaux*. But he was beginning to think and feel, and make different choices.

Maybe it wasn't destiny that he remain alone in his world of wealth and adventure. He could have married Judith, but she would have produced offspring and left him alone to venture forth in the world, to wherever his amusements took him.

Rachel was different. She made him connect even when it terrified him, even when it brought a rage to the surface which was his father's legacy.

He closed his eyes and placed his head against the back of the chair. Maybe life wasn't at his beck and call. Maybe it was a force that was even bigger than the great Noel Magnus—a force even bigger and more powerful than his father had been.

And maybe, just maybe, if he trusted the look in Rachel's clear blue eyes, and followed the honesty in her voice, maybe life was much more merciful, too.

"After breakfast, shall we go see about buying that building?" Noel asked across the table the next morning.

Rachel looked up from her plate. The children had already eaten breakfast and were now quietly playing in the parlor, out of distance to hear the conversation.

"I could ask my lawyers to find the owner for me. We could settle the deal today." Noel glanced at her, hesitancy in his eyes.

"Are you really going to do this? Do you mean it? Especially when I know it will be costly—"

"I'm heir to the largest newspaper in all of New York. Why shouldn't my money go for good works?" he reasoned.

"But good works come at a price..." She paused meaningfully. "And the good works should continue even if their benefactress must return to her homeland." She stared at him, wondering if he understood.

"I'll set up a trust. The orphanage will continue in perpetuity. My lawyers shall arrange it all."

She burst out with a smile. "Then we must begin. Too soon may not be soon enough for some of the children who need shelter."

He stared at her as if dazzled. "I'll send a note right after breakfast."

"We'll let the children name it! Oh, I can't believe it! I finally feel I've a purpose for coming here. Something good is about to happen, I know it."

"I know it, too," he said under his breath, his gaze not leaving her.

Pushing away her plate, she grabbed a piece of hotel stationery and a freshly whittled pencil. "We'll have to have a nursery. Rooms for the older children, and lots of play space. A schoolroom, rooms for the housekeeper and the teachers..." She chewed on the end of the pencil.

He laughed. "You look like a schoolgirl yourself, worrying over her examinations."

"I went to school once." She nodded. "It's true. When my mother was alive, she had the pennies to pay for it. I went for two years before she died and I went to live on the whaler with my father." She gave a wry grin. "After that, my father tutored me. He didn't believe in education for females, but there was little to do on an ocean voyage but read. He had no choice but to continue my education so that I might stay out of his way."

He lifted one eyebrow. "I always wondered how it was that this young woman on Herschel could read, add, and subtract better than any captain of a whaling ship."

"Everything you'll ever need to know is in a book somewhere. Once I knew that, the world opened up to me." She took the pencil tip from her mouth. "So I must insist the females in our orphanage be as educated as the males."

"I have no objection, but you know it will be controversial."

"Fine. Maybe some others will open up another orphanage just to prove us wrong in our thinking. The most important thing is that no child be left to starve on the streets."

"I never knew this compassionate side to you, Rachel."

She glanced at him, then grinned. "You never stayed around long enough to see it, sir."

"*Touché,*" he said quietly, never taking his eyes off her.

Edmund removed the holy papers from their custom-made sleeves of vellum and wood. The Franklin papers were his finest possessions. Each paper found on the tundra, hidden beneath a pile of rocks that looked for all the world to be an ancient druid cairn six thousand miles from home, had cost a life. Edmund had been willing to pay a fortune to any fool able to make the journey to the north and trail Franklin's last documented days until, bereft of men, the venerable explorer had taken off on his own and died in an unknown place that had still to be discovered. At least by anyone living.

Edmund's expression hardened. He was convinced Rachel's father knew Franklin's resting place. The man wouldn't have parted with The Black Heart, not even when he was frozen and delirious. He would have died with the thing around his neck if just for the sentimental fact his wife had presented it to him upon his departure.

And now the opal was Magnus's. The woman, too, was his, and along with her the information.

A surge of jealousy hit him. It was rare he ever became infatuated. His interests were only two: Franklin and topping Magnus. Lust was used for a bevy of mistresses who suited his fancy at the time. His passions had never been the all-consuming fire that flared every time he saw Rachel Howland's face, or thought about the way she looked when he'd forced her to admit Magnus didn't love her.

Magnus wasn't worthy of such a creature, but the man had yet to gain what he was really owed. *The New York Morning Globe* was the finest paper in the entire country. His own father had founded it, then lost it to the tyrant Magnus. His son, Noel, hadn't worked for it, nor did the lout appreciate it. The *Globe* was merely the means to his folly—exploring the North.

To lord it over him, Edmund had seen to it that he acquired most of the Franklin papers. Some—particularly those at the end—were nothing more than scrawled fragments of wandering thought: he loved his wife, he missed his dog, he wondered if the Queen would honor him after death. Nonsense thoughts that lent no poetry to Franklin's dire situation.

But the point was that Edmund had most of the diaries—Magnus did not. And when Magnus decided he must set out to right the balance, Edmund had enjoyed thwarting him with The Company of the North, his own insidious company that manipulated the lives of every white man above the 53rd parallel.

But now, just when his vengeance seemed near, he wondered if Magnus would even care if Edmund Hoar found Franklin first. Every day the wretch was back in Northwyck, Edmund had expected to hear the announcement about Magnus's great plans to return to the North and continue the hunt. But the announcement had yet to be forthcoming. Magnus, it seemed, was too caught up in his latest passion, his beautiful Rachel.

Rachel. She was even burning within him. If he found out for certain Magnus wanted her, he would go insane. She held too much for him. Too much beauty, too much information, too much delicious ice, for him to ever think dispassionately about her.

But if Magnus loved her, Magnus would lose her.

If Edmund couldn't win in the race to Franklin, he could very easily win the Rachel prize. There, the winner of the game wouldn't win by gaining her; instead, the loser would be determined by who lost her.

Rachel's life was held by the thinnest of skeins. And the loser was bound to be Magnus.

Edmund placed the tattered pieces of paper in a line on his desk, in chronological order as best as he could determine. Above, on the wall, was a map of the Arctic. Inexact at best, with even the latest information, but a map nonetheless. Glittering across the face of the map were ruby-studded pins that marked the points where Franklin's journal entries had been found. Ruby-red silk thread lay out the torturous wanderings of Franklin as the circle he walked became tighter and tighter.

As if marking the spot with an imaginary X, his finger traced the points between York Factory and Fort Nelson. The last journal entries had been found there. If he could determine that old man Howland had found the opal there, Edmund knew he could find Franklin. He would be somewhere within the circle.

And the only guide who could take him there was Rachel.

CHAPTER TWENTY-THREE

Rachel tied the wide taffeta bow beneath her chin. Glancing in the mirror, she was amazed at the transformation.

The sophisticated *Fanchon* hat was bonneted and ribboned in sea-green, but inside the brim, Auguste had trimmed the piece with claret-colored rosebuds to frame her face. A sea-green satin button held a fan of Alençon lace to one side, finishing the work of art.

She, Rachel Howland of the Ice Maiden Saloon, was not worthy of it. Nonetheless, she smiled at her reflection. The wonderful hat lent color to her pale cheeks and danced a delightful sparkle within her eyes. Truly, the hat elevated its wearer. She could finally understand why Monsieur Valin was so sought after. When most dressmakers allowed the accessories of their gowns to be fashioned by others, Valin insisted that the entire outfit be dictated by himself. He wouldn't tolerate a peach-colored silk organdy morning gown to be topped by last year's maroon velvet leghorn bonnet. He was an artist in full; he was as good at choosing the right bonnet as he was at sketching a ballgown.

Picking up her lace gloves and violet beaded purse, she entered the parlor where Noel was waiting.

He looked up. If he noticed her bonnet, he didn't seem to show it. His gaze never left her face. In the past day, it was as if she was a crystal-clear stream, and he, a man dying of thirst.

"Are you ready?" he asked solicitously.

She smiled. "As ready as I'll ever be to meet with a half-dozen lawyers."

He chuckled and opened the door.

"Good-bye, Rachel," Clare said furtively from the parlor door.

Rachel went to her and hugged her. "We won't be long."

"They're in good hands, Mrs. Magnus," Mrs. Avery, the plump wife of the maitre d', came to the door with Tommy who stared silently, forlornly, at Rachel.

"Betsy has been summoned. She'll be here

tonight, I promise." Rachel nodded to the older woman. "In the meantime, you'll be fine. Mrs. Avery has had twelve children of her own. She'll know what to do with you in the short time I'm gone."

"Hurry back," Tommy said under his breath as if he didn't want Noel to hear.

But Magnus heard anyway. He glanced at the boy, clearly bothered. Finally he placed his hand at the small of her back and ushered her out of the suite, a grim hardness to his jaw as if he were trying very hard to work out an unsolvable problem.

The tall, handsome, gray-haired lawyer handed Rachel a portfolio from across the massive mahogany table. All around sat a jury of other lawyers, each one more anxious to please than the last.

"Mrs. Magnus," the man announced, "along with title to the property and signing privileges to the accounts, you can be assured that every dime of the trust will be overseen by this firm and that no irregularities shall ensue. We manage all of the *Globe's* funds and Magnus here doesn't give us one minute of rest until each penny is accounted for. We expect the same diligence from you. In fact, we would be insulted if you didn't visit us quarterly so that we may have the honor of escorting you to luncheon here in the city." The distinguished man bowed, then resumed his seat at the table.

Rachel innately trusted the man. He and his brethren seemed to take their profession seriously.

"Please take a moment to look everything over. We'll leave you alone until you have questions." One by one the lawyers filed out until it was just Rachel alone with Magnus at the far end of the sea of mirror-polished mahogany.

"I know nothing about finance. Nothing," she said to him, feeling lost behind the leather portfolio of inexplicable documents, most written with long Latin phrases.

"Let me go through it with you." Magnus sat next to her.

She wondered if he was as aware as she was that his leg pressed intimately against her thigh beneath the table.

He picked through the documents, reading them as if jaded to their language.

"This one is the title to the building." He laid out a large vellum sheet with engraving. "We'll open you your own vault drawer at the bank. You can keep it in there."

He pointed to several other papers, mostly alike. "These lay out the trust. They give you sole signing privileges to the accounts. There's one for the building, restoration, and maintenance, one for the household to be managed, the other account is for special needs—something we might not have thought of—such as hospital care for the young ones." He closed up the portfolio, but not before her hand reached out and stopped him.

"There's one other paper in there," she said, pulling the document out.

He inhaled a deep breath, as if bracing himself. "Yes, there is another one. I had hoped to tell you about it later."

"What does this document state?" she whispered, scanning the voluminous fine print.

"It gives you your settlement."

"My settlement?" she quizzed, staring at him.

"Whether we ever truly marry or not, this document gives you funds for your personal use, regardless of your status. In short, Rachel, if you live by our bargain, at midnight on the thirtieth day of playing my wife, you will become a very rich woman." He pulled the engraved document out of her hands and shoved it into the portfolio.

"You didn't have to do that, Noel. I'm not Judith Amberly's parents. Nobody would have come knocking on your door on my behalf, ever." She held his gaze.

He looked away, suddenly angered. "I did it. I won't answer why I did it. But at midnight on day thirty, whether we decide to marry or go our separate ways, you will be very wealthy and truly independent. If the fates play out that you should stay with me and marry me, then so be it. But if you do not choose to be by my side, you'll have the means to go anywhere you choose. You'll never again want for money. Never." He tied up the portfolio and slid it across the table to where the lead barrister had sat.

"Thank you," she said quietly. "But I don't

see why you owe this to me. I'm the one who caused damage to you."

"Yes. And you gave me the opal. And here it is." He pulled The Black Heart out of his watch pocket and pressed it into her hand. "It was your father's legacy to you. He probably didn't know what he found, but nonetheless, he gave it to you and you've rights to it." He released a long breath as if he'd held it a while. "Enough said."

"But this was payment—"

"No more payment. The accounts are cleared. Besides—" He gave her a long, appreciative look. "Besides, I like how it looks on you. You wear it well, Rachel, curses and all."

She studied the stone warming in her palm. "Yes, and what about the curses? I don't want anything terrible to happen to Tommy and Clare or..." She stopped herself. "Or anyone," she finished cautiously.

He snorted. "Curses are for idiots, Rachel. They explain in a neat little stone package all the tragedy around us every day." He took her chin in his hand and raised it so that she would meet his gaze. "You think those two little wretches you lifted from the gutter were put there because of a curse? No, they had no such fame, no such luck. It was just the dark side of the human condition that put them out there; and it was the grace in your soul that lifted them out of it."

He took the opal necklace from her hand and clasped it around her throat. "The Black

Heart is no talisman of doom. A thousand white men have died wandering the tundra. Only Franklin was rich and titled enough to make his disappearance noteworthy. His fate had nothing to do with this beautiful stone. And I say now, such that the stone can take on a curse, it can take on grace, too. I cast upon it now the same kindness that you have within you. The same that saved Tommy and Clare from the clutches of hell."

She looked down at the opal lying gently next to the vertical row of sea-green silk buttons that covered her bodice. The blue-green iridescent fire seemed to burn anew against the color of the gown.

"It doesn't seem cursed now," he said softly. "So, will you honor me by wearing it?"

She looked at him for a very long time. "Yes," she finally answered, for some reason feeling as if the ghost of her father had just come upon her and wrapped his arms tightly around her.

"Then come, let's take a tour. I'll show you already how much your orphanage has changed." He helped her from her seat.

She gave him a curious look, but she could tell he wouldn't explain himself until they arrived where he wanted to take her.

Rachel was stunned by the building once called Vincent Orphanage. In just a matter of hours, the derelict building was crawling with workmen who hammered and painted without pause.

"Rachel, I want you to meet Stokes. He's worked behind the scenes on every project I've been involved in. I told him I wanted this place up and running in a matter of days, and he's the only man to do it."

A wizened gnome of a man, sawdust on his black silk waistcoat, walked toward them, the smile cracking his face showing extraordinarily well-preserved teeth. "Mrs. Magnus, let me say what a pleasure it is to finally meet you. You're a legend in New York. I know Magnus very well. Like to consider myself the brains if not the brawn behind his successful Arctic expeditions. I never thought I'd see him find his match until I was told about your—your—well, your extraordinary arrival." He took her outstretched hand, bowed to it, and the smile grew wider.

She was speechless. With all the bustle and noise around her, she prayed her silence would be forgiven.

"If I may," Stokes added, "the men and I gathered up a modest amount of funds to help out the little street Arabs here." He reached inside his waistcoat and pulled out a leather bag stuffed with coins. "I'd like to give it to you, Mrs. Magnus, on behalf of everyone working here, and most of all, on behalf of the orphans." He winked. "Getting those hoodlums off the street will certainly make the place safer once more."

Noel looked at her, one eyebrow raised in

derision. Whispering for her ears only, he said, "I think I certainly can say that the streets here are already safer by two."

She almost laughed.

Gathering herself, she took Stokes's outstretched bag of coins. "Your generosity is most appreciated, sir," she said. "I can assure you I'll see the money put to good use."

"Thank you, ma'am." Stokes grinned.

"Speaking of hoodlums, I think we'd best be off, don't you agree, Wife?" Noel said, placing his hand securely on her back.

She wanted to throttle him, but he was, after all, right. Tommy and Clare were hoodlums, but they were still children. They needed her; she didn't want to be away long. Until Betsy arrived, she knew the two wouldn't feel secure with a stranger.

"Indeed, we must be off. Thank you so much, Mr. Stokes. I hope when your work here is finished that you'll join us at Northwyck for dinner." She smiled graciously.

He bowed over her outstretched hand. "I would be honored, Mrs. Magnus."

Noel led her down the front steps and into the awaiting carriage. When they were settled, she realized he was staring at her.

"What is it? Is something wrong?" she asked him as he sat next to her, his thigh bumping against her heavily skirted knee.

"I was just marveling how well you play my wife."

She felt a blush heat her cheeks. "I hope I wasn't wrong in inviting Stokes to Northwyck."

"No, it was a touch of brilliance. Everyone will think I married a woman with graciousness and charm. I couldn't ask for better, not even if I had truly married you."

She said nothing. His words, as flattering in some ways as they were, suddenly made her feel depressed. She was just *playing* wife, and she would have to remember it. Perhaps after thirty days the situation would become real, but until then, she would have to keep in mind that all they were doing was performing an experiment.

"Tonight, we'll be dining at the hotel with Mrs. Astor. Apparently, she's planning some kind of fabulous ball in October, and wants to make sure we return to town for it."

Her eyes widened. "After the debacle at Mrs. Steadman's ball, I never thought she would speak to me again."

He snorted. "You have nothing to worry about. Caroline Astor prays at the altar of old money, and mine is as old as Petrus Stuyvesant's."

She sat back, deep in thought. It seemed strange to be invited to a dinner to talk about a ball that she might very well not attend. October was weeks away.

"Why are you suddenly so quiet? What's going through your mind? Antipathy for Mrs. Astor?" He grinned. "I concur completely."

"Do you know what night the ball is to be?"

He shrugged. "October twelfth sticks in my mind. October twelfth at the Academy of Music, I believe it is."

"Just as I thought," she said quietly.

Scowling, he studied her. "What did you think?"

She looked out the window hoping to cheer herself with the windows of the passing shops. "Midnight of October twelfth. That's the thirtieth day, Noel. Mrs. Astor's ball marks the end."

She waited but he didn't comment. By his silence, she didn't know if she was inexplicably relieved or saddened.

CHAPTER TWENTY-FOUR

Rachel stared uncomfortably into the cold eyes of Miss Judith Amberly.

As was the custom for married couples, Rachel was placed at the opposite end of the dining table from Noel and made to extract conversation from the strangers around her. She could have managed except for the icy silence of the woman whom everyone knew had been jilted.

At the other end of the table, Mrs. Astor ruled with pugnacity. Noel sat at her right. Willy B., as Noel referred to him, was absent, sending his apologies from his yacht where it was said he confined himself with his mistresses.

To Rachel's astonishment, Judith's mother sat at the other end and laughed gaily with Mrs.

Astor. It was the first moment of pity Rachel had had for the girl. The money Noel had settled upon the family must have been the price of Judith's shame to the penny.

"We ladies shall retire. If you'll excuse us," Mrs. Astor said, standing.

It was the moment Rachel was dreading. Now that the interminable dinner had concluded, she would be forced to confine herself with the women at the table and endure their barely hidden insults.

The men stood while the ladies gathered their shawls. The dinner—by New York standards, as Rachel found out, was an intimate gathering of fifty—was held in the same ballroom where Edmund had trapped her. As if haunting her, the oriel stood empty except for the pair of hotel footmen who sentineled each side of the opening.

A double parlor adjoining the ballroom was lit with two enormous gasoliers. The ladies swarmed into the glorious rose damask room and one by one lounged upon the rococo furniture as if exhausted.

Hesitantly, Rachel went to Caroline Astor. She said, "If I may, I'd like to check on the children. If you would excuse me?"

Mrs. Astor looked at her with studied blankness. "Of course you may," she said, patting her de rigueur bun of lustrous brown hair.

"Thank you," Rachel whispered, filled with relief as Judith's eyes followed her to the door.

Tommy and Clare ran up to her as soon as

she entered the suite's parlor. "You're still up? You should be in bed!" she laughed as they nearly toppled her to the floor.

"I just arrived. How good it is to see you so well, love," Betsy said as she went to her.

The older woman hugged her, and Rachel found tears in her eyes.

"There, there, we won't do this again," Betsy said as she wiped Rachel's eyes with the Venetian handkerchief tucked into her sleeve.

"I'm sorry. I just wondered if I would ever see you again," Rachel said, laughing at herself.

"And I, too, love. You can't know how worried we all were." Betsy frowned. "I'm sorry I didn't give you the money you needed. I just hoped time would help. If you'd needed to leave so soon, I would have given you the funds just to make sure you had some. I beg of you, please tell me next time before you flee and leave us all beside ourselves!"

"There won't be any need for that," Rachel told her, stroking Clare's plaited hair.

"So you won't ever be going again?" Betsy lowered her voice. "Did he make it official, then? At last!"

"Unfortunately, nothing has changed." The corner of her mouth tipped in a sad smile. "We're to give the marriage until midnight of October twelfth. If it seems to be working, we'll make it formal. If not, I'm off to Herschel with the children. And, I might add, Noel's given me my own funds. This time when I leave, I won't need to bother

291

you or anyone for the means. They're at my disposal."

"Oh, no." Betsy lowered herself to a chair and looked as if she'd been struck. "The fool. He doesn't know what's good for him."

"Perhaps not," Rachel answered lightly. "But this also gives me the chance to decline. I might not want to tether myself to him, you know. He's certainly not perfect," she said, a catch in her throat.

Betsy looked at her and shook her head. "He is certainly not perfect. But he loves you. And I do believe you love him. For that, he should be unspeakably grateful and run to get a marriage license. He needs you, Rachel," she said solemnly. "I do believe you shall survive without him, but I fear as strong as he is, he will not fare so well."

An oppressive silence filled the room. Then Betsy glanced at the children, whose eyes were heavy with needed sleep.

"What am I doing chatting away when you two look to be ready to drop to the floor! Off to bed with you, and in the morning we'll take a nice stroll through Washington Square and buy some oranges." She stood and followed the two toward their room. Before she left, she said, "Rachel, love, if you need anything, you let me know. As much as I adore Magnus, I confess I'm on your side now in this battle."

Tears sprung to Rachel's eyes again. "Thank you. Ever so much. But there's nothing else to be done. It's in the hand of fate now."

Stoically Betsy said, "Then so be it," before she followed the children to their beds.

Rachel quietly let herself out of the suite. She returned to the ladies' parlor just as the women were gathering their things before returning to the men. Quietly she waited at the door in order to follow them back to the ball-room.

"She entrapped him, and that's all there is to it. How else does a bar wench get a man like Magnus except on her back?" Judith Amberly's mother said in an aside to Caroline Astor.

Rachel drew back against the door at the tittering of giggles. No one, it seemed, had noticed her arrival. Now, as much as she hadn't wanted to return, she wanted it even less, seeing how they were openly disparaging her.

"The Amberlys and the Magnuses were destined to link," Mrs. Astor said, her voice as imperious as ever. "I will never cease to be disappointed by that creature's arrival. Noel's father, if he were alive, would have made the man stick with his kind."

"Magnus couldn't admire her as he did Judith," Judith's mother chimed in. "It serves the man right that the Prince of Wales is coming to the ball, and he's destined to bring several dukes along with him. I swear Judith will make a more triumphant match than with Noel Magnus."

"Of course, my dear. We should have seen to it long ago," Caroline assured her. "When

293

the man was thought dead, I still don't know what made Judith wait."

"She waited for what Charmian Harris gets every night," one of the ladies whispered to another, all within earshot of Rachel.

"What was that, Katherine?" Mrs. Astor shot at the woman.

"Nothing at all, Caroline. Shall we return to our husbands?"

Rachel stepped back from the doorway so that none of the women should see her standing there, privy to their conversations.

To a passing footman, she quickly penciled a note asking for leave of the party because of illness. Then taking her wounded feelings with her, she left for her rooms.

Once there, however, she found she wasn't sleepy. Betsy had retired with the children; there was nothing to greet her in the parlor but a cold hearth and Magnus's decanter of whiskey. Pacing the carpet, she ran the women's words over and over again in her mind until she was ready to run for a glass.

"They told me you were unwell," Magnus said, his tall frame filling the doorway to the suite.

She stared at him, still moved by his handsomeness in a black cutaway and bottle-green silk waistcoat.

"I didn't think there was much point in remaining. Mrs. Astor doesn't like me, nor I her."

Noel grinned. "She doesn't like anyone

but those who can further her social aspirations. I applaud you on your taste."

She nodded, then turned away to look into
the stone-cold grate. "They are angry about
Judith, as they should be."

"She was a brilliant match for me. I suppose
some will resent it for a while. Until she saves
some impoverished English earl from his
gambling calamities, and lords her title over
the lot of them."

She made no comment.

He stared at her for a long moment. "Are
you ill? You're too quiet this evening."

Shrugging, she said, "I guess I'm more
tired than I thought. I think I'll retire to my
room."

"I had your things moved to my room. If we
have this bargain—if we truly believe we
should live as man and wife these few weeks—
then I thought it unreasonable for you to
have a separate room."

She stopped and stared at him. "I cannot
share your bed indiscriminately. We are not
truly married and you—you—" *Do not love me,*
she wanted to say but couldn't.

"If this is to be a trial, then we must live as
we would if we were truly married and I would
have my wife at my side." His voice took on
an edge of displeasure.

"Then you must ask Judith Amberly to
move her things in here."

"What does she have to do with anything?"
he demanded.

Rachel stood her ground. "She was the one you courted on your few trips to New York while I waited for you each fall at Herschel. Let her take the risks of a trial marriage."

Angering, he snapped, "Was ours a courtship? My father forced her on me like a medieval handfast long before I met you. We had the longest engagement on record, I believe, and any normal girl wouldn't have waited so long except to get her hands on a fortune."

It was possible that he was lying, but she now wondered if he wasn't telling her the truth. He'd always spoke of Grisholm's approval of Judith, but Magnus's father was dead way before he'd first arrived in Herschel. She, in her jealousy, had never put the two facts together until now.

A sudden rush of relief swept through her. The betrayal that had hung over her head for months was now dissipated.

"So, what wicked thoughts are trailing through your mind?" he demanded. "Are you finally allowing me to see your envy of Judith?"

"I'm not envious," she answered, but it was still only a half-truth. Judith had had everything she had not: protection, money, and, lastly, a bonafide engagement to Magnus. Rachel would trade all of the bargains and duplicity in her relationship with Magnus for one clean engagement—provided it had a happier—and quicker—ending than Judith's had.

"There are times I actually feel sorry for Judith," she admitted, grudgingly. "But then

I remember all the money, and all the people looking out for her, and I know she'll be fine."

"You'll be fine, too, Rachel."

She stared at him and gave him a bitter smile. "Of course I will."

Frustrated, he said, "What do you think kept me from finally taking her hand in marriage? Tell me," he insisted, his words harsh.

She shook her head. "I haven't any idea."

"It was the memory of you waiting for me up at the Ice Maiden."

"But the memory didn't force you to ask for my hand in marriage, did it?" The tension of those last weeks and the night suddenly got the better of her. She couldn't stop the hurt from seeping inside her when she thought of herself waiting for him while he took his time in New York to continue the sham courtship of the more suitable woman.

Sighing, she stomped toward her old bedroom, determined to sleep there even if she must do it in her chemise.

He blocked the doorway. "This trial is not pretend. I said you're my wife, Rachel, and I will have my wife warming my bed."

"I will not," she defied.

Anger bolted through his expression. "If you will not, then perhaps I should give you the taste of the life of a real society wife and take my pleasures elsewhere?"

"With Charmian Harris?" she said, anger flashing in her eyes.

"Who else?" he retorted. "Isn't that why a

man keeps a mistress? So that he might have a sympathetic ear when his wife is being difficult?"

"If you think to have a marriage like that, then I shall be happy to decline the offer of an engagement. And I shall congratulate Judith Amberly on her near escape!"

He stared at her, his eyes glittering with anger. "I want you next to me when I sleep."

"If you want a woman next to you in bed, then you'd best stay the entire night with Charmian Harris. And be about it quickly before she locks her door for the night," she shot back.

He stared at her, his face hard with fury.

"So be it," he finally spat before grabbing his hat and slamming the door to the suite.

Running to the window, she peered through the crack in the draperies. Outside, a hired carriage pulled up. Noel dashed inside it. The dark bonnet of the vehicle swayed in its rush to be gone from the hotel, and from her.

She let the drapery fall back.

Thinking she should feel better than she did, she went to the dark unprepared room with the idea of going to bed. Without ringing for her maid, she unhooked her dress and corset, and slipped beneath the cold sheets. But her thoughts became haunted by Charmian Harris, and the picture of Noel kissing her, holding her, unhooking her corset. When the sound of the harlot's imagined giggle finally overrode the noise of the carriage traffic on Fifth Avenue, Rachel's only choice was to bury her face in the pillow so that it might silence her tears.

CHAPTER TWENTY-FIVE

False modesty is better than none.
— Vilhjalmur Stefansson
Arctic Explorer

Edmund fingered the burlap hood. Next to it lay a heavy satin neckcloth; he determined it would make the best gag. A coil of hemp was next on the table, with fibers soft enough not to damage delicate skin, but strong enough to hold a struggling woman.

His plan was becoming clearer. He had the ship ready to sail. The carriage was ready to take his prey to the ship. A sledge and dogs were already aboard, ready to take him to Franklin. The harsh environment of the North gave him no pause. He'd never been there, it was true, but he owned an entire company that thrived on supplying that section of the world. If an illiterate fur trader could master a trip to the Arctic, then Edmund could master it in elegance and comfort. He was, after all, a man of education and breeding.

He just needed the night. Timing was everything. He couldn't just knock on the door of Northwyck and ask to take the lady of the house for a stroll. Rachel wouldn't come with him, and as much as she questioned Magnus's devotion, Edmund knew well enough to leave Magnus's possessions alone.

To stalk the man's wife might mean Edmund's own demise, and he wasn't willing to risk that.

No, he had to think. When they were in New York City would be best. That way he could spirit Rachel right aboard his ship and set sail immediately without giving Magnus warning.

But he was handicapped not knowing their schedule. The few Northwyck servants willing to have their palms weighted with coin were quick to report the whereabouts of the master and mistress, but even they didn't know what was coming next. Right now, Noel and his wife were both in the city, and it was just this evening that Edmund had been informed of the event. It was all too little, too late.

A knock came at the library door. His butler entered with a silver card tray.

"This just came, sir." The English butler bowed and handed Edmund the vellum card.

Edmund read it, then tipped his head back and began to laugh. A miracle had just fallen into his lap thanks to Mrs. Astor.

Flinging the invitation to the Academy of Music aside, he went to his desk and penned his reply. Indeed, he would be at the illustrious ball to be given in honor of the Prince of Wales. It was the social event of the century and anyone who had aspirations to be within the social elite would be there. No one who was invited would dare miss it.

Not even the defiant Noel Magnus and his beautiful new wife.

Noel opened the carriage door and stood on the sidewalk. He knew the townhouse well. He himself had bought it. Charmian had grown tired of her country house, and tired of city hotel suites. She'd persuaded him they'd both be more comfortable in her own boudoir, and so he'd given her her desire because she'd always eased so much of his.

The door was the same, pedimented in brownstone, painted dark glossy green. The door knocker was just as he remembered, the bronze lion's head with the heavy ring in its mouth.

He took the steps two at a time, at once feeling rash and yet hesitant. It had been a while since he'd seen her. The last expedition to New York had been spent garnering supplies and making ready the ship that would finally find its way back to Herschel. That last time he hadn't the patience to linger within his mistress's arms. He'd wanted to get going. To go to...

He shut his eyes. He'd wanted to return to the Ice Maiden. To be captured again by Rachel Howland's terrifying beauty and neediness.

He'd always known she wouldn't fit into his world. The test was proving it. She didn't want him with Charmian; she was jealous of Judith. He laughed to himself darkly. Jealous of both women and with no reason. His alliance with Judith had been planned by his father with all the obsessive detail of a Niccolò Machiavelli. Noel had been barely eighteen when he'd been told his destiny was the skinny girl back in New York City whose family name was correct enough to mask the Magnus wealth and obscenities.

There had been time enough for a proper engagement. Noel was to be trained in the family businesses. Old man Magnus finally died and left him in peace, but not without baggage, the heaviest of which was Judith Amberly, now a whispered-about spinster who was still pressing for the wedding date when she could revel in her luxuries and dutifully look askance at his indiscretions.

The Arctic had called him, but even more strongly, New York had pushed him away. The open tundra was freedom to his hunted soul. The trips back to the city for supplies became fewer and fewer. Finally, when he knew he'd been presumed dead, he'd felt no need to return home and correct the mistake. Everything was still running without him. The presses still printed newspapers, his accounts still ran flush with the profits.

It would all wait without him. Maybe forever.

But it hadn't had forever, because Rachel had beat him to it.

His eyes opened. He stared at the knocker

beckoning him to take his pleasure with another.

Cursing under his breath, he walked back down the slate steps and back into the carriage that had yet to drive away.

"Take me to the hotel," he snapped when he shut the carriage door.

Behind him, the townhouse grew smaller and finally melded in with the others in the uniformity of the block. But he didn't look back. He didn't care. He would never see the thing again even though he owned it.

She had ruined him for any other woman. When he closed his eyes, Rachel was always there, staring at him with those infinitely mortal blue eyes full of hope and longing and fear. He couldn't look away. There was no other choice but to give in to her, or face the rest of his life as his father had, detested, angry, with no more company than his own diseased mind driving him to the gates of hell.

"Rachel," he whispered, needing her name on his lips.

He knocked at the backboard to make the carriage go faster, then he leaned back against the seat and pictured her again, as she was at the chapel ruins, her hair tangled, her lips parted in a soft gasp, giving him a pleasure that was five times the weight of all gold because it was born from the seeds of love, and not lust.

He was afraid. His father's ghost lurked inside him, making him cold when he should weep, making him fierce when he should break. He feared he could never love Rachel

as she deserved, and she might never understand the torment. Judith and Charmian were
better suited for him. He'd been forged by his
father never to love, and they cared not a
whit if they were loved.

But not Rachel. Rachel demanded feeling.
She deserved everything a good man could give
her.

And suddenly, he wanted desperately to
be that man.

Rachel felt the hand on her hip, and the
weight of Noel's body as he sat on the edge
of her bed.

Half in dream and half awake, she clambered
to a sitting position, aching to throw her arms
around him and tell him how happy she was
he was back, but something stopped her. Perhaps the terror that she'd find the scent of
another woman on his lips and in his clothes.

Instead, she drew back against the carved
headboard and stared accusingly at him in the
dimness of a low candle.

"What have you come for?" she asked,
hating the edge in her voice, hating the dis-
trust.

"I—" He closed his mouth.

"Please leave," she said, pulling the bedclothes to her chest, hiding the scanty batiste
chemise she wore.

He said nothing. He didn't move.

A melancholy gripped her. She might never
have him fully. He was bound by the life he

lived to fracture his affections between wife and mistress. It was nothing for him to roll from the welcome thighs of his lover, then expect to be greeted as warmly by his wife. But she didn't want that life, and now suddenly she could see his point that she didn't belong. And maybe never would.

"Is it down to this?" she rasped, her voice thick with depression. "Must you come after me even though you've had your fill with another?"

"Rachel—"

"Leave me be, Magnus."

"No, Rachel—"

"Yes. Leave me be, or I'll take my money and leave this night."

He stiffened as if her words stabbed him. Then he stood, his tall frame towering over the bed where she clung to the headboard.

Without warning, he reached out and touched her cheek as if he yearned for her. She didn't move as his hand stroked her, back and forth, soothing in its gentle strength.

"I didn't go to Charmian. I couldn't."

"I don't believe you. She's your mistress. You've always had other women even when you said there was only me. You lie, Magnus. You lie, and every time I believe you." She pushed away his hand and dashed the tears from her eyes.

"Believe me now, I didn't go to Charmian. Look at the hour. I haven't had time."

Slowly, she turned her gaze to the parlor door. Beyond, the tall case clock was about to ring two o'clock. He'd been gone less than an hour.

Despairing, she said, "This time perhaps you didn't go, but there will be another time, and then another. My past with you will always be ruined by Judith, and my future with Charmian or whatever girl replaces her." Her shoulders slumped. "You told me I would never fit in this wretched society life. I think now I believe you. So go, Magnus. Leave me alone. I don't want you here."

"The bargain was you would live with me as my wife. I paid mightily for these thirty days. I'm not going to be cheated out of them."

She raised her head to make out his expression in the flickering candlelight. His expression was focused and steadfast.

"I don't want to sleep in your bed," she told him defiantly.

"Why?" He leaned closer. "Because you're afraid to be tainted by the filth of another woman? Well, I tell you upon everything I ever believed in, I did not go to Charmian tonight. I came back here because I wanted you next to me. You and only you."

"I will not spread my legs every time you snap your fingers. That was not part of the bargain."

He pressed his face to hers. "I'd never expect you to. If you give your body to me, you must do it willingly, generously, lovingly, as you've always done it. I will not force you. *Ever.*" He lifted her chin and captured her gaze with his shadowy one. "But I will demand that your place these thirty days be at my side. Day

306

and night. I will not compromise." He released her and straightened.

She waited, her breath caught in her chest.

"Put me down, Magnus," she hissed as his arm swooped around her waist. He lifted her as if she weighed no more than a newborn bear cub.

"I'll put you down, Wife, in our room, where you belong."

His arm turned into an iron band. She struggled, pulled and wiggled all the way through the parlor until he dumped her unceremoniously on his bed.

"The old Magnus of the North is back. The barbarian. The brute," she spat at him.

He laughed and yanked at the barrel knot of his tie.

"I don't want to sleep with you," she said as she tried for the door.

He stepped between them. His gaze slid to her face, then down slowly to her chest. Beneath the transparent film of her chemise, her nipples were clearly outlined.

"I suggest you return to bed, Rachel. I believe you're cold," he said as he unbuttoned his waistcoat and threw it on a nearby chair.

She wrapped her arms around herself, all the while looking desperately for a wrapper.

"Lower the gas, will you?" he asked.

"I will not—" She didn't finish. He slipped off his trousers and shocked her with his nudity.

Naked, his back raw with fresh scars, his torso

rippling with a steel grid of muscle, he looked like the magnificent god of war. He strode to the gas sconces and turned the key until there was barely a flame.

"Get into bed, Wife."

"I won't," she said, holding her arms across her chest and refusing to look at him while he displayed his maleness like a long, swinging axe.

"Come." He grabbed her and held her against him.

She released a long frustrated moan and tried to beat on him.

He was impervious to insult or violence. Without pause, he slid beneath the covers, taking her with him.

"Good night, Wife," he whispered against her hair.

She wanted to bite him, but it was impossible. His front was against her back, his arm held her fast against him like a medieval chain.

He kissed the top of her head.

She held her ground, waiting for the assault. He was aroused, perhaps by her closeness, perhaps by her warmth. His manhood pressed against her bottom, but he didn't move to take her. Instead, he kissed her nape, shifted slightly as if to get comfortable. Within seconds, his breathing became deep and even. He was fast asleep.

Fury built inside her. He was a brute to throw her in his bed like she was a sack of straw, then curl beside her, taking her warmth, giving her nothing.

Determined to leave, she tried to rise, but the arm manacle held fast. Soon she was worried she'd wake the sleeping giant that had fallen lax against her buttock.

And she was warm. So very warm. So very deliciously, seductively warm.

Weariness drifted over her like a cloud of morphine. She wanted to stay awake but it was impossible.

For thirty days, her destiny was to play wife to this man beside her. The price would be a grand orphanage that would care for Tommy and Clare's mates, and an account of her very own so that in time, if she should choose, she could be free of Noel Magnus, Herschel Island, and anything else that might prove to be a disappointment.

Wrapped in warm, hard male muscle, she wondered if she indeed hadn't gotten the better end of the deal. She could endure for a mere thirty days. In the meantime she would see to her orphanage, and she would show Magnus she was not his puppet. In the morning she would look into a trip to Paris. She'd read about the City of Light. Or perhaps she might travel to St. Petersburg, or Rome. There was an entire world outside the Ice Maiden Saloon, and without her realizing it at first, she now knew she had the ability to see it all.

"Go to sleep, Rachel. Quit plotting," came the gruff voice at her back.

She squeezed her eyes closed. "I hate you, Magnus."

He kissed her shoulder, then lay back and resumed his sleep.

"And I love you," she whispered once she was sure he couldn't hear her.

CHAPTER TWENTY-SIX

Weeks went by at Northwyck. Dreamy, impossible weeks that made Rachel feel as if she were living another woman's life.

Stokes came up by train and spent several days going over the changes to the building. Every afternoon Rachel and Magnus spent hours in the Gothic palm-lined solarium discussing the minutest detail of what would be needed for the children. Already a portion of the orphanage was opened and children were finding their way to it in hopes of a meal and a safe place to sleep. A staff had been hired from a cook to a house physician to care for the street Arabs who arrived. Rachel was most pleased that three children had found adoptive homes just from the publicity of Mrs. Noel Magnus's good works.

The evenings were spent with Tommy and Clare by the fire. Autumn was coming early if the evening chill was any indication, so they ate in the library most nights, the four of them cozier than they would be in the enormous dining room.

After supper, Magnus had decided the children needed to learn chess. Tommy held back, instead choosing to cautiously watch Clare learn the game. But after several games, he, too, wanted to try, and Rachel was pleased to see how well his street strategies worked with knights, kings, and pawns.

When it grew late, she would read a story to them, usually Scott or Dickens, until their eyelids grew too heavy to stay open. One night Clare took the initiative and crawled onto Magnus's lap for storytime. Rachel almost laughed at the expression on Noel's face. He looked as if one of her porcelain-faced fashion dolls had come to life and done the same thing. Clearly uncomfortable, he nonetheless let her stay there until her head lolled back against his chest and she was sound asleep. So he lifted her with his sure, strong arms and carried her up the stairs, and he himself tucked her into bed. Rachel watched him then go back to the library and retrieve Tommy who'd fallen asleep in a chair. He carried the boy with the same gentleness he'd used for Clare, and tucked him in as well.

"I think you'd make a very fine father, Noel," she had whispered to him while he shut the door to the nursery.

He'd stared at her then, a strange emotion crossing his face that she swore looked like unspeakable relief.

The nights should have been the most difficult, but Magnus kept to his bargain. Her things were moved from her bedchamber to his. Nightly, Mazie helped her undress in her dressing room until she appeared in a prim white gown, ready for bed.

Noel was the master of restraint. His only demand of her at all was that she be next to him in his enormous bed when he was ready to turn out the light with the gas key. Cuddled next to him, she slept as peacefully by his side as she had ever slept. Safe and secure. Waiting and praying for midnight of the thirtieth day to make the dream real.

The only pall over their existence resided in the parlor. Six feet tall, affixed to the chimney breast, much too large for the elaborate carved tracery mantelpiece, was the unsmiling oil portrait of Grisholm Magnus. Often, Rachel would peek into the parlor and find Noel there, staring at the portrait as if drawn to it by some strange spell. Father and son had much the same face, the same large muscular build, the same scowl. But the eyes were very different. Grisholm had pale-blue eyes, striking in their clarity against his cropped mane of black hair. Magnus must have received his mother's eye color, for his were ten times warmer than the sea-ice color of his father's.

Rachel longed to get rid of the portrait. It obviously didn't fit the chimney breast or the mantelpiece. The edges of the enormous portrait stuck out beyond the wall. She yearned to put it in the attic and forget about it. Let the untold generations to come who didn't know old Grisholm and couldn't be affected by his cruelties find him. They'd dust him off and laugh at his naive antiquity, blessed to never feel the sting of his presence.

But as much as she wanted the thing gone from view, she didn't know how to broach the subject to Noel. Grisholm was his father. For all of Noel's emotions on the subject, the strong one of love was mixed inside them all, forever torturing him with the idea of what should have been, what could have been.

Finally, with caution and prudence, she brought the subject up with Betsy. The two women were in the kitchens filling vases with bronze chrysanthemums to freshen up the corridors. Outside, the children played in the kitchen gardens. Noel was nowhere to be found.

"Do we have any more artwork in the house, Betsy? I've been thinking of ways to lighten up the parlor," she mentioned while filling a long copper watering can from the pump.

"I don't know. It's been so long since I've looked in the storage rooms, I don't even know what's there," the housekeeper replied.

"Let's take these upstairs and go look, shall we?" Rachel held her breath.

Betsy gave her a warning glance. "You might find some skeletons. Are you ready for that, love? This has not been the wonderful place you and the children have made it."

"I know," Rachel answered softly. "But let's exorcise some more demons, shall we?"

The two women carried the vases upstairs to the landing. Then Betsy lit a chamberstick and they ventured up another two floors until they reached the storage rooms in the eaves of the high-pitched gabled roof.

The windows were sooty from the numerous chimneys and probably not cleaned for twenty years. The chamberstick came in quite handy in illuminating the dark eaves of the various rooms.

"Where to begin?" Rachel commented, staring across a sea of old trunks and linen-draped furnishings.

"I know where," Betsy said gravely, shifting her hoop through the narrow corridor of trunks.

Rachel followed, curious to see what she was about.

Betsy came to a small walnut trunk with chains wrapped around it, scratching the fine wood. On a small tarnished plaque screwed to the top of the trunk was the engraved name in script: CATHERINE.

"This was her dowry trunk. When she left, old Magnus had it chained up and demanded it be thrown into the river." Betsy looked at her, her face pale and dancing with the light from the sputtering chamberstick. "Somehow the old man must have changed his mind, or the servants disobeyed him and found it easier to hide up here. But nonetheless, here it is, unopened since Catherine left here never to return."

"Can we open it? The lock looks rusted," Rachel said, fingering the heavy chains.

"Magnus has the key, but he doesn't know

it. It's inside the drawer of his desk, affixed to his father's watch fob. I think Nathan and I are the only ones in the house who know it."

"Why, there might be some wonderful things here for Magnus to have. He doesn't even know the trunk exists." She looked at the older woman. "I'll get the key. We'll see what treasures lie here and give them to Magnus as a surprise. I'm sure he believes, like everyone else, that all his mother's belongings went into the river."

"No doubt, but—"

Rachel interrupted her. "What's over there in the corner? It looks like a rocking horse."

She walked over to the object and undraped it. Indeed, it was a leather rocking horse, replete with a well-worn yarn mane and long, arching rockers. She tipped it; it still rocked.

"That was Magnus's. He loved the toy. Rode it in his nursery constantly." Betsy frowned.

"But why so glum? What a delightful thing." Rachel turned to admire it once more.

"Again, love, you're bringing up bad memories here. Magnus did love his rocking horse, but when the old man decided he was too old to ride it anymore, up here it came. Noel was forced to ride a real pony in its place."

"Every little boy wants a pony. Noel even promised to teach Tommy to ride," Rachel countered.

"Yes, but Noel was barely four years old when the old man presented him with a mount. The boy was expected to be an expert rider, according to the old man. I'll never forget how he would ridicule him for riding atop his little wooden rocking horse."

Rachel looked over at Betsy. The housekeeper had tears in her eyes.

The question came slow and difficult. "So, what did his father do to him, Betsy?"

"Every time the child fell off, old man Magnus took his riding crop and beat the child, sometimes clear across the face, while the boy just lay in the dirt trying to recover his breath. The wretched man would beat his child until the boy would remount the pony and try again. The tears and screams did not touch him, I tell you. Grisholm Magnus said it was the only way to teach the boy. He wanted the fear of *not* getting back into the saddle to be much worse than the fear of simply falling off." Betsy paused for a long moment, as if to choke back tears. "Needless to say, Noel learned to ride at a record speed. Even now I believe that's at the root of his fearlessness. The frozen Arctic can't daunt him as long as Grisholm Magnus is long gone from it."

Rachel suddenly felt defeated. All the cheer and delight she'd experienced from exploring the storage rooms had been drained from her. She lowered herself to a trunk and put her hands over her face.

Betsy's arms went around her. The scent of her lilac water was comforting. "I shouldn't tell you these stories. I doubt Magnus wants you to know."

"Oh, God, Betsy, I want to love him. I want everything that's good for him and for us all. But I don't know how to erase terrors of so long ago. I just don't know how."

Betsy put her arm around her. "Wounds heal. The mind can forget if not forgive. Give Noel something good to focus on, and he won't look back. I'm convinced that you and Tommy and Clare are just what he needs to accomplish that."

Rachel stood. Looking back at the innocent rocking horse, she said, "Let's leave this place. Perhaps if I find the key, Catherine's trunk will hold happier memories."

"It can hardly be worse than what we already have," Betsy confirmed before blowing out the candle.

Rachel poked her head into the library. It had taken days for her to find the opportunity to be alone, but that afternoon, Noel announced that he and Tommy would be duly occupied. Instead of allowing the stablehands to work with Tommy on his equitation, Noel decided he should take a part as well.

After a light meal, Clare went with Betsy to the parlor to practice her tatting, and Noel and Tommy left to go ride. Rachel took her opportunity. She didn't want to be caught shuffling through Noel's desk. Her goal was the key to Catherine's trunk still attached to Grisholm's watch fob.

She went over to the large desk. Opening the

shallow top drawer, she spied the watch immediately. It was cast to the corner as if it held no more value than the empty ink bottles that rattled along with it.

She picked up the gold watch, opened it, and, with sadness, read the ornate inscription inside the cover:

G—Love forever—C

She placed the cover back over the watch face as if painfully turning from an inscription on a tomb. A tiny brass key dangled from the fob chain. Unable to disconnect it, she took the entire contraption with her to the attic.

The door hinges creaked to the shadowy attic room. Rachel lit a candle and placed it on a nearby dresser. Evening was approaching. From high in her perch, she could barely see the two mounted figures in the field where Magnus and Tommy rode their horses.

The key fit the keyhole, but it didn't turn. Decades of neglect had left the lock rusted. She wondered if the adventure was destined to fail when the lock bar sprang open.

Suddenly nervous, she took a few seconds to gather herself. Then she opened the lid, unsure of what lay behind it.

She hadn't expected to find a portrait. The trunk was not overly large, but fitted expertly inside the interior was a velvet lined painting of a beautiful woman. She wore a puce satin gown with wide padded sleeves that made a mockery of the current fashion for fittedness.

Her hair was sable brown, rolled into a cascade of curls that fell to her nape. Most striking were her eyes, the same sherry color that Magnus possessed, but they were looking away, as if caught by a fascination far in the horizon.

Unwedging the portrait from the interior, she was surprised to find the original puce satin gown folded beneath it. A matching pair of gold bracelets adorned with a dozen lavender jade cabochons fell from the folds of the skirt. Upon closer look at the portrait, Rachel found the bracelets adorning Catherine's wrists at the bottom of the picture.

Catherine was young in the portrait. No more than twenty. Rachel suspected it was her betrothal portrait, painted before her wedding and Magnus's birth. The frame was a mystery. It was of a later style, made of the same mahogany carved tracery that composed much of the woodwork at Northwyck.

Suddenly Rachel made a realization. Catherine's portrait was framed with the same Gothic motifs that were carved into the library mantel. The piece had probably been reworked to specifically hang there and grace the master's private dominion with his young wife's beauty. When the portrait was taken down, old man Magnus must have substituted his own terrifying but poorly fitting image to take its place.

The candle sputtered and waned. She realized the time had gone without her noticing. Noel and Tommy would be back from the stables. She didn't want them looking for her, because suddenly an idea formed in her head.

Unfolding the gown, she placed it over her front and tried to gauge the size of its original owner. Catherine was taller than herself, and less generously endowed in the bosom, but given the wide style of more than three decades ago, Rachel knew Auguste Valsin would have plenty of satin to work with in order to restyle the gown and make it fit.

Gathering up the bracelets and the gown, she left the attic for her dressing room. Noel would never see the items. Tomorrow she would have the gown sent to New York and have it finished before the ball at the Academy of Music.

Already she could barely contain her excitement. Again and again she pictured the look in Noel's eyes when he first saw her in his mother's gown; the warm glow of appreciation melding into a pool of tenderness and nostalgia. By resurrecting Catherine's image, she might cast out the terrible haunt of Grisholm, and bring Noel into the future with hope and optimism.

She would get one of the footmen to exchange the portraits the morning of the ball as they were on their way to the train depot. That way the anticipation of her Cinderella transformation later that night would be that much more momentous.

She only hoped she could keep the secret of her surprise long enough to make sure Magnus never suspected anything.

CHAPTER TWENTY-SEVEN

The horse arrived with bells woven in its charcoal-gray mane. Prancing around the paddock, its dappled rump brushed to a shine, the animal looked like a prince's steed that had somehow stepped right out of the pages of a fairytale.

Tommy's eyes lit up as he walked around the animal. A stablehand held the high-spirited mount's halter.

"Magnus, he's beautiful. Just beautiful," Rachel gasped, nearly as awestruck as Tommy.

"He comes from the best stable in all the state. Stokes promised his bloodline was impeccable." Magnus stood to the side, his gaze never leaving Tommy.

"Can I ride him now?" Tommy asked.

Rachel watched him look at Magnus. For the first time ever she saw a child's joy on his face, and suddenly she wanted to wrap both of them in her arms and hold on to the happiness that bloomed within her.

"I think Magnus should break you both in slowly. He looks like a handful to me," she cautioned with a laugh.

"But I can do it myself. I don't need your help, Magnus, truly I don't," Tommy announced, a hint of the old toughness in his voice.

Noel chuckled. In the bright morning sun, his teeth gleamed white. Dazzling.

Rachel's breath caught when he glanced at her.

"Whoa there. Rachel's right. You'll have to take some time. He's all yours for the keeping. But you two need to get to know each other and reach an understanding before you go galloping off into the forest."

"That's right. You need to be careful, Tommy," Clare piped in. She stood almost behind Rachel. Nothing had been devised yet to persuade the girl to lose her fear of horses. Once, during a nightmare, Rachel remembered holding the little girl as she screamed for her mother who'd been crushed beneath a wagon. It seemed likely that that was how Clare had ended up on the streets. Still, once awake, she hadn't wanted to talk about it, and Rachel knew no more, except that Clare worried incessantly when Tommy rode, even under Noel's instruction.

Magnus took Clare in his arms and held her up. Coaxing her gently, she was finally able to reach out her hand and touch the animal's velvety charcoal muzzle. But when the animal jerked up its head, fear again rose inside her, and Noel let her wrap her arms around his neck, and he carried her away to a safer distance.

"Come. We've got Mr. Harkness waiting in the schoolroom. We mustn't keep him waiting." Rachel held out her hand for Clare. The girl took it without hesitation.

Tommy was much more reluctant. He stared after the animal so much, it took twice as long for her to get them in the house from the stable.

"Do well in your lessons, and we'll see to saddling him up before supper," Noel said as the children departed up the stairs.

"Perhaps Mr. Harkness can help you name him, Tommy," Rachel said.

"But I already have a name."

"Is it worthy of the finest horse in all New York?" Noel challenged good-naturedly.

"Indeed, it is," Tommy said gravely. "I'm going to call him Magnus."

Rachel felt her heart swell. She stood dumbfounded watching Tommy follow Clare up the stairs. It took her a long time to look at Noel. As she expected, she found joy in his expression, mixed with a strange kind of devastation.

"I think Tommy has found an idol," she commented softly, unsure of his mood.

He refused to meet her gaze.

"Of course," she added, "boys will do such things when long in the company of a man they admire. One who is kind."

His eyes turned to her. "My father was not kind."

"I know," she whispered, suddenly chilled.

"I idolized him."

The words were delivered with all the coldness of a confession.

She held his gaze and thought back to the letters Betsy had given her. The rigidly polite tone of them had always bothered her. He'd been too young to address his own father as Mr. Magnus. Now she could see that there was more in those letters than had seemed apparent. His feelings even then had always been so much more than just hatred and despair. To make them worse, they'd also been tainted with love and worship.

"It's all right, Noel," she said, the words out before she could stop them.

He gave her one long, difficult stare, then left to cloister himself in his library.

She watched him leave, her very soul aching with the need to care for him.

But instinctively she knew he needed time alone. His emotions needed sorting. The healing would come when they were all finally detangled like a ball of multicolored yarns.

"Where is that boy? He missed supper and he was supposed to continue with Mr. Harkness on his arithmetic." Betsy stood in the doorway to the conservatory. "Is Tommy with you?"

Rachel looked up from her sewing. Her forehead furrowed. "Has Magnus seen him?"

"He's still holed up in his library. He refused a tray when I had one sent up at five. I don't think the boy is in there."

Outside the far windows, Rachel could see the sun was setting. The autumn-gold fields were filling with long purple shadows.

She put aside her Berlin work and stood, a foreboding falling over her like a pall. "I'll get Magnus. I'm afraid the boy might have gone off and done something foolish with his new horse."

Betsy looked sick. "I was thinking those same thoughts myself. Yes, get Magnus."

Rachel half ran, half walked to the library. Hardly bothering to knock, she opened the door and found Noel sitting in his leather chair, his eyes fixed on the portrait of Grisholm.

"I think Tommy's gone off to the stables. I'm sorry, Noel, but Betsy and I are worried he might have stolen a ride on the new horse. I—I have this terrible feeling—"

Noel bolted from his chair. He gave Rachel a nod of fury, then he went for the stables with Rachel picking up her skirts and trailing after him.

She arrived at the stableyard in time to find Noel galloping madly atop Mars toward the east field. At the top of the ridge, she could see Tommy quite clearly, doing his best to control his new mount even though he was going at top speed toward a fence he couldn't possibly clear.

"Tommy!" she gasped. Her breath stopped.

Magnus pulled alongside the green horse and rider. He reached out and yanked back violently on the nearest rein. The dappled gray rebelled at the harsh pull on its mouth. He gave a buck and sent Tommy toppling out of the saddle and onto the ground.

Rachel ran toward them, but they were so far away, she feared she would never get there.

Noel jumped from Mars's back, then Rachel stopped dead in her tracks.

Tommy scrambled to his feet, but stood like a yearling frozen in terror of a beast. Furious, Noel stood over Tommy, riding crop raised in anger. The picture of it sent hackles down her neck.

Suddenly she realized she was running again, but this time not to care for Tommy, but to protect him.

She was almost to Noel before she realized how still he stood also, riding crop raised, the picture of his father years before. As if in a trance, he stared at his hand gripping the whip, and not her arrival nor Tommy's running to her affected him. But then, as if it burned him, he hurled the crop to a far patch of grass.

"Oh, God, are you both all right?" she blathered, tears streaming down her cheeks for both Tommy and Magnus.

"I think he's just had the air knocked out of him," Noel said slowly, staring down at Tommy who was wide-eyed and breathing hard, a little of the defiance knocked out of him as well.

Rachel held the boy tight in her arms. In her concern for Tommy, she didn't notice Noel mount Mars, then depart as if the devil himself was jamming his spurs into the stallion's sides.

"Where's he off to?" Tommy asked.

Rachel stared at the diminishing silhouette of horse and rider, hot tears still running down her face. "I don't know," she whispered. "I don't know."

Noel didn't return to the house until well after midnight.

Rachel heard his commanding walk in the passage. She hadn't been able to sleep. Instead, she curled up in a leather chair in the anteroom, reading by the light of the hearth. Worrying about Magnus, she couldn't keep her mind on the page in front of her.

He didn't see her as he entered the suite. Grim-faced and tired, he went directly to his dressing room. His boots fell to the floor with a deafening thud as he removed them.

She rose from the chair and clutched the two edges of her violet silk wrapper. Walking softly along the carpet, she went to the doorway to his dressing room still unobserved.

He stood at the mahogany-and-marble washstand, dressed only in his dusty trousers. From the mirror, he spied her behind him.

"I think it would do you good to take a hot bath. Shall I ring for one?" she asked as any good wife might ask her troubled husband.

"No." He turned back to the washstand and splashed cold water onto his bare torso. The drops glistened on his chest hair in the low flickering gaslight before he took a linen towel and wiped them off.

"Did you have a fine ride? The moon is out again. Almost full," she said lightly.

"I didn't notice the moon." He dropped the used towel into a mahogany bin.

"I'm sorry."

Her words fell between them like a wall. He didn't want pity; she knew it only too well. But she was sorry. Sorry for his father, the scare he'd had that afternoon, sorry even that he hadn't taken the time to look up and see the fine October moon playing hide-and-seek with the clouds.

He glanced at her, noticing the way her hands clutched the edges of her wrapper to her. A bitter laugh escaped him.

"Is something funny?" she asked, hope rebirthing inside her.

"How ridiculous it all is. You here at North-wyck. I should have resolved this matter of you being here weeks ago. By now I could have resumed my search for Franklin, instead of wasting my time here."

"If you want to find Franklin, you can. I'll help you."

"Help me?" he scoffed. "You? Standing so insignificant and vulnerable there in the doorway?" His gaze raked down her body. "Look at you, holding your wrapper together as if that could stop any man who truly wanted to breach you."

"I may not be physically your match, but *I am* your match, Noel. *I am,*" she repeated softly but steadfastly.

He held her gaze. For a long moment he said nothing, then, "You belong here more than I, Rachel." He looked away. "I can't stay here any longer. I can't endure it."

She went to him, panic filling her. She couldn't watch him end all their chances by fleeing. "I belong with you."

"I've decided to head North again. Right away. It'll be freeze-up soon. With dogs and a sledge, I could be at Fort Nelson by spring."

"Tell me when we leave," she pressed.

He laughed again darkly and drew her aside. "Of what use could you be?"

Fear of losing him had kept her silent, but she would fight now if she had to. She couldn't watch him leave without taking her. All along, she hadn't wanted to discover that her allure was paltry in comparison to information, but finally, using the last carrot she had to dangle in front of him, she said, "I think I know where Franklin is."

His head whipped around. He locked stares with her. "What's this? You know?"

"I think I know. Because of where my father found the opal."

"You knew all along where he found it, then?"

She nodded.

"All this time you kept it from me."

"I planned on telling you on our wedding night, but since that has yet to be, perhaps I will tell you now."

"You must—so that I know where to go."

"I'll take you there. After midnight, the thirtieth day of our bargain."

He stared at her. "If you are using this to force a proposal out of me, you should have

329

done so sooner. But even so, I could be accused of marrying you just for the information about Franklin."

"I didn't want to tell you before until I knew there was a chance you could love me. But now I know. And so be it. All that is meant to be will happen," she said solemnly.

"You lean too heavily on destiny, Rachel, and destiny can be cruel," he said.

She smiled softly.

Going to him, she stood on tiptoes and placed a kiss on his hard mouth. "I know it in my soul you were meant for me. You threw the whip away, and then I knew you were not destined to be your father. Never."

He was silent. A range of emotions crossed his face, from pain and anger, to something else. Something unnamed and yet wondrous.

"You may find you rue the day you longed to be my wife, Rachel," he said, taking her nape in his hand and lowering his head for a kiss.

"Never," she moaned, then pressed her mouth to his like a woman starving.

Slowly, his other hand parted the fortress of her wrapper. His palm slid warm across her breast, cupping the nipple. His fingers teased it until it was hard and aching for more.

"It's well past midnight," he whispered against the pulse in her throat. "We've less than twenty-four hours to live out this infernal bargain. I say we dispense with it."

She felt his hands slide over her shoulders, taking the feather-light silk wrapper with it. The garment landed at her feet, a shimmering violet pool. If there was any more protest left within her, it was gone by the time his teeth grazed against her nipples and his mouth captured one, sending sensation rocking through her all the way to her back.

He straightened and kissed her mouth again, running his fingers over her slick nipple. Taking her hands in his, he forced her to work the buttons on his trousers before he slid them over his hips and buttocks. Naked, hard, and wanting, he took her hand and pulled her into the bedchamber, greedily pushing her back onto the bedclothes. There he loomed above her, gazing down at her nudity as if it had been wrought by the angels.

"Dreams of you like this kept me alive, Rachel. So many times I could have given up and frozen to death there on the tundra, but I always pushed on because of the promise of how you look right now." He lowered himself to her and placed his hand between her thighs, the other at her cheek. "Love me," he whispered, hotly licking the vulnerable hollows of her neck.

The torment was more than she could take. His hand roughly parted her. Somewhere in the fog of pleasure, she felt him settle in between her thighs.

"When we marry, Rachel, you'll be required to be a lady. Be one with everyone else, but here, in this bed"—he locked gazes with her, his own dark and heated—"here, I demand you throw off those chains. I want to hear you moan your pleasure; I want to freely take all of you, and to do that, I demand that you give of yourself freely, totally, as I will."

He penetrated her fiercely, and without warning.

She threw her head back, wondering if her smallness could even accommodate his size, but then, his hand rubbing her damp nipples, his tongue pushing and thrusting inside her mouth, she was left dizzy with sensation.

The need inside her built until she was running her hands down his buttocks, pressing him to go harder and faster. His thrusts tempted her until her loins burned with need. His chest hair rubbed against her large, sensitive breasts as he rocked her.

Suddenly, in her mind and body, she felt herself slide across a plateau.

Crying out, she knew she'd reached the edge.

If he'd left her at that moment, she would have felt like she'd slammed into a wall. Instead, his possession was full and absolute. With two rock-hard thrusts, he drove her into a freefall of pleasure. The force hit her with wave after wave of sensation until she could barely hear him groan her name.

Afterward, weak and panting, she stared up at him as he still worked over her. His eyes were glazed with unfulfilled desire. His expression was rigid with intensity.

He met her gaze, then kissed her once violently.

Pumping into her, he whispered the words that sent him into ecstasy, "Take me, Rachel. Take me forever."

Rachel awoke early the next morning, still wrapped in Noel's embrace. The scent of their lovemaking clung to the sheets like dark perfume. It had been almost dawn before he seemed to have dulled the edge of his wanting. He'd taken her so many times, she was left with a lush erotic soreness between her legs.

Extracting herself from his arms, she rose and went to Noel's dressing room for her wrapper. It was still on the floor, a puddle of shimmering violet. The servants had yet to arrive with the morning coffee to clean up the rooms.

She secured the wrapper around her waist with the ornate fringed belt. Silently, she opened the door to the passage and disappeared up the stairs going to the attic.

The painting of Catherine sat askew in the open trunk, untouched since she'd last visited here. The piece was an awkward size to carry, but she managed it, going down flight after flight until she reached the first floor.

It was going to feel good to rid the place of Grisholm. She rang the servants' bell. Soon Betsy arrived in the library, her frilly headpiece hairpin straight despite the early hour.

"Goodness! You gave me a start. With Magnus returning so late last night, I expected you both to sleep late," the woman exclaimed when she saw Rachel.

"I have a surprise for him." She pointed to the portrait of Catherine. "Could you call a

333

few footmen? I want to put Grisholm up in the attic where he belongs."

Betsy assessed the situation. She nodded, but then said, "Are you sure about this, love? Something strikes me wrong here. I wonder if we're not fooling in an area best left untouched."

"He couldn't have an attachment to his father's painting. I daresay he won't be upset to have me take it away," Rachel told her.

The housekeeper thought on this a while. Seeing no way to refute the logic, she left and returned with two hefty footmen. They carried away the ominous portrait as if it were no more important than a dustcloth for the furniture.

"Now, let's see her back in her true place." Rachel stood upon a chair. Taking the portrait in her hands, she affixed it to the spot above the mantel. It was a perfect fit. The carved mahogany tracery around the mantel also framed the chimney breast, but Grisholm's portrait had covered it. The tracery outlined the ornate Gothic picture frame exactly. Northwyck's architect had clearly devised the two to fit. They were now together again.

"How I remember," Betsy cooed from the doorway. A sadness drifted through her expression.

"She was there before, wasn't she?" Rachel gazed up at Catherine. The woman sat young and placid for all to see. But there was still a pall over her expression. Youth and inexperience would soon doom her to be crushed beneath a tyrant. Her face, with the pallor of her cheeks and the slight downward tug at the corner of her lips, seemed to foreshadow her destruction.

"But she was beautiful, wasn't she?" Rachel marveled.

"That she was. I think it made her son love her all the more," Betsy clucked in despair. "He missed her so terribly."

"Well, let him miss her no more, for here she is, almost lifelike once again." Rachel spun around to face Betsy. "Yet, you mustn't whisper a word of this to him, Betsy. I want to surprise him."

"But when do you plan on doing so? You're both leaving for the city today by train. The Academy of Music ball is tonight."

"I know, but I thought to let him glimpse the change just as he's walking out the door. To let him know that a more wonderful Northwyck awaits his return."

Betsy gave her a wry smile. "I hope it works, love. Truly I do."

Rachel went to her and hugged her. "If there was justice, Betsy, the portrait above the mantel here would be of you. You were more a mother to him than Catherine. I know that. But she did give him those terrifying, wonderful eyes of his. For that she should have a place of honor."

The housekeeper smiled. "You honor me, love, but in the meantime I've got to fly. Nathan said he would oversee your trunks getting to the carriage, but I've got to manage the chits in the kitchen so that they get your breakfast trays upstairs in good time."

"Then let me return to the bedchamber. Give me five minutes, then send our trays up."

Betsy pressed Rachel's hand as she was leaving. "Good luck," was all she said.

Rachel slipped off the wrapper and slid back into the bed. Noel was rousing. He rolled toward her. As if by instinct, he covered her with his heavy muscular arm, and pulled her against his body.

Breakfast arrived within minutes. A knock came at the door with Mazie announcing their trays. Noel grunted and two chambermaids walked in and placed the silver trays on a round quatrefoil-embellished table in the center of the room.

They exited as expediently as they arrived.

Rachel looked across her shoulder to her lover. Noel lay against her, his gaze pinned to her.

"Good morning, beautiful Rachel," he said, nipping her nape with his teeth.

"How did you sleep, sir?" she asked with a light tone she prayed masked her embarrassment at her nudity.

He lay back against the pillows and rubbed his muscle-gridded torso like the satiated heathen he was. "Not a finer sleep can I recall."

"Good. Because our breakfast is here. It's time we got ready for the train."

He rolled toward her again. His hand rested on her back, where his fingers began caressing her soft, bare skin. "Breakfast can wait, I think," he nuzzled.

"The train to New York cannot, I'm afraid," she said matter-of-factly.

"Then we must make good use of the time we have," he whispered, sliding one hand beneath her side and greedily cupping both her breasts at once.

"Have we time?" she gasped, amazed at his ready arousal.

"You tell me," he shot back diabolically as his hand slid to the sweet triangle between her legs.

"I'm not sure," she moaned, her head rolling forward in her weakness.

"Then, allow me, Rachel," he said softly against her hair, "to show you how expedient a man can be when he wakes up next to a beautiful naked woman."

He did.

The trunks were hauled down the servants' stairs. Rachel had Mazie assist her into a midnight-blue traveling dress with black silk passementerie ornamenting the sleeves and bodice.

Noel waited for her in the antechamber, clad simply in black trousers and jacket.

She waited until they were in the downstairs foyer before she took Noel by the hand and led him into his library.

He laughed and looked down at her playfully. "What is this?" he asked, toying with the swirls of braid over her chest. "Are you up to a dalliance even though we've yet to get to the train?"

She pulled his head down and kissed him. It seemed so natural to be with him, to laugh with him and lay with him. They had to be right for each other, because no other man would do after him. He was everything to her, and she prayed that at midnight, he would see their bargain had been worth keeping, and so was she.

"I've a surprise for you, my love," she said softly in his ear.

He smiled and kissed her back, his sherry-colored eyes dancing with refracted joy. "And what is it?" he asked.

"Look up. Over the mantel." She held her breath.

He raised his head. The smile on his face froze, then fractured as if it was of glass and dropped from a very long height.

"What is this?" he asked, his voice hushed with incredulity.

"It's Catherine. Your mother."

"Why is she here?"

"Betsy and I found her in a trunk upstairs. I wanted very much to get rid of your father's portrait. Imagine my surprise when I realized this portrait not only fit the space here, but had been designed to hang over the mantel."

He stared at the portrait. Rachel wondered

if he was ever going to speak. Finally he turned from the picture and strode to the servants' bell.

"Go to the carriage, Rachel. Wait for me there."

She heard his words, but they didn't quite register. Suddenly unsure, she asked, "What do you think of my surprise, my love?"

He glanced at her, then at the two footmen who arrived at the door.

"Take this portrait down and burn it," he ordered coldly.

Rachel gasped. "Noel, you can't mean it. She's been gone from you for all these years—"

Snapping his head around, he glared at her. "What do you mean by raking up the past like this? The woman left me here to fend for myself. She was weak and she was selfish, not fit to be called a mother. I've no need to look at her face any more than my father's."

"No, Noel. I'm sorry, so sorry," she whispered, her words clogged with tears. "I had hoped to surprise you."

Fury flashed through his features like lightning. "Surprise me? You damn well surprised me. You just reminded me why I left this place, why I didn't want to marry Judith, or anyone for that matter. Anyone," he rasped, staring at her.

"You can't mean this," she sobbed while the footmen woodenly obeyed his orders and removed the portrait from atop the mantel.

"You question my sincerity?" His mouth

tipped in a cold grin. "This is what I think of her, your idea, and marriage to a bitch like her in general." He snatched the letter opener on his desk. With brutal force, he stepped to the footmen and slashed the portrait in two, then three, then countless shreds. All the while Rachel protested and wept, pleading with him not to be so harsh.

"Come. I don't want to disappoint Mrs. Astor," he said when the footmen had left with the garbage that had once been a beautiful portrait.

Fallen to the settee, Rachel looked up with a tear-stained face and shook her head. "What use is there in going? There's no joy to be found between you and I today."

"I have a standing in the community. I have a responsibility to the great newspaper which is *The New York Morning Globe*. You don't seem to see the duality of my existence, Rachel. I long to be free of this life, of this place, and when I am up North, I'm both. But yet, while I'm here, I'm determined not to disappoint. I tried not to disappoint Mr. Magnus, I tried not to disappoint my mother. Both forsook me. But my wealth and my standing never have. To them, while I'm here, I am true."

She lowered her head to her hands. Everything had gone wrong. It was like she'd set off Roman candles and seen all she'd worked for go up in flames. "Please, Noel," she begged, "I didn't mean to dredge up bad memories. I only wanted to replace Grisholm and thought you would like the change."

"I'll stare at Grisholm Magnus any day, Rachel." A muscle bunched in his jaw. He looked as if he wanted to beat her. "He was true to his nature, true to his cruelty. As abusive as he was, he never lied to me. He never tucked me into bed and kissed my forehead and told me he would protect me from the monster who lurked downstairs, then left me in the middle of the night. No, Mr. Magnus never did that. He was never that cruel."

She'd heard too much. Placing her hands over her ears, she buried her face in the settee, all the while longing to flog herself for the error in judgment.

"Get up. We're leaving for New York," he said coldly.

She took a long, hard breath. "I cannot."

"They believe you're my wife. You have no choice but to come."

"I cannot, Magnus. I cannot," she pleaded.

Viciously, he pulled her from the settee. With his iron arm around her waist, he dragged her out of the library and shoved her out the door, toward the waiting carriage.

If Nathan and Betsy saw the debacle, Rachel didn't know. She was pushed inside the carriage. Noel clambered up beside her and the carriage was off at a gallop for the train depot.

"Noel, this moment will pass. You'll see I didn't mean to dredge up these awful memories," she told him, her hands out in supplication even as they swayed violently. "One day, you'll forgive me and then we can go forward as we were meant to do this morning."

"I'm off to the Arctic, Rachel. I want to be gone from this place."

"Then I shall go with you."

He stared at her. "You're now entrenched here. I don't want you with me, reminding me of things long dead, as you did this morning."

"No..." she whispered, unable even to cry.

"Take Northwyck, take my whole god-damned fortune." His words were laced with bitterness. "I only want to be free. I want to be away from this place and live like a man should. Free. Free, damn you!"

"I won't stay here without you," she pleaded.

"Go ahead, play the merry widow. You'll find some lout along the way to bed you and keep you warm at night. You don't need me any longer. And I, you." He steadfastly looked out the window.

She stared at him in morbid silence, her eyes filled with cold, unshed tears.

The awful moment would pass. They would arrive in New York, and with the new scenery, he would forget his malice. His words couldn't chase her away, only he could. And he'd yet to place her on a ship and tell her to be gone from him, for that would be what it would take for her to leave him.

She slumped down in the carriage seat and tried to think of all the good things that would take his mind from her awful error. The ball would prove to be beautiful, a delight to the senses. They would sip the finest champagne and eat the richest caviar. Soon, the terrible moments would melt into finer ones and he'd

342

see he still needed her, that his words had been wrought of the moment, not of the truth.

Then suddenly another wretched thought occurred to her, and she was overwhelmed by a webbed shroud of depression.

The dress for the ball. She'd sent Catherine's dress to be refitted for the occasion. She had nothing appropriate to wear to the ball but Catherine's puce satin gown, reworked but recognizable.

She could not attend in that, so she could not attend at all.

"Noel," she whispered in a tear-etched voice. "I fear I'm going to be ill tonight. I think you'll have to make my excuses as much as you'd like me to attend."

He stared at her, the anger still burning bright in his eyes. "You'll attend or suffer the humiliation."

"Of what?" she asked, not wanting to know but finding no way to avoid it.

"Of me attending with Charmian Harris in your place. That should cause a stir."

Going dead inside, she turned away from him and stared out at the fleeing landscape.

She had lost. There was no denying it. She had lost the situation, and him. If he'd loved her at all, it was now buried beneath the cave-in of his hatred for everyone else. In her weakness, she feared she could never dig him out. So she had lost. The time to retreat had finally arrived.

CHAPTER TWENTY-EIGHT

"M rs. Magnus, it's time I dressed you for the ball." Mazie stood in the dressing room of the hotel suite, consternation on her face.

Rachel paced the ornately patterned wool carpet until she swore she was wearing it out. They'd arrived at the Fifth Avenue Hotel in timely fashion. Magnus had promptly left them there with the trite excuse that he needed to do some shopping before the evening's festivities.

As much as Rachel didn't want to think it, she knew he was going to see Charmian. Perhaps he was going there to lay in her arms, to find succor where she offered none. He might even be nursing the hope that his "wife" would not be up to attending, and he could cause scandal by taking his mistress instead.

She stared at the dress that was bound to signal her doom. The puce satin had been exquisitely refitted for the occasion with a new crinoline and puce silk netting over the skirt. The long, old-fashioned sleeves had been cut down to mere poofs adorned with satin bows of the same pale pink-gray. It was a triumph of skill and design. Auguste had been beside himself with excitement when he arrived at the hotel to show her the heirloom dress he'd so masterfully brought up to fashion. He'd almost keeled over backward when she told him she couldn't wear it and he must somehow find her an appropriate gown she could wear to the social event of the decade, and he must do it in less than an hour.

Of course, it could not be done. He was sick to have to refuse her, but not as sick as she was when she knew she had to accept his apologies and let him leave so that she could finally dress for the ball.

"Are you ready, Mrs. Magnus?" Mazie asked softly, the worry in her eyes reflecting Rachel's own. "Mr. Magnus's instructions were clear. You were to be ready at eight."

"I know." Rachel gnawed on her lower lip.

"Before he left, he sent me this box. He simply said you were to be wearing the things inside it at the ball."

Rachel took the violet posy-papered box. Lifting the lid, she saw her old black satin corset with the lilac-colored bows. Nestled within the deep ridges of satin-wrapped steel lay The Black Heart.

She stared at the two objects, anger and resignation warring within her. As much as she wanted to give up, she couldn't let Charmian Harris take everything she ever wanted. She had no choice but to be ready at eight and take a chance Noel might forget the horrible thing she'd done.

She handed Mazie the black corset and presented her back to her.

Swiftly, mercilessly, the maid laced her into it until Rachel felt the world sway and grow dim.

Noel had returned and was dressed before Rachel could bring herself to leave her dressing room. At precisely eight o'clock, when the bells of the mantel clock were still ringing, Rachel entered the parlor, clinging to the shadows, ashamed and afraid.

"Let me see you," he ordered in the same black mood as he'd been in the entire train ride south. Sitting in a chair, a glass of brandy held loosely in one hand, his very stance commanded her to obey.

She stepped in front of him, no smile or warmth on her face. Following his gaze as it moved down her face, she held her breath as it fell to the unmistakable chevon-pleated bodice.

"Christ, what are you doing to me? Driving me mad?" he bit out, now refusing to look at her.

She fought back tears. "I'm sorry, Noel. I have nothing else to wear."

He stood. All at once, in a rage, he hurled his brandy glass into the fire.

She was startled by the violence of it. "Please, Noel," she begged, going to him.

He shook his head and pushed her aside. "Get your wrap. We don't want to be late," he ordered.

Releasing a quiet sob, she took an ermine-and-velvet cape from Mazie, who stood cowering in the dressing-room doorway.

"And bring the wretched stone," he cursed.

Mazie dashed into the dressing room. She handed the opal to Rachel, then retreated back into the shadows.

"Put it on," Noel growled.

Rachel tried to fix the clasp, but her hands were shaking. Taking it from her, he placed it around her neck. His touch was gentler than she'd expected.

He stared at her long and hard. The opal glistened between the two swells of her breasts that the corset held tight. For one brief impossible moment, he reached out and ran his thumb across the stone, stroking her cleavage with it.

"Now let's go," he announced, again refusing to look at her.

She choked back her despair and went through the door he held open for her.

The Academy of Music was a fairyland of pink rose petals strewn across the banquet tables and women flitting like bells in and out of the main hall. The opera boxes were adorned with Union Jacks and the stage had been extended to serve as a dance floor. From above, the ballgoers merged into a sea of taffeta and diamonds, each woman anchored by a man in formal black.

Any other time, Rachel would not have believed her good fortune, to be amongst the country's elite who curtsied for the Prince of Wales in the receiving line. The Academy of

Music was beyond her imagination while she'd lived up in Herschel. The dazzling gowns that she gazed at now would have made the *Godey's* ladies run in shame of their shabbiness.

The most perfectly presented was the young matron behind the ball: Mrs. Astor. She wore a suitable brown matelasse to match her dark sable hair. Around her neck gleamed a diamond necklace that was said to have belonged to Marie Antoinette. With her imperious bearing, Mrs. Astor looked much like the queen herself in the receiving line, standing next to the famous, barely twenty years of age and homely, Prince of Wales.

"Why, there you are, Magnus! How's the famous search for Franklin?" A heavyset man with impressive lambchop whiskers met them at the end of the receiving line.

"Astor, how are you?" Noel asked, accepting a glass of champagne for him and Rachel from a passing waiter.

"Fine. Fine. The wife's been busy, as you can see." He rolled his eyes. "Thank God for the *Roustabout.* Say, why don't you come up to Newport in the spring and take a spin on the new yacht?"

Noel grinned.

Rachel was heartsick at how handsome he was; handsome and untouchable.

"I'll have to postpone that, Astor. I'll be leaving for the North in a day or two."

"What? Are you mad? You plan on leaving this luscious wife of yours to fend for herself again?" William Astor took Rachel's hand and kissed it. "How are you, my dear?"

She tried to smile but the sadness in her soul couldn't be surmounted. "Very well," she answered a bit too brightly. "Thank you so much for asking, Mr. Astor."

"You'd best stay home and protect your wife, Magnus. More than one man has commented on how lovely she is. Edmund himself has made it known throughout the city how desirable he finds her."

She looked at Noel, hoping to see jealousy, possessiveness, anything that might indicate his passion for her still burned.

His expression was implacable. "Edmund can hardly manage his company and his expeditions. I think it dubious he could manage my wife, too."

Astor broke out in a loud, boisterous laugh. His wife glared at him, still at the prince's right in the receiving line.

"I'll count you in to be the next captain of the *Roustabout* come April, Magnus," Astor said jovially before departing.

Alone with Noel, Rachel looked down and realized in her depression, she'd finished off her glass of champagne. Another waiter passed and she demurely took another glass.

Trying to sip the drink this time, she looked around and found a man staring at her from the door to the staircase. It was Edmund Hoar, looking his usual elegant best.

Magnus had seen him, too. The men stared at each other for an eternity before Edmund called the draw and disappeared into the crowd.

"There you are! Why, goodness, don't you look stunning in that gown, Rachel. Wherever did you get it? It's so demure and yet lavish. Caroline is beside herself with jealousy!" Mrs. Steadman beamed at Rachel like a long-lost aunt. Her gown was of pale-yellow lace making her more of a Valkyrie than she already was. The two-ton brooch of emeralds and sapphires in the shape of a large peacock feather fit her bodice and her style perfectly.

"And you, you lout!" she announced good-naturedly to Magnus. "Why have you not brought your wife and lovely children to the house for a call? I'm quite put out with you. You return from the dead and cloister yourself in that magnificent house of yours as if you and your bride are on your honeymoon. Very bad form, Magnus. Very bad indeed!"

Magnus smiled again just like a wolf with beautiful eyes and enticing jaws. "Gloria, you haven't taught me manners yet, and I daresay, you never will."

Mrs. Steadman tittered a laugh. "If you weren't so ridiculously good-looking, Magnus, we would have shunned you years ago—and you would have deserved it!"

He tipped his head back and laughed.

Mrs. Steadman took her arm. "Just for that, I'm taking your wife from your side. I've several gentlemen who would like to ask her for a dance. You can see her anytime, so you mustn't be selfish."

Rachel felt herself be led away by Mrs. Steadman. She looked back just once.

Noel stared at her.

Their gazes locked, and for one sweet second, Rachel almost thought he was angry Gloria Steadman had spirited her from his side.

Rachel danced until her feet ached. If it hadn't been for Betsy's careful instructions, she wouldn't have known the schottische, or the more scandalous waltz. But even though the Prince of Wales himself had asked her twice, and every man who escorted her around the dance floor was scrupulously polite and considerate, she longed for Noel's arms around her. And he was nowhere to be seen. Not making mundane conversation with the matrons in the boxes overlooking the floor, nor in the passages laughing at an off-color joke with the other barons of industry.

Then, like Cinderella, she was suddenly, painfully, aware of the hour. Eleven strokes of the enormous French clock that echoed in from the main hallway, and she knew the hour was upon her. Midnight of the thirtieth day.

No matter how many gentlemen asked to dance after that, she had to refuse. All she wanted to do was to search the crowd for Noel. But every tall, handsome gentleman she was sure she recognized would turn around and her face would fall. It was not him. It almost seemed as if he had left the ball without her.

"My dear, what's happened? You're suddenly so quiet and solemn I'd think you'd just received news of a wake." Mrs. Steadman stopped the waiter and handed Rachel another glass of champagne. "Drink this. You're clearly too sober."

Rachel took the proffered glass, but she was definitely not too sober. Depression and liquor were a bit too compatible. Now, though she stood steady and her words were not slurred, she knew she was going to need a strong arm to help her up to the carriage for the ride home. She only hoped the arm would be Noel's.

"What time is it?" she asked, unable to see the clock over the ballgoers' heads.

"Why, it's almost midnight. How the time has flown!" Mrs. Steadman marveled.

Rachel leaned against a pilaster near the main hallway entrance.

"Gracious! Are you ill?" Mrs. Steadman asked.

Rachel shook her head. Physically, while she'd imbibed a little too much, she was in truth fine. Spiritually, she was crushed.

"Shall I call you a maid?" the matron inquired.

"No. Please. I just need to find Magnus. It's going to be midnight soon. It's so very important that I find him. If I don't find him at midnight, then I must leave. I can't stay here any longer."

With a shaking hand, Rachel held on to the banister, determined to go upstairs to search each box and find him. Their bargain be damned. It was midnight of the thirtieth day and she would still have him. If he chose to cast her aside now that the magic hour had arrived, then he must tell her to her face, and not abandon her to the champagne and society she could live without.

"Where is the girl going?" Mrs. Astor asked Gloria Steadman as Rachel ascended the staircase in front of them.

"Oh, we have to find Magnus for her. The dear is distraught. She said she had to find Magnus by midnight or she was leaving on her own." Mrs. Steadman lowered her voice. "The way she acts, I do believe we've another heir on the way."

Mrs. Astor set her chin. "I won't have any displays here, Gloria. Not when the Prince of Wales is here."

"Then go find Willy B. and tell him to round the old boy up!" Mrs. Steadman's face brooked no disobedience.

Caroline Astor narrowed her lips, then did as she was told.

Rachel went from box to box as patrons turned to stare at her forlorn figure scanning the crowds. She knew they found it odd that Mrs. Noel Magnus was wandering the ball looking shamelessly for her missing husband. That was not done in this circle, because the worst sort of scandal could ensue should she find the man.

But she didn't care. She'd had too much champagne, and it gave her a bravery she didn't normally have. If she found Noel embracing Charmian in a darkened corner of one of the boxes, then she would swallow her horror and despair, and accept that as his choice. And at last she would know his choice and be free to search for a way to lose her wretched love for him.

But he must tell her to her face he didn't want her. He must tell her to her face he didn't love her and never would. Then she would take her life back and find fulfillment where she could, with Tommy and Clare, with the orphanage. There would never be another man for her. She could love no man as completely as she loved Noel, but she would take what her life offered and she would make the best of it. Because that was who she was. She was Rachel Ophelia Howland, and he would tell her his choice to her face. She would not let anyone take the coward's way out.

She turned the corner of the passage. No one was there. A back staircase was empty of servants rushing up and down.

She turned around and made to leave, but suddenly a shadow fell upon her. Her way was blocked by the silhouette of a tall, slim man.

"Have you lost him, Rachel?" came Edmund Hoar's voice, soft and seductive.

Desperately trying to sober herself, she took a step back and held on to the cheap wooden railing of the servants' stairs. "Let me pass, Edmund."

"But my darling beautiful girl, surely you're done with him now. After all, where has he gone? He's gone off with some other wench—"

She tried to run past him, but he caught her and pushed her back.

"—some other wench to whom he's probably giving a delicious banging right as we speak—"

"No."

He looked down at her almost tenderly. "Rachel, love, let me steady you. I think you've had too much to drink." His hand went into his jacket pocket.

In her fear and insobriety, she couldn't quite figure out what he was doing. She went to call out to someone—anyone—at the ball who seemed tantalizingly in full force just around the corner, but her words never had the chance to come through.

His hands went around her head. In terror, she found he had a gag on her mouth.

She pushed at him, scratched him, but she couldn't make any effective sound. He easily pinned her to the stair railing and tied the gag tight.

Her breathing was quick and shallow, like a hunted rabbit's. He seemed to enjoy it. He caressed her face almost lovingly before his hand lowered to the chain around her neck. Viciously, he pulled the opal off her and pocketed it.

"Let's get her to a carriage," he said to a man who appeared behind him. The man was dressed as a servant. Rachel's eyes went wide as she saw the man held out a woman's cape with a large, obscuring hood.

Edmund reached into his jacket once again. With a gleam in his eyes that told her he was not deluding himself that he offered her comfort, he kissed her, perhaps for the man's benefit, perhaps for his own. He tongued her cheek, then her throat, then her breasts.

Finally his hands went over her head again, this time with a burlap bag.

Everything went black.

Magnus watched the rain spatter across the panes of glass of the casement window. The downfall was light at first, then grew heavier. Below the open window, the street was crammed with carriages. A commotion ensued as footmen and drivers found cover beneath the lowered front bonnets of the cabriolets.

Behind him the ball went on in all its glittering splendor. The cabinet alcove was well known to the regulars at the Academy of Music. High on the third floor, rakes were known to meet their mistresses there—usually dancers from the opera—while the wife sat in her box below, irritated at her escort's mysterious disappearance.

He himself had had a moment or two with some baggage touring with the opera. But now he was just grateful the Prince of Wales was too important a draw for even the licentious. The alcove was empty, a dim haven where he could think.

She looked beautiful tonight. Even in his mother's old gown, she glowed with a radiance he'd never seen. The opal gleaming between her breasts cast her skin a porcelain pink, her blond hair coiled against her nape gave her a sensual air—the very bondage of it made him ache with the desire to free it and run his hand through it as he'd done before.

He closed his eyes. Guilt made him gird himself. He'd been too hard on her, but the portrait had been difficult. He thought he'd never look upon the face of his mother ever again, never again have to relive the emotions she'd left imprinted upon him. When he'd seen the painting of the woman, his shock had been absolute.

And then there was the gown. Another error in judgment, but still, just an error. In truth, if he viewed her by others, she was delightful in it. The color was a subtle backdrop to her pale beauty. The fit was flawless, though a little too snug in the bosom. Auguste Valsin must have known it would drive a man crazy.

Gloria Steadman was due for a comeuppance also. She had no right to take Rachel from his side. He found it cathartic to have her with him even if he was angered. Watching her depart, seeing the young bucks queuing up to have a dance with her, left him inconsolable. No man had a right to her. She was his. His alone.

Rain, cold and real, sprinkled on his face. He opened his eyes and rubbed the moisture away.

There was no getting around it; he couldn't let her go. Even though he'd fooled himself into thinking he could do without her, tricked himself into believing he could ease his guilty conscience by setting her up with accounts, the truth was, he needed her. He was a big strong man who'd conquered the fearsome North, but whose past had left him as damaged and fragile as a crystal goblet. But she coaxed him away from his petulance and temper. She promised healing if only he would let himself heal. And now he knew he must let himself do it. For his sake. For all their sakes.

Below him, he heard the gong of a clock. There was another, then another in long succession.

He held his breath. It was midnight.

The games and bargains were now officially ended. The manipulations were through. He would have to tell her how much she meant to him and plead with her to stay by his side, or he would have to face losing her to his own self-indulgence of temper.

Indeed, he was not worthy of her. She'd been patient when he'd been a bear; she'd been loving when he'd been helpless to love her back. She'd defied him, duped him, outwitted him, and now brought him to his knees. She'd insisted to him all along the way that she was his match, but she was fatally wrong. She was not his match. He could never, ever live up to being worthy of her, but suddenly with the last stroke of midnight, he knew he wanted to spend his lifetime trying.

"Magnus! There you are! Everyone's looking for you!" Mr. Astor cast a long shadow in the alcove as he stood staring at Magnus.

"I'm here," Noel said, walking toward the passageway.

"Your wife, it seems, has left you, Magnus."

Noel stopped dead. He stared at Astor as if the man had just lifted a pistol and shot him in the chest.

"What are you talking about?" he demanded.

William Astor began to sputter. "It was the damnedest thing. She told Gloria and the wife that she had to find you by midnight or she wouldn't stay here any longer. Now she's nowhere in sight. What do you think was going through her head?"

Slumping against the wall, Noel took a moment to shake off the haze of dread. He knew very well what she'd meant. The bargain had come and gone, and she'd decided to do without him.

And he damn well deserved it. But he was a persistent bastard, and he would have another try just as soon as he could get to the hotel and proclaim his feelings for her. Just as soon as he could get down on his knees and beg her not to leave him to his barren existence any longer. Just as soon as they could get to a justice of the peace that very night and he could make her his legally and forever.

"Good God, man, slow down!" Astor gasped as Noel took off down the stairs.

CHAPTER TWENTY-NINE

"Yes, sir. She left here, all right. She seemed ill, I think. She leaned on the man with her as if he were holding her up. Her face was all covered by the green hood to her cloak. I didn't know what else to do for her but find her a hired carriage, and they took off."

Magnus stared at the doorman as if he wanted to throttle him. "Get me my carriage at once."

The short elderly doorman nodded furiously. He snapped to a boy, who went running down the line of carriages.

"She'll be all right, Magnus," Astor said, still huffing from trying to keep up with him. "The wife says she thinks she just might be addled because she's with child. You know how these women get when they're with babe. You've already had two children with her."

Noel's face took on the harsh planes of devastation. Without another word, he clambered into his carriage that had pulled up and ordered it back to the hotel.

"It's not possible she's not here. It's not possible," Betsy insisted.

Magnus stared at her, the muscles bunched in his jaw.

Betsy's expression mirrored the rising fear

on his. "I'll agree she's a woman with her own ideas, that is true. But even if you had this bargain and it was to be finalized tonight, even if all went wrong and she left you as perhaps she should have months ago, I tell you, it's not possible for her to not be here now."

Betsy went to the door of the suite. She opened it and thrust the light of a candle into the darkness.

Tommy and Clare lay deep in sleep in their beds, innocent and oblivious to the drama around them.

"She would leave you, perhaps, if you drove her to it, Magnus, but she would not leave them. I'll go to my grave believing it."

He turned away, unable to show his face to Betsy. "My own mother left me. Why should she not take the funds that I gave her and leave two children who are not even of her own flesh?"

Betsy laid a gentle hand on his jacket. "The flaw was in your mother, love, not in you. I've told you that for years, and now you must believe me. Catherine was shallow and weak. She could not endure your father, and to leave him she was willing to part with you. But shallow and weak is not Rachel. She did not leave these children willingly, Magnus. She did not."

"Then where is she?" he demanded, a strange crystalline light coming to his eyes that seemed almost like tears. "Has she taken on a lover?"

"When would she do this? And where that

the servants and I wouldn't know about it?" Betsy scoffed.

"I was gone from here for six months. For all I know, she may have played the merry widow in my absence." He lowered himself to a chair and placed his head in his hands. "There was a man with her when she left. You must tell me true, Betsy, did she take a lover while I was gone?"

"Impossible! If she had I would know it, and I tell you she loved you. She never looked at another man. Not even when Edmund Hoar came around and made himself obvious that he wanted to court her did she turn her eyes. She threw him off and told him in no uncertain terms she was still in mourning for her husband."

Magnus straightened and stared at Betsy. For several seconds, he sat perfectly still, his incredulous expression turned inward in thought.

Then, without warning, he rose and went for the door.

"What are you thinking, Magnus? What is going through your head? Oh please say it isn't what's going through mine. Please tell me so I have something to tell the children when they awake."

"Franklin," he gasped, his eyes dark with worry and torment.

He looked back at Betsy, then stormed out the door for the docks and Hoar's own ship, the *Arctos*, that he prayed was still moored there.

"She left, sir. Pulled anchor not half-past midnight." The lone stevedore pointed toward the docks. "I niver seen a ship so quick to sail. She was preparin' all evening."

Magnus stooped and picked up a burlap bag that had been thrown onto the docks where the gangplank of the departing ship had been. He picked a long strand of blond hair from its interior, then he stared east toward the night horizon. No ship was outlined in the moonlight. The *Arctos* was gone.

A carriage pulled up on the docks. Stokes leapt out of it, breathless. "Magnus, I got a missive that said to meet you here. What's wrong?" he asked, his face old and lined beneath the lone gas lamp that flickered overhead.

"Rachel's gone," Noel said, still staring east as if the ship would show itself if he willed it. "I fear she may be with Hoar." He turned to the man. "You're the only one I can trust. Get supplies to my ship as soon as you can. I have to have her ready to sail north now."

"You know he took her North?"

"I think he believes she can take him to Franklin. The only way to get to Herschel this time of year is by sledge. Hoar's never done it himself, but his crew will know they have to dock in Halifax and head out for Rupert's Land with dogs."

"I'll get everything you need. I helped put

together the other expeditions, remember?"

Magnus turned to the older man. With a low rasp, he confessed, "This one is much more important."

Stoke nodded. "I'll move heaven and earth. You'll sail within the hour, my friend."

CHAPTER THIRTY

Rachel sat in the bowels of a ship, bilge water spraying in on her from the rudder. She shivered in her sodden cloak and struggled against the rope that tied her wrists, but to no avail. The rope was knotted by a seaman. It was secure. The ship rose and fell again and again, negotiating the North Sea waves. Her father had been a whaler, ships were in her blood; she was thankful that at the very least she wasn't made sick by the violent heaves of the vessel as it made its way up the Atlantic seaboard.

Despair more thick and black than the impenetrable darkness had fallen over her. The night of her abduction, she'd struggled the whole way to the ship while Edmund had barked orders to his manservant. Once the ship had sailed, Edmund had told her she would be put into the captain's cabin with him, to share his bed.

With the gag finally removed, she'd spit

right into his face. He'd slapped her and ordered her to the bilge until she broke.

She still hadn't broken. Not even now, days later, when she was weak from hunger and cold. Death was preferable to becoming the plaything of a monster. Death was preferable now that she'd been taken from Noel, and at the horrible precise hour when he would think she'd made her choice to leave him.

She'd made her peace that he wouldn't come after her. He didn't know she was spirited away by Hoar. She had no doubt Noel believed she had all she could stand of him, and had left the ball of her own accord. She could certainly do it now that she had her accounts, and he would think she'd disappeared to find a better life with someone less difficult.

For days she had wept on and off again about her hopeless situation. She would never see Noel again, nor Tommy and Clare. They might mourn her passing for a while, but eventually, the children would grow up not remembering her; Noel would find a wife who fit his world and his moods, and he would cease to think of her. They would be fine, but she, she was destined to die a lonely death fighting her captor with her last shallow breath whispering the name of her beloved.

She sank against the ice-slicked bilge boards, laying her head back in misery. Her instincts kept her fighting for life, but it was getting more and more difficult with each passing hour. Delusions began accosting her. Nightmares of Noel marrying another sent her spiraling down into an inferno of hell. He'd never told her he loved her. Her deep regret would be that she hadn't lived long enough for that, but now it was impossible. Fate seemed to prescribe that she wasn't destined to survive the ordeal Hoar was putting her through. She was bound to die, and more and more it seemed it was imperative she do it quickly before more misery could be inflicted upon her.

Without warning, the door to the supply room opened. An old, grizzled sailor stood there, a cruel grin on his face.

"Let's go, gel. Mr. Hoar wants to talk to you." He reached over and unlashed her hands. Grabbing her by the arm, he pushed her in front of him to the passageway.

They climbed two ladders. Her wet cloak weighted her down and tripped her up. Every time she stumbled, the sailor shoved her forward again relentlessly.

They finally came to a polished walnut door at the stern of the ship. It opened and she was thrown into the interior.

She landed on a soft Tabriz carpet. Looking up, she noticed the wainscoting, the large fitted bed, the cabinets were all made from the same polished walnut. Cranberry-red wool curtains covered the portholes, keeping out the drafts. At the bay end, there was a banquette covered in the same red wool. Edmund Hoar sat on it, eyeing her.

"They tell me you haven't been eating your hardtack," he commented, all the while peeling a bright fragrant orange with a knife. Finished, he tossed the peels and the knife on a figured walnut desk built into the wall.

"How long have I been here?" she demanded, her voice low and scratchy from disuse. With no light coming into the bilge, she hadn't been able to count the days, but she suspected there had been many of them. Even now it was hard to tell the time of day. The curtains covered the portholes, and the oil lamps affixed to the wall burned brightly, but these things could have been to keep the warmth in the room, not because the sun didn't shine outside.

"We've been out a week. We're on our way to Halifax." He ripped open the orange.

She almost fainted from the scent of the citrus oil and sweet pulp, it had been so long since she'd had real food in her stomach.

He held out a plump section of the fruit. "Take this. Eat it. Understand that there's plenty more here for a girl who can cooperate."

She got to her feet. "If your plan is to starve me into submission, then I tell you right now, I'll choose to die first." She lifted her head defiantly, though she was dizzy and unsure in her weakened state of her ability to stand.

He laughed. Studying her, crushing the orange between his small teeth, he said, "Look at you. You're wet, you're hungry, your fine gown is nothing more than rags. And yet you still think you can win."

"I will never tell you where Franklin is. Never," she spat.

Swallowing, he rose from the banquette

and loomed over her. "My men in The Company of the North asked around. They said your father took only one trip the last ten years on Herschel. He went to York Factory courtesy of the Hudson Bay Company to see if he could deal in beaver pelts brought up from the forests of the Yukon. So there I have it, girl. If he found the opal, then he did it around York Factory or up at Herschel."

"I won't tell you anything."

He ignored her. "York Factory is first on our wonderful tour. Then, if we find nothing there, we go on to Herschel."

"You plan on doing this in the middle of winter?" she scoffed.

"I've men enough to get me there."

"You'll die."

Angered, he lashed out. "I run the whole territory. Who are you to tell me what I can and cannot accomplish?"

"You'll need dogs and a native guide to get you anywhere on that trip in December."

"I've got dogs in the hold and more in Halifax."

"How do you plan on finding Franklin beneath all the ice and snow?" She finally laughed. It felt good to ridicule him. He was going to die right along with her, and perhaps that was justice after all.

He stood and grabbed her, shoving her against him.

She moaned from his rough hold, but refused to give him the satisfaction of looking away.

"I've got reams of Franklin's writings that

were left on the tundra," he snarled. "I've plotted his every step save the last. The Homeland Cree will know about the bones of a man, if there are any out there. They can find him snow or none. And they will point me in the right direction once they know how miserable they'll become should my Company of the North decide not to make their summer supply stop at Fort Nelson."

"Why do you still want to find him? You have the opal"—she looked slyly at him—"and the curse that goes with it."

"I want it all, do you understand me?" He stared down at her, his hand harshly following the contours of her face. "Grisholm Magnus took everything from my family that would have been mine. I'll see his son dead before I'll allow him to be victorious over Franklin...or you."

She closed her eyes. She wasn't going to hold out much longer, but she was still standing. "How rich this all is. Grisholm Magnus took from both of you. I daresay he'd find it amusing, your rivalry with his son. Frankly, the villain that he was, I don't know who he'd be cheering for."

"It doesn't matter," he whispered. "He took and I shall receive. I have you, and the international fame that will come when I find Franklin, and Magnus does not."

"Ah, but Noel has one large advantage over you, Edmund," she commented.

"Which is?" He tightened his clench on her waist.

"He knows where Franklin is. You do not."

His sharp intake of breath told her she'd shocked him.

Smiling wanly, she stepped from his embrace and lowered herself to the wool-covered banquette. It was a lie, of course. She hadn't told Magnus. But Hoar didn't know that. It was her revenge.

"You'll tell me or—" He closed his mouth.

She smiled. "Or what? Kill me? Go ahead, kill me. You're starving me, freezing me, hurting me. Why not kill me? Then this agony is through, and you will have lost."

He stared at her, wild-eyed for a long moment. Then he said, "Don't you ever want to see your lover Magnus again?"

She thought long and hard. Her whole life was nothing without Magnus, but returning to him wouldn't change much. Not now when she'd have a difficult time proving she hadn't left him of her own volition. If she could even return to Northwyck, he might even show her the door, explaining how he'd married in her absence, and that they had no more future together. All would be lost then, and the fight to survive and return to him would have been for naught.

"I will not tell you where Franklin is," she reiterated.

He took the opal out of his waistcoat pocket and threw it at her. "If you will not tell me, then the curse shall be yours. You'll see your lover die before your eyes for your transgressions."

The opal caught in her skirt. She gazed down at it, marveling at how brilliant it looked despite its dark color and the dim light of the oil lamps.

"Are you willing to watch Noel die, Rachel?" he whispered into her ear.

She wanted to laugh, but no longer had the energy. "How shall you touch him, Edmund, when you're far in the north Atlantic and he's back in New York?"

"He's not back in New York. He's following us even now."

She looked up suddenly, afraid he was joking and the shot of hope that coursed through her was nothing more than a sham. "What do you mean? How do you know?"

He studied her. "Up top, they've been watching a ship for days. It's following exactly behind us on the horizon. These are wretched waters this time of year way up here. The only ship that could be behind us is his. There's no other one."

"Magnus," she said, racing toward the porthole. She lifted the heavy wool curtains to peer out. But it was night after all. Nothing could be seen but inky waters.

"You'd need a glass to see the ship in any case," he said, lowering the curtain to chase away the sudden draft.

She digested the new information. As much as she hated to rally false hope, the thought of Magnus somehow coming for her gave her back her strength and her will to fight. If everything was not lost, and he did care for her, so much so that he was coming to save her now, then she would be sure she was still around when he did arrive.

"Is that all you want from me, the directions to Franklin's bones?" she asked him.

Hoar grunted. "How simple this would be if that were all." He found her waist again and he pulled off the sodden cloak.

Catherine's infamous ballgown was in tatters. The netting over the satin skirt was shredded, the hem was soiled and torn. The poofs of sleeves were flattened. The black satin corset that had fit tightly to the point of obscenity was now loose from too much wear and her own lack of food.

But he didn't seem to see her disgrace. His gaze lit upon the gown's chevron-shaped bodice, and his hands seemed to itch to touch the flesh that still generously filled the low neckline.

In a flash, she turned and grabbed the small knife he'd used to peel the orange. It glittered in her hand as she spun around from the desk.

He stared down at the weapon, then smiled. "You think a small knife will stop me from taking you?"

"It will slow you down," she reported. "Furthermore, the way I plan to save myself is through a bargain. Would you like a bargain, Edmund?"

He said nothing, as if he were calculating how much he should trust her.

"I'll tell you where I believe Franklin is. But

upon our arrival in Halifax, no sooner. There, I'll give you the information, and you shall release me so that I might go with Magnus."

He looked down at the knife, then up at her face. "Why should I console myself with half the spoils when I can have it all?"

"You'll never have me." Her own gaze lowered briefly to the knife. "If I must slit my throat to keep you off me, I will."

He locked stares with her. "Put down the knife, foolish girl. I have all the riches he has. More if I can step up whalebone production this year. You'd do no better with Magnus, so come to my bed. Set your sights on pleasing me and sparing your life."

"If you like riches, Edmund, then take this, too." She tossed him the opal. "Now the only thing you can lose is your money."

He rubbed the stone in his hand, then deposited it back in his waistcoat. "As you wish."

"Then we have a bargain?"

"Come and we'll—"

She thrust out the knife to keep him back.

He stopped. "Do you plan on killing everyone on this ship with the wee knife, Rachel? I think your plan is too ambitious."

"I plan on protecting myself and gaining my freedom once we dock in Halifax."

She looked across the desk. There was a key lying on it. She took it and slowly moved to the door. When the key fit, she said, "I think our conversation is over now, Edmund. You have my bargain and now I'm tired. I think I'll spend the rest of the voyage by myself." She stepped from the door to allow him to pass. "Now go."

"You're putting me out from my own quarters?" he hissed.

She smirked. "These are the captain's quarters. You've never even been as far north as Halifax, though you own this ship." She motioned to the door. "So go, and think hard on our bargain. Once Magnus catches you, he'll go hard on you."

"Such faith in your lover. I long to see his mortal weaknesses finally do him in," he cursed.

"He has no weaknesses," she told him smugly.

He whispered back to her before she slammed the door, "We'll see. Because he now fears for *you!*"

She rammed home the bolt in the lock with the key. Making sure she was locked in tightly, she took the key and put it down her bodice for safekeeping.

Looking around, she saw the large platter of fruit and cheese placed on the end of the desk. Taking an orange, she curled up in the bed and began to peel it. The fruit tasted impossibly sweet and wonderful. She would revere the smell of oranges for the rest of her life.

Lying back on the pillows, she closed her eyes for some much-needed sleep. If she had hope inside her again, perhaps she could revive the same fighting Rachel who ran the Ice

Maiden with spitfire and a will of iron. Now that she believed Magnus was coming for her, she could handle the dire situation. And she would survive just to have Noel hold her in his arms once more.

Exhausted, she fell into a deep sleep, oblivious to the bustle up on deck, or of the fact that the ship quite solidly put down anchor.

The time for reckoning had come, but she was fast in slumber, unaware that the ship had arrived in Halifax, or that Edmund stood over her bed, watching her after he'd entered the cabin with a second key.

CHAPTER THIRTY-ONE

Rachel didn't know how many weeks they'd been with the sledges, but the sunlight was fast dwindling with each passing day, and the endless forest of black spruce was becoming sparse; the trees themselves were smaller and more twisted, barely able to survive the intense cold that shattered the sap inside them.

Just as she was shattered inside.

Wrapped in caribou as the rest of their party was, she rode on the sledges some hours, and then, when she could no longer take the cold and the endless bone-pounding ride of the wooden sledge, she begged to walk next to the dogs if only for a while. The days went by and she grew more and more grim.

She hadn't expected to see Edmund staring down at her when she awoke in Halifax. But her knife was gone, and she was told she was welcome to the key placed in her bodice, for there were others.

She'd expected him to rape her. The terror of it rose in her throat like bile, but the onslaught had never come. He explained to her that he was in a hurry. The ship behind them was but hours away and they would have to start for Rupert's Land right away.

Once they reached the docks, a train of wagons awaited them filled with dogs and their supplies. They would take the wagons and mules as far north as they could until the ice covered the ground and they could continue much faster on the sledges.

Since then, she hadn't been bothered by Edmund. The trip exhausted him. He seemed in no mood to tussle with her when his feet were cold and their supplies were too heavy for the dogs. The days were filled with attrition and want. Their only passing was marked by the invaluable bundle they had been forced to leave on the tundra that day in order to keep up their time before the food ran out.

They were probably going to die and Rachel knew it. Edmund Hoar was indulged and inexperienced. The trip through Rupert's Land was a disaster by any account and they had yet to endure the worst of the journey to York Factory, where they would encounter winds past one hundred miles per hour and temperatures easily falling to forty below zero.

In her melancholy, she told herself that her few brief moments of hope had been premature. She had no real reason to believe Edmund's words that Magnus trailed them. His haste was apparent, but Edmund could be rushing for countless reasons other than a murderous lover on his heels. The fact that the trip was ten times more harsh than he'd ever imagined, and that he whined about his discomfort constantly was enough to make anyone rush.

He might have lied about Magnus, and it served her right. Magnus had just been a dream anyway. Now as she returned to the land she loathed, she could see she belonged there. Her destiny had been artificially forged in Northwyck, but now nature was taking over. It seemed fitting she should die in the wretched tundra. She should die of cold and hunger and a loneliness she'd never thought possible until she forced herself to accept the fact that Magnus had never been able to love her, and now never would.

A hand pushed her forward. Behind her walked the same cruel-faced sailor who'd brought her out of the bilge. He proved to be a hard taskmaster. Every time the cold made her feel warm and sleepy, a walking dead woman, he shoved her awake and forced her to trudge. For what reason, she didn't know any longer. They walked only so that they could meet a belated death elsewhere. Alone. As Franklin had met his.

Ashes to ashes, dust to dust, ice to ice.

And then they'd all be gone.

Magnus rode the dogs hard, unencumbered by the need for companions. He was baptized in the ice of the North. Like the natives from whom he learned, all he needed were his dogs and his knife and he would thrive in the hell in which most would perish.

Nothing stopped him. He was determined to get to York Factory before Hoar. There was no telling where the party was that had headed out before him. In the vast stretches of primeval forest that was slowly giving way to the desert of tundra, Hoar's expedition could be fifty miles to the east or west of him at any given time, and Noel knew it.

But the memory of Halifax was enough to drive him harder and faster than he'd ever gone before. Several outfitters had seen the party from the *Arctos* take off and told him they were headed to York Factory. They also told him of the woman who went with them. She was fair, with blond hair and a beautiful face. But what they remembered most was that beneath her furs, she wore a raggedy puce-colored ballgown, torn and dirty, with no crinoline.

Magnus's heart had stopped upon hearing the news. He was on the right track, but descriptions of Rachel, thin and pale, didn't rest well with him. It was a tough journey to York Factory. Once there, he knew they might be stranded for several months. But he knew the Hudson Bay Factor well, and his lovely wife. They would care for them as long as he and Rachel needed to stay over the winter.

But Hoar wasn't going to need such care. Magnus was determined that he would be buried beneath an ice heave before long. If Grisholm Magnus was anywhere inside his son, he was there now in the murderous glint in Noel's eyes.

Edmund would die for his sins. He'd kidnapped the only woman Noel had ever loved, could ever love.

For that he would pay the ultimate price.

"We'll stop here!" Hoar cried out in a fifty-mile gale. The sky was dark, though it was hardly teatime.

The men and dogs circled into a camp. Trenches were dug in the snow and caribou tents erected, but the snow was not deep. There was little protection from the constant wind and the bitter cold.

Exhausted, Rachel helped dig her sleeping hole. She longed to huddle by the oil stove that the cook had already lit, but she wouldn't do it. To protect herself, she stayed as far from the men as she could. One night, one of the men had tried to sneak inside her makeshift tent. Edmund had heard the ensuing scuffle as Rachel struggled against the rapist.

Edmund had had the man pulled from the tent and shot on sight.

Even now the men stared at her with fear. Her salvation.

"Get the wood," Edmund commanded her, his face lit by the bright burning light of the camp stove.

Leaving camp, Rachel consoled herself with the fact that Hoar didn't look the pampered gentleman now. Instead of appearing rugged and masculine with the growth of facial hair and the burned skin, he looked sickly. There were deep black circles beneath his eyes. The tip of his nose was shaved off in his inexperience with the cold. The skin was raw and black around the edges where it had frozen and thawed, causing excruciating pain.

They were running low on food and fuel. Again, in their inexperience, they'd burned the oil stove to make their food quickly while deep in the black spruce forests. But now the tundra was pulling near. There was virtually no wood to be had, and they would suffer for it before they ever arrived at York Factory. Rachel tried to educate them on the matters, but Edmund dismissed her and her years spent on Herschel. She was a foolish woman. And he'd had the most hardy men in New York brought on the expedition so that they would travel in comfort.

Comfort was mean and cold in this climate. But it meant survival, and she didn't believe they had long for that once the fuel ran out to cook their food. She could survive on *muktuk* and seal blubber—she'd eaten it before—but just as Franklin's letters left on the tundra revealed, the men on the expedition would test the elements and starve before eating raw flesh.

The wind died down for a moment, and she took the opportunity to walk deep in the twiglike spruce stand and gather what wood she could find above the snow. If she was allowed a knife, she could have cut willow branches, for these trees were still lush enough to stand at eye level. But no knife was allowed her, another handicap to their survival.

In the distance she heard the baying of an Arctic wolf. Behind her, the light of the camp stove sparkled like a star fallen into a field of ice. It could be seen for miles on the flat, low land.

Wishing fervently for an escape but knowing that to leave the party now would ensure her doom, she continued her task, wandering farther and farther from camp. If she'd been a coward she would have stayed closer to the light. They were too far south for polar bears yet, but barren-ground grizzlies roamed this part of the Hudson Bay. They were not unknown to be found foraging in the middle of the night. To make a kill at any time was their way. But she refused to be afraid. The respite from Hoar and the rest of the repulsive crew he'd brought along was enough for her to venture forth and risk a bear encounter.

She stopped and heard the faraway howl and yipping again. For some reason, the sound bothered her. Arctic wolves generally didn't make so much noise so close to dusk. The sound was more like a man's dogs being settled down for the night.

Looking in the direction of the noise, she took several steps before she was grabbed and a hand was slapped over her mouth.

"Hush, hush," the man soothed.

Her entire body trembled. She recognized the voice but in the darkness couldn't yet make out the face she knew so well.

"Have you come for me? Truly?" she asked, fighting back the tears that would only freeze in the intense cold and damage her eyes.

"I seem to be spending all my life chasing after you," Magnus said, holding her close and tight.

In unspeakable relief she fell against him, sure she would never be able to break from his arms again. They stood for minutes in silence, their arms locked around each other's unwieldy caribou-clad figure.

"Come. I'll feed you at my camp. We'll be in York Factory in less than a week and the factor's wife will see to it you're cared for." Magnus forced them to part. He took her by the hand and led her away from Hoar's camp.

"We'll see them again at York Factory," he said to her. "I'll take my revenge then. But first I'll see you cared for."

Mutely, she allowed him to take her to his sledge and dogs. From his camp she could see the fire of Hoar's stove miles away. It was how he'd finally found her.

"We can't take the risk of a fire here. But there's a ridge only a mile or so ahead. We'll camp there in comfort." He piled her with polar bear hides and rehooked the dogs.

"Noel, I feared I was going to die with Edmund," she blurted out, faint with cold and unspeakable happiness.

He leaned over her and placed a warm, deep kiss on her mouth. "I decided to die by your side instead. Do you disapprove?"

Numbly she tried to laugh, but the effort was too much.

He studied her, clearly worried at her fragile health.

But she was not worried. He'd come for her. She'd survive now. Nothing could make her give up save a knife to her throat.

"Do you love me, Magnus?" she whispered so quietly, she was sure he hadn't heard her. When she didn't receive an answer, she kept talking, half delirious. "For I love you. I was going to meet you at midnight and beg for us to continue..."

She wanted to sleep. Suddenly finding herself warm beneath the lush white furs, she nodded off, but not before she heard the words echoing on the north wind, "I love you, Rachel. I love you."

CHAPTER THIRTY-TWO

O then
Pause on the footprints of heroic men
Making a garden of the desert wide
Where Parry conquer'd death and Franklin
died

—CHARLES DICKENS

Rachel sat by the stove in the library at York Factory, a cup of caribou stew in her hands. She was still listless and weak after being there for several days, but her strength was returning by the hour.

"Would you like some more tea? Or some scones?" Miss MacTavish, an older Scotswoman long accustomed to the rigors of the North, studied her with a kind eye. "The babe needs his nourishment," she admonished, placing another hot scone on a plate next to her.

Rachel smiled in gratitude. If not for the tender ministrations of this woman, and of the Factor himself, she might have died. She and Magnus arrived at York in record time. Even now she could picture the depot looming in the frozen distance, its high cupola a welcome sight after so much hardship.

But as soon as they'd arrived, the pains began. Horrible contracting agony that forced her stomach to grip like iron. It was clear to her that she was pregnant, and the sorrow of losing Magnus's baby was almost more than she could bear.

But beneath Miss MacTavish's care, with bed rest, warmth, and good food, the miscarriage never occurred. Rachel placed her hand on her belly every night like it was a talisman, as if wishing for her baby's health could make it so. But superstitions and fear crept upon her. She was once again back in the North. Life was fragile; the way perilous. The social cost of a bastard baby couldn't be weighed the same as it would be back in Northwyck. The stigma would come later if she returned there, but until then, she was among those who wouldn't cast stones upon her and would help her keep the desperately desired new life inside her.

"Do I hear dogs?" she murmured, raising to go to the tiny window in the Factor's house.

Miss MacTavish sadly shook her head and pressed her back into the seat. "You mustn't worry. Noel Magnus will be back as soon as he can."

Rachel wanted to weep but couldn't expend the energy to cry. As soon as Noel had seen her well on the way to recovery, his baby staying put inside her womb, he'd taken off to find Hoar. She had begged and pleaded for him to take out his wrath when the men made it to York, but he was impatient to seek justice. Hoar had almost cost him everything that mattered to him, he'd explained, and now he would pay.

"You must get your mind off your troubles. Would you like a book to read?" the woman asked her.

Rachel looked around the room at the astounding shelves covered in books. It was the most impressive library of first editions, from Dickens to Sir Walter Scott. Every book that had ever been brought to the settlement had been left in the York library, dating back to the eighteenth century.

But she felt no desire to read until Magnus was back. Nothing, it seemed, could take her away from that focus, until Miss MacTavish began rattling away in conversation.

"Did you know I was acquainted with your father?" the older woman began, settling down across from her in the other Windsor chair. "Indeed, when he last visited York, there was talk of an engagement. Now, I don't pretend to say things went so far as that. He went back to Herschel and I departed for Red River to teach, but I always held out the hope he would return." She smiled at Rachel. "Do forgive me. I mean no disrespect for your mother. It's that I always held a fondness for your father, and now that he's gone and buried, I don't think I'm being disrespectful in telling you this."

"I had no idea," Rachel said, her gaze studying the woman. She would always have a fondness for Miss MacTavish after all the kindness she had shown her. "But I think you would have been good for him. In any case, you may have well saved his grandchild, so perhaps I should consider you family now even without your marriage to my father."

"Oh, how lovely of you, my dear." The woman seemed to tear up. "I have no real mementos of your father. Just the Franklin letter that we keep here in the library. But I've read it all, every line, just to know he did the same."

"A Franklin letter?" Rachel repeated, astounded.

"Yes. Would you like to see it? Your father said he had no use for it, and Factor Hargrave, when he was in attendance here, thought to put it in the library."

"May I see it?" Rachel gasped.

"Of course." Miss MacTavish rose and went to a shelf crammed with titles. Inside Dante's *Inferno* she slipped out a yellowed piece of paper.

"He said he found it while hunting reindeer. It was weighted down with rocks." She handed Rachel the paper.

Her heart beating wildly, she read the short diary page. In long, weak script, it said only:

March, 1847

Heading north to find the HMS Terror. I leave The Black Heart to curse me no more...

Sir John Franklin

Rachel lowered the letter, at peace with the revelation. Her father had found the opal and the letter at a cairn on the lowlands, but they were never going to find Franklin near York. He'd wandered around, and moved north. And his bones lay somewhere in the vast tundra, probably not to be found for decades.

" 'Tis astounding, is it not, how long and far the man wandered." Miss MacTavish poured both of them another cup of tea from the silver samovar left by the Hargraves.

Rachel sipped from the cup handed to her, content that one part of the mystery was solved. But now her thoughts wandered to Noel, and she ached to have him back. The land had taken Franklin. Magnus was mortal, too.

Magnus rode into the camp without fear. No persons moved about even though the sun shone low on the horizon and the caribou tents were still staked into the snow. The scent of burned dung fouled the air. The wind stilled as if in respect for the dead.

He got off the sledge. Mounds of snow came alive as the expedition's dogs took their last strength to see who the newcomer was. He tied them to his sledge and threw them some frozen char. Most of the dogs wouldn't make it to York, but their fur had served them well in the days of cold and hunger.

He opened the flap of each tent. Body after body was huddled inside, frozen, white faced, eyes closed in sleep. The men circled around a stove that had long since run out of fuel. With no wood to burn, the men had used dried dung until that, too, had run out. The wind had quickly sapped the rest of the life from them, with no more energy to keep them warm.

He found Hoar in the last tent.

Stooping down, Magnus was surprised to find him still alive and staring at him, his facial skin peeled away by the frost.

"You've come for me, Magnus," he said, slurring his words.

Magnus stared. The hatred in his expression burned away to pity. "Your obsession with Franklin has finally brought you to Franklin's end."

"Take me with you. I can make it," he pleaded.

Magnus set his jaw. "You would not have shown me such mercy. Nor my wife."

"Take me—take me—" Hoar begged. His hands, frozen into black-fingered stumps, tried to hold on to Magnus.

But the effort seeped away the last of his life. He died, his grip still on Magnus, his eyes wide with terror as he met his just Maker.

EPILOGUE

Rachel held her heavy, rambunctious son in her arms while the ceremony took place. The head curator of the New York Museum placed the opal in a black velvet case that was lit constantly by an overhead gas lamp. Beneath it was a plaque that stated simply:

THE BLACK HEART

A gift of Mr. and Mrs. Noel Magnus

Captain Leopold M'Clintock handed Magnus the key to the case. He locked it, then in turn handed the key to baby Noel who cheekily threw it to the floor. The party laughed and Clare picked up the key for her new infant brother.

"Quite a day!" Rachel exclaimed to Noel when he placed his arm around her to look at their donation.

They'd been home less than a month. For the sake of her health and that of the baby, Rachel had given birth at York Factory. Now the baby was six months old and reaching for everything, especially his brother Tommy and sister Clare.

It hadn't been much of a wedding, but when they'd arrived back at Northwyck, Noel summoned a minister. They rode to the crumbling ruins of the old family chapel, and there Noel pledged himself totally to Rachel. Few guests had been in attendance to account for the late date of their marriage. Only Betsy and Nathan, Tommy and Clare had stood as witnesses. The minister had had his palm so well lined with gold that he'd even consented to changing the date of their wedding so that it would coincide with the older children's presence.

Now, miracle that it was, they were a family.

Magnus had refused to speak much of Hoar, or the condition he'd found him in, but some ghosts were best left buried, and Rachel had ceased to ask about it.

At the museum, though the building was crowded with spectators and dignitaries, Rachel felt as if there were no other people around. Noel looked at her with his warm gaze, and suddenly all else seemed to melt away but her love for him, and his for her. They'd endured a lot together, and now their match was for eternity.

"I love you," Noel whispered to her, smiling. The baby reached for Daddy, and he took his son in his arms.

Tommy and Clare stood in one corner of the museum, regaled by the famous Captain M'Clintock who had announced his find of the lost Franklin expedition on King William Island while they were stranded in York Factory.

Rachel turned to her husband, who stared at the captain and the two children. She touched his arm and asked softly, "Are you disappointed it wasn't you who found Franklin? Tell me true."

He kissed her boldly and openly in front of the distinguished crowd of visitors.

Ignoring propriety, he held her close to him and their baby son. "Instead of the bones of a dead man, I found life. I ask for no more," he said.